Frank Penny

&

The Rise of the Red Flame

THE FRANK PENNY BOOKS

Frank Penny

&

The Rise of the Red Flame

Jeremy Elson

First published in 2023 by Oddsocks Puddles Publishing

The moral right of the author has been asserted.

Cover image copyright © Glyn Bateman

ISBN 978-1-7396613-2-8

A catalogue record of this book is available
from the British Library.

Any resemblance to persons fictional or real,
living or dead, is purely coincidental.

Jane – no you, no Frank Penny. Thank you for believing in me.

Before

The Beginning

Revenge should never be served cold. *Never*.

It must scorch and sear and boil. It must rip and wreck and destroy. It must be delivered with a raging fist, fire to burn every forest to ash, smite every city to cinders and tear away the flaming fury that coiled around every limb of her slender body until it had undone everything they had done to her.

Even then, it wouldn't be enough. Nothing would ever be enough. There could never be enough blood in all the realms to satisfy her crushing thirst, her desire to even the score.

Nothing would survive her. She wouldn't let it. For every ounce of wrongdoing they had inflicted upon her, she would shed a ton of raging fire upon them. She wouldn't let them plead their case nor beg for forgiveness.

Forgiveness was like handing your last coin to a beggar, easily given but soon regretted, regretted by those weak enough to look their enemies in the eye and think they were capable of caring.

Not her. She didn't care. They didn't care. No one cared.

She'd moved beyond that years ago when they'd watched her fall and break into tiny pieces and no one stopped to try and mend her.

They thought her beauty belonged to them, something to possess, something to covet, something to trade. They'd used her, eaten her up and spat her out into the gutter with the rest of the filth.

The images were inked on her brilliant mind even though she'd tried so hard to lock them in a box, but the lid would never stay shut for long and soon they would return, unbalancing the scales and now it was time for the debt to be paid. A hundred times over. A thousand times over. For eternity.

That's what the voices told her.

That's what they'd been telling her for years.

Soft whispers, dark whispers in her head that kept her safe, the guardians of her thoughts, sometimes muddled, sometimes malign but always keeping her safe.

In calming tones they told her, one day, she would inflict her revenge. That it would be purer and more beautiful than the face she saw in the mirror, the one she clawed at incessantly to rid herself of her guilt, the one she always talked down from the ledge, that struggled to find the peace that rode easily on the backs of everyone she knew.

Revenge should never be served cold.

Nor would it.

She hid it well, fooling even those that she held closest. They didn't know of her building resentment, her increasing inability to shut the voices out, the voices that had begun to aim their dark murmurs and curses at everyone she cast her piercing eyes on.

She never showed it, found concealment easy in the dark warmth of her smile, her laugh, her wayward nature. The world had bent her to the unruly, created a beast that could barely tame itself and tugged ceaselessly at its leash as she got older.

And the voices wouldn't leave her alone. Not as she roamed through the heather and hills around the lake close to her home, not when she screamed and shed tears, pushing her hands into her eyes to keep them out, and never in the quiet of the night when sleep couldn't find her.

She fought the kitchen knives and skewers and won. Mostly. But the darkness always loomed, from nowhere, threatening to tear her apart, showing her no mercy, crushing her inside until she cowered in the corner of her bedroom, begging it, begging them, to leave her alone, pleas that always went unanswered.

It took years, long years, but she finally learned to embrace them, to control their influence. Just. Not quite. Sometimes.

She allowed them to become her friends, her accomplices. Allowed them to live uncomfortably in the far corners of the mind but, by letting them, there would have to be a trade, a devil's bargain and, just as with most things in her young life, she knew she would pay the price for it.

She grew older, restless, and began to question their promises but the voices told her to be patient, that time would bring its rewards to her door, would bring her what she deserved. So she'd waited. Waited until the world was at its most vulnerable and when power would fetch its greatest premium, continually walking the tightrope of her dark moods, growing her abilities, refining the contours of her energy – all of which were in her blood, the dark, untamed, unforgiving blood of many generations.

Blood that she shared with no one.

Bad blood.

Then chance dealt her a fortunate hand when the quiet, green-eyed girl who'd seen her by the lake taking out that day's crippling anger on a pile of stones brought her the one thing in the world she actually needed. She hadn't known at the time, but fate had certainly been diligent that day, and very kind.

She'd loved Jenny. Loved her with brutish intensity, with savagery; for a while anyway.

Jenny's innocent, unblemished touch took away her troubles, her kiss brought daylight and silenced the rabble but she found the pain difficult when she wasn't there, when those that dwelt inside her head began to fight back.

And Jenny was easily led into countless unruly and rebellious confrontations with authority, she pushed her further and further just to see how much their love could take, how far it would stretch, wondering if she was trying to break it intentionally just to hurt her, to push her away.

But it rode out all the hollows and Jenny's kindness rubbed off just a little, a warmth and comfort that sat uncomfortably on her skin.

But her love always seemed to grow tired, urging her to move on and she'd left Jenny for others, many others. She never regretted it, never thought about it but never understood why she always ended up hating herself because of it.

When Jenny's mother had given up her fragment of the Simbrian she knew she'd arrived at her calling, that her suffering had just been a road that had led her to that moment, as if her life had reset, that she had been reborn and she could see, hear and taste the world and everything in it differently, for the first time.

It was then that she knew how gifted she'd become and understood why. How the years of building her abilities had led her to this point, to the perfect plan, one that could only be hatched in the darkest and most devious of minds.

A mind like hers.

Only she could detect the scent of the seven guardians. Only she could decipher Everbleed's prophesies. Only she could weave her way through the silent forest to rob Irundi of one of its great treasures and she and only she could conjure a plan so utterly breath-taking in its complexity, so audacious in its cunning and totally beyond anyone's grasp.

The voices loved her, told her how brilliant she was. Utterly brilliant and utterly terrifying.

But she couldn't do it alone. She knew she needed him as her accomplice. Needed his consent to bring about the end and she knew he would follow her, knew they all would if she'd asked them.

She knew what they wanted, what she needed to give for them to nod their weak heads and think they were special to her. A slow shake of her long, blonde hair, a fond sultry look from her vivid blue eyes that veiled the raging fire behind, that hid her scars. It was an easy bluff and all that was needed to deceive their shallow minds.

He was no different, but he would be perfect, and willing. He'd taken no persuading and, in her own way, she loved him for it.

So she told him her plan.

***

She checked herself in the mirror. The beauty had never faded. That was all anybody saw, failing to look through the mask, always falling for the disguise.

It was too easy, much too easy, but why make things difficult.

Behind her, the stately room in the middle of Alsha Kar seemed trivial, furnished with the grandeur of past kings, opulent beyond her impoverished childhood dreams.

The burning reds and shimmering blacks. She'd forgotten colour, couldn't remember the last time she'd stopped and admired nature's palette, how her world had faded to brown and grey once she'd begun, once her plan had brought her here.

Never had she dreamed of such comfort, nor did she want it, or deserve it. For her it was simply part of the passing landscape on the way to achieving her goal, it was the privilege of those who she sought to obliterate, those she blamed, for whom her fist clenched in anticipation.

She was both tinder and flint. The green landscape with its curving hills, thick forests and singing rivers would burn, cities would become dust and, finally, so would those that didn't deserve its comfort.

There would be no forgiveness and, for the world, there would be no happy endings.

1

THE MEETING

Frank woke himself with his own cry, immediately bolt upright, feeling himself drag in a long, dying breath as he willed himself awake, coughing until his lungs ached and his guts burned.

He opened his eyes wide to be met with thick darkness, feeling for the brutal hands around his throat before he felt the wash of relief of a condemned man pardoned as the noose is tightened.

As nightmares went, this one rinsed him. Pushed under the water until his last breath left him and he'd surrendered to the crushing darkness, the face of the person who would end him and wrestle the title of Simbrian heir from him. His own father. Dagmar Dag.

He pushed himself round, urging himself to consciousness until he became aware of the wind and rain battering the life out of his bedroom window, sending an unusual sense of gratitude sweeping through him as he realised he was in the attic of Polly's teashop. Alive.

He braced his elbows on his knees and pressed his eyelids together, calming the short breaths that had travelled with him through the blur of waking but the image of Dagmar through the flowing water of his drowning wouldn't leave him.

He fought the urge to fall back to sleep. The soft, freshly laundered bedding called to him, but so did the demons of his dreams. He fought some more, gripping to the wakefulness, despite the wholly unsociable hour.

The window wrestled against the squall that threatened to break its glass. Frank reached within himself, determination coursing through his adolescent muscles until he got to his feet just as the town clock struck two. He took a moment to compose himself, to adjust to the dark. A few deep breaths before he quickly dressed and headed softly down the two flights of stairs to the front door.

He was late.

***

Out on the street, Cas, Gabby and Anya waited, cowered in a shop doorway. Scant shelter against the relentless sour wind and obstinate rain that had settled over Rhaeder during the last few days as the autumn began to usher in its tougher, colder cousin. A miserable night to be out and about, a sure dark omen of the task that lay ahead of them.

Frank noticed them bracing rigid against the weather, coat collars turned up, hands in their pockets or thrust under their armpits, the slightest of nods from each of them as he approached through the torrent, their faces dark and wary against the black shadows of the night, rainwater trickling in slow droplets from the end of each nose. A miserable night for sure. Dark omens for sure.

'What kept you?' said Cas, pulling his coat tighter as if it would do any good. No smile.

'Sorry,' said Frank. 'I got held up.'

'At two in the morning?'

Frank shrugged. He looked to the sky, pinching his eyes to slits against the ferocity of the rain in the vain hope it might clear, that it might help them in what they had planned, but it looked back at him and laughed, throwing more misery right down their throats.

They knew what they needed to do; not a task for the faint hearted. They'd discussed it in the days following their return from the horror of the silent forest, but not one of them looked like they had the stomach for it, not on a night that shed demons from above and promised nothing but bother.

They hadn't gone back to the confines of Excelsus. What was the point? None of them wanted to, none of them felt a life on a straight road fit anymore. They walked in the wake of Irundi, an experience that had left its indelible mark on them, left hidden scars, deep scars and had brought all of them closer to death than was healthy for four teenagers.

Moonhunter had told them they needn't return, that she would cover for them while they finished what they'd started. She was more interested in what had happened to Frank's mother and had sworn not to tell anyone, given her blessing. She knew greater things preyed on their young minds, drew them down the darkest alleyway the end of which was cast in the bleakest shadow. It was a one-way street, one down which they'd been travelling for over two years, one where they could feel the end getting closer though it still kept drifting maddeningly out of sight, the final pieces of an impossible jigsaw that continued to elude them, hiding in unreachable corners.

Adventures with good and glorious outcomes were the thing of folk stories, written by the victors with wandering memories. The reality couldn't have been more different. It had left them battered and tired, a sour taste coating their mouths and the relentless pursuit of the Simbrian had done none of them the slightest bit of good.

Anya gave her glasses a pointless wipe and patted her right thigh. A subconscious reflex, a matter of instinct. A tell-tale sign of the weapon concealed there, the one that had cut down Morrin and added years to her youth. Frank knew there was at least one more hidden in her boot. Perhaps one knife is never quite enough.

Thick droplets fell slowly from Gabby's lashes. Her eyes, the colour of wet soil, meeting his. Fixed, determined, her body bound up against the bitterness of the weather. She looked like she'd rather be elsewhere. They all did.

'Ready?' she said.

'Are you sure we have to do this?' said Cas.

The others ignored him, not even the usual raise of the eyebrows, and moved off, leaving Murgatroid Square to its shadows and nightmares, and melted into the narrow backstreets of the town.

2

IN

No souls walked the streets. Only the crashing rain dared to venture onto the roads and pavements, battering a frantic, endless rhythm.

Fast-flowing rivers of rainwater sped easily down the gutters and around their feet. The storm-water drains had exploded against the torrent, overflowing beasts that growled in heavy plumes that frothed with wild unforgiving in the night.

No ordinary storm, not like a petulant child's tantrum – best ignored and soon ended – this was cold and murderous, merciless and grudge-bearing, bitter and relentless.

They kept their footsteps light, dancing across the pathways to avoid getting their feet soaked, through the back-alleys where the downpipes on buildings, blocked and choked by sodden clumps of brown and decaying leaves blown through by the wind, had backed up to the rooftops, sending roaring cascades crashing down to the darkness below.

The town should be completely dead, but it lived with the sound of the storm that seemed determined to impede their progress. But nothing would and Frank hoped they could use the weather as their bad-tempered ally to execute their task quickly.

Gabby was swift and sure, leading them to the side of the building.

They'd been careful to take an obscure route, doubling back on themselves, prolonging the wretched soaking, just in case they were being watched, being followed. Paranoia followed the Simbrian around like a lost puppy, but nothing was out tonight – nothing except the invisible monsters that hid themselves on corners and in the doorways of their minds, trying to unsettle their nerves, forcing them to keep one pace ahead.

Frank felt his insides jitter as Cas pushed the window up, the silent sash moving gracefully upwards from when he'd worked on the lock the previous day and, without words, they climbed in one after the other.

A wave of dry gratitude engulfed them, left them dripping like split gutters in the small, unlit room. Gabby grabbed a handful of her long ringlets and wrung them out as the others tried to rid themselves of as much water as they possibly could. Frank peeled off his dripping coat and placed it in a corner on the floor as Cas shut the window, stifling the thudding from out in the street.

Frank blew the raindrop that appeared anchored to the end of his nose. The rain had chilled him and evaporated much of his enthusiasm and the silence each of them demanded and the dry confines of the room did nothing to raise his mood or his hopes that they were going to follow this through with any level success.

He rubbed his palms up and down his upper arms. Brisk movements to ignite some warmth. He blew out his cheeks, reached into his pocket, pulling out the Elemental ball together with a small square of white cloth.

'Light,' he said, watching as the sphere clouded, a swirl of vivid aquamarine and dusty white, punctuated with pin-pricks of yellow sparks, igniting the primitive sleeping power it possessed as it stalled, then lit the room with an intense white light that had Frank and the others looking away.

Frank spread the cloth out in his other palm and dropped the ball into it, wrapping it with a curl of his fingers, damping it to a steady glow.

A look at the tension on the faces of the others. He could feel it on his as he attempted to push aside the constant thoughts of getting caught, and the consequences. He gave them a moment to steel themselves, to make sure each of his friends had hurdled the storm sufficiently before they moved out. There was no rush.

After a few minutes he checked them. All ready.

'Let's go,' he said.

3

EMPTY

Anya led, checking her blades again, her soft, smooth movements as stealthy as a jungle cat. Silent. Concentration took hold of her as she stopped them at the end of the corridor with a calm raise of her palm, listening to the darkness, before stepping out and heading towards the staircase that would take them to the first floor and Jackson's office at the front of the Council building.

They'd been there just once, following the discovery of Markowitz's body after she'd been relieved of Everbleed's prophesy by Dagmar. They all knew the route, that the Council offices were guarded day and night and that they'd need luck to smile on them just this once, although Frank knew relying on luck as your partner was like jumping from a cliff while tied to a rope, without having checked the knot.

Fortune had a habit of favouring the intelligent while turning its back on the stupid and he hadn't stopped to ask which category this fell into.

But Jackson had something of theirs - their book. The book that appeared to have the whole mystery of the Simbrian bound in its small and battered pages. They had to get it back. Thief.

The storm rocked the building. The blackest night Frank could ever remember had them scurrying like mice to Jackson's office door. Anya didn't bother checking to see if it was locked, she just pushed the handle down and shouldered the door open with deep resounding thud, earning looks from the others although Frank was sure nothing but the howling wind would wind its way through the offices to anyone who cared to patrol its corridors. The storm was, indeed, a friend.

Cas blew warmth into his hands, then locked the door, an instant precaution to buy them valuable time if anyone came looking.

Then they got to work.

No time to talk, no time to linger, no time to take in the finer aspects of Jackson's surroundings that the light from the orb revealed. The smell of polish on the crafted furniture, the thick comfortable pile of the carpet, the gilding on the window frames, all the finery that Jackson wrapped himself up in. None of it mattered. What mattered was getting their property back.

It didn't take long. Cas could sniff out a hiding place as easily as drawing a breath, but it wouldn't have taken a genius to find it.

It was the obvious place for Jackson to have a safe. So obvious a blind man would have seen it. Arrogance always seemed to follow the powerful as much as it followed the foolish and would eventually see either undone.

The steel-grey eyes, a match for his beard, gazed across the room from the portrait, staring directly at where Jackson sat each day presiding over Byeland and spreading his own myth that he was a man for the people. A myth he firmly believed, no doubt.

As Gabby and Anya lifted the large frame off the wall Frank looked into the eyes of the man that had had his grandson steal their book and felt nothing but the corruption of power, the sort his gran had warned him of.

The painting told him what he already knew; to have a portrait of yourself commanding your office, then store your valuables in a strongbox at its back was the height of vanity. To think you were untouchable.

It wasn't just an image, but a reflection of the ego of the man who sat at the top of the chain, holding on to power, jealous of youth, thinking he could do what he pleased without a thought for the shoulders on which he stood.

They placed the picture carefully on the floor against the wall, its musty smell stretching out into the room. Cas stood before the heavy iron strongbox recessed into the wall, held in place by weighty bolts. A combination lock and sturdy handle looked back at him. Frank could taste the tang of metal, could feel its weight on his hands just by looking at it.

Cas gently ran his index finger around the edge of the small door, then pushed the handle down. The heavy thunk of thick steel echoed through the room. He looked at the others with a shrug of his shoulders. Frank could barely believe it. Unlocked.

Cas gave the handle a light tug, the door swinging towards them under its own weight. Frank held the light up to the opening and peered in.

Empty.

The safe was empty. Frank assumed there would be something – coins, banknotes, gold bars, confidential papers, important documents of government. But no, nothing but cold, grey metal and a bunch of lost hopes.

'Bastard,' muttered Gabby.

Cas ran his hands around the inside. Nothing. Jackson's smug face looked up. Frank could hear him laughing at them, admiring his own little victory. He loosed an irritated breath before kicking the point of his boot between Jackson's eyes.

'Perhaps it's at his house?' said Cas. 'Although he's bound to have a couple of massive dogs.'

Frank wandered over to Jackson's desk, cursing and sighing through his teeth. He placed the Elemental ball down and picked up a bottle of ink that sat lonely on the top before throwing himself into Jackson's exquisite, padded chair. He felt his tired limbs unwind, easing in the comfort of the soft quilting of the seat and back as he stretched his legs under the desk.

He gave the ink a shake, wondering if he should empty it over Jackson's face, before placing it back down on the purple leather inlaid into the oak.

The empty desktop stretched out before him, a desert of corruption and duplicity. The fact that there was nothing on the desk brought an uneasy twist to Frank's stomach. He'd expect a busy man like Jackson to be bothered by a multitude of requests or demands from the corners of the country, from towns needing help with their roads, to lawmakers claiming his time to consider their ideas, to the poorest seeking assistance. All would bring a deluge of papers and documents, all would require time and trouble, but it looked like he'd cleared his desk, packed everything up and wasn't coming back. Now, *that* was troubling.

A look down had Frank glimpse something hidden in the shadows in the foot-well, propped up vertically against the dark of the pedestal. He pushed the chair back and bent forward, a closer look revealing a single piece of paper, inviting him to reach down and pick it up.

He pulled it out from the shadows and held it for a moment before unfolding it and laying it flat on the desk, feeling his eyebrows knit. He felt Gabby at his shoulder and looked up at her as she stared at the flame-red wax seal on the empty envelope, a seal that bore the familiar but vile image of a scorpion.

He turned the envelope over.

Neat, upright writing in a well-schooled hand was inked firmly into the paper, addressed to Governor Alfred Jackson, marked private and personal, for the addressee's eyes only.

Gabby reached over and took it, showing it to Cas and Anya. He could tell they were all thinking the same thing: Why had Jackson received a personal letter from Kzarlac, and where had he gone?

4

THE PEACOCK

Frank sunk back into his bed, soaked and frustrated, the needle from Jackson's office sticking him, and awoke to receding grey skies and even darker thoughts of Jackson's motives.

A letter from Kzarlac, Byeland's sworn enemy. It could mean anything. A threat, an offer, a trade deal.

Despite the antipathy between the two countries, the machinery of commerce still kept turning and Frank understood there would be dealings on a certain level, even with Byeland's fiercest adversaries. Lucrative trade deals didn't necessarily go hand in hand with full-frontal aggression, but deals were still struck and money was the soothing ointment that those with fortunes to make gladly applied.

Someone was making money from them and Frank didn't need to move the pieces on the board many times to understand who that might be.

Norris was always cussing and blustering on the subject, lecturing the breakfast table on the few who benefitted from creaming money off the top.

But Frank had an unshakeable feeling that whatever had been in the envelope had led to Jackson emptying his safe and clearing his desk. No other explanation would fit and Frank had lost his appetite for coincidences.

Their Simbrian quest was stacked high with them. Coincidences were just the thin layer under which one could always find careful plans or luck or mistakes and this was no different.

He could feel his sour mood through his tiredness, the hot feeling behind his eyes that stung every time he rubbed them in a sorry attempt to haul himself awake from the meagre hours he'd managed to sleep, although the sweet smell of cooking breakfast gave him a welcome shove.

He swung himself out of bed, the effort drawing a groan and a twist of his neck, and sat for a moment staring at the crumpled mound of damp clothes, discarded willingly in the small hours in his desire to get back under the covers, to feel the warmth and dry and comfort of his room.

Breaking into the Council offices might have seemed a waste of time in the moments of the empty safe, but it had thrown him some interesting questions and he might just be pointed in the direction of the answers by Norris.

Hearty, home-cooked food beckoned as Frank dressed, taking a moment to run his finger around the dark circles under his eyes as if they might rub off before roughing up his hair and heading downstairs.

He could never get enough of Polly's cooked breakfasts, packed with all the calories a teenage boy needed first thing in the morning. The greasy ooze from the sausage and bacon, the earthiness of mushrooms and the sweetness of tomatoes was the thing of teenage dreams and, following the night's outing, Frank devoured everything on his plate like a hen pecking at freshly thrown corn, to Polly's raised eyebrows.

'My goodness, Frank,' she squawked. 'Your legs hollow?'

Frank jerked his head and pulled on a smile, feeling the onset of fullness in his stomach, stifling a hefty belch with a fist over his mouth as Polly caught his sideways glance to Maddy who had barely managed a few mouthfuls. Polly reached over and took his plate.

'Good job I cooked a bit extra. Seconds?'

Frank nodded and stretched, a reminder of him sitting in Jackson's chair in the clutch of the storm. He looked at Norris whose attention was firmly on that morning's *Broadsword* which he clasped with one hand while absently trying to impale a sausage with the fork he held in the other.

'Blasted Huish fisherman,' he muttered so Polly wouldn't hear. 'Claiming some sort of rights in the Morra. That's been fished by Byeland for centuries, now they want to turn up and claim a share.' He looked at Frank. 'Trouble's brewing, Frank.'

Tell me something I don't know, thought Frank before saying: 'I'm sure Governor Jackson'll sort it.'

Norris gave a hmph and a snort, still doing some fishing of his own with his fork, the sound of metal prongs on crockery rat-a-tatting across the table.

'You look what you're doin',' said Polly with a thick hint of irritation.

Norris appeared not to hear, grunting as his attempts at spearing the sausage finally ended in success.

'If I wanted to speak to Governor Jackson, how would I go about it?' Frank felt himself bristle at his own words. Whenever Jackson wanted to talk to him he seemed to have no trouble seeking Frank out but it was unquestionably not the same in reverse. Norris kept looking at the paper and took the end off the sausage with a snap of his teeth.

'With difficulty, my boy,' said Norris. Frank felt a vague roll of his eyes. 'I'm afraid you'll have to go through Mrs Frost.' Frank's mind flashed to the last time he'd looked into the icy receptionist's compassionless eyes when she was having him handcuffed and dragged away before being thrown into the cells. Not something he wanted repeated. 'But I wouldn't worry at the moment.' Frank raised his eyebrows. 'Mr Jackson's away on business. Not sure when he'll be back.' Frank felt the frustrated sag in his shoulders. 'Got Malarkey in charge. How that woman ever got to be so senior, I'll never know.'

But Norris's voice faded as Frank began to nod inwardly – not just coincidence, then. Safe empty, their book in hand, a letter from Kzarlac, away on business. A questionable cocktail.

Norris munched at the other end of his sausage.

'Where's he gone?' Frank felt the sharp tone of his of voice as its edge nicked Norris. 'Sorry. Do you know where he's gone?'

'Can't say I do, Frank. His assistant came down to the office yesterday and told us that Mr Jackson had been called away on urgent business and Malarkey would be holding the fort. Dropping the fort, more like.'

Norris chuckled at his own joke as he turned a page before looking back at his plate, embarking on a round of hasty mushroom spearing.

'Would Spyro know?'

'I'm not sure. I don't know. Maybe. All I know is that his grandson's looking after his house – shouldn't say that, really, but Mrs Hattersley was telling me –'

'Ralph Jackson?' Frank's interruption had Norris looking over his glasses.

'Why, yes,' said Norris. 'You'll know him from the academy. Jumped up glamour-boy. Peacock doesn't quite describe him. Looks like he's destined to be my boss someday, heaven help us. His grandfather already seems to have him under his wing and it's causing some to do more than raise their eyebrows, if you know what I mean. If only Mr Jackson knew a thing or two about what he's really like.'

But Frank's focus was already running three strides ahead. Ralph Jackson; the vain, strutting heir to the throne, stealer of girlfriends, stealer of their book. Well, what d'you know. Was that the tuneful sound of a score being settled he could hear? Perhaps it was time to pay him a visit.

Even peacocks could be plucked.

5

THE PAYBACK

The location of Jackson's house in Rhaeder wasn't the closely guarded secret it might have been. In fact, Frank had wandered along the upmarket street, gazing idly on the evenly spaced sycamores, admiring the carefully swept pavement and roadway and its closely clipped grass verges on a number of occasions during his time in the town.

It was a different world to Murgatroid Square and the narrow, rat-infested backstreets that that led from the eastern end of the town.

Each of the square, double-fronted houses sat back from the road as if it would be unthinkable for them to be any nearer to the passing public. High walls and hedges provided a further step back into seclusion for the wealthy, private owners. There was no doubt that poverty and hunger had never walked along these roads.

To anyone from the poorer parts of town it may have seemed a touch intimidating but, once Frank had filled the others in on the details of his conversation with Norris, about the arrogant house-sitter that awaited them, they didn't hesitate. They quickly drained their rhubarb shakes, thanked Mr Laskie and headed across town.

The high iron gates of Jackson's house fronted the short driveway that ran to a shiny, ink-black door under an elaborate portico flanked by two gothic pillars that sang to the tune of authority to those who approached.

The damp legacy of the previous night's storm had left the sky full of strange colours but had brought a quiet, still day and the sun set the gravel on the driveway sparkling as, through the gates, ambled the languid figure of Ralph Jackson, a pretty girl on his arm.

From his hiding place, Frank's gaze fuelled the fire of animosity and deepened the pit of revenge. He focused his eyes. It wasn't Libby, he'd have recognised her instantly. The girl that clung limpet-like to Jackson's bicep like she'd won a prize at the fairground was waif-like with hair like the bleached face of the sun at the height of summer.

Frank clenched his teeth at the smarmy grin, the broad confidence that smelled like honey to the swarm of Rhaeder girls from whom Jackson could have his pick. He was determined this would go well, though not for the Governor's grandson.

As Jackson dipped his hand into his pocket to retrieve his keys, Frank walked out of the shadows at the side of the house and up behind him, unnoticed, and waited until Jackson held the front door key to the lock.

Before Frank could say anything, Jackson's female companion appeared to sense him standing behind her and pivoted, her fingers tightening on Jackson's arm, drawing herself into him as she looked round, a gasp escaping from her pale lips, lips that Jackson was undoubtedly planning on acquainting himself with once inside the house.

Jackson turned, key still in hand, looking poised and combative, his alarm quickly giving way to a short breath of contempt through his nose as his lips curled into the smuggest smile Frank had ever seen.

'Get off my property, Penny,' said Jackson with a superior jerk of his head towards the gate. 'Go on. Piss off, you peasant.'

Frank ignored him.

'Finished with Libby already?' he said. 'Or just spinning as many plates as you can manage?' The girl turned her head to Jackson, who shrugged her off. Frank looked at her. 'He was taking my girlfriend off me just a week or two ago. Perhaps she's back on his menu tomorrow. I'd find a more trustworthy horse to ride if I were you.'

The girl blinked back at him. Frank couldn't tell if she had suddenly lost interest in Jackson or felt she was about to get in the way of the storm that had started to brew on the doorstep but, whatever she was thinking, she let go of Jackson's arm and headed up the path and away, just the clicking of her shoes and no look back.

Jackson screwed his face up. Frank cracked a grin sharp enough to get under Jackson's skin.

'You just cost me a blissful afternoon, Penny.' He took a step forward, making a grab for Frank, his other fist clenched. Frank backed away as Jackson came for him. 'What was it about my last lesson that you've forgotten, you little piece of shit?' Frank just flashed his teeth in a wide smile in the hope it would wind Jackson up even more. He wasn't disappointed. 'It'll be my pleasure to smack that look right off your face.'

'Oh, promises, promises Ralph,' said Frank, folding his arms. 'But all I want is a bit of information off you, then we'll leave you alone. That's all.'

Frank watched as Jackson let his words sink in, looking like he couldn't figure out if Frank was joking. A moment hung in the air long enough for Frank to avert his eyes over Jackson's shoulder, making Jackson turn his head, looking behind him.

Anya stood with her feet apart, arms crossed over her chest, looking like she would tear his head off if he made a wrong move. He looked back at Frank.

'What's this, got your little girlie to try and scare me?'

He laughed. A slow, well-heeled laugh with all the hallmarks of privilege, his look embedded with arrogance as if being born with a good-shaped face was an achievement to be endlessly proud of, though Frank detected an air of uncertainty as Jackson glanced behind him again, absorbing the steel in Anya's eyes.

'Had you down as a coward, Penny. Seems I was right.'

Frank resisted the temptation to invite Anya to give Jackson a short demonstration of her abilities, sharpened in the company of Esryn and the Black Flame, and simply cocked his head and clicked his tongue.

'Now, now, Ralph. Sticks and stones.' Frank inspected his fingernails before crossing his arms again, indifference on his face. 'I just need to know where your granddaddy is, please.'

Jackson snorted.

'Are you stupid? Why would I ever tell a little scrote like you?'

Frank shrugged.

'Fair's fair, Ralph. I give you my girlfriend, you give me what I need to know. Then we're quits, okay?'

Jackson's face darkened.

'Piss off, Penny. Go back to school or, even better, back to Smithwood. Leave the important matters to people who know what they're doing. And you didn't give me Libby, I took her.'

Jackson's arrogant tone had Frank burning inside. He felt himself twitch. How he wanted to hurt him there and then. Hurt him badly. He watched as Jackson turned and, with a degree of delicacy, walked past Anya who kept her eyes imprinted on him. Frank stared at his back, a glance and a raise of the eyebrows to Anya.

'So, we're not quits, then?' said Frank.

The click of the front door opening had Jackson taking a step backward, his key still in his hand. Frank had to push back a chuckle as he imagined the look on his face as the door swung open. Cas and Gabby stood on the inside. Jackson squared his shoulders.

'Can't find it,' said Cas to Frank over Jackson's head.

'Get the hell out of my house,' said Jackson. 'I'm going to get the law onto you for breaking and entering.' Despite the appearance of the others and the numbers against him, he was still calm and superior. He turned back to Frank. 'This is priceless. I can't wait to tell my Grandfather and I can't wait to come and visit you all in jail.' His tone was sure, feet planted easily on the high ground.

'Fine,' said Frank. 'And while you're at it, why don't you tell him you've been entertaining goodness knows how many young girls in his house while he's been away and, oh, there's the small matter of that.' Frank nodded back to the doorway, making Jackson follow. Cas held up a small brown paper bag with a slight shake of the wrist.

Jackson clenched his jaw. 'Or do you want me to tell him you've been keeping a stash of dreamweed in his house?' Jackson couldn't rip his eyes from the bag, looking like he was sifting through his options. 'Cas is really good at finding things. *Really* good.'

'I'll just say you planted it,' said Jackson, certainty beginning to crumble on his tongue.

'I don't think that'll wash, Ralphie.' Frank took a few measured strides, folding his arms as he stopped alongside Jackson. 'You see, we know who supplies it to you and who knows how much more is in the house? You see, Cas is really good at hiding things, too. *Really* good.'

It hadn't taken much for Norris to spill what he and his Council chums knew about the Governor's grandson, telling Frank it was well known that Ralph had an appetite for smoking drugs. In fact, once Norris had started, just as Frank expected, he couldn't stop himself, eager to offload not just his own opinion, but that of the whole Council staff.

It appeared that, throughout the halls of power, nepotism went hand in hand with deep resentment and Ralph Jackson was the recipient of both.

Then, a brief visit to see Blackburn on the way to Laskie's that morning had yielded more. Frank couldn't believe it when, after telling the inventor about his aversion to Jackson, he'd confirmed Norris's story about Ralph having a brewing habit for low-level illegal substances and revealed a friend of his had provided a supply. Frank didn't want to push on Blackburn's connections, but found his inventor friend was happy to drop a barrel-full of information about the Governor's grandson and the unsavoury elements he mixed with, sporting an obvious matching dislike for the entitled ex-head boy of Excelsus, giving Frank the handfuls of ammunition he needed to spring their little surprise.

Jackson's jaw tightened and his lack of a smart response told Frank he was holding a lid on his temper. Frank had him cornered, smelling the sweet sweet aroma of revenge for Libby.

'What's up, Ralph? No more cards to play? Well, unless you're going to tell me your granddad knows all about your dirty little habit, I'd say you're holding a dud hand anyway.'

Jackson snarled.

'Piss off. All of you.'

Frank shrugged and turned to go.

'Have it your way, Ralph.' He stopped and turned round. 'Oh, there was something else; Gabby?'

'I'd say trying to get this stuff into Excelsus would put the brakes on any ambitions you might have to follow in the family footsteps,' said Gabby. 'But I hear you've been doing just that.' Frank held his chin up, breathing in the scent of payback. 'Any idea how something like that would be viewed by the authorities? Or those headline hunters at the *Broadsword*? I'm just trying to imagine if good old grandpa Alfred would stand behind you.' She held her finger to her chin. 'Hm, tricky one.'

Jackson's jaw dropped. Frank watched the high ground disappear from under his feet.

'Maybe Aurora Moonhunter would like to know, what do you think, Gabby?' said Frank, meeting Gabby's eyes.

'Now that you and her have become quite close, I'd say she'd be quite accommodating, wouldn't you? A matter of who you know, not what you know. Know what I mean, Ralph?'

Her teasing tone didn't hide the barb.

Jackson looked at Frank, looking like he wanted to dare him to even try it, a step that he must know would, at the very least, ruin his self-serving prospects of ascending through the ranks of the Council, although Frank suspected he was the type who could fall in his own shit and end up getting others to clean him off before heading to the next undeserving matter that would see him get a leg up.

'Or you could just tell us what we want to know and we won't,' said Frank. 'That might be a more appealing option?' His eyes locked onto Jackson's. 'What do you think?'

The storm raged behind Jackson's stare.

'You bastard, Penny.'

Jackson clenched his fists, but Frank stepped up to him, his face inches from Jackson's finely cut jaw so he could feel his angry breath, feeling the wash of victory sweep through his body.

'You know, Ralph, the problem with you is that you think you're untouchable, that you're better than me. But you can't see a thing through your own ambition, can you? Your arrogance is your blind-spot and you should always be careful who you go messing with. Now, where is Governor Jackson?'

Jackson clenched his teeth, a seething hollow of having been outsmarted carved out below him. Frank stared at the hatred in his eyes but wouldn't allow himself to back away. Still Jackson hesitated, then let out the long breath of a beaten man, realising no one was coming to the rescue. Through his reluctant, gritted teeth he said:

'He's gone to Garrim.'

Not a response Frank was expecting.

'Garrim? Why?'

'He has a house there.'

Another unexpected answer.

'That's not what I meant.'

'I don't know. He must have some business to see to. He didn't say.'

'How long's he gone for?'

'A week, maybe a bit longer.' Frank waited, allowing Jackson to suck on the uncomfortable silence. 'What? He just asked me to look after the house while he was gone.'

'That's it?' said Frank.

'That's it, I swear.' Jackson's nerves showed themselves through his high cheek bones. Silence from Frank. 'Look, I don't know why he's gone. He just packed a bag and went.'

'By himself?'

'Yes.'

Frank looked at the others, noting the question on their faces, before stepping back.

'There, that wasn't so difficult,' he said. Jackson bit down on a response. 'Oh, just one more thing.'

Jackson seethed, looking like he wanted to rip Frank's head from his shoulders, blindsided as Anya stepped toward him and, before he could react, floored him with a combination of painful blows to the face and abdomen. Jackson sank like a felled tree and lay curled up and coughing at Frank's feet.

'Now we're quits,' said Frank. 'But breathe a word of this to anyone and we'll be back for you and, next time, Anya will demonstrate how sharp her blades are.' Frank looked down at him with the bittersweet tug of vengeance. 'I won't ask if you understand because, if you don't, you're more of an arrogant fool that I thought.' He looked up. 'Let's go.'

6

THE UNEXPECTED VISITOR

Governor Jackson has a house in Garrim? The arsehole of Byeland, where lawlessness stepped hand in hand with dishonesty, where you'd only venture if you were looking to cross the border into Kzarlac, looking for trouble or to get your kicks in its many gambling dens, taverns or brothels that hugged its streets.

The few days they'd spent in its company were enough to make them think twice about a quick return and their brief dalliance with the sleaze and depravity of Garrim confirmed that Jackson hadn't bid farewell to Rhaeder and headed there with a holiday in mind.

The obvious question was, why?

Frank would understand if he had owned a front-facing beach house in Copperhead Sands, but to have chosen the dark, foul backstreets of the urban wart that was Garrim had him scratching his head but, then, even the best kept dogs are inclined to get fleas now and again.

More important than the make-up of Jackson's property portfolio was that it looked like he'd headed there with their book. His reasons for taking it unknown but he could detect the scent of the Simbrian on the tail of Jackson's journey east.

Frank knew they had to follow, knew the late autumn would herald the onset of poor weather around the high peaks, the border and the mountain pass, adding to the unpredictability of Garrim, thoughts that had him worried before they'd even started thinking of a plan and you had to have a plan, however rubbish, and trust you could see it through.

Time wasn't their ally. It never had been. It had always run ahead of them, never looking back and now it sprinted out of sight towards the Longshadow mountains, daring them to follow to Garrim. But the only transport had left that morning and the next one wasn't for another two days and two days was too long. Too much thinking time. Too long for them to think of what might be waiting for them as they anticipated taking wary steps back into the festering pit of the border town. Too long for them to dwell on what Jackson was doing.

They couldn't wait, didn't want to wait, but they were all out of choices, and it doesn't do to be out of choices.

The delay just drew on Frank's impatience, although a short pause might be for the best. Their haste had seldom brought the best of rewards. Too often they'd jumped in without taking time to peer into the waters and nearly paid a high price, perhaps the Simbrian pool was just too murky but as the day passed all he could think of were a hundred reasons why Jackson had travelled to the borderlands without telling anyone why and not one of them gave him an ounce of comfort.

An autumn wind had picked up, unlike his mood, and his pleasure at the sight of Ralph Jackson spluttering his guts up on his doorstep had quickly waned on their heels as they'd left the grand house.

He kicked at the dust in the street, casting a sullen figure – head down, hands deep in his pockets – as he left the others and headed back to Polly's, not sure how he'd be able to stretch the preparations for their journey, feeling the time leak much too slowly through his fingers, the thought of a few nights in Garrim beginning to gnaw at his nerves.

The teashop was packed to bursting. As Frank pushed the door open the singing of the wind outside was quickly replaced with the high hum of friendly chatter, together with the aroma of fresh pastries and freshly-brewed coffee, which broke him from his thoughts.

Polly and Maddy busied themselves with a full complement

of clientele, neither of them looking his way as he weaved his way between the red and white chequered tablecloths and headed through the shop, head down, and through the door at the back which led into the kitchen, keen not to be noticed, keen to be on his own to think. To stew.

He shut the noise behind him, puffing out his cheeks, the sound from the shop reduced to a soup of blurred conversations but, before his mind could reap the comfort of the quiet, he was aware of someone else in the room, sitting at the dining table across the far side.

He looked up, his eyes on the figure in the chair. The familiar sharp, grey features looked back with no hint of pleasure at the sight of him.

'Aunt Rachel.' Surprise obvious in his voice. 'What are you doing here?'

She studied him as a schoolmistress studies an errant pupil. No smile, just her familiar look of disappointment and disapproval, as harsh as the draw of her hair, pulled back in a ruthless ponytail. She tapped a rhythm with the flat of her palm on the table, the other nursing a cup of tea.

'Nice to see you, too.' A pinched look. 'Shame it's here and not back at home.' A challenging raise of the eyebrows and the familiar tell-tale signs of her brand of confrontation. Had she come all this way for a fight? Frank felt a mild sense of alarm. He turned his head, sweeping the room with his eyes. 'He's not here,' said Rachel, severity across her words. 'Brigg's away, so he couldn't leave the farm.'

Her unexpected appearance and the immediate reference to his dad stoked his fire.

'I've been busy,' said Frank with a shrug.

It was a lame response but one he was sure she'd rise to. His eyes dared her for a response.

'Too busy to write? Too busy to pop back for a few days?'

Another shrug had her narrowing her mouth.

'I wrote,' he said, clipped and blunt.

'Your dad's worried about you.' Her angular face lanced him.

'So he left it to me to come and check that you were alright. I told him —'

'Well, I am,' said Frank with brewing adolescent arrogance. 'Now you can go back and tell him that.' He knew he'd tasted his own anger too soon, that he should have taken a moment but the only thing he could think of was that his dad hadn't felt it important enough to make the journey himself, regardless of the awkwardness that would have brought. After all the deceit, the lies, he couldn't bring himself to see the boy that wasn't his true son. 'Tell him to come and see for himself if he's that worried, which he obviously isn't.'

A muscle in Rachel's jaw tensed. He knew she didn't deserve the challenge, but she'd already dug deep beneath his skin. Even so, he pushed down the thought that beneath her words she was right, that she had picked at the scab that told her he'd stayed in Rhaeder for his dad to pay some kind of price.

He knew his absence was, in part, his way of dispensing punishment and his dad deserved every ounce of it. The other part was the wound that refused to heal. His reluctance to confront the truth, the truth his dad would confirm, the truth about the blood that flowed through his veins.

Dagmar's blood. Blood that marked him as the Simbrian heir.

'Don't take that tone, Frank.'

She was sharp but calm, the way she always dealt with Phoebe but Frank knew from his years of upbringing that she was always just an errant word away from a rush of blood. Phoebe often pushed her beyond the edge but he'd always stopped short of discovering her wrong side despite having witnessed it as an amused bystander.

The door from the teashop opened and Polly rushed in, cleaving some relief into the frost-bitten temperature in the room.

'Hello darlin',' she said. 'You see we've got an unexpected visitor.'

She dealt a wide grin toward Rachel who somehow managed to force one in return.

'So I see,' said Frank, his voice flat and unapologetic.

Polly looked at him, then to Rachel and back again. The ice in the room froze another degree.

'Cutlery,' she said. 'That's what I came through for. Cutlery.' Polly quickly grabbed a handful of knives and forks from a kitchen drawer. No eye contact. She turned. 'Well, I'll let you two…yes, I'll let you do whatever. Goodness me it's busy.'

Then she was gone, unwinding herself from the discomfort of the kitchen and back into the shop, away from the knives and daggers yet to be thrown. Rachel turned back to Frank.

'You don't have to be so rude.'

'I must have picked up some hints and tips from you along the way. It's a shame to waste the opportunity to use them.'

Rachel clenched her teeth. Frank felt himself pushing her to the edge.

'Don't take that attitude with me.' Her words were slow and precise. 'Your dad's had to put up with a lot, bringing you up while running the farm wasn't easy.'

'Well I'm doing just fine without him, okay. Tell him that.'

He was sure he could sense the grinding of her teeth, the tensing of her muscles, like the bending of a branch to the point where you know it's going to snap.

'I think you owe him an explanation for your selfish —'

'Selfish? I think he's cornered the market on selfishness. Tell him that, too.'

He noticed her tighten the grip on her mug.

'I think that's enough. He deserves better —'

'He deserves everything he gets.'

Rachel darkened in the face of Frank's petulant teenage spirit. He could feel her spring being wound another notch, suddenly flushed with the enjoyment of it.

'You owe him an explanation, as well as a darn sight more gratitude.'

'I owe him nothing.'

The barb in his voice was sharp, but Rachel didn't flinch. She drew in a few long breaths and narrowed her eyes at him.

'You owe him everything. He raised you as if you were his own...'

Her voice cut, too late. Her tight lipped look showed she'd caught herself out. He'd prised open a crack, not knowing he'd find something so unexpected. Now a silent barrier descended. Frank stared at her. She knew. All this time, she knew. His temper flared.

'You know.'

The rise in his voice had Rachel tightening her grip on her mug as he took a step forward.

'You know,' he said again.

'I...'

Frank waited, fascinated how she was going to explain her way around this one but as Rachel met his stare with her usual hard face, something inside him sparked.

'You devious bitch.' The words tumbled out before he had time to regret them. 'You and Dad are in this together. *Aren't you.*' His words pitched off the walls. Silence from her. 'I should have known. The Penny's bring me up inside a pack of lies and all you can do is come here and try and shame *me* into apologising. Well you can just piss off back to Smithwood and take your deceit with you.'

'Who told you?'

Her snarled question just added a bucketful of fuel. No apology, no remorse, no explanation. Just a brazen attempt to draw Frank out. Frank shook his head.

'What matters is why *you* didn't tell me. Why *he* didn't tell me.' The ferocity of his words kicked the room. 'You selfish, scheming cow. You come here with your fake care and concern while keeping your secret from me all this time.'

He didn't care if he was being unfair, that he'd started to push buttons he might regret. He knew he should be more grateful, knew it wasn't her fault but her defence of his dad, knowing what he knew, what they all knew, had stepped in the way of his own common sense.

Rachel got to her feet, knocking her tea over.

'How dare you. I've put up with you for long enough and you're no more grateful that that whore of a mother of yours.' If he thought she was going to back down, admit to her part in the deceit and offer some form of apology he was clearly mistaken as he felt the words bite him. Her face twisted, snapped. Rage contorted her already harsh features into something unrecognisable, something he'd never imagined lay lurking inside her. She rounded the table, stood two paces from him and raised a finger to his face. He fought the urge to back away. 'I remember the day she turned up with you. Just turned up out of the blue and handed you over and Lawrence agreed to keep you like the besotted fool he was. She knew he'd do anything for her and she used him, just like she used everyone. She dumped you and took off to bed the next poor bastard she could get her claws into. Such a filthy whore —'

Frank railed, kicking against her precisely targeted words, taking a small step forward. 'Don't you dare speak about her like that. Don't. You. Dare.'

'Oh, go on, Frank. Dare me.' A storm erupted in her eyes. 'I'll do as I damn well please. You never knew her. I did, and I wish I hadn't. She bound my brother with her beauty, the spell she laid upon him. Him and all the men she bedded. Then she dropped him and moved on and I just had to sit and watch as she broke him into little bits.' She prodded her finger into her chest. 'I was the one left pick up the pieces as she danced her way in and out of our lives. Whore. No sooner had she ground Lawrence under her heel, she moved on to...'

Her words faltered as something different gripped her face.

'Dagmar.' Frank finished her sentence for her with a lift of his chin, noticed the widening in her eyes, the dilating of her pupils at the mention of his name. 'So —'

'He was *mine*.' Frank felt a hot spike of uncertainty flush through his veins. Had he heard correctly? '*I* loved him. Dagmar was mine but she had to take him. That...that *slut.*' She spat the words, hard. Like the taste of his mother coated the inside of her mouth in bitter, unpleasant dregs. 'That whore. She just dumped your father and went after Dagmar and, surprise surprise, he fell for her charm too, just as they all did. With her shimmering her way into his bed he wouldn't as much as look at a drab stick like me. Plain Rachel Penny. She was a snake; lured them all, dug her poisonous fangs into everyone she met and wouldn't let go, not until she'd got whatever she wanted from them. She never loved him, not like I did. She wasn't capable. But he fell for her, I could see that from the moment he first laid eyes on her, since she first flashed her wild, unforgiving eyes or wound that noose of golden hair around his neck. So utterly predictable for someone so unpredictable, just like she'd done with Lawrence. But she didn't want him, she didn't want any of them. She just wanted something from them. She'd take her men from others with a flick of her lashes and without a single thought for any of the carnage she left behind. None.'

Her breathless tirade knocked the wind from Frank. So many words thrown he couldn't process them.

'You loved Dagmar?'

'What? You think me incapable? From the first time I came to Rhaeder. He was Lawrence's best friend, went everywhere together and I'd tag along. Then I couldn't think of anything else when I went back home.'

'But what about Simeon?'

'What about him?' she snapped. 'I don't deserve him. I don't deserve what he's done for me.' Her eyes lost their focus. 'Dagmar. He was so handsome, so kind.'

'Kind?' Frank huffed the word.

'Yes, Frank. But like any young man his head could always be turned by the tricks of someone like Rebecca Forbes. She stole him, left Lawrence love-struck and flapping in the dirt. She'd come back to him here and there, goodness knows where she'd been, full of the bloody pox I should imagine, but he'd always be so grateful to see her, so dependent. She was like the worst kind of drug and she always left him broken.' She paused, wiping her mouth. 'Then one day she turned up. With you.' She could barely get the words out. She looked him up and down, simmering in her eyes, looking at him like she wanted to wipe him away. 'She told me that you were Lawrence's, but I wasn't convinced. Knowing her, you could have been from any of her many men but Lawrence didn't even question her lies and agreed to bring you up.' Frank bit down. 'She left you with Lawrence and just headed off, again. Call her a mother? No mother would do that but, then, she only loved herself.'

Frank could feel each claw of her voice at his throat as it tried to rip him to shreds. Before her stood the child of the one person she loathed and the unstoppered hatred flowed in untethered torrents. She paused, composing herself again, yet Frank could still see the naked emotion tumbling from her.

'All I wanted was for Dagmar to notice me. I did all I could in the face of that serpent. Things I shouldn't have. I...'

Her voice trailed off. She looked at her shaking hands. Something different passed across her face. Frank caught it for the slightest moment but there it was. Guilt. The faraway look of guilt. He'd seen it on Edwina Chetto's face and in Moonhunter's tired eyes and now recognised it like an old friend.

'It was you,' he said. 'You gave away my Dad's part of the Simbrian.' No reaction. Confirmation. 'Your family's legacy to protect the world. You took it and gave it to Dagmar so he'd, what? Fall in love with you?' Silence. 'Didn't you?'

She raised her eyes to his. Now they were full of hate. Hate for him, hate for his mother, hate for herself. Her face twitched.

'And I'd do it again if it meant I could have him.'

Tears raged in her eyes. Frank shook his disbelieving head, trying to think of any reason why she would even contemplate giving Dagmar the fragment of the Simbrian, to steal it from her own brother. But he knew how love could make people behave, how it could shed the shackles of their senses, take them to the other side of the line. He thought back to his mum and Moonhunter, how they had been prepared to kill to keep their young love intact. Rachel huffed contempt at him.

'I had a suspicion you might know.' Her words caught Frank by surprise. He looked back, drawing more from her. 'Your dad was worried about you when you came back from your first year at the academy. When I asked him what was wrong he wouldn't tell me, so I knew you'd found out about the Simbrian. He said you'd mentioned something about the old caretaker, but you didn't let me in. Got that little skill from that freak of a mother, did you?'

Frank felt his face drop as his mind took him back to his bedroom at the farm, then to Moonhunter's office when the Head had identified the seer's marks on his temples. It was her. Not Simeon. All along he'd suspected Simeon. He was the obvious choice, where all the fingers pointed but, now he thought about it, she'd been there both times the marks had appeared.

'You read my mind?'

Rachel loosed a laugh under her breath. Frank found himself staring at the floor.

'It's not just Lawrence that can boast unusual skills. It's my speciality, although I never got an invitation to Excelsus.'

'I thought it was Simeon.' He looked back up. 'I thought it was him who stole Dad's part of the Simbrian, and you let him take the fall for that, as well as letting Dad think it was him.' Frank shook his head. 'You let Simeon take the blame for all these years.' A satisfied, unapologetic nod. 'And he...what? Went along with it? For you?'

'Like I said, I don't deserve him.'

'You think?'

'Love has many forms and he is devoted to me.'

It was difficult to take in. Simeon, the willing fall-guy for his deceitful wife, the man Frank had been quick to blame, quick to believe what his dad and Spargo believed, yet he had been part of the life-saving rescue for him and his friends from Balal and her blood-thirsty band of Sapirai and had expected no thanks for it.

Frank could see how his naturally miserable disposition and withdrawn manner made him an easy target, but Simeon had just sat back and taken it. Did he really love his wife that much? And how could everyone be so wrong about him? The abysmal way Simeon had been treated added one more layer to the lies, the whole unsavoury pack of lies, and the fault for that lay squarely at his aunt's feet, stoking the heat under his skin.

'And Dagmar did what?' He could taste the venom on his tongue, sense the building mockery. 'Took it and sent you on your way.' Her face tightened as Frank grasped a nerve and began to squeeze. 'He didn't want you, did he?' He sensed her start to boil. 'You stole something so important to your family, who'd kept it safe for generations and gave it to Dagmar and for what? So he could reject you like the cold, unwanted coward you are. Well, you got what you deserved. You talk about my Mum but you're no better. If fact, stealing from your own brother and getting someone else to take the rap for it makes you far worse, you selfish bitch.'

Frank had no time to react as she slapped him across the face with the force of a raging tempest, knocking him sideways. Tears clouded his vision as he tried to gather his senses.

She hit him again. Harder. Shockingly hard. Murderously hard. For such a slight woman it was difficult to imagine she could wield the palm of her hand like it were brick.

He could feel the full weight of her rage as the pain whistled around his skull. He wrapped his head in his arms to stop the searing pain of the third blow if it came but all he heard was the guttural sound of Rachel's growling breaths. He stepped back, his hand against his stinging cheek and looked into her dark, dark face.

'You're just like her,' she spat. 'Bad blood. You're full of *her* bad blood.'

7

THE PAIN

Frank sat at the lakeside, the cool autumn breeze that washed down the shallow valley picking at his hair, a salve to his bruised mood. He knew his mind should be focused on the trip to Garrim, on finding Jackson, but it kept wandering down the dark alleyway that was the confrontation with his aunt, the way she looked at him, what she saw in him – a reminder of the bitterness and loathing she still felt for his mother, of what he represented. *Bad blood*; if only she knew what blood ran in his veins.

He could still feel the smarting of his cheek as if she'd just hit him, the razor-cut from her words that repeated in his head fogging his concentration, despite his attempts to push them aside.

But it wasn't just the poisonous words she'd reserved just for his mother. She'd known, had always known and he would never forgive her.

As far as he was concerned she could piss off back to Smithwood and tell his dad that he knew all the lies, save him the job and the awkward confrontation he'd been avoiding for months, then he'd never have to go back to the farm again.

His gran sat next to him, wrapped up in her old grey cardigan, sleeves pulled to the wrists to hide the Prismian ink that lurked beneath, tapping her foot on a flat rock against the easy silence that sat between them. Ingozi sat leaning into Frank, occasionally sniffing at his mug of hot chocolate. Warmth to the chill of Frank's thoughts as he sifted stones through the fingers of the other hand.

Leaving Polly's for a couple of days for his gran's comfy cottage in the wilderness before he travelled to Garrim with the others hadn't been the most difficult of decisions in the face of his acid aunt. Rachel had travelled all the way from Smithwood under the veil of checking he was okay, yet she'd ended up throwing unremitting spite about his mum and her words had left their mark. An unplanned end to a wasted journey.

He'd never known, would never have guessed, the secrets they kept or what people would do for love. His dad's love for his mum, Rachel's love for Dagmar, Simeon's love for Rachel.

The truth about how Dagmar came by his dad's fragment of the Simbrian was hard to stomach. So easily given. Was that the first one, the one that had sent Dagmar on his hunt for the others, that sowed the seeds of Dagmar's obsession? If so, the cost had been terrible.

But both Moonhunter and Spargo and now Rachel had cast a shadow on his mum's character and he found it a difficult image to shake. Moonhunter had described her as complex, unholy. Spargo as wild, unleashed, dangerous, words that didn't fit the mother he'd always conjured in his head, the one he thought of every time he looked at the locket that hung around his neck or listened to the stories his gran told him.

His gran had created nothing but charming, mischievous pictures of her, deepening the sentiment with every tale while avoiding any reference to the picture painted by others that knew her.

His mother had stepped into the lion's den voluntarily, taking the piece of the Simbrian that Moonhunter's mother had willingly passed to her straight into the jaws of Kzarlac and all that meant for the safety of the world and, whichever way he cut it, he was sure she knew what she was doing, that the whole thing wasn't just the random act of a young woman even though the risks were beyond measure.

Who would do that? Why would she do that? It seemed like an act of foolishness and one thing he was certain of, through all the stories, good and bad, was that his mother was no fool.

He looked out to the lake, squinting against the dipping sun, knowing the time had long since passed for him to try and get to the bottom of the many unanswered questions. If anyone knew, the old woman sitting next to him knew but it appeared that truth was a difficult commodity for his family to deal with.

He drew in a reluctant breath in preparation for a difficult conversation.

'Why did Mum go to Kzarlac?'

Frank's question from nowhere had his gran's silence speaking for her. He didn't look at her. He continued to sift the stones in his hand, occasionally catapulting one as far across the contours of the water as he could, hot chocolate lapping over the side of his mug.

She offered no answer, no denial. Frank let the snare of silence tighten, the easy peace fading, the emotion in his throws rising.

He turned to her. He was used to her granite exterior, the harsh rock-face she wore like her favourite jumper but there was something in the lines on her cheeks, the creases around her eyes and lips that held varying shades of sadness. There was a frailty about her that he'd not noticed before.

'Why?' he pushed.

Why had she taken her piece of the Simbrian right into the throat of the beast who made it his ambition to seek the ultimate power for himself?

She closed her eyes, then looked down to Ingozi, now laid out between them, and rubbed his ear slowly between her thumb and forefinger.

'I don't know, Frank,' she said.

It was no answer, delivered from under the veil of weariness and Frank felt himself draw in a long breath. He put his mug down before pressing the heels of his hands into his eyes then raked his fingers through his hair, clasping them together around the back of his head. The sour taste of Rachel's venom still in the back of his throat.

'Is there something about Mum that you haven't told me?'

Iris gave a barely discernible shake of the head. Frank looked out over the water. The last thing he wanted to do was to upset his old grandmother, or get on the wrong side of her, she didn't deserve that but, at the same time, she was the one who knew his mum best.

He glanced at her. She looked out across the hills, stoically focused on the landscape, but he could tell she knew he was looking at her, looking for answers behind her unmoveable façade.

'I love the stories you tell me about her,' said Frank. 'You know I do. It's just that everyone else thinks she was different to how you see her. Like she had this whole other side.'

'Bloody opinions.' She huffed long and hard. 'You'd be best tell whoever it is where to stick them.'

She growled the words like a tiger who'd been poked hard with a sharp stick and Frank wondered whether he'd be better backing off.

'But —'

'She was your mum, Frank.' A softer edge to her voice.

'What does that mean?'

'It means you should remember her fondly. I know she wasn't there when you were growing up but —'

'Exactly. I never knew her, Gran.' He looked at his aged grandmother, her features tired and grey as the autumn clouds. 'I know you want me to hear about her carefree and spirited side, but I want to know the other stuff, too.'

'Why, Frank?'

Frank paused. An admission in his gran's words. He knew he had to choose his words carefully, not to reveal too much.

'Because I appear to be chasing her shadow, without any idea why and no clue of what she was or what she was capable of.' He looked directly into her old, sunken eyes. 'I need to know. Please.'

She looked away, her arthritic fingers grasping at the ends of her sleeves, the stern expression returning, a face hewn from stone. He knew that look. It was the look of a book closing, the door shutting. Frank drew in a breath. She was impossible.

He got to his feet and looked down at her. She refused him a look, making an obvious sweep of the valley with her eyes. After a disappointed pause, Frank turned to head back into the cottage.

'I'm sorry,' said Iris before he took a step, words that hadn't been given lightly. Not from her.

She didn't look at him, just stared out at her own thoughts. She waited, knowing he'd sit down and wait for her to unfold in her own time. Frank took a moment, then resumed his seat next to her, still she watched the emptiness, ignoring him.

'I'm sorry,' she repeated. 'Perhaps I should have told you, but I didn't think it mattered. It doesn't matter. She's no longer here and I thought it was more important for you to hear about your mum's bright side, her rebellion, her carefree passion. Not *that* side of her.' She looked at him, saw the question in his face, giving a sigh in response. She closed her eyes tight as if searching for the words. 'All of us are cut from the same cloth, Frank. It's in all of us to do right and wrong, show the light and the dark. We have sides to us that are good and sides that are less so. Then there are the sides that we don't show to anyone, that we keep hidden. Parts that we pray will never show themselves.'

She paused, taking in a deep breath as if preparing herself for something she'd never thought she'd have to do.

'We're all the same, Frank. Each of us fights our own demons. Rebecca did. Sometimes we win, sometimes we lose.' She looked down into her lap. 'Rebecca fought hers. Fought them hard. She built a vault of remarkable talents, but there's a trade, something that must be given, as day gives way to night. Sometimes she'd beat them, but sometimes they'd break her into bits.'

She looked away, a faraway look to the faraway hills, rolling gently out of sight like the vision Frank had had of his mother up until now. His gran continued to stroke Ingozi. Broad, soft sweeps of the hand to brush away the memories.

It was as if she'd opened a box that she'd struggled hard to keep closed for years, revealing a trove of unwanted words she didn't want to admit were wrapped tightly to her daughter, as if she was exposing a vein of weakness that was best kept away from prying eyes.

'Light and dark,' she repeated. 'She was too clever for her own good. Everbleed's blood has some difficult shadows running through it and it seemed to flow stronger and darker in her. Sometimes I thought she was filled with a strength and power that nature itself couldn't summon, sometimes she would just want to me to hold her for hours and wipe away her tears while she fought and struggled from within, a place where a young, innocent mind shouldn't have to dwell or linger and somewhere she kept me from entering. So many times. Too many times. She'd claw at her face and beg it to stop and there were times when I found her curled up in the corner of her room, shaking like a wretch and … I couldn't help her.' Her eyes watered and a single, solitary tear ran slowly down her cheek. 'I couldn't help her,' she whispered, a plea for forgiveness uttered too late.

'I'd watched her grow up, been her guide for twenty years, yet there was a side to her that I didn't recognise, a darkness that she kept from me.' She looked up. 'When you have children, there comes a time when you realise you can't stop the world from hurting them. Protecting your child and motherhood are fused at the core, an unbreakable bond. But I was helpless in the face of whatever was deep inside her. Helpless.'

Frank listened, although he wouldn't have called it listening. It was more than that, as if he was experiencing everything that his gran was saying, reliving it with her word by word, by the images she created as she spoke, of his mother curled up, her frightened breaths trying to find comfort in his gran's bosom while the darkness she wrestled with couldn't be contained.

It was a tough watch but it came with understanding, understanding why his gran had shielded him from his mother's distress. She was right, he didn't need to know. The box would have been better kept locked, the key discarded.

'Was she okay?'

He didn't know what else to say.

Iris nodded.

'I think so, eventually,' she said. *Or maybe she just hid it well.* 'She seemed less troubled as she got older, more in control. She was so strong-willed, utterly defiant – got that from me – but she was the restless sort, always something on her mind, needing to be elsewhere, always full of ideas and plans, wanting to take on the world, like all youngsters do.' A warm smile graced her face. 'Perhaps that was her way of coping, keeping busy and I was glad she was so independent, thought I'd done my parenting job well. When she met your dad I thought, hoped, that would settle her down a bit but there was something that had already caught her roving spirit that she couldn't shake. She'd been like it ever since she broke up with Jenny.'

Frank felt his mind fog. He thought of Aurora Moonhunter recounting the details of her passionate, unruly relationship with his mum, a relationship that faded once she had been exposed to the Simbrian and taken the fragment from her friend's mother. *The beginning of an obsession.* An obsession that had eventually taken her to Kzarlac, to Dagmar. He looked out over the water, his silence asking her to go on.

'She became distracted. Spent more time in the town, became more secretive. She'd always had a habit of getting a little obsessive about things. Don't get me wrong, you know I've always said it's important for kids to have their secrets. I had mine, but this was different. I'd ask her what was on her mind but she'd just give me that smile. Her beautiful smile. So lovely, but a disguise.'

She managed a weak smile. Frank managed one back, catching the sorrow and shadow in his grandmother's eyes.

'The joy of Rebecca's sweet and mischievous side began to fade. Something had taken hold of her and I couldn't wrestle it from her and I knew one day she'd want to leave here.' A tip of her head to the cottage. 'Still, I wasn't prepared. No mother ever is.'

'Did she tell you where she was going?'

Iris drew in a long breath.

'No.' Said with a thick slice of resignation. 'She just said there was something important she needed to do.' She noticed his look. 'I didn't like to ask her too many questions, Frank. If I did I knew she'd close as tight as a fist rather than tell her old mother anything. I was the same. You are too, don't deny it.'

Frank couldn't. He'd taken his dark mood and secrets all the way to Irundi and back and his silence had nearly cost his friendships with the others. Secrets he had in plenty. Secrets he'd had enough of.

'Then she left.'

Three words that felt so final. Frank couldn't begin to imagine what she must have felt to see her only child disappearing down the solitary track, heading away from the safety of her home and the mother who cared so deeply, wondering where her wayward daughter was going or when she would return, if ever.

'But you saw her again?'

Iris nodded.

'She'd come home occasionally. Stay for a few days. I'd ask her about the cuts and bruises but never a straight response, not that I expected any different. But she was changed. She was young but something was ageing her, drawing her away again. I could tell whatever she had done, she had more to do, somewhere else to be and off she went again.' A shake of her old head. 'Then she came back. For the last time.' The crack in her voice was barely detectable, but Frank caught it, noticed the dry tone and the watering of her eyes as she paused, taking a moment to compose herself. 'She told me she was going to Kzarlac and that she might be there for a while. I knew she knew Dagmar Dag and I could tell that whatever she was involved in had something to do with him. For the days she was here that last time I saw some of the girl I thought I'd lost. She'd help me in the kitchen, sit and talk with me out here bunched up close to me as if she didn't want to leave my side. She'd walk Ingozi around the lake and the trails she'd trodden as a child and when she left she held me for longer than she had since she was able to walk.' Iris stared down between her feet, lacing her fingers together between her knees. 'Looking back on it, she was saying goodbye to me, like she knew she wasn't coming back.' An agonising pause, eyes glazed and tearful, looking at nothing. 'And she never did.'

8

THE JOURNAL

Talking about his mum was never good for Frank's sleep. It seemed that the more he heard, the worse it became and although he'd had to prise the information from his gran, there was part of him that regretted it as he fought the bedcovers in the darkest pockets of the night.

The dark side of her unsettled him, made him search himself for similar traits, for the troubled part of his mind that he was sure lurked inside him somewhere. After all, if you look for the downside you're sure to find it, eventually.

Despite what his gran had told him, he was yet to understand anything about his mother's motivation, the thing that drove her to Kzarlac, to Dagmar.

She'd borne his child, conceived without telling him and, in the process, sent the perfect flow of blood into Frank's veins, blood that marked him as the Simbrian heir and with all he'd been caught up in from Hums to Irundi, from Excelsus to Zanmir's eye, he couldn't shake the feeling that none of it was mere coincidence.

He knew that even the most difficult of journeys could end at the brightest of destinations, but it was clear that the path his mother had taken had found a more treacherous route that had her enduring the darkness and ending up dead. A route that she'd specifically chosen for herself.

Doing anything except staying put under the blankets in the cottage wasn't something that entered his mind the following morning, but what should have been the realm of teenage laziness brought restless and pointless forays into his imagination, an imagination that dwelt on images of his tormented, restless mum.

He cast them aside, only to have them return minutes later to keep elusive rest from him until his struggles had him out of bed and heading down to the tiny kitchen to pump icy water onto his face in an effort to shake some life back into himself.

There was no sign of his elderly grandmother or her equally time-worn dog, perhaps she hadn't slept either. Perhaps she never slept well. Perhaps her nights brought a different sort of darkness and had done since that day, long ago, when her only child disappeared from sight.

Frank wished he could see the loss of his mum from his gran's point of view, to understand the pain she kept locked inside, that tramped the hills and lakeside alongside her each day but, though he had witnessed her grief for the first time, if he was honest he was having trouble assembling the parts of his own feelings to have the time for other people's concerns.

He took a few weary steps to the back door, pulled it open and walked, barefoot, down to the shore of the lake. The early morning was warm. A smear of autumn colours was waking with the rising sun – fading purples and lilacs oozed from the heather under the browns and tans of the dawn.

In the distance he could easily make her out. The small but sturdy woman standing at the lakeside with her faithful dog sniffing the ground around her ankles. She looked over to him. Frank raised his hand; if she saw it she ignored him but she started back, short, brisk strides like she was trying to get away from something, though Frank knew she could never outrun it.

'Couldn't sleep?' said Frank as Iris marched towards him like she was on military manoeuvres.

'Me? Goodness, no.' She stopped in front of him. Where Frank had expected her to be blowing out her cheeks, she seemed not the slightest bit out of breath. 'We always walk by the lake at first light. Helps clear my head.' Which the day before had appeared about as clear as the mud that crusted her boots, despite years of early morning strolls. 'Sleep well?' Frank gave a slight shake of the head. 'Ah well, I'll get some breakfast on.'

With that, she headed into the cottage. Frank followed her in.

The next minutes were spent with Frank wincing as Iris bished and bashed pans and plates to within an inch of their existence, making him wonder how she had any crockery left, before she presented him with scrambled eggs.

She hummed and whistled throughout, a distraction perhaps, the start of another day-long attempt to stop the demons from settling, one that would likely end in failure.

'I'm meeting Cas and the others in town this morning,' said Frank as he tucked in. Iris sat opposite at the small table, sipping tea. 'We're heading to Garrim.'

'Garrim?' No real surprise in her tone. 'Well, you just be careful. Foul, pit of a place. Brims with dishonesty and lures you with empty promises. Shake hands with anyone there and you'd best count your fingers and thumbs afterwards. I take it you're going to be up to no good?'

'No, not really. We had something stolen. We just need to get it back.'

Iris gave a slight dip of her head.

'Then make sure you're quick about it. Folk there will just as much take crowns from a child as anyone, or worse.' She took a sip, looking at him over the brim of her cup. 'You need to take care, Frank. I'll warn you that those who you might get on the wrong side of will use the very worst tricks and stop at nothing to make you theirs.'

'Don't worry, Gran, we can handle ourselves.'

She lowered her cup and cradled it in both hands. She wore her granite exterior well.

'That's as maybe,' she said. 'But we all have our weaknesses, a soft underbelly that a well-directed blade will easily slice open. We all have something to lose, or something we'd put ahead of ourselves, well, most of us. You should beware the man who has nothing to lose and even more wary of those who stand to lose everything.'

'What about you?' said Frank. 'What do you have to lose?'

She tightened her lips, then looked down into the ink-green liquid in her cup.

'Like I said, most of us.'

Her eyes misted, a slight crack in the granite telling Frank she already bore the scars of something absent from her life and, despite her get-on-with-it attitude, he knew she'd been adrift for more time than was welcome. As Millington Johns had told him – *we all bear our scars, some of us on the outside, but all of us on the inside* – and some scars never quite heal.

'Do you ever wonder what happened to her?' His question had an edge. He wanted to know, but knew he was using his grandmother to close the door on his own curiosity.

Iris shook her head.

'I used to, Frank. What mother wouldn't?' Her smile was filled with melancholy. 'But I stopped a long time ago. Now it's just me and the passing of the days.' Ingozi looked up at her, his sad eyes a match for her mood. 'And you, of course, you old fleabag,' she said to the dog.

She looked at the back door, still open against the strengthening sun, as if she was waiting for the sound of long-forgotten footsteps, for a face to appear through the entrance, for the warmth of a familiar voice to brighten her day.

'I kept looking for her last journal,' she said. 'When she didn't come back. I thought it might give some clues or tell me the story of what she was up to. I took to tearing the place apart to find it.' She looked to Frank. 'That's when I found the letters from your dad. But I couldn't find it and I realised that I would tear myself apart if I didn't let it go. Like I say, Frank, you get busy living or you get busy dying and I realised I needed to drink from my own medicine bottle. I still think about it now and again, maybe it would have given an old woman a few answer before she dies, eh?'

'She didn't leave it in the house?'

'No. When I think about it, she had it with her the last time I saw her, so I suppose she took it with her, although it was quite a small one. Had this unusual purple leather cover, so I think I'd recognise it if I found it. Like I said, it's a while since I stopped looking.'

A small book with a purple leather cover. Not necessarily words to make the hairs on your neck stand up, but there it was.

Frank felt himself go hot and cold at the same time. He'd had his suspicions for a while, but his gran's words stamped it in large, red letters, adding a new link to the Simbrian chain.

It was her, Rebecca Forbes.

She was the ghost they'd been chasing these past few years, the woman who never once let them glimpse her identity. But there had never been anything tangible that tied the elusive sorcerer, who found all the guardians and plundered Irundi, to his mother.

As far as he knew, she'd simply gone to Kzarlac with a piece of the Simbrian, that was all he could be certain of about her Simbrian journey, her obsession as Moonhunter had framed it.

But in the few words uttered by his aged grandmother he knew it was her, knew she'd found them all, robbed Irundi of the key of darkness and conceived the conundrum that was the book that Hums had dropped in the grounds of Excelsus.

She'd found them and warned them against the evil spread of Dagmar's ambition. She'd somehow made the first Simbrian live and breathe, then sent herself to her death while she left her infant son in the hands of someone who wasn't the natural father.

Frank pushed down on his desire to swear, thankful that his gran's eyes were still fixed on the door.

He stared into space. Focused, unfocused, trying to connect the strands that hung loosely before him.

He was sure he was right. The visit to each guardian to lay her warning before them made vivid by Edwina Chetto and Sapphire Hark. He recalled their descriptions, the blonde beauty, the resemblance to Frank. The bells in his head chimed in realisation as it started to make sense and poked at him for not realising sooner.

He didn't need to stretch his imagination too far to understand she'd most likely visited Hums and Menetti and used her full range of abilities to somehow reach into Irundi, with all its safeguards, and snatch the key.

Qaas and Esryn's description of the visitor, the target of their spite and vitriol, for whom they had nothing but murderous words, also ran to the same rhythm. The hated sorcerer that had taken Irundi unawares, plundered its treasure and laughed over her shoulder as she headed away.

He just couldn't imagine what sort of person she would have to be just to do that.

His mother was so tightly wrapped around the core of the Simbrian it was hard to peel back the layers. She'd been as close to Dagmar as she could. Shared his bed. It was just a small step to realise she knew what Dagmar was trying to recreate, to use the power for his own ends.

His mum had never died in an accident, that was coated in Lawrence Penny lies.

She'd obliterated herself, along with the Simbrian and left them to pick through the wreckage. She'd left him without a mother, deliberately, consciously, never allowing him the opportunity to feel himself in her arms, her breath in his hair, the touch of her love on the nape of his neck.

Clarity and concentration left him as he realised he couldn't do it, couldn't unravel the long thread he'd just been handed, the thread that would have an answer at the end of it. The answer that would tell him why.

9

THE WAIT

The transport didn't leave until mid-morning. Even so, Frank was back in the town early, standing at Mr Laskie's door as the old man opened it and turned the sign from 'closed'.

Frank was ushered in like an old friend, Mr Laskie uttering words of welcome through his rotting teeth and thick accent as Frank ordered coffee and slung himself and his shoulder-bag into the cushioned booth to await the arrival of the others.

He hadn't meant to be so early, but he was up just before sunrise so that he could slip into the academy grounds and release Tweedy, the hawk through whose eyes he could see, sending her up and east as their ally.

He wasn't going to repeat the mistakes of the silent forest, and having her sharp eyes above the sullen mountain rooftops of Garrim might give them an edge and help them track Jackson down if he was still there.

It couldn't hurt and it was a plan, of sorts, and you have to have a plan, however rubbish, and trust you can see it through although dragging the bird to unfamiliar territory, where pickings would be slim with the possibility of larger predators loitering around the mountainside felt a bit like a one sided decision.

He was tired. He yawned so wide he thought his jaw would dislocate. Sleep had been running in the opposite direction since their visit to Jackson's office and had sprinted further following his bust-up with his aunt and he knew Garrim demanded a clear head and sharp wits, neither of which he could summon with any confidence.

Frank squeezed his eyes shut and mustered a long breath in an attempt to rouse himself.

'More coffee, Frank?'

Mr Laskie stood at the table, ghosting in unnoticed between Frank's lethargy and constant yawning, brandishing a steaming pot.

Frank nodded and watched as Laskie quickly and efficiently served him a brim-full of welcome wakefulness before heading back to the counter.

The time swam in treacle and although it was less than an hour before Anya showed up, it felt considerably longer and Frank knew his fourth coffee wasn't really doing him any good.

Thankfully, Cas and Gabby arrived soon after, allowing Frank to tell them about the time he'd spent at his gran's, confirmation that his mum had written the book and that she was the one who had visited the guardians and Irundi before dispatching herself in the hellfire of the first Simbrian.

None of them appeared even slightly surprised; that part of their senses had long since dulled. They all had their suspicions and to have Frank confirm it was just underlining her role in the whole sticky mess.

'That sounds rather heroic,' said Anya.

'Spare me,' said Frank.

He felt the bitterness in his words. He knew he'd rather have had his mum by his side, in his life as he grew up. Not some single-minded super-sorcerer who left him alone to embark on a self-indulgent quest of her own to save the world, if that was what she was doing.

It may appear heroic to others, but they weren't him, they hadn't lost her, hadn't thought every day what she might have felt like, sounded like, smelled like. What it might have been to have her hold him when he fell, to lay his head in her lap in a field of wildflowers and listen to her childhood stories while she stroked his hair, feel her breath, hear the softness of the clouds in her voice as she told him that she loved him and see her sweet untethered smile when he said it back.

He knew you could fall over and bruise your knee, that it would sting for a bit, but only people really hurt you and it all hurt too much. Too much.

'So, she left the book so that we, or whoever found it, would use it to protect the guardians,' said Cas. Frank nodded. 'Although a fat lot of good we've done on that front.'

Frank swilled down his last mouthful of coffee, feeling its bitter bite at the back of his teeth.

'That's why we need it back,' he said. 'Otherwise we won't know who the seventh guardian is or if it's going to tell us something else.'

'That bastard, Jackson,' said Gabby. 'I never trusted him.'

Nods around the table, rising tension at the thought of heading east.

'We have the key, though,' said Anya. 'And the heir.'

Three glances in his direction. Frank felt himself frown with his inward groan, wished it away. He was no nearer understanding his part in the confusion that was the Simbrian and he'd stopped trying fit it all together – his mum, her relationship with Dagmar, the book – any of it.

The whole thing was just a twisted jumble of disconnected things although he knew there was a pattern somewhere, a pattern that would make sense of what was going on. And the book had ended up in his hands. Now why didn't he think that was some kind of coincidence, and coincidences he'd had enough of.

'We should get to the square,' said Gabby, pushing her chair back. 'We can't afford to miss the transport.'

She was right, but Frank could smell the reluctance on all of them, feeling the hour of execution upon them, knowing there was no turning back once they boarded.

As she got up Gabby reached into her pocket, a sideways look at Anya.

'That reminds me,' said Gabby. 'Here, take this.'

She handed Frank the short length of iron they'd lifted from

Irundi. The key of darkness, the insignificant looking object that was anything but. The one thing that allowed the Simbrian heir to fire the Simbrian.

Some deeds seem easy when you think of them, but the consequences can sometimes be frightening and, in very few cases, catastrophic. In this case, it would be both.

Kester's plan meant the key, the heir and the Simbrian all needed to be in the same place, a safeguard of sorts, a way of muddying the waters for anyone stupid enough to try and follow its trail. Stupid, or clever beyond measure – Frank knew which side of the fence his mum stood on, perhaps a different side to him and his friends. 'Put it in the possessor,' said Gabby. 'It'll be safer in there.'

She looked him in the eye. For a moment Frank wondered if she felt the weight of the key, its influence, bearing down on her, keeping her awake at night as it did him but he could see the depth of her determination to keep him safe. She didn't have to say it, he just felt it, felt it in all of them.

He took it from her. Heavier than it looked, an arrow the only marking etched into it, pointing to one end of the key with the silent instruction to insert, to bring the Simbrian spitting and screaming into the world, whatever that meant – to inflict or to heal, to drown or revive, to bring light or dark.

He didn't know, there were no instructions, just a jumbled mess of guesses which he hoped he'd never have to thumb through.

He took out the small pouch and loosened the drawstring. It contained the Elemental ball and a small set of lock-picks that Cas had given him, items only he could retrieve.

With a long intake of breath, he placed the key inside with a silent prayer that he'd never have to get it out again.

They all stood. There was no joy at the table, not the carefree plans that teenagers were supposed to inhabit. No lazy trips to the beach or laughing at each other through the calm and sun-kissed streets of Rhaeder.

Garrim awaited them. Like visiting your least favourite relative, only an objectionable aunt wasn't likely to get you beaten up or rob you of all your money.

10

GARRIM

The sprawling dark patch that sat in the mountain pass looked like someone had taken a shit between the high peaks and not bothered to clear it up.

Buildings in indistinct shades of grey and brown and black clung to the rising cleft in the rock, anchored to the north and south of the pass that led through to the border crossing over the river Jixx to Kzarlac. As views went, it wasn't one to be inspired by.

Given their brief history with the town, it was inevitable that the approach to Garrim would bring shivers at the unwelcome sight of its smoking chimneys and promises of threats and menace as the daylight dwindled. Frank had returned there many times, but only in his dreams and never did he imagine he'd be back so soon so the streets could take another swing at him.

Even from a distance, all it did was dredge up unwanted memories. Frank was unable to shake the pin-sharp images of their previous encounter with the lawless border town as the transport pitched in yet another large pothole, before it came to a clattering halt outside the Troll's Cudgel on the outskirts, leaving them staring into the mouth of the depravity and mayhem that spread itself across the heavy shadows of its filthy, unpleasant, narrow streets.

Gone was the high summer sun from their last visit that at least had made an attempt to breathe warmth and a small degree of normality through the towering peaks and down into the town, replaced by the dour, restless late autumn sky that wrapped the mountains in blues and greys and blacks and left the rooftops slick and the town angry.

The chill mountain air spilled from the blankness and swept down through the streets, demanding they wrap themselves up. Damp and danger clung to every surface in a greasy film and beckoned them in. The biting wind found chinks and holes in the rocks and made them sing and sigh and wail, a mournful choir to announce them.

Everywhere Frank felt the cold stare of the town on them as they left the transport behind and headed through the close warren of the suburbs, wondering which of its unwashed inhabitants would try their luck with four out-of-town teenagers and whether the slime, Manville Symes, would get wind of their arrival and finish whatever unfinished business he might feel he had with them.

As destinations went, it wasn't one to be inspired by.

But this time it was different. They were different. They'd run this road before and bore the scars of their encounter. Experience dwelt within them and the wetness behind their ears had long since dried. Even Cas had purpose on his face and despite the undertone of hostility in their surroundings and the slight chiming of his nerves, Frank wasn't as scared as he thought he might be. Their experience in the silent forest had numbed any sense they had of courting danger.

The stink of piss and sweat came at them from all sides as they eased their way through the grime and filth towards the central part of town, avoiding the vulgarity of the main drag, the tightness of the streets leeching the waning light away.

They ignored the dark looks from the shadows in the doorways and from small groups of hustlers leaning against the damp, crumbling brickwork of the buildings, sizing them up, probably deciding whether to lay out a well-rehearsed scam or just try and mug what looked like four young strangers on unfamiliar turf, heading to the southern mountainside.

Frank could taste the tang of the bedrock on the roof of his mouth, a constant reminder of the rugged peaks that kept Garrim held in isolation from the rest of Byeland.

The fading light turned up the growing cold that had already started to pinch Frank's fingertips and he thrust them further into his pockets to stop it spreading.

The smell of woodsmoke reminded him of home, of the farm. He pushed aside the image of him and Phoebe sitting in front of the fire drinking hot chocolate and toasting marshmallows while firing insults at each other with ever-increasing venom. Fond memories. A different time.

By the time they'd started up the side-streets of the south-summit, the sun had left Garrim behind, leaving only dim mustard lamplight to guide them through the labyrinth.

Unease was constantly at their shoulders, following them closer than a limpet hugs a wet rock. The air thinned, becoming progressively clearer as they left the stink of the levels behind, but the cold crept along with them with no promises of leaving them alone.

The streets narrowed further, the incline of the pathways, made slick by the mountain air, increased step by step, biting Frank's calves until the familiar sight of the hanging pub sign outside the Gargoyle's Head, tucked anonymously away, cast some of the tension away.

DUCKETT

Gabby pushed at the heavy wooden door which swung open with the grace of the calmest swan.

The smell of aged oak, earthy hops and coal-soot ushered them through and into the small bar, the few faces from the shadows of hidden corners between the dark twisted timbers turning their way as they crossed the threshold.

Eyes lingered but returned to their ale and cards and conversations without a second glance. Broad flames, licks of orange, lazed in the fire. Warmth curled around their bones, as welcome as hot soup in mid-winter and twice as nourishing.

Gabby wiped the damp ringlets of her hair and led the others to the bar where the broad figure of Cossens stood chatting and laughing with a woman who glugged at her pint and fluttered her eyes.

He noticed them instantly, a natural instinct for a Garrim bartender. He jerked his chin at them and said something inaudible to the woman, who turned and gave them a disinterested look before taking up her glass making her way across the tavern floor to an empty table near the fire.

'Back so soon,' said Cossens, bracing his formidable forearms on the polished surface of the bar, his gruff voice indifferent. 'Most folk are wise enough to learn from their first experience.' He loosed a slight laugh to himself under his breath, the muscles lining his thick neck straining to stay in the confines of his collar as he surveyed each of them in turn. 'Beer?' Nods in answer. 'Find yourselves a seat, I'll let Duckett know you're here.'

That was it, no questions about why they'd just turned up,

no questions about what they wanted. No one asked questions in Garrim.

They found an empty table in a quiet corner, the sort of spot where they would draw least attention and sat, nursing their drinks among the murmurs and muted conversations from the few regulars dispersed around the alcoves, nooks and niches of the small inn, none of whom appeared bothered by their presence, although Frank knew strangers in the Gargoyle would be duly noted.

'This place hasn't changed,' said Cas. 'Never thought I'd be so pleased to see it again.'

'We're not,' said Gabby, gnawing at her nails. 'We're not here by choice.'

Cas shrugged and took a mouthful of beer, followed by a long wipe of his sleeve across his mouth. The fire cracked and bucked. Gabby was right, they would never set foot in Garrim unless they had to and Frank cursed Jackson for dragging them back.

The broad shoulders of Duckett brought a welcome distraction from the darker edge of their thoughts and silence. He cut an impressive figure as he walked over to their table and pulled up a chair which groaned as he sat. His round, cheery face and bright yellow shirt seemed at odds with the rest of the town.

He leaned back and folded his arms, powerful biceps straining against the sunny material of his shirt, blue eyes sparkling at them.

'Well, well,' he said. 'I must say I'm surprised. Didn't think I'd be seeing anything of you once you'd left here in the back of Symes's wagon.' He scanned each face. 'You should keep better company.'

'Believe me,' said Gabby. 'The company of a rat would be better.'

She shivered. Frank glimpsed her memories. The foul, festering excuse of a double-crosser had Gabby glancing to the door.

'Snow's forecast,' said Duckett with a sniff and a flick of his eyes to the window. 'That's normally enough to put anyone off coming here.'

He looked at them expectantly, Frank putting the question to his words.

'There's something we need to do here,' he said, leaning in, keeping his voice low. No response from Duckett, it would have been simple to guess that one.

'Someone we need to find,' said Cas.

Duckett's eyebrows lifted slightly.

'People don't come to Garrim to get found,' he said, pulling his chair closer to the table. Again, his expectant eyes asked the question.

Frank felt himself tense, they had no issues with Duckett, but – to tell or not to tell, to trust or not to trust. Once something was said, you couldn't unsay it. The game couldn't be retrieved once it had been given away. Hums had said they needed the help of adults but Frank was learning the hard way that age was never a guarantee of wisdom or honesty, both of which were hard to detect, both of which were a rare commodity in Garrim.

Gabby saved him the bother.

'We're looking for Governor Jackson,' she said in a near-whisper.

Frank looked around at the tables, to the shadows on the faces, the hushed voices and beer glasses. No one appeared to be paying them any attention. Now Duckett's brow furrowed.

'Here?' Their faces gave him the answer. The lines on his weathered face bent as he cracked a smile. 'Jackson never comes to Garrim.' His eyes swept their faces. 'Back in Rhaeder he may well be a big shot, but not here. The Townmasters have long since run this town, before them it was bandits, cutthroats and criminals, most of whom still walk the streets and they don't answer to no one but themselves. This is Byeland in nothing but name, has been for decades, so the authorities tend to steer clear – and that includes your Mr Jackson. What makes you think he's here?'

'That doesn't matter, we just know he is,' said Frank with a quick glance to the others.

'Well I doubt he's running a game of nines and kings in any of the card houses along the Ditch.' Duckett could hardly contain his laughter but doused his mirth when he failed to draw smiles from any of the teenagers.

'We need to find out where his house is,' said Anya.

'His house?' Duckett looked near to uncontrolled laughter, once more, as if he was following a lengthy joke and was anticipating an excellent punchline. 'I very much doubt —'

'He does,' said Frank. 'Can you help us find it?'

Whether or not Duckett appreciated Frank's directness was hard to tell, his expression unchanged as Frank's demand hung between them.

Duckett laced his fingers, cracked a smile and his knuckles before his face turned more serious.

'Look, we're out the way enough here that we're rarely bothered by the Townmasters or the Watch,' he said. 'But the streets have eyes and ears in the smallest of cracks and I'll lay short odds that Jackson, *if* he's here, will have greased the right palms so, if I were you, I wouldn't go about town asking the wrong sort of questions to the wrong sort of people. Information is currency here so, if the wrong people get to know why you're in town or, worse, who you're looking for, it'll attract trouble and we'll be getting some unwanted visitors.' He looked around the bar, still no one paid them any attention. 'You'd best keep your heads down for now.' Duckett's eyes gave a glimpse of the tougher, ex-military man behind the cheerful veneer. Street-wise and no nonsense, the precise qualifications to run a pub in Garrim. He looked for their agreement, met with slight nods. 'Good. I assume you need somewhere to stay?' More nods. 'Right, I'll get Cossens to show you upstairs and I suggest you stay put for a day or two. Keep the curtains pulled.'

'So you'll help us?' said Gabby.

Duckett got up.

'I suppose I could put out a few feelers.'

12

CLOSER

The inn had a few rooms just about fit for the passing traveller, assuming they would ever stumble across the place, stuck down a back alley in the southern sprawl of Garrim.

All were empty.

Not much on the south-summit side to draw in the weary passer-by as the eager grasp of winter neared and Frank doubted if Duckett ever played host to many overnight guests from out of town when there were inns situated down on the levels, right up against the main action, gifting easy access to the host of pleasures.

The Gargoyle's Head was just another gloom-filled drinking house where the locals could eke out one more day in the blackness of the border town, finding solace at the bottom of a glass.

But, in the face of the approaching snow and the constant chill wind, it was warm and Frank drew a small amount of relief that its quiet position away from Garrim's spiced attractions, if you could call drink, gambling and sex attractions, would keep them away from the prying eyes of the town and, in turn, that would keep them safe, if safe was a word that was used in Garrim.

Cossens led them, hauling himself slowly up the narrow stairs that creaked in annoyance under his muscular thighs as they headed up then along the tight passage of the first floor landing, the bent wooden corridor barely wide enough to accommodate his hefty frame.

Each room was small but comfortable and Frank took the last along the passage.

A bed, a table, a mirror and perhaps the smallest hearth Frank had ever set his eyes upon. Despite being crammed in, the welcome sight of a comfortable bed lifted Frank's spirits as he threw his bag down and emptied his pockets onto the small table that stood under the windowsill. The possessor – the keeper of his secrets –, a few silver crowns, two Dahke passes – one from his mother, one from Dagmar, brought in event they needed unfettered access into Kzarlac, though Frank prayed they'd be left unused and that Jackson hadn't simply passed through Garrim and headed straight to Alsha Kar, leaving his trail cold.

The small, leaded windows looked down on the street but barely let any light through and leaked cold like the steady drip of a broken tap. Everything in Garrim was cold but Cossens quickly had flames bounding upwards in the small grate before heading back to his bar duties, leaving Frank to sink into the bed as the room fought to thaw itself.

The bedclothes, though frayed and blemished, were the freshest thing he'd smelled since he had arrived on the outskirts of the town although they didn't have the fiercest competition and he felt the call of his fatigue as he lay on the mattress and closed his eyes, too tired to concern himself with Duckett's reaction to their assertion that Jackson was somewhere in the town.

He didn't realise just how ludicrous it sounded to a Garrim resident and couldn't blame their host for all but laughing in their faces, wondering if he really would ask his network of contacts or just leave it to them and their imaginations to conjure the old man from the backstreets.

At the same time he tried to dismiss the notion that, in making the journey, he was running from his past. All the symptoms were there – the avoidance of any contact with his dad, his dismissive and pointed answers to his aunt's questions and demands, the bleak and turbulent pictures his gran had painted of his mother, the festering thoughts and conversations in his head that never ended well and now the glaringly obvious realisation that the spectre they'd been chasing from guardian to guardian and through the silent forest to

73

Irundi was her.

And while he ran from his past, he knew he had to keep hiding from his future.

The Simbrian heir had a price on his head, one someone like Dagmar would mortgage all the land in Alsha Kar to pay if he ever found out and though his secret was safe for now, it felt very much like it was held up by the flimsiest of threads. Run, hide, run, hide – just the thought was enough to exhaust him.

He opened his eyes and stared at shadows across the whitewashed ceiling, wondering just how long he could keep running, that he might run for the rest of his life. Exhaustion was the least of his worries.

A light knock at his door had him turning his head and drawing himself up, the worn wooden headboard creaking as he pushed against it. The door squeaked quietly, revealing Gabby on the threshold.

At the sight of her soft eyes something inside him shifted. Momentarily he felt the shackles of his thoughts fall away. Jackson, Garrim, his dad, his mum, his aunt – it was as if their hostile flame had been extinguished as Gabby stepped into his room and sat on the bed, swinging her legs round and stretching them out before shuffling herself up alongside him, bumping her shoulder against his.

She had a familiar look on her face, a mix of the faraway and the uncertain, the one he'd seen many times since their last encounter with Garrim and through their best-forgotten brush with Balal, their stay at Irundi and their mauling at the hands of Qaas, all of which had been far harder on her then the rest of them.

They shared a moment of silence, watching the healing movement of the fire.

The last time they'd sat together like this, Frank had just spilled his inner secrets, expecting her to punch him, to rip into him, to never speak to him again – a reaction he fully deserved – but she'd wrapped him in her arms as his emotions got the better of him and it was she who had healed the deep, dark rift that he'd cleaved in their friendship during the weeks before, when his bleak moods and inner struggles had made him almost impossible to be around. Now something inside him wished she'd do it again.

She'd barely been able to look at him in the escape from the silent forest but she'd given him understanding the moment he'd needed it, where he deserved none, had shown her softer side from beneath the tough exterior to bring them back together and now he felt closer to her than he could ever have imagined and his world was a better place for it.

The world was always a better place when people got along. Especially when it was her.

She laced her arm through his, her hand resting gently on his wrist and leaned into him, her warmth bleeding quietly into him.

He listened to her breath, felt the slight prickles on his skin. Whatever it was inside shifted a degree more.

'You okay?' he said.

Gabby shrugged in response. Frank leaned away, creating a small gap between them and looked at her. She looked back, her tawny eyes on him, something on her mind, for sure.

'Gabby?'

She shrugged again and let out a breath.

'I don't like it here,' she said.

'Me neither. I'd rather be at the beach,' said Frank, drawing a smile. 'Somewhere warm, at least.'

She squeezed his wrist slightly.

'Maybe we can go when all this is over,' she said.

'No maybes,' said Frank.

He ran his fingers over the back of her thumb and across the heavy bangles on her wrist; felt himself flush slightly.

He wasn't sure it would ever be over, but her words invoked an image in Frank's mind. He and Gabby – long sunny days; carefree days, days the like of which he couldn't remember, days reserved for other people, normal people.

A smile – part happy, part sorrowful – moved his lips. He and Gabby in different times, where destiny had rolled their dice another way.

'Sometimes I just wish we were all living normal lives,' she said, a lead weight on her words. 'Don't you?'

He moved his shoulder back against hers and she leaned her head on it. He tilted his head so he could feel the warmth of her hair on his cheek, felt her hand on the back of his, felt the skip in his chest.

'Yeah,' he said. 'A normal life would be just great.' *And completely impossible.*

'Just think, if you'd never come to Excelsus you'd be none the wiser and be as happy as a farm boy.'

There was playfulness in her words.

'And you'd be teaching the art of sorcery in a far-flung exotic country or something like that.'

But then I would never have met you.

'Hopefully, as long as they don't mind us dirty Prismians.' She looked up at him. He found he couldn't look away, didn't want to look away. 'Or perhaps I'd have found myself in Smithwood and become a farm girl.' A teasing raise of her pierced eyebrows, another image played in his mind. 'How about that, Frankie?'

'I'd pity the poor sheep.'

She gave him a quick slap on the back of the hand, her face laced with mock indignation.

'How dare you, Frank Penny. You never know if my skills extend to the expert handling of a sheep dog. I'm sure my Mum knows an enchantment for that sort of thing.'

For a moment he wasn't in a small, dingy bedroom in the southern reaches of Garrim, stuck waiting for a glimpse of a grey-bearded thief in amongst all the other thieves in the impossibly cold and dark warren of streets and alleys of the worst place he'd ever set foot in.

For a moment he felt untroubled, like a bird released from its cage, singing out its cheery song to summertime on a warm breeze that stroked his face. A teenager's dream of being with someone you cared for, someone you...

'I wonder what we'd be like if things were different,' he said. 'If we'd met, but none of the Simbrian stuff existed.'

'Who knows? Perhaps we wouldn't get on.'

'You are kind of fierce looking, maybe you'd have scared me off.'

'If your grumpiness hadn't put me off first,' she said, setting the unfamiliar sound of laughter off in the tiny bedroom. 'I'm sure fate would have played us some lucky cards and we'd have ended up...' Gabby let her words trail off but Frank felt her push herself against him, her smile pleasant and relaxed. Maybe he knew what she was thinking, maybe she thought the same as him, but he wasn't about to ask. 'My Grandmother used to say that things turn out for the best for those who make the best of the way things turn out. She told me life was difficult, but there's no reason to be scared of it.' She worked her fingertip over the back of his hand. 'Maybe things would have turned out okay. Maybe they still will.'

'I think, sometimes, you have to scare yourself,' said Frank. 'My Dad said that Mum was the sort who lived life right to the edge. No regrets. Seems like he got that right.'

She turned her head to him, her face no more than a few inches from his. He could feel her breath, imagine the taste of her mouth, imagine what it would be like to...kiss her.

'No regrets,' she said, closing her eyes and moving her lips closer to his.

'Can't get my fire going.' Cas appeared in the door, Gabby quickly pulled herself away and sat bolt upright. 'Oh, sorry, am I interrupting something?'

13

FOUND

Frank thought he would feel like a caged bear in his tiny room, miserable and pacing but found the confines of the Gargoyle's Head strangely comforting and safe.

Safety was the one thing he was most grateful for above all else – above the close company, above the decent, hot food, above his roving desire to get out on the streets and look for Jackson himself. Safety was a premium product in Garrim.

Duckett's carefully aimed request that they stay put while he whispered in a few ears was easily heeded in the passing hours of the following day, either in their rooms or in the back kitchen of the inn and Duckett's sitting room that were the landlord's private space, out of sight and, mercifully, out of earshot of the bar.

The right opportunity to finish his conversation with Gabby hadn't presented itself. Although he'd slept well the first night, he'd woken to thoughts as bright and blue as the skies that hung over the town as he pictured the two of them together.

He knew he should have pushed them aside but he couldn't. That was just about as easy as ridding himself of the blood that flowed through his veins. Everbleed's blood. *Bad blood.* But it was Prismian blood, a part of his fabric that bound him more closely to Gabby yet one he wished he could rid himself of, one that provided the unwelcome fuel driving him onward to his destiny.

But each time he thought of the future, of when the Simbrian nightmare had finally finished, he arrived at a dead end. There was no point looking past the next day, to dream of what may lay beyond, past the confines of Garrim, the winter, the green shoots and welcome warmth of spring. Not for him. The Simbrian heir, after all, would need to be slain by those with greed and power in their minds and here he was, just within reach.

On the second morning the sky had become bored with the colour blue and its mood had darkened to a frothy grey, threatening to shake its fist at the town as its clouds tumbled around the peaks.

As Frank watched from his bedroom window he felt a similar shift in his temperament, noticing how the turbulent air began to ink itself in, uttering promises of what it had to offer as the day moved on. It felt like the town was asking them to hurry themselves, bullying them into either doing what they came here to do or to go home and the feeling did nothing to lift his spirits.

He dressed and knocked for Gabby who appeared at her door looking like she'd been wrestling a bear all night and lost.

'Breakfast?'

Gabby ruffled her hair and yawned like a cat. 'Already? Give me a few minutes and I might actually wake up,' she said, picking at the corner of her eye.

Frank felt his stomach swim. His gaze lingered, a little too long. 'I'll get the others, then.' Gabby rubbed a sleepy eye before shutting the door on him. 'See you downstairs,' said Frank, muted, to himself.

He stood for a moment, placing himself on the other side of the door, drawing in a deep, satisfying breath as his imagination got the better of him before moving down the hall to knock for the others.

They sat at the bar, early beers idling in glasses before them, watching as Cossens demonstrated how he could crack walnuts between his bicep and forearm.

The tavern didn't open for business until the later part of the morning, or when either Duckett or Cossens decided and this gave the four students the freedom to hang around the tight, meandering timbers while Cossens went about his duties, occasionally providing impromptu entertainment, appearing to enjoy an audience and the attention.

As the barman swept the remnants of a shell into his palm, the click of a key in the door had them all turning. Through came Duckett, braced against the cold, the fading dust of light snow levelled on the heavy coat that hid his broad shoulders. He tipped his head at them as he lingered by the fire.

'Looks like we're due some,' he said to Cossens who jerked his head back in response. 'Good job they've finally cleared the storm drains.' He noticed the expectant looks as he took his coat off and placed it on an empty stool. 'We had flooding here last week when that storm passed through. All three drains that run under the town were blocked, see. They all flow out to the cliffs and into the Jixx and they're meant to keep the meltwater off the streets. Bloody Townmasters are more interested in keeping their money in their filthy hands than they are on spending it for the upkeep of the town.' His voice trailed off at the disinterested faces of the four teenagers. They weren't there for a briefing on the drainage system of the town.

Duckett pushed his shoulders back and took the couple of strides to where Frank and the others were seated, pulling out a barstool and perching himself on the edge.

Cossens handed him a glass of water which he emptied in three easy glugs before wiping his mouth on the back of his hand. He looked at Frank.

'Well, what do you know, it appears you're not on a fool's errand after all.' Frank felt himself straighten. 'Seems your Mr Jackson does have a place here in town.' He looked at Cossens. 'Never knew that. You?' Cossens gave his head the slightest of shakes. 'I bumped into that good-for-nothing Geez hanging around on the Ditch this morning. Strikes up a conversation offering me a supply of ale his brother's brewing up on the north-side – a tank load of piss and shit with a taste to match, no doubt – couldn't get rid of him, but when I suggested he should leave me be and flog it to the Council in Rhaeder, he said he could just pour it through the letterbox of Jackson's house, here. Thought he was right funny.' A shrug of his impressive frame, adjusting himself on his seat. 'Seems that sometimes the things you're looking for have a habit of finding you first. Course I had to take a barrel of the stuff before he'd tell me where the damn place was.' He looked a Cossens. 'Tip it straight down the gutter when it arrives.'

The mood at the bar turned sharp.

'Where?' said Frank. 'Where is it?'

Duckett narrowed his eyes at the edge of Frank's abrupt tone, but Frank wasn't about to apologise. Information, that's all he could think of. Information that would see them get their book and turn their backs on Garrim.

'He doesn't mean to be rude,' said Gabby, making Frank roll his eyes. 'What he meant to say was would you be good enough to tell us where we can find the lovely Alfred Jackson's house?'

Frank held in a breath as Gabby's impish grin calmed him. He gave her a slight shake of the head and she stifled a yawn back to him.

'Well, Gabby,' said Duckett. 'Seeing as you asked so nicely, Geez told me he's got a small house on the high north-side.' He held out a folded piece of paper. 'Last street up. Seventh house down from the east.'

Frank noticed the frown on Cossens's face, as if Duckett had just wafted a bad smell over to him. Anya was on her feet, the instant scraping of stool legs as she did. She checked her thigh, then her boot – her new routine, and one blade is never quite enough.

'Time to pay him a visit, then,' she said, adjusting her glasses and brushing her hair from her forehead.

The others got to their feet, drinks unfinished, but Duckett put a hand on Frank's shoulder, forcing him still as he went to pass.

'A word of warning, Frank, before you go charging off.' His voice was low and level, a thick seam of gravity running all the way along it. 'I'd be careful, if I were you. The streets can be dangerous, and I don't mean the ice. Word is that no one's seen your Mr Jackson. Looks as if he's keeping himself firmly to himself and powerful people always a habit of moving in the gutter when it suits them. But if he's decided to come here to conduct whatever business he has to conduct, I'll warn you that there'll be something unsavoury about it.'

Words to be heeded from one who knew the rules of a deadly game.

He held Frank's stare long enough to let his warning stick. Frank nodded, understood. Jackson wasn't here on official business, of that they were already sure. The letter from Kzarlac, the speed of his departure from Rhaeder, the disappearance of their book told them that the grimy, bitter elixir of Garrim had the head of Byeland Council mixing in very different circles, one of which they were about to step into.

14

THE HOUSE

The snow had already begun to thicken, falling in lethargic, disorganised clumps, but didn't want to hang around, disappearing as soon as it found the darkness of the street, fleeing the noxious pathways like rats at the scent of the cat, finding no time to settle, preferring the comfort and familiarity of the rooftops.

A bitter wind from the east, from Kzarlac, had claimed the town early and dark clouds, thick with the promise of heavier snow, blown through in great billowing knots, hung heavy from the sky, hurrying their feet down the south mountainside into the crook of the town as they headed to the levels and over to the north-side and the address Duckett had given them.

They skirted the edge of the Ditch, the worst of what Garrim had to offer. The town's main street, on the level ground between the two steep inclines of the mountainside and the jagged peaks that looked down on it from each side with an ogre's easy menace.

It was alive night and day, pitted with hustlers and traders, pushers and pickpockets, drunks and punters. The seedy hum from the gambling houses, drug dens and brothels pitched in the air around them, trying to claw at them, to drag them in and rob them of their coin and any innocence they had left.

The air was a dense, foul cocktail of cheap perfume, sweat and coalsmoke which chugged from the line of braziers set at regular intervals around which knots of unpleasant-looking folk gathered to rub away the chill.

Everyone looked drunk. Fat, lazy and drunk, with no calling but lechery and idleness, dishonest or ready for a fight and the cold, biting air hung heavy with the threat of violence on each corner.

The Ditch ran to its own tune, a tune that never stopped and nothing was either desperate enough or clever enough to put it to sleep.

Each tasteless frontage, each gaudy interior, the good-time girls and touts flaunting themselves in the doorways and the sound of bawdy music were all specifically designed to do one thing and one thing only – part as much money as possible from anyone who found their way, willing or unwilling, onto the strip.

Frank gave it the briefest of looks and moved on. The place was best avoided.

The address Duckett had written down wasn't far, nothing in Garrim's warren of streets was far but the town, with its long fingers, kept good its promise to slow their progress with deep suspicious scowls from anyone loitering in the streets and approaches from the dark eyes of sleazy men and women tempting them, touting for them to spend their money.

They pushed everything back. Sidestepping and ignoring, purpose in their feet as they left the flat of the mountain pass, the Ditch at their backs, and headed up the north mountainside as the sky blackened and the falling snow thickened, wetting the streets further, bringing the uncomfortable beginnings of numbing feet and irritability.

The clouds, now the colour of the blacksmith's anvil, had begun to lay siege to the mountains, darkening Garrim and stirring the snow that emptied from the sky in ever-increasing chunks and by the time they'd found their way to the north-eastern reaches, the cold had begun to ice the pavements, urging caution in their boots.

The northern incline was steeper than the south and the sour wind found them easily, numbing Frank's face and ears, giving no respite, making him wonder if they were ever going to get to the uppermost street until, finally, they reached the entrance to a dark, narrow lane, although alleyway would have been a more fitting description.

A row of small terraced houses disappeared to darkness despite the hour, their backs flat against the curve of the rising mountain that towered like an impatient giant behind them, holding the buildings firmly in their place with the flat of its hand, yellowing light from a single street lamp barely making an impact. Only shadows lived here with the rats. It looked like the perfect place for a jump.

The stink of rot and piss from down the alley had Frank pushing against his gag reflex, had him puffing out long clouds from his lungs. Why Jackson would own a house way up here in the thin air, down a stinking side-street with all the grandeur of a pig rolling in its own shit was against all logic.

'This makes no sense,' said Frank with a shake of the head.

'On the contrary, mate,' said Cas. 'I think this makes complete sense.'

Frank pulled his thoughts, nodding as he realised Cas was right. It was hidden, completely out of the way, somewhere where no one would even think or dare to roam. Where Jackson could hide away with the certainty that, while the crowds festered and occupied the Ditch, no one would trouble him.

The shittiest house, in the shittiest street of the shittiest town. Perfect. That's why it made sense.

'The question is – why?' said Gabby, bunching her shoulders as a chilled gust slapped and chafed them.

Frank took tentative step into the shadows, his breath long in the dim light offered by the street lamp.

His hesitancy had Anya drawing one of her blades before Gabby stepped ahead of him and started slowly down the alley, counting the doors on the right as she went, stopping at the shabby entrance to the seventh.

Layers of thick, black paint, worn and scuffed, peeled from the weathered wood. Large cobwebs clung to the upper corners like frost, the lock dull and pitted with the stains of rust and neglect. All the windows were boarded, held so close and tight by tough nails it looked like you'd need a dozen men to shift them. The place looked forlorn and forgotten and like no one had been through in a very long time.

Frank didn't think. He just knocked. Hard. His frozen knuckles painful on the solid wood, his rising anger at the self-important Jackson in his fist.

No response, not like he was expecting one. He hammered again, battering the door into submission until his clouding breaths came fast. Raised eyebrows from the others.

'Got that out of your system?' said Gabby. Frank couldn't resist a smile.

They waited. Nothing stirred from within. Nothing from down the deserted street as they watched for any sign of movement, of twitching curtains or opening doors at the echoing racket. Nothing.

Frank would have been surprised if anyone actually lived here, such was the bleak and abandoned feeling that leaked from the gutters, coated the pavement and slithered away down the mountainside with the rest of the filth.

Cas checked around the weather-beaten boards covering the downstairs windows that sat either side of the door then looked at the others with a shake of the head. Frank gave the damp wall a frustrated kick with the sole of his boot.

'I'd like to say he's just out,' said Anya. 'But I think we can all tell no one's been near this place for a while.'

Anya didn't have to say it, it was as clear as the meltwater from the mountain peaks that only the rats had been anywhere near Jackson's bolt-hole and even they weren't hanging around, so what was going on? Frank tried to put some sense to it but found his thoughts clutching the air.

Perhaps his arrogant arse of a grandson had lied, perhaps Duckett and his dodgy contact had it wrong. Whatever the answer, Frank felt the familiar rush of heat start to cloud his head, that ill-tempered feeling, the one he had a difficulty putting a lid on.

They stood in silence; cheerless and cold, very cold.

Frank could feel the grinding of his teeth and, despite the refuge the alley provided from the snow, the wind still bit at his fingertips to add to his darkening mood.

He glanced at the others, watching them continually blowing on their fingers and into the palms of their hands to keep Garrim's harsh mountain air at bay, each minute sucking the scant enthusiasm that had started to wane once they knew Jackson hadn't come to his house, increasing the longing for Duckett's fire while snow and dejection fell from the sky, settling over them in a low-slung, shivering cloud.

'Any suggestions?' he said to the unease on their faces.

Head shakes all round to the whistle of the wind and the distant noise from down the mountainside, from the Ditch.

'What if he's not even here?' said Gabby.

'Then we'll make certain Ralph Jackson understands the consequences of being a lying bastard,' said Frank.

'Although he looked kind of rattled,' said Cas. 'I didn't get the feeling he was feeding us a line.'

Frank agreed. Jackson junior had definitely been shaken and they'd given him good reason to tell the truth, and Anya had given him five better reasons for them not to go knocking at his door again, so what were they missing?

He looked up and down the alley once more.

'Let's get out of here,' he said. 'This place stinks like shit. So does this whole thing.'

15

The Plum-Coat

The trudge back down the north slope was silent and miserable. The wind blew frosted crumbs of snow against their ruddy cheeks as Gabby led, scowling at the ground, keeping to the edge of the town, giving them the occasional, broken view across the deep gorge at Deadman's Scar and the bridge across to the fortified border post, the entry point to Kzarlac.

Frank stopped, squinting to the east. The thought that Jackson hadn't come to Garrim, but had simply passed through to their country's adversary, to Etamin and Dagmar, chilled him further, if that were possible, and the thought that they were wasting their time bothered him more than his frostbitten fingers and the herald of worse weather. An omen. Something to remind them of their hopeless position.

Jackson's house was boarded and soulless, shut tighter than a hunter's trap. He could be anywhere but if he was in Garrim, Frank knew their only option was to go hunting, despite Duckett's plain counsel, but hunting in the black shadows and alleyways of the border town would need sharp eyes, keen wits and a barrelful of good fortune and good fortune was another rare commodity in Garrim. He checked the faces of the others.

'Anybody else feeling lucky?'

On their previous visit just a few months back they'd spent no time in the centre of town, preferring the security Duckett had provided at the Gargoyle's Head and they'd only managed to scout the east-side, to the Jixx and the border beyond. There had been nothing to lure them down to the centre or the fringes of the mountainsides and Garrim offered no welcome to four teenagers, wet behind the ears and heading to Kzarlac, equipped with nothing but their wits and innocence.

But in the short space since then things had changed and what gave him a breath of hope was that *they'd* changed. They'd seen the sickening face of evil in both their frightening encounter with Etamin and the breathless but hopeless challenge to the revolting Balal, deep in the silent forest.

Irundi had scarred them and Anya had killed to protect those who had come to their rescue. They'd grown up quickly, too quickly, and the forces that had shaped them sat squarely on their shoulders, urging them to finish what they'd started, sending them into the grip of the town and the Ditch.

Away from the deserted higher reaches, Garrim thickened and dripped with the clear scent of dishonesty, coated in debauchery like treacle, ensnaring those who ventured through its door. Walking its infested streets had a different feel than the terrifying solitude that they endured at the whim of the Sapirai, but the similarities were unmistakeable.

With every step on the wet cobbles Frank felt eyes on him, expecting an unwanted approach, targets of a scam or mugging, that they would attract attention from the wrong people, not that there appeared to be any right people anywhere.

The gambling dens didn't need to fight for position along the length of the Ditch. They left that to the drunks, the thugs and the dispossessed. You could take your pick from the dozens of establishments and not be disappointed. All designed to sap your body and snatch your money.

Duckett had told them how the ranks of the decadent and immoral had previously been confined to the backstreets in a corner of the lower north-side to make the more depraved elements of society easier for the Watch to monitor but, following the last major outbreak of ice-pox ten years ago, the Townmasters decided to move them to more central, front-facing positions, dressed up and presentable as a deliberate scheme to encourage more visitors, more people to part with more of their crowns so they could take their share of taxes and restock the town's coffers.

But Duckett had spat when he told them an unfortunate but predictable side effect of the move was that those who governed the town, together with the Watch, had gradually but inevitably become increasingly corrupt, with more than a few of its number keeping their palms silvered with vested interests along the Ditch, blurring the lines and leaving much of the activity unregulated and lawless.

Money spoke in alluring tones and the law enforcers, or some of them, had decided to learn its language and put themselves above the law.

As they worked their way off the slope and into the centre of the town, the swirling snow leading them towards the swell of people, the tart smell of coalsmoke and sweet whiff of dreamweed, Frank knew the only thing they'd missed, as they'd climbed into the back of Manville Symes's filthy wagon, was the opportunity to get scammed or beaten up.

They reached the levels, cold slush slopping in their footsteps, frost pecking the ends of their toes. Slim alleyways disappeared to the dark and the mountainside at intervals along the Ditch, the occasional glimpse of pale flesh as men took advantage of street girls unable to find safer work in one of the many brothels that sat comfortably between the dens and taverns. It seemed clear that visitors to Garrim were able and willing to indulge themselves in whatever style of debauchery their sordid imaginations could dream up, as long as they could pay for it.

Large braziers, set at regular intervals along the street, glowed orange among the crowds, some of whom huddled close in tight clusters, others stopping briefly to hold their palms to the shimmering warmth before moving along to find their thrills among the seedy comfort of the array of tightly packed buildings that promised delights for a few, misery for many others.

The street seemed to move both fast and slow. The sound of dice and chips falling, like the tail of a rattlesnake with the slower rat-a-tat-tat of the ball on the luck-wheel acted as a lure to bored travellers, tourists and locals and although the Ditch smelled different to the filth of the backstreets, perhaps by design so punters weren't put off, the air still breathed heavy with the subtle threat of violence, chilled to its roots by the whistle of the wintry wind.

Surely Jackson wasn't down here barging shoulders with the dregs, but the Ditch promised anonymity to anyone rash enough to step in its way and the mass of bodies in the thrall of the strip told Frank their task had become impossible as they headed slowly along the road, alert for signs of the missing Governor, alert for signs of trouble.

He didn't need to tell the others to stay close. The past few months had left them primed for misfortune and bother, both of which kept themselves uncomfortably near and stepped happily in their shadow.

The Ditch was no different. Groups of men and women, some well-dressed, some looking like they stank of week-old piss, stood idly against the walls or in vomit-splattered doorways laughing amongst themselves but Frank could sense the sideways glances as they passed, laced with unspoken threats, eyes sizing them up, lingering longer than necessary.

Each doorway oozed its own brand of temptation; bait for the unsuspecting, charm for the willing, all of which worried Frank, and he wasn't the worrying kind.

They managed to negotiate themselves half-way down the strip, their instincts keeping them alive to any schemers, still no sign of Jackson, when Frank immediately smelled trouble as someone peeled off from the roadway and approached them.

Dapper in his tailored plum long-coat and black velvet top-hat, the tall man oozed intimidation down to his fine boots that sucked at the forming slush.

His jaw needed no further chiselling and his eyes, the colour of cornflowers, struck him handsome but Frank knew that books with pretty covers could still give you nightmares.

The man grasped the top of his black cane with both hands and planted it on the ground in front of them. A signal for them to stop. An immediate show of authority. Two roughs at his back looked on. The man broke a smile, showing his row of bright, straight teeth behind the scar on his lip. There was something of the Ralph Jackson about him that had Frank holding his breath.

'Looking for work?' His questioned aimed squarely at Gabby and Anya, eyes flickering over them, lingering an insulting moment. 'Two young girls like you would fetch a fair price at the Drum,' he said with a nod of the head back down the street. Gabby's face darkened, her fingers scratching at her forearms, drawing the man's eyes. 'I know men that would part with good coin for the fawn skin of a Prismian girl.' He reached out a hand which Gabby instantly and violently batted away, replacing the man's smile with a snarl that he sucked in through his teeth.

'Get lost,' said Frank, taking a step forward, his foot pressing deliberately on the toe of the man's polished boot. The man grabbed a fistful of Frank and shoved him back as the heavies on each side closed. He wrapped a gloved hand around his walking cane and pressed the metal tip to Frank's chest. Frank brushed it aside only to find it returned with a purpose, the cold steel biting him between the ribs.

'There are many things you can get in Garrim, you lout,' he said. 'And believe me, lost is not one I would recommend to those unfamiliar with its streets.' His blue eyes devoured Frank. 'Although it is something I could arrange, if you're not careful.'

Anya pushed her coat back, showing the sheathed blade that hugged her thigh. The man sniffed, looked her up and down, obviously unimpressed. No matter what the code of the street, this smelled like violence.

This time the man tapped the top of his stick on Frank's chest, hard enough for Frank to feel it drumming through his back and down his spine, unsettling and sinister.

'Watch yourself, lout,' he said. 'You can easily hide yourself in Garrim but, on the other hand, it can be difficult to keep out of sight.'

He gave Frank a slight shove, deliberately knocking Frank's leg with his own as he did, making Frank lose his balance, sending him back a few steps before he fell on his backside in the cold muddy slush, drawing looks from those passing, looks that melted away quickly, grateful it wasn't them in a heap on the street.

The man's mocking smile wasn't lost on the others as Frank quickly got to his feet, the faint swish of steel on leather as Anya pulled out her blade. The man turned his head to her.

'Be a good girl and put your toys away,' he said, a look of schoolmaster disappointment on his face.

Anya locked her steely eyes on his, a look of business, a look Frank knew well but, the way Frank saw it, now was a good time to back down and disappear. They'd already drawn enough unwanted attention to themselves within five minutes of landing in the Ditch and escalating the quarrel was the strategy of fools.

Frank looked at Anya and gave a slight shake of his head. She re-sheathed her weapon.

'Kids,' said the plum-coat. 'Always the same, thinking you know it all. Let me tell you, no one knows it all here.' He looked each of them up and down. 'Strange. Four ferrets in a man's world. Makes me wonder what you're doing here.' He looked at Cas. 'Mummy and daddy down the Peaks getting tanked up on that piss they pass for whiskey?' He turned back to Frank. 'Or trying something new with the girls in the Red House?'

A warped smile lit his face. Silence from the teenagers. Frank just wanted away. A glance at Gabby, the familiar look on her face told him she was biting down on her temper. Time to go.

He stepped away from the man and his heavies with the care of someone trying not to wake a new-born, signalling to the others with a flick of his head. Gabby, Cas and Anya followed on wary feet, while the man in the plum coat watched them with unblinking eyes.

Frank could feel them on his back as they headed back down the Ditch and to the south-side, only looking back when they knew they were a safe distance from their aggressor who called out with a lift of his chin:

'I'll see you around, lout.'

No, thought Frank, he wouldn't, because he wouldn't be coming back to the Ditch even if Jackson himself sent them a hand-written note inviting them.

16

THE KITE

Their brief flirtation with the Ditch had been yet another mistake, another hard lesson on how the world works. Not a place for the cowering or the meek.

The main drag was more gutter or sewer than street, where people cast off their normal lives and became something else, something they don't want others – wives, husbands – to see. A place where people came and went like the tides and willingly slipped through the cracks and stayed where they didn't belong.

As far as Frank was concerned, they could keep it all, sup it up all day long until they puked it up face down in the filth in readiness for the next go.

Whoever had raised the town from the rock of the Longshadows had moulded it into the very definition of unruly, where the man in the plum coat and all those around him could breathe new meaning into menace.

Duckett had advised them against venturing to the Ditch. Words that rang loud, pitifully ignored like all good advice given to teenagers. Frank wished they'd heeded his wisdom, wondering if his warning should extend to the whole town, which now seemed tame by comparison, and they should just leave and return to a normal life, the kind of life he and Gabby had spoken of, one set aside for others.

He was sure Cas would agree, although Anya would sooner head to the training grounds of the Sandulum assassins to further her abilities. Even that seemed like a preferable option compared to sitting and waiting and waiting some more. A game that might have no end, but couldn't be over soon enough.

Early the next morning Frank sat on his own at the bar, as grim as a mourner at a funeral, drumming a bleak rhythm with the tips of the fingers on one hand while the others curled themselves round a glass of whiskey, all but a mouthful left.

His sixteenth birthday had come and gone, much like Jackson, devoured by the town. Celebrating was the last thing he wanted to do in Garrim so he'd let it slip past without even mentioning it to the others who he'd left to their slumber while he reflected on their unfortunate episode the previous day.

The new day had him yearning to be solitary and being by himself gave him an element of peace, something he had been lacking for weeks, something he needed to clear his head which might lead to him thinking of a plan although he doubted he had it in him, unable to catch a thought and hold onto it.

Cossens emerged from the cellar, dropping the shiny wooden trapdoor which slammed, causing a shudder through the empty bar though Frank barely acknowledged it, swigging down the remnants of his drink, feeling the fire in his belly.

'Feelin' better?' said Cossens, his deep-set eyes prodding Frank.

'Not really,' said Frank, pushing his glass across the bar with a dip of the chin toward the bottle that stood just out of reach to the side.

'Then another won't help,' said Cossens, his leaden stare still on Frank, who gave the glass a further shove.

'I thought this was a pub?'

He tapped the rim of the glass with his index finger.

'It is, and I thought you had to be eighteen to drink in a pub.'

Cossens raised his brows.

'In Garrim?' said Frank. 'You're joking.'

Cossens eyed him, then set about checking the beer taps.

'I've seen more than a few youngsters thinking they'll find their answers at the bottom of a whiskey glass and until now none of them have, so take some advice from me, Frank, don't wander too far down that path. It's normally a one way street and one way streets have a habit of leading to dead ends.'

Frank bit down on his teeth, staring at an invisible dot on the surface of the bar. He knew Cossens was right, but hated the wisdom dispensed like he was still a child. He tapped his fingers on the bar and got up, feeling the pull of the fresh air to clear his head and feed his solitude.

'Off out?' said Cossens. Frank looked back, but said nothing. Cossens braced his forearms on the top of the taps. 'A word of caution. The Watch appear to be a bit more sniffy than usual.'

'Then I'll keep out of their way. What do they look like?'

'Bunch of blokes. All plum coats and tall, black hats. Think they own the levels.' Cossens's words sent a shiver through Frank, had him reconsidering. 'They're the eyes and ears of the Townmasters, looking out for any brewing trouble but also on the make. Townsfolk tend to steer clear.' Steer clear – good advice, late advice. Frank looked at the door. 'Never see much of them up this way, they tend to stick to the centre and around the Ditch, that's where they make their money. But the word is it seems they're being a bit more attentive at the moment. Something tells me it might have something to do with your elusive Mr Jackson so, if I was to go out looking for him, I'd make sure I kept my head down and my mouth shut.' He paused for effect. 'Or not go out at all.'

Cossens's eyes lingered on Frank for a moment, letting his advice sink in. Frank nodded his appreciation as Cossens turned and headed out the back. Frank looked to the door, tossing around the barman's words and decided he'd be better staying put.

He stepped back to the bar, swiped his glass off the top and, ignoring Cossens's other piece of advice, reached across, grabbed the half-full bottle and poured himself another whiskey before sliding off his stool and walking the few steps to the fire that lazed in the hearth.

Frank threw himself into a chair and blew out his cheeks, hard. He stretched his legs out and flexed his feet, soaking up the warmth, grateful that he'd not headed out for another bout with the weather that was sure to suck him joyless.

He swirled the amber liquid around in his glass, wishing he could spit it in the smug face of the watchman they'd encountered the previous day, knowing he wouldn't get the chance and, even if he did, he'd probably end up getting skinned or tossed into the Jixx from a great height.

He wanted to be far away from the Ditch, from Garrim, but they weren't the type of thoughts that would help them find Jackson.

He took a fiery swallow, feeling the pinch of the liquor on his lips and at the back of his throat. Perhaps they should leave it, leave him. Perhaps they should just going back to Rhaeder. Perhaps now was time to quit. He'd discuss it with the others and was confident they'd see sense.

After all, what was the use in just sitting in the Gargoyle's Head day after long, boring day waiting for fate to deal the cards? Chances were it would be a shit, losing hand anyway and it wasn't the only thing Garrim was likely to swindle them out of before it sent them packing.

It would take their wits, their self-respect and any innocence they had left, which he could fit in the palm of his hand. Yes, perhaps now was the time to quit.

He closed his eyes, soaking up the weariness in another mouthful of whiskey. It was far too early to be drinking alone but that's what Garrim expected, how it charmed you with its promise of riches at the tables and drew you into its grip. Like Cossens had said, there were no answers in his glass, only the knowledge that you'd end up eager for the next drink, and the next.

They'd found nothing and their objective felt further away that when they had begun. Tweedy hadn't sent him anything. He'd tuned in now and then but, just as with Jackson's house, the pot was well and truly empty.

He felt sorry for his hawk, alone and cold in the unfamiliar air. Despite thinking it was a good idea back in his bedroom in

Rhaeder, now he wasn't sure what he'd hoped to achieve by bringing her with them. Surveillance, but of what? He couldn't spend the entire day watching images of the Ditch through her eyes, and he couldn't expect her to sit on the exposed rooftops in the dreadful wintry conditions, continually whipped and battered, awaiting his command while he soaked up the warmth of the fire in his room.

It felt like she was his prisoner, forgotten, and she needed to hunt, to keep her strength and the pickings up in the mountains were slim indeed.

Frank loosed a long breath and put his half-empty glass on the floor in front of the fire. He leaned forward, pressing the heels of his hands into his tired eyes, drawing in the scent of coalsmoke, gathering his concentration before summoning the kite.

An image appeared as he closed his eyes. She was sitting on a high rooftop at the western end of the Ditch. The hawk's keen vision, pin-sharp, gave him a sweeping view along the street despite the flurries of snow being blown in from the east. Even this early, the Ditch was busy, its twenty-four hour lifecycle continued, ticking over unchecked. The draw of the card tables and splash of liquor in the glass didn't stop for the weather, the night or the throng of pleasure-seeking patrons.

He could sense the bird's discomfort, her yearning for home, the padding from one foot to the other the keep the cold from her legs.

One last scan, just one, that's all he'd ask of her, just to see if Jackson showed himself before he'd send her on her way back to Rhaeder and the safety and care of Professor Huxley. It was only fair.

Tweedy's eyes zoomed in, closely following the familiar loose life of the street, picking out the faces that dared show themselves to the first throes of daylight.

Townsfolk staggering off the back of an all-nighter looking to their homes or to the gambling dens to continue their quest for a change in their fortunes, men with their arms draped around the good-time girls, traders with warm sweetmeats and steaming kettles to tempt those with sore heads and rumbling appetites. The glimpse of the occasional plum long-coat. But no Jackson.

A further, slow skim of the Ditch was equally unsuccessful despite Frank's heightened anticipation. Finding anyone in the shadows or in the sea of bodies was impossible. Jackson was a small fish in a very big ocean and it added grist to his already surrendering thoughts that the whole journey might have been a waste of time. Perhaps Duckett would turn up something else, soon, before the deepening resignation he was beginning to feel got the better of him or he started getting an irreversible taste for alcohol.

In any event, it wasn't in his nature to keep Tweedy shivering on the rooftops and, with a dispirited sigh, he gave her the command to head back to Rhaeder.

He felt her ruffle her feathers, preparation for taking to the skies but, as she took a last look across the Ditch to the patchwork of coloured frontages before turning her head to the clouds above Garrim, Frank caught a glimpse of someone in the street. Someone dodging through the crowds in an anonymous grey cloak, someone familiar and completely unexpected.

17

THE LID

Quickly, he commanded the hawk's keen eyes back on the crowded road below. He felt her irritation, a swipe of talons from the cold, hungry bird far away from home but Tweedy settled and performed a slow, careful sweep back along the length of the Ditch.

Frank wandered the street with her eyes, desperate to pinpoint the figure he was sure he'd seen, the person he was sure he'd recognised but, at the same time, as he dug down into his mind, balancing the possibilities, wondering if he'd been mistaken. After all, how could they be here? But now the sea of bobbing heads brushed irritation onto his skin as he failed to make them out in the wash of white and grey and the push and shove of the early morning.

He urged Tweedy to keep her focus, pushing against the bird's instinct to take flight. Her devotion only stretched so far. With difficulty he tried to push his frustration to the side and kept looking, hoping he would see them. Nothing. No sign. Grey cloaks were plentiful in Garrim.

He crushed his eyelids together, pressing them until his eyes hurt, until the images of the street burned and blurred until there, there they were, just in time to see a glimpse of a face looking back, pulling their cloak tighter against the cold air before they disappeared into a gambling house at the western end of the Ditch. It was them, no doubt. No doubt at all.

He released the bird from her duty and commanded her back to the sanctuary of Excelsus. He could feel the hawk's relief as he ditched his glass and sprung to his feet before hesitancy grabbed him.

He should get the others. No, safety in numbers hadn't

exactly been their ally the previous day, alone would provide better camouflage.

He grabbed his coat, realising that being decisive wasn't the same as making good decisions and, against all good sense, headed out into the chilled and corrosive air of the town.

The final blow of snow breathed and huffed at him as it waned on the wind. The early morning sky was a bruise of greys and blacks with dents of blue and white beginning to appear, announcing bright sunshine that glazed the rooftops below him and on the north mountainside opposite, setting the ground hard and making a hazard of the descent through the patchwork of backstreets, although a glance to the east and the looming dark clouds told Frank that the tap would soon be turned back on.

Heading into the town by himself had his nerves chiming at the thought of more men in plum coats. Cossens had been clear. He wondered how just walking down a street, minding your own business could be so damn hazardous.

Down the frozen slope to the levels, the freshly glassed surface determined to delay him, to knock his balance and crack his kneecaps. The low thrum of voices wove back up the mountainside, getting gradually louder, drawing him in as the ice splintered under his feet.

Down through the twisted spires, the decaying brickwork and the ice-battered houses. Down through the constricted streets and hidden alleyways until he reached the junction at the mid-point of the Ditch.

He turned the corner, determined not to hesitate, something he was sure would draw attention to himself and ploughed on through the crowd, head down, collar up, hands in pockets, avoiding eye contact with any tout or bare-fleshed vamp that thought him a target, wary of any of the plum-coats, doing his best to blend in, and plotted a course to the far end of the strip.

He dodged between the bodies, careful not to slow or knock into trouble. He kept away from the braziers and doorways, where people naturally congregated in threes and fours, scouring the street or deep in conversation, not stopping until he stood before the gold-fronted pleasure house that had been Tweedy's final act, his breath clouding in short bursts.

Above the open double-doors a large sign – The Lid – welcomed clients and punters over the threshold to spend whatever they had left of their wages.

Glittering posters on either side, adorned with the symbols of card suits, dice and the numbers on the luck-wheel promised good luck and a good time. A promise dealt to the public by every doorway along the entire dishonest length of the street.

Beyond the bright, gilded doors, Frank could see a foreign land, the gambling tables where cards were being laid, dice thrown and fortunes lost. Everything about the gaudy show pulled against his instincts. He didn't want to go in, but his choices had deserted him a while ago and Garrim had robbed him of his common sense.

As he reached for his courage, a young woman, no more than a year or two older than him, dressed in nothing but a green, thigh length satin shift that left nothing to his young imagination, approached him from the door. She was pretty in a desperate sort of way. Her near-white hair descended in a long plait, sweeping over her even paler skin, blotched blue and pink with cold but still she somehow forced a smile from her prematurely sad face, the sickly scent of cheap perfume wafting from her bare shoulders.

Anywhere else she would have easily stuck out but, here in Garrim, she was as commonplace as a leaf falling from a tree in autumn.

'Looking for a good time?' she said, the well-worn line, coated in mock sensuality, falling flat at Frank's feet. She fluttered her eyelashes as he looked beyond her, through the doors. Her hollow eyes followed his gaze. 'The cards are lucky today. Especially for a handsome young man like you.'

He could have thought of a response, attempted to be polite, but he was damned if he was going to make the effort.

She reached her urchin hand to the lapel of his jacket, sifting the material through her thumb and forefinger, another subtle attempt at temptation as a cold breeze blew down the Ditch. The young girl tensed against it, her bone-white skin paling even more, her body suddenly taut as a bowstring. Frank nodded to the door, anxious to be off the street.

She took him by the arm and led him the few steps to just inside the doorway. The spike of thick chatter in the streets was cut to a low-level hum from the tables, the tune to which misery danced and money was lost.

The inside of the Lid was comfortably warm and looked larger than it appeared from out in the street – and significantly cleaner, not that it had much competition as Frank checked the filth on his boots, wondering if he should wipe his feet on the large mat that sat at the threshold.

The square front gave way to a circular interior of smooth, whitewashed walls, yellowed by the light from numerous lamps set at regular intervals that gave the unexpected feeling of comfort and warmth, a ploy, no doubt, to make anyone think twice about heading back out into the foulness of the street and the grip of the weather.

Across the floor, among the thin haze of tobacco smoke that hung across the room like the silken trap of a spider's web, a dozen or more tables filled the space, all attended by dealers in smart, gold-braided waistcoats and drawn-on grins, each of them keeping the host of players in the grip of the green baize of whatever game they were running, not allowing the punters' attention to roam anywhere but to the card or dice or wheel in front of them while short-skirted young women wove through with trays of drinks to keep the players in their seats. A twisted wooden staircase folded around itself at the rear of the room.

Despite its friendly appearance, it still oozed of alcohol and stale tobacco. Some things, it seemed, could not be washed away with a gloss of paint and the promise of money.

Frank noticed that the room was completely windowless. No

one could be allowed the luxury of knowing how much of the day had passed or have a sense of their empty lives slipping gradually out of sight. The loss of wealth and dignity should, evidently, continue unabated, without the distraction of the dying day.

The only people that took any notice of him were a number of gorilla types who stood at intervals around the room. Once their violent eyes had checked him for trouble, deciding there was none, their attention went back to the tables, to the players, looking, Frank presumed, for any sign of the swindler, the rogue with marked cards or loaded dice although he was sure the house played its own con on the unsuspecting.

'Why don't you buy me a drink,' said the young woman in sultry tones, lacing her arm through Frank's, working her well-rehearsed routine.

He didn't reply. He scanned the room looking for the unexpected entrant to the club, the one who had entered twenty minutes ahead of him. Perhaps they'd left already, maybe he'd been mistaken. After all, he was at a loss as to how they could be there.

His eyes fixed on each face in turn. The customers, the staff and those who wandered between the tables, checking familiarity until the lightweight pull of something in his jacket pocket broke the spell.

He grabbed the waif-like wrist before it had time to slide back out and turned to face the girl, her sallow eyes, bereft of the sparkle that should have inhabited something so young, fashioned with surprise and guilt.

He squeezed his fingers tight, feeling her bones, surprising himself at his own strength, then let go as he caught the gasp from her pale face.

Cas was forever telling him to be aware, to read the signs of a potential pickpocket. A stranger coming too close, being familiar, engineering a chance encounter. She bore all the hallmarks and he'd been prepared the moment he'd seen her lay her eyes on him.

She held his stare, then a quick, anxious look to the brutes around the room.

'Please,' she said, her voice quiet, her eyes watering a touch. 'Don't —'

She stopped as Frank put a reassuring hand on hers.

She was barely older than Gabby or Anya yet, up close, the dark circles that hung on her eyes made her look twice their years.

Long hours working from a young age in the gutter had already begun to take their toll and Frank didn't want to think about how Garrim had taken advantage of her or the depravity she might have endured in her short life. She'd probably spent half her lifetime working her way up to whatever her position was now. A life on the tightrope, and Frank wasn't about to make her lose her balance and cast her deeper into the cess-pit.

He dipped into his pocket, producing the leather purse that had been her target before pulling the drawstring and withdrew a silver crown. He pressed it into her palm. Her young eyes dipped then shone as she looked at him, a question on her lips.

Frank gave her a pitying smile and turned back to the room, his eyes scouting the tables again - from the dealers to the players, to the heavies, cashiers and those fielding drinks to the clients as they exchanged more of their money for the next stack of playing chips – one by one until they landed on one familiar face toward the rear of the large room, where Sapphire Hark, a former guardian of the Simbrian who he'd last seen bleeding to death at Dagmar's hands, stood dealing cards to the unsuspecting people of Garrim.

18

THE LUCKY GUARDIAN

Her hair was longer, tidier and she looked significantly fresher than the haggard young woman they'd met in the black-ink quarter of Alsha Kar, but it was unmistakeably her.

A coat of lip-gloss and a tight-fitting dress under the tailored waistcoat made the best use of her features, tools for attracting and keeping those with coin to spend, just what a gambling den in Garrim desired.

But she was alive – she should be dead, had to be dead. The last time he'd seen her she was being dragged away by Dagmar's men, unconscious, having been relieved of her fragment of the Simbrian. Dagmar had been clear of what end awaited the former guardian and it didn't involve dealing cards in the Lid.

With the urchin following in his wake he was at the table and planted on a stool before she noticed. Even then she didn't look up, just dealt cards to the other two players, sat further along, like she'd been doing it for years. To her he was just another in the long line of punters she allowed to shift between the hope of quick money and a lucky morning and the desolate pit of destitution and loss of self-respect.

Frank looked down at the faded green baize of the table-top, sensing the pale young girl had moved with him from the door and stood at his shoulder, perhaps in the hope she might get a further hand-out but more likely to keep him spending both his time and money in the confines of her employer's circular walls before offering to claim some of it for herself with sexual favours.

He watched as Sapphire collected up playing chips of the two

107

gamblers. Another losing hand, another win for the house.

He placed a silver crown on the table, an exchange for playing chips. Only then did she pay him any attention, lifting her eyes to his as he drummed his fingers on the playing surface.

Her painted-on smile hung for a brief moment before sliding quickly to the floor as he watched her pupils dilate, her hesitant eyes widen whether in shock or surprise he couldn't tell. She'd recognised him without hesitation, he was sure of that.

Immediately her eyes wandered the room, the pale skin of her throat started to redden. Frank looked behind him, to the heavies that patrolled the room, to the players dancing to the rhythm of the falling dice. No one appeared interested in him, or that he'd sat at her table. Just another player, just another soft touch in the maw of their house of misery and no one cared, just as long as he stayed and spent.

He watched as she drew in a long breath, suddenly nervous as she fumbled with the coin he'd placed on the table in front of him and replaced it with a pile of white and red playing chips before her artificial smile at the other men at the table had them asking for a new hand with a dip of their heads to the deck of cards that sat before her.

She shuffled the pack. A series of clean, assured movements, though Frank detected a slight tremble in her hands.

'What the hell are you doing here?' she hissed through her teeth.

No eye contact. Still Frank drummed.

'I was going to ask you the same thing.' He kept his voice low, conscious of the girl at his back, wary of his secrets, wary of drawing the wrong sort of attention. 'You're meant to be dead.'

A sideways glance from the man two seats away. Still she kept her eyes off of his.

'You need to leave.'

A nervous glance around the room, voice still through her teeth. Frank could sense the tension in her body, looking like she was fighting the urge to flee.

'Are you dealing or what?'

The testy voice from one of the card players had both Frank and Sapphire looking sideways. She jerked her head in apology, offered the scantest of smiles and sifted three cards for each player, sliding them across the table, pausing at Frank, her eyes asking him the question. Frank nodded and she dealt him a hand.

'Dagmar said you were no use to him,' said Frank, a little louder than intended. 'And we all know what that means.'

More looks from the other players. Frank looked back, a hard point to his stare, a silent demand they mind their own business. Both held his gaze, a brief silence holding the deadlock and brewing bother before one of them pushed his stool back.

'Come on. Let's go somewhere where we can get a proper game.' The man looked at Sapphire. 'Somewhere where the dealer values our money and a hand of jack-in-the-hole.' He looked at Frank. 'Plenty of those about.'

Both players got to their feet, sweeping their remaining playing chips into the palms of their hands with a rattle and a clink, angry scowls at Frank before they headed to the cashier's desk without a look back.

Frank kept his eyes on them as they were stopped en-route by a dark woman in an elegant black, floor-length dress who wore a pinched look of officious authority. The anxious look from the young girl at his back didn't go unnoticed.

'Shit,' said Sapphire through her teeth as the woman, still in conversation, glanced her way. 'Look, I need this job,' she said, collecting the discarded cards. 'So, just go. Please.'

'Then just tell me what happened and you'll never see me again.'

Sapphire's eyes flicked from Frank to the woman in black, a hint of the haunted look she'd worn in Alsha Kar masked the reluctance in her eyes.

'You need to go,' she said, but Frank anchored himself tighter to his seat, watching as her jaw tightened, knowing she wouldn't be going anywhere. He'd make sure she counted every minute of her long shift with him as her sole player. He dipped his head.

'You'd better deal,' he said.

Her eyes dwelt on his, then looked behind him and back again. She squared the deck in her hand, her fingers fidgeting on the edge of the cards, but didn't throw any his way.

'He let me go.' Her words, whispered through her teeth, caught Frank out. She noticed. Frank's look had her shrugging her shoulders. Dagmar didn't let anyone go. Sapphire Hark's existence made no sense, to have a former guardian of the Simbrian wandering the streets presented all manner of potential complications and when Dagmar had said she no longer had a use, it didn't take much imagination to know what he meant. 'I was unconscious when he dragged me from my home, remember?' How could he forget? 'I woke up in a small bedroom, not some filthy dungeon like I expected.' Her eyes kept flicking over his shoulder. 'Then a couple of servants came and cleaned me up, fed me and told me to wait.' She drew in a long breath. 'Then *he* came in the middle of the night. I thought he was going to cut my throat, but he told me not to worry and he was going to let me go if I agreed to his bargain.'

'Which was what?'

'He told me to lose myself somewhere, anywhere, and get on with my life, free from the Simbrian and, in return, I was never speak of the Simbrian again. I hated the thing in the first place, so it wasn't exactly a difficult decision for me. So I agreed.'

'And?'

'Then he gave me some clothes and money and had an escort take me to the border.'

Frank felt his mind race. Dagmar killed people, he brewed havoc, he watched the world burn, having set it on fire himself. He didn't set them free. Especially not a prize piece of the puzzle such as Sapphire Hark. He'd killed Ludlow Hums, killed Montrose Menetti. His mother had been in the same position, wielded a fragment of the

Simbrian at Dagmar and, as far as he could tell, she, too, had paid the price for it.

'I don't believe it,' he said, but there she was.

Again, Sapphire shrugged, placing the deck on the table.

'And you think I do?' she said. 'I wasn't going to ask any questions. I just did everything I was told as I was taken to the border crossing thinking that, at any minute, someone was going to slit my throat and dump me in a ditch but once we got there I was given some papers to change my identity and they let me go. Believe me, I know what luck is and it doesn't sit at any of these tables and I left all of mine in the back of a wagon between Alsha Kar and Garrim.'

'And you decided to stay here?'

'It's easy to lose yourself in Garrim. No one asks too many questions and as long as you keep your head down and the punters happy, no one gives you any bother. The pay's okay and I get food and lodging. Certainly no one knows who I am and it was easy to get a job. So, what are you doing here?'

Frank turned a playing chip over in his fingers.

'I'm looking for someone.'

'Me?'

'No. Someone else.'

'Good luck with that.'

'Alfred Jackson. Governor Jackson.'

Sapphire shrugged, a movement that told Frank all she knew about the head of Byeland Council after years in hiding in Alsha Kar. Her eyes darted over Frank's shoulder, locking onto something behind him. She tensed.

'Shit.'

She picked up the cards and made a show of trying to make herself look busy, shuffling the deck as Frank turned his head to see the approaching woman who'd been talking to the two players a moment earlier, purpose and trouble in her short, determined strides. The sort of look on her face that tells you you're about to meet some bother.

She rounded the table and stood at Sapphire's shoulder. She was older than she'd appeared from a distance, built like the figurehead of a ship, carved by a generous hand. The dark skin on her small, round face had been leathered from years amongst the peaks and tobacco smoke. Her hair, blacker than her dress and her elbow-length gloves, was neatly pinned into a harsh bun and she wore her no-nonsense expression like a king wears a crown, immediately setting Frank in the cross-hairs of her eyes.

'What's going on, Melissa?' she said, her voice as hard as the morning's frost. A glance from Sapphire to Frank. 'Anything the matter?'

'No, ma'am,' said Sapphire. 'I just got talking to this young gentleman. I was about to deal him a hand.'

The woman's eyes never left Frank, a look coated with suspicion, a whip about to crack. Frank felt the faint heat under his collar.

'Is he bothering you?' Her voice already spoiling for a fight.

'No, ma'am.'

'Are you sure?' She appeared determined to find something to allow her to turn on Frank.

'Yes, ma'am.'

Frank felt himself shift on his stool, her natural authority anchoring itself to his skin. Trouble was the last thing he needed but this had it inked in large letters.

'You were so distracted that two of our regular customers walked out. Did you notice?' Sapphire looked down the table to the empty stools and cursed under her breath. The woman let the silence thicken. 'Do you want to keep your job?' A tight nod. 'Then remember the idea is to welcome clients to the table and have them play for as long as possible, preferably all day. We don't provide them with cheap drinks and even cheaper girls for our health. Understand?'

Frank sensed the young girl at his back shift uncomfortably.

'Yes, ma'am.'

'Very well. I'll have to report this to Mr Narvi. We can't have our regulars heading down to the Mountain Palace. They'll never come back.' She sniffed and looked at Frank. 'Although, for you, I think this game is over.'

'I haven't even started,' said Frank, tapping on the column of playing chips on the table in front of him and tossing her a disarming grin which failed to ignite any warmth on the woman's face.

'You've been sitting there for ten minutes and you've only played one hand, that's not how I run things. Like I say, you're finished here. And you look a little young.'

'Young? This is Garrim and I'm probably older than some of the working girls you have here.'

A half-turn of his head to the young girl who stood a pace back, picking at the sleeves of her flimsy dress. The woman bristled, then glanced over Frank's shoulder, no doubt fishing for the attention of the doormen. A slight twitch of her head to two of the heavies had Frank reaching into his pocket for the Elemental ball.

He looked at Sapphire whose eyes pleaded with him not to cause trouble.

Trouble for him, trouble for her.

After giving her away to Dagmar, after being responsible for having her relieved of the artefact her family had kept safe for centuries and left her for dead, Frank knew he owed her. He stepped from his stool, a last look at the former guardian before he turned to go.

The waif stood to the side, hopes of a long stay in the warm of the den dashed with the certainty of more hours standing frozen in the doorway being ogled by drunks and fending off those looking for something other than a stay at the tables.

Frank adjusted his jacket, preparing himself for the bitterness of Garrim's early morning air but as he stepped away from the table the woman raised her finger and said:

'I think a quick word from Mr Narvi before you leave.'

19

NARVI

A glance to the door told Frank he wouldn't be leaving just yet as a pair of thick-set doorman eyed him from the entrance, paid to do the woman's bidding and not ask any questions.

If he was anywhere else he may have considered the odds of making a run for it, out into the thick current of people and away, but the town was already telling him it didn't like him that much and any luck he was looking for was stuck firmly to the tables around him and most of that was clearly already being lost by the bucket-load.

'If you would follow me,' said the woman before turning to the young girl. 'Back to work, Lily.' A flick of the eyes towards the entrance.

Frank gave the young girl a shallow smile which she returned with sorrowful eyes before heading to the door to catch her death and the next in the long line of willing punters.

A nod to a security guard had him stepping to Frank's back, ushering him towards the twisted black wooden staircase at the rear of the den on the heels of the floor manager. Frank didn't look back to Sapphire Hark. She was, after all, dead.

The woman led him up without a glance back. Her short, clipped steps in keeping with her character – humourless and abrupt.

Each stair squeaked like a well-worn concertina as they bore her weight, then Frank's, in quick succession. He could feel the heaviness in his boots, the feeling that comes with wondering what vision of hostility awaits at the top of the flight, behind the cold, white door that appeared as the staircase wound round to a small landing, knowing there was no way back.

There was no indication, no sign announcing who might be on the other side but Frank didn't think a visit to the office of the owner of a Garrim gambling den would be anything but an experience he'd rather not be having. The woman knocked and entered without acknowledgement, leaving Frank outside like a schoolboy caught thieving from the headmaster's office.

The heavy had positioned himself at the bottom of the staircase and gave the occasional glance up, daring Frank to try his luck and make a run for it. Frank was already learning the hard way that luck was a rare and fine thing, as was hope but, now, both appeared to be in short supply.

'What is it now, Mrs Burns?'

The curt and hostile tone of a busy man not wishing to be disturbed arrowed through the door and landed into the thick of the Lid. Frank felt himself tense, he'd been in enough edgy situations to recognise when things were likely to go badly. This, he was sure, was going to be one of them.

People in foul moods always relished having others to take it out on, someone to help batter their temper away and here he was, squarely in the firing line.

'Have you had that leaking gutter fixed yet? If there's anything likely to put a client off from coming through my door it'll be the feeling like they're being been pissed on as they walk past. They can pay good money for that down at the Fallen Angel, if they care, and more besides.'

More belligerent tones cranked up Frank's nerves before he just made out the hushed tones of the woman's voice, obviously announcing his arrival to the quarrelsome owner who would, no doubt, have him pissed on all the way back to Rhaeder, and more besides.

The moment of silence was broken when the woman returned to the small landing, her weathered face looking him up and down before she stepped aside from the open door and invited Frank in with a barely discernible nod and a sideways flick of her head.

Frank rolled his eyes and took a few steps forward into a small office where a man sat behind a large desk, the surface of which was invisible under the scatter of papers and documents, his small pewter eyes, brimming with irritation, already trained on the teenager, his arched fingers at his lips on which sat an impressive moustache, grey, waxed to fine points, a match for his mood and his long slicked-back sliver hair. Frank felt any remaining comfort of the outside world slip from his grasp as he heard the click of the door closing.

The room leaned in on him. The office walls were stacked with books, lined from floor to ceiling on three sides with no space to spare. Leather-bound tomes, thick and thin in a dull array of colours squeezed the crammed spaces and drew his attention. The fourth wall was a study of strange assorted objects lining a number of clean and polished oak shelves. The sweet smell of soothing liquor swam up from the glass on the man's desk.

'I like to read,' growled the man, noticing how Frank's eyes darted over the spines of his impressive collection of works.

Frank jerked his head as the man slowly pushed himself up, a long, languid action of a man who would have preferred to have remained seated and was finding it hard to refrain from violence.

Frank looked upon his black shirt and jacket, cut with quality, expensively tailored, noted the easy way his long limbs moved, lithe and comfortable, like he was being poured from a bottle with a long neck, a strange cocktail of elegance and menace. Like a snake.

He stepped in front of his desk and perched himself on the paper-strewn top but Frank's eyes were drawn to something behind him – the effigy carved into the chair back where he'd been sitting. The vulture symbol of Excelsus academy, coloured in gold and purple, stared back.

If he noticed, the man didn't show it, nor did he appear that interested as the lines on his smooth, pale face buckled as he frowned at Frank, the steely-grey of his eyes dismantling him slowly. His natural poise and look of authority would have easily graced a military general or, ironically, the head of the Council, offsetting the hint of tiredness that came with running a gambling den in the rat's-arse end of Garrim.

A long exhale through his nose before addressing Frank.

'Mrs Burns says you're making life difficult for one of my dealers,' he said with a look towards the woman who stood at the door.

'Two customers left due to his distracting Melissa, Mr Narvi,' she said with deference and a slight bow of the head. 'They headed to the Mountain Palace.'

Narvi folded his arms and tightened his lips, looking down at his feet. A pause and a smooth shuffle of his mirrored shoes to show who was in control.

'Not your lucky day,' he said.

'I'm surprised you believe in luck,' said Frank.

'Oh, we must believe in luck,' said Narvi. 'How else should we explain the success of people we don't like, hm?' His eyes glinted like the edge of a straight-razor. 'Luck or no luck, my business is built upon the satisfaction of those who enter,' he said. Not the taking of their money, then, thought Frank. 'Mrs Burns runs a tight ship and I have a reputation to uphold. I won't tolerate anyone disrupting what goes on out on the floor and bad news travels faster than an outbreak of ice-pox here in Garrim.'

Frank didn't quite know what to say, but the last thing he wanted was a lengthy lecture from the owner of a gambling den who, by definition, would be connected to all the wrong people, the Watch included, and would lose no sleep in having him gutted and thrown into the newly-cleared storm drains. Trouble was closing in on him and had him looking for the quickest way to exit and return to the others on the southern slopes.

'I'm sorry,' he said. Narvi tilted his head back slightly. 'Can I go now? I promise not to bother you again.'

Narvi didn't respond. He gripped his chin between his thumb and forefinger and stared down his nose at Frank, letting the quiet hang for a moment. He cleared his throat.

'Your name?'

Frank stilled. Information of any sort was currency in Garrim and he wasn't about to give this man anything to spend.

Narvi didn't wait. He just turned his head and looked idly to the door.

'Mrs Burns, can you let Melissa know she's relieved of her duties and throw her out onto the street. Right away, please.' He folded his arms again, stone cold conquest lined his expression, revealing in an instant his talent for pushing the right buttons. 'You can go,' he said to Frank, with a nonchalant shrug and a flick of his head.

A perfunctory nod from Mrs Burns as she pulled the door open and went to leave. No waiting for a response from Frank, no questioning the instruction, no pitying or thought for the consequences. Just the compliance of an executioner swinging the axe.

'No.'

Frank heard the edge of the plea in his voice. Narvi held up his hand to stop his floor manager and raised his eyebrows. No other reaction, such was his certainty of the outcome of his little game. Just like those played at his tables.

'Icarus Emerald,' said Frank.

Narvi raised his head.

'And what are you doing in Garrim, Mr Emerald?'

'I'm on my way to Kzarlac,' said Frank. 'Just passing through.'

'Ah. Just passing through.'

'That's right.'

Narvi pursed his lips. Another pause.

'Then be sure to give my regards to your father, Soren, won't you?'

Narvi gave an exaggerated nod, a smile cracked on his face, the sort of smile that told Frank he'd just been undone by his own words. Narvi clicked his tongue and shook his head.

'You see, Soren Emerald and I go way back,' he said. 'So you won't be surprised to know I'm also acquainted with his son. And, would you believe…' He leaned forward and lowered his voice. '…you look nothing like him.'

Frank felt himself flush, a slow closing of his eyes revealed his own stupidity.

'Would you like to have another go? See if you can get it right this time.'

Frank turned his head and stared at the wall for a moment, silent curses in his throat. Narvi waited, silent as someone who could wait all day if it pleased him, like anything would please him.

'My name's Frank. Frank Penny.'

Frank felt the shiver of disappointment in himself. Just giving his own name felt like a betrayal of sorts and handed the advantage to a man he'd only just met. The air stilled as Narvi looked him up and down, something stirring behind the eyes of steel.

'Well, well, Frank Penny. And why are you in town?'

He brushed an invisible speck of dust from his sleeve and folded his arms.

'Holiday.'

A thin serpent's smile tugged the corners of Narvi's mouth. He dipped his head.

'Alone?'

'Yes.'

'And where are you staying?'

'Somewhere I'll be missed if I don't go back. Why are you so interested?'

Narvi barked a laugh before his face darkened, directing a black, sinister look at Frank, lowering his voice just enough to allow Frank to understand whose hands his fate was in.

'Why do I think you look like trouble?'

He measured the words.

'Because you spend too much time looking in the mirror? I don't know.'

It was the response of a fool. Fighting in someone else's

backyard might work when you have the option to run, but Frank knew he should have learned his lesson about baiting a bear when it's blocking the exit from its cave. Narvi huffed a laugh as he stood, pulling himself to his full height. Despite his age, his broad shoulders and fine cut cast an imposing figure and Frank felt himself go hot. Narvi lifted his chin and peered down his nose.

'You should keep your young wits about you. The Watch sniff out troublemakers and I've been around long enough to do the same.' He raised his hand to his face, framing his chin with his thumb and forefinger. 'Maybe I should report you. They have different ways of getting the answers to their questions.'

'What, just because I came into your place and spoke to one of your dealers?'

Narvi huffed again and screwed up his nose. He dipped his hand into his pocket and produced a one crown playing chip, coloured yellow and black and played his fingers over it before flipping it across the room. Frank caught it.

'On the house,' said Narvi as Frank turned it over in his hand. 'Keep it as a memento or take it to one of my competitors and bother them.' Frank looked up. 'What I mean is, clear off out of my casino and don't come back.'

'And if I don't?'

Not a good response. Narvi took a stride towards him. A slow, elegant movement that had Frank backing away a step. Narvi cleared his throat.

'Then I'll be clear. If I see you in here again, I'll cut you into small pieces and throw you into a barrel for the rats.' He didn't ask Frank if he understood, his message as clear and cold as the icicles that clung to his leaking gutters. Narvi looked at Mrs Burns. 'If you can show Mr Penny to the door.' He turned back to Frank. 'And throw him into the street.'

20

The Servant

Mrs Burns led Frank back down the stairs and to the door. Her brisk gait and clicking heels had him running to keep up, a quick glance to the table where Sapphire Hark dealt cards to five new punters. She didn't look up.

There was no sign of the waif at the door, making him wonder if he'd missed her at the crowded tables in the den or if she was engaged in another, basic way of keeping the Lid's satisfaction guarantee as part of Narvi's trade in misery and the exploitation of anyone unfortunate enough to cross his path.

He didn't linger; anxious to be away, keen to let Gabby, Cas and Anya know he'd discovered the rejuvenated guardian stashed anonymously between the tables at the Lid under the watch of Narvi, and her confusing story of her brush with Dagmar.

His relief at being back out in the street, away from the poisonous air in Narvi's office was short lived as he caught sight of two of the Watch idling by a brazier a few strides down, chatting and warming their hands. He had no reason to fear them, to think they would give them any trouble but Narvi's succinct message now had him on his guard and had left him with a feeling that trouble was posted at every corner aiming for the target on his back.

Despite the watchmen, Frank took a moment to sweep his eyes up and down the Ditch, an opportunity to look for any signs of Alfred Jackson, trying to pick him out in the sea of bodies – the thinnest needle in the Garrim haystack. Even so, he felt the surge of anticipation at the possibility of catching a glimpse of the Governor, the same feeling that lived in the belly of every player at every table at every gambling house, before the dice are rolled. There was nothing, another predictable loss, another predictable disappointment. The feeling after the dice have fallen.

He swore under his breath, grinding his teeth and scuffing his boot in the cold muck as the first spots of fresh snow began to fall before turning his collar up and heading away with a mixture of relief and frustration.

He had to concede that, when they left Rhaeder, he thought finding Jackson would be straightforward. In his mind he saw them confronting the old man, getting the book and heading straight back whereas the truth of the matter was they were no further forward than when they'd left Ralph Jackson in a heap on his grandfather's doorstep and, so far, each turn along the Garrim's streets had been met with dead ends or threats.

He peeled off the Ditch at the first opportunity, though his progress back up the south-side was slowed by his constant checking for the spectre that lurked in the shadows at his back. He cursed himself for feeling so paranoid but his unsavoury encounter with Narvi had him guarded and his instinct was to protect his friends and keep any hungry wolves away from their door.

He made sure his route back to the Gargoyle's Head wasn't direct, taking to different streets that all looked the same – same dark and battered buildings, same filthy, stinking gutters, same threats in the shadows of the doorways – each one retreated to places where the mid-morning light couldn't reach and although he'd always had a vivid sense of direction he found himself struggling to decipher the web that spread up and out from the levels.

The constant looking behind didn't help as he moved south, along and up, occasionally doubling back. Thoughts that he was being followed wrapped themselves around his shoulders, pulling him in like an old friend. He batted them away until he was sure that the only thing that was following him was the icy wind and the feeling that his tally of enemies in Garrim just kept on increasing.

As soon as the streets hushed, Frank stopped and pressed

himself into a doorway, cloaking himself in shadow, and waited, mastering his breathing. Ice framed him against the door. Had he imagined someone behind him? He peered out. No sounds. No movement. No one.

Frank cursed himself for letting Garrim get into his head but knew danger crept in the wake of the Simbrian, like rats in the sewer. The silent forest had left its scars.

Once he was sure it was safe he stepped from the doorway, pulled the collar of his jacket up further and headed up the slope. His feet clanked on metal as he passed over a heavy iron grate, bolted between the paving slabs, below which the sound of running water sang to the street. An access point to one of the storm drains Duckett had mentioned, throwing the chill of meltwater up into the already freezing morning.

Frank looked down, giving a shiver at the thought of the grate giving way, of falling in then looked back up at the sound of footsteps and hushed voices. He saw two figures coming towards him, bound up in their heavy coats, deep in conversation, heading down to the levels. The men walked on the same side of the road as him, making it difficult for him to cross without attracting attention to himself.

Acting naturally suddenly became an awkward pantomime, like he was wearing all the wrong clothes. He could tell he was doing a terrible job of trying to blend himself in as he walked toward them, retracting his neck into his upturned collar like a startled tortoise, passing them as quickly as he could, eyes on the pavement in front save for a curious glance.

Frank locked eyes. Half a second, less.

Percy, Dagmar's personal servant, looked back.

Shit. Frank looked right ahead. Ten paces, then a turn of the head over his shoulder. Percy mirrored him. Frank caught his ashen face before the dark of the street swallowed him up.

21

THE DRINKER

'Alive?'

What else did he expect them to say through their puzzled faces? As they sat in the Gabby's small bedroom at the front of the tavern, Frank recounted the full episode, his conversation with Sapphire, the brief, unsavoury meeting with Narvi and his certainty that Dagmar was in town.

'But that makes no sense,' said Anya. She sat in the window, her eyes trained on the street below, her mood sullen, ready for what the day might bring. 'We thought she was dead from the moment he had her dragged from her house. Why would he let her go? And why would he see to it personally in the middle of the night?'

It didn't sound like the Dagmar they'd become familiar with. The Simbrian and death skipped hand in hand from the black citadel in Alsha Kar and had no end to its reach. Information and secrecy were woven through Dagmar's quest. That he would let her go, out into the world with the potential to derail him was at odds with everything they'd learned.

'He must know about the curse,' said Gabby. 'He must know that she wouldn't be able to talk about it.'

'Do you really think he'd take such a big chance?' Anya's question hung in the air. 'She would be free to track down her family and expose everything that Dagmar was doing. No, it makes no sense.'

She was right. It didn't make sense. They knew Dagmar as a careful, particular planner. Mix that with his reputation for wielding his sword across the throat of anyone who crossed him and the outcome was like flipping a two-headed coin.

'We should go back and ask her more,' said Gabby.

'I'd rather not,' said Frank. 'I like all my limbs attached to my body and do you really want to be loitering along the Ditch waiting for her shift to end?'

Gabby exhaled a frustrated breath but Frank could tell she knew he was right. His solo foray to the Lid had had them all shaking their heads at him and numbers weren't going to make the odds of success any better, especially as Percy would tell Dagmar of his presence in town.

He'd blown their cover, not that they'd been doing a good job of keeping themselves below the parapet but now it felt like they'd donned bright red hats and stared down a phalanx of archers.

'So, are we just going to wait here?' said Gabby.

They looked at one another. No answers. Keeping to their rooms was something that was easy to say but nearly impossible to do.

Following Frank's brush with the owner of the Lid and the unwelcome incident with the Watch, they could all see that Duckett had their interests nailed to the tavern wall, but time would just seep through their fingers and if the ghost of Alfred Jackson was wandering the streets of Garrim they had none of it to spare.

Restlessness was fast becoming their unwanted friend on the promise from Duckett that he would find out something that would confirm Jackson's whereabouts, but Frank could feel the walls starting to close in on him.

Sitting in Gabby's room made it worse. It was the smallest the inn had to offer with just enough space for a bed which nestled uneasily between the door and the window which overlooked the narrow street, below. A small fire warmed them. Just.

'My Nan used to own a canary,' said Cas, breaking the silence. 'I guess this is how it used to feel and at least it had a mirror.'

'My room's got a mirror,' said Frank. 'Believe me, the canary wouldn't have been any happier.'

'Perhaps we should go back to see Sapphire,' said Anya, eyes still on the street. 'I could go, if you want.'

Frank looked at Gabby and shrugged his shoulders, maybe she was right and of all of them, Anya could handle any bother the best.

He opened his mouth but any response was interrupted by a light knock on the door which swung open on squeaky hinges. The huge frame of Cossens filled the doorway. He braced his broad hands on the doorframe and leaned into the crowded bedroom as if he was used to seeing four people crammed into it.

'There's a man downstairs,' he said, eyes on Frank. 'Looking for you.'

Gabby sat up. Frank felt a surge of nerves, he felt it in the others. No one knew they were there, or where they were staying and Cossens would have given anyone from the Watch the edge of his tongue and shown them the street.

'Who?' said Gabby.

'No idea,' said Cossens with a hefty shrug. 'Scrawny looking guy, looks like the sort who likes to keep himself to himself. Can't say I've seen him in here before. He wouldn't give his name, but he knew you were here, despite my attempts at bluffing. I'm as sure as I can be that he's not with the wrong people, if you catch my drift.'

'Is he still here?'

Cossens nodded. 'He just asked me for a beer, took a seat in the corner and asked me to ask you to join him. If you had nothing better to do, that is. That was a couple of hours ago and he's still there, so I thought it was best that you knew. Make of it what you will. If he's still here at closing, I'll have to chuck him out but he looks like he's in for the afternoon and most likely the evening.'

With that, Cossens dipped his head at them and left.

A note of tension rang out through the small room. None of them knew quite what to say, as if a despised relative had just walked in and no one felt like striking up a conversation.

'One of us should go down and take a look,' said Gabby. A deliberate look at Cas.

'Okay,' he said, with a lift of the eyebrows, raising himself from the end of the bed.

'Make sure he doesn't see you,' said Gabby.

'Thanks for the advice, just as I was going to put on my bright pink party gear, buy him a drink and ask him about his holidays.'

The tight-lipped look from Gabby was returned.

'Give me a few minutes.'

Cas returned quickly, just enough time for him to dash down the stairs, peer through the few drinkers and dash back to Gabby's room, met with faces a mix of expectant and curious.

'He's still there,' said Cas, breathy.

'Friend or foe,' said Frank, although neither seemed like a welcome option. Both could cause them problems.

'Depends on which end of the spyglass you're looking through,' said Cas. He looked at Frank. 'Even I couldn't miss the unmistakeable profile of your uncle Simeon.'

22

SIMEON

Cas's words caught Frank like he'd been snared on a large bramble. He didn't need to ask him if he was sure. Frank was immediately on his feet and heading down the narrow stairs.

He could tell Simeon clocked him as soon as he was through the door, tracking him with narrow eyes all the way across the tacky, beer-stained floor.

He sat in the farthest corner, black and shadowed, hunched over his full glass. His long, dark, lank hair, twisted and matted like a spill of treacle, fell around his narrow, gaunt face. Cas was right, there was no mistaking him.

Simeon adjusted himself in his chair, back to the wall, as Frank approached, greeting him with a dip of the chin, as if he'd been expecting him. His sunken eyes raised a little, looking over Frank's shoulder as Cas, Gabby and Anya followed Frank's path through the tables.

'Frank,' he rasped. He scanned the others, the corners of his mouth twitching. 'Strange place to meet.'

Even then Frank noticed how he didn't look at him, that he kept his eyes firmly on the door and the drinkers and the faces and the movement, no doubt checking and re-checking for trouble, for a sign of ill-will or potential wrong-doing or a rat in their midst who might sell their whereabouts for the right price to the wrong people.

Frank glanced back across the bar, to the corners and alcoves among the blistered timbers. For all the noise it was quite empty. Only a few people were scattered at the tables and no one paid them any attention.

'Don't tell me this is your local?' said Frank.

Simeon smiled like a viper that's just bitten its prey.

'You joining me for a drink?' he said.

Simeon jerked his head at Cossens and signalled with his fingers, a nod in return.

They sat, Simeon's eyes sifted the bar again, waiting to see if anyone showed interest in their little gathering. Frank could sense a natural edge to him, like the taught, drawn string on a bow, ready to slice anyone who crossed him while appearing nothing but relaxed and responsive. An odd cocktail. A deadly cocktail.

Simeon leaned back in his chair, inviting Frank to speak.

'Why are you here?' said Frank.

Simeon remained passive.

'Strange question.' He leaned forward, shifting smoothly in his seat. Frank knew what weaponry was concealed under his uncle's ebony cloak. The Black Flame weren't creatures to stray from their training or habits. 'I live here,' he said. 'Garrim is my home.' There would have been a time when the words would have surprised Frank, but that part of his senses had long since been dulled. 'And I find hiding in plain sight to be one of the more interesting aspects of human nature. You'd be surprised how effective it is, that and I only frequent places where the beer isn't too watery.'

His attempted humour slid off him uncomfortably.

'You followed me?' said Frank.

'Let's just say I like to keep my eye on things and most things happen along the Ditch.' He looked up as Cossens brought a tray of drinks, lingering for a second. Simeon's look of thunderclouds in his direction had him locking eyes, a dip to the barely-noticeable monogram of a black flame on Simeon's collar before retreating to the bar. 'And if you wait long enough...things happen. People come and go. Same faces, mainly, but, every now and then...' He let his words trail off as Frank wondered who else had been unfortunate enough to see him that morning. He'd been careful, he was sure, but knew you could be careful boiling a kettle and still get burned.

'So you're staying here. At the Gargoyle.' Simeon widened his weasel's eyes, letting them wander up to the ceiling. They kept quiet. 'Hm, Duckett's a good host, runs a good ship. Not so much trouble up on the south-side. Never see the Watch up this way.'

He licked his lips. Taking up his glass and relieving it of a mouthful, eyes not leaving the spot over Frank's shoulder.

'I take it you're not here gathering more information for Irundi?' said Cas.

Simeon let out a laugh under his breath.

'I think we all set light to our bridges where that's concerned,' he said. Another look behind them. Frank went to turn, to see what had caught Simeon's interest. 'Don't,' he hissed under his breath, his hushed warning met with a shrug of Frank's shoulders as he resisted the urge.

'Then what?' said Gabby.

'You mean other than checking you are all okay.' A glance at Anya. 'Especially our rookie. How are you? Still alive, I see, which is always a good thing.'

Anya smiled.

'I'm okay, thanks.'

Simeon somehow managed to further narrow his eyes, searching beyond Anya's response.

'Killing Morrin was a courageous thing,' he said. 'But I dare say it will have left its shadow. They all do.'

Anya didn't respond, though Frank detected a slight slackening of her face as Simeon handed her an important insight into the other side of an assassin's work, the one that went unspoken lest it crept up and grabbed you by the hair. There was undoubtedly a trade for taking a life, a trade that Anya's youth wasn't prepared for and Frank could only imagine how its shadow might rot you from the inside.

Simeon took a gentle sip of beer.

'I come home from time to time,' he said. 'To empty the mind. This is one of those times. I think the silent forest requires that of you.'

No disagreement, making Frank wonder if they should have left Jackson alone, taken more time to recover from their ordeal at the hands of Balal and Qaas, but they'd been out of choices and it doesn't do to be out of choices.

'And you never quite know what might come to you while you wait,' said Simeon. 'Let's just say information runs with the strangest of crowds and, here, there are none stranger.' A pause. 'I see your old friend Dagmar is in town.'

'But not *your* old friend,' said Frank, a glimpse of his aunt in his mind.

If Frank thought he'd catch Simeon off-balance he was wrong. Simeon cleared his throat.

'No,' he said. Another sip of beer, another look across the bar. 'No,' he said again. 'I thought we were similar, back then, but it turns out we were very different.' He noted the question on their faces. 'There are those of us that were set on a path to protect the Simbrian and those that chose the pathway to control it.'

'Protect?' said Frank.

Simeon looked at him through limp strands of hair.

'That's right,' he said. 'The four of us – me, Dagmar, Spyro and Lawrence. We all had the best insight from our time as the golden intake. We four know more about the Simbrian than just about anyone, except Baggus perhaps.' Frank felt himself shiver as the names spilled off of Simeon's tongue. They were bound together. Four scholars of the weapon Etamin sought. 'Spyro chose to defend it by becoming part of the inside machinery of Byeland, ensuring his own inevitable rise to the top from where he could access everything the Council had. Secrets, communications. Traitors.' He caught the look on Frank's face. 'Don't let that affable fly-boy exterior fool you. Spyro's as cunning and ruthless as any fox. Twice so. I chose to gather information from the wider world and pass it to Irundi, following my training in Sandulum. I'd also pass bits to Spyro.'

'Does the wider world include Kzarlac?' said Gabby.

'I've had the pleasure,' said Simeon with a thin smile.

'And Dagmar?' said Gabby.

'Chose his own path, a different path, clearly.' Simeon's eyes darted to the door as it creaked open and one of Duckett's regulars staggered in. He brought himself down, adjusting himself in his chair a touch. 'We never really got on. Our paths haven't crossed that much, not directly anyway, since Excelsus. He's quite difficult to get behind and, of course, we have some history.' Simeon's eyes glassed slightly across the table. Something behind them gave Frank just a glimpse of something torn, that time hadn't mended. Love that had been tainted but not discarded and now hung somewhere out of Simeon's reach.

'Was he always the same unpleasant bastard?' said Frank.

'Strangely enough, no,' said Simeon. 'He was quite the lamb. Terrific with a sword and an intellect just as sharp, but quiet and withdrawn, followed in Lawrence's shadow.' A look. 'Not quite the case now, though. All along we all agreed that the Simbrian should never see the light of day but we all know how snakes shed their skin. Looks like Dagmar fooled us, or Etamin got inside his head and all of a sudden the world is a more dangerous place and the work I do becomes more interesting.'

'Makes you wonder how he can be so wrong, for someone so clever,' said Frank.

'Wrong?' said Simeon. 'Is there such a thing?'

'What do you mean?' said Gabby. 'We're all lectured on the difference between right and wrong from before we're out of the cradle.'

A slight shift of Simeon's eyes to her.

'No one ever sets out to be the villain, Gabby,' he said. 'Everyone thinks they're on the side of the right, it's just a question of which end of the battlefield you're looking from.' He sniffed. 'Do you think Etamin Dahke considers herself to be treading the wrong path? That her cause is less worthy than yours or mine, hm? Of course she doesn't. Only those who write the history books have the benefit of telling us who was correct and then it's mainly the victors. But there are two ends to the spyglass. Believe me, whatever Dagmar's plan, he'll know exactly what he's doing and won't falter from the path he's set because he thinks he's one hundred percent right, as we all do.'

'Then what about my Dad?' said Frank. Still the words tightened his chest.

Simeon twitched his long nose.

'Ever the mystery, Lawrence.' Simeon regarded Frank and chewed the inside of his lip. 'Ever the mystery.' He paused, tapping his finger on the table. 'All the talent, the knowledge, the prospects, the offers but stepped away from anything to do with protecting the peace.' Now he stared, unflinching, at Frank. 'And let the world shit itself into oblivion. Now why do you think that is?'

Frank felt himself shift in his seat, taking an uncomfortable swig from his glass. He felt the eyes of the others examining him as he searched for an answer but, in the face of Simeon, Frank stalled, wondering if he had a point.

'He said he didn't want anything to do with Jackson or the Byeland elite once he'd finished at the academy. Can't say I blame him.'

Simeon stroked idly at the stubble on his upper lip, musing.

'I guess that might be right. I must say he's not given me any cause to think otherwise when I've been observing him at the farm. Always seems...content, disinterested. But then...'

He let his reflection hang and Frank felt the familiar seeds of doubt being planted by his uncle. Suddenly the lies, the deceit, the treachery all loomed, throwing uncertainty his way as if every word ever uttered by Lawrence Penny was tainted, to be treated with suspicion, even when there should be none.

'Dagmar called him a coward.'

A shrug from Simeon.

'A little strong,' he said. 'Although Byeland could have certainly done with his help.'

'I like to think he lost interest,' said Frank, hesitating over his defence of his dad.

A sage nod from Simeon.

'Perhaps.' A pause.

'I have no reason to think otherwise,' said Frank, although he immediately thought that was a lie, his dad had given him reason enough to have the finger of suspicion wagged in his face. Simeon gave a shallow nod.

'A man doesn't have to believe everything he hears, Frank, and love and suspicion don't dwell comfortably together. I should know.' Frank searched for a response but found nothing. 'You're probably right,' said Simeon. 'Looking back, he may have been a bit too caught up with his *other* interests.'

'You mean my Mum?'

Simeon did his best to hide a grin, even though Frank thought it was an odd experience for his face.

'Well now, if there was ever someone that knew how to hold a man's attention.' He cleared his throat with a rasp of phlegm before looking at Anya. 'So, why are you here?'

Frank looked at the man who just a month ago had been an odd stranger and the object of constant contempt bordering on hate at the farm all the time he was growing up but had since been a key part of their flight from, and survival of, the silent forest. A trained assassin, sculpted in the art of killing, to be relied upon. He asked for nothing in return. Unlike the businesses in his home town, there was no tab to pay, no favour sought or banked and no scores to be settled.

He'd misjudged the sallow sack of bones that was his uncle. His dad hated him, always had but hadn't known the truth, hadn't ever understood what his sister had done and how Simeon had covered it up because of his misguided love. Perhaps the best of men.

'We're looking for someone,' said Anya. 'He has something of ours.'

Simeon absently fingered his glass. A nod and a grunt to Anya.

'Well I doubt you'll find them in the Lid,' he said with a humourless look at Frank. 'I'd stay away from that place if I were you otherwise you'll have the Watch on your backs, if you haven't already. Narvi doesn't take to interference, or so I've heard. Never met him. He's the quiet type, but they can be the worst.' He looked at Anya. 'Good place to lose yourself, Garrim. Blend in. No one asks too many questions. Who are you looking for?'

'Alfred Jackson,' said Anya, expressionless.

Simeon licked his lips. A lift of his eyes to the room.

'A big fish for such a small, inexperienced crew,' he said. 'What is it he has?'

'Something he had his grandson steal for him,' said Anya.

Simeon loosed a chuckle which caught in his throat.

'Ralph? That weed-puffing good-for-nothing? I'm surprised Jackson hasn't had him shipped here, he'd fit in rather well, don't you think?'

Frank couldn't disagree. If it served Ralph Jackson, he'd be in Garrim on the next transport, pressing the right flesh and jumping into the beds of the influential. If he'd learned anything about the Jackson family it was that a dog could live in a fancy house, but would just as soon tread the gutters if it could get itself fed.

'Can you help us?' said Anya.

Simeon just raised an indifferent eyebrow, his eyes wandering over their shoulders again, then suddenly alert, like a switch had been flicked and he'd gone from the chatting drinker to the primed assassin in half a heartbeat. A predator that's just caught the scent of its prey.

He pushed himself slowly to his feet, his eyes tracking something behind Frank who turned his head to see the door to the tavern being pulled shut from the outside.

'Look, I might be able to help,' said Simeon through his distraction. 'Meet me outside the Patchwork Frog tomorrow at eight bells. I may have something for you. Now, if you'll excuse me.' He reached into his pocket and laying a few crowns on the table. 'Duty calls.'

With silent feet, he swept across the floor and was out through the door, blank faces in his wake.

23

THE DITCH

If Garrim's demeanour in the middle of the day cast a threatening shadow over those unfortunate enough to walk its streets, the dark, damp evening brought a whole new meaning to intimidating.

It drew out a greater number of thugs and pickpockets like a healer draws poison from a snake bite. They lurked on each corner while the well-dressed hawkers from the row of salacious establishments trod the streets, engaging with travellers and tourists in well-rehearsed attempts to attract them into their employer's den to relieve them of as much of their money and dignity as they could, moving from one to the next, not the least bit put-off by a quick rejection or a swerve to the other side of the street.

The ooze of charisma mixed easily with the undertone of violence, people robbed and charmed all at the same time and many fell for the convincing chat of those that sold promises of fortunes and pleasures. Even the lowest dog loves having its ears scratched and the Ditch was the ideal place for it.

But the Ditch had bitten them once, Frank twice, and venturing back felt like yet another bad idea in a long line of bad ideas, despite Simeon's offer of help.

Entering the main drag had Frank's senses chiming at the thought of the Watch or the host of pushers latching on to them or, worse, Narvi's thugs looking to work out their aggression, remembering his promise of a slow and painful death should Frank make the stupid mistake of returning to the Lid.

The low light from the street lamps and the glow from the

braziers threw an unsettling, ghostly glow across the street. They kept their eyes on the ground, avoiding any sort of signal that might invite attention. Even then, a young woman dressed in purple silks and calf-length jackboots grabbed Cas by the arm in a failed attempt to divert him to the tables in one of the gambling houses.

The evening had brought an unwelcome drop in temperature, but the bustle from the throng sent an unhealthy warmth through the air. The burning braziers steamed the street down the whole stretch, lighting the way and sending coalsmoke into their lungs as they fought the heightened sounds of revelry. The night, and the darkness it brought, shed an unusual mix of excitement and tension, even for those used to its visit.

But one of the advantages of Garrim was the anonymity it promised. The fact that no one knew them or why they were there was a salve to the itch of the town and Frank felt them glide seamlessly towards their rendezvous with Simeon, arriving across the street from the Patchwork Frog earlier than he had wanted, bringing unwanted problems.

Now they faced waiting, exposed to the open eyes of the Ditch.

Whatever Garrim was, it never stopped moving and to still anywhere along its streets was to invite attention, probably the wrong sort or, even worse, trouble.

They could ride it out, attempt to blend into the background, but the street's eyes were everywhere, picking out the unwary or innocent. For those with the wrong motives, there was no fruit so sweet as the one yet to be tasted and, loitering on the pavement, Frank felt ripe and good for the picking.

'Let's carry on and come back,' he said to nods.

They returned as eight bells sounded above the menacing mix of voices, music and apprehension. Frank felt the bunching in his shoulders and the heave of his breath. Just standing to the side of the road put him on edge as the strip revved to full swing. They idled by a brazier in the hope some of its warmth would leech into their bones.

They waited. No sign of Simeon. Frank kicked the toe of his boot into the filth, feeling unwanted eyes on them.

'Why don't Cas and I wait over there,' said Anya, nodding to the other side of the street, appearing to sense the potential problem. Frank nodded. 'And if there's any problem, we'll head back to the inn and see you there, okay?'

Another nod from Frank, more of a reflex, until her comment sunk in. She was primed for trouble, could sense it in her assassin's bones even though they had only come down to meet Simeon which, in itself, was no cause for concern. Except each step taken on the streets of Garrim came with the potential of a trip hazard and Anya recognised the aggression in the air for exactly what it was. No chances to be taken, especially following their previous stroll into the teeth of the Ditch.

Anya linked arms with Cas and walked through the slow river of people, hanging by a different brazier further down, warming themselves against the increasing chill that crept down the mountainside as the dark of the evening deepened.

Frank pressed into Gabby who wove her arm through his and around his waist, pulling him close, giving him comfort while his eyes scanned the street for his uncle. Gabby looked at him, reassurance in her eyes, no sign of the trepidation he felt. Perhaps she just hid it well.

His mouth was dry, sour, and he'd quickly become sick of waiting, and it wasn't like a member of the Black Flame to lack punctuality. The faint sound of alarm bells started somewhere in his head.

'Something's wrong,' he said to Gabby above the voices jabbing the air from the gaudy doorways where good-time girls laughed and shivered, but she didn't hear him, she just stood looking across to Anya.

Frank followed her eye-line, noticing how Anya had tensed, how she looked around her with the care and apprehension of a deer feeding close to a predator, anticipating something, something bad, her seer's senses tweaked.

She mouthed something to Cas who looked over before quickly melting away into the crowds. She looked across to Frank and Gabby, then back into the stream of people before hurrying across, approaching them quickly.

Let's go, she mouthed with a swift jerk of her head just as five men in plum coats slithered themselves easily from the depths of the crowd and stood surrounding the three teenagers, closing in slowly, corralling them like cattle.

All of them looked primed for a fight. One of them, short and wiry, clenched his fists eagerly around a set of brass knuckles as a taller man stepped forward. The familiar square jaw and scarred lip studied Frank.

'Hello lout,' he said with a confident show of his teeth.

There was no sign of the walking cane he'd berated Frank with before, just gloved hands which he flexed by his sides as a veiled threat.

Gabby backed off a stride before a hand on her back had her still. Anya was on the balls of her feet, her hand reaching to her blade.

'Don't even think about it,' said the watchman. A nod to one of his associates had him gripping Anya by the shoulder, his hand going to her thigh, withdrawing the weapon slowly, his touch lingering longer than it should before Anya pushed him off, resisting the urge to break his nose.

'You can't do anything,' said Gabby. 'We're just standing here minding our own business. Surely even Garrim's law allows that.'

'Yes, but you'll be pleased to learn that your presence is required elsewhere.'

Elsewhere? Elsewhere in Garrim was somewhere unpleasant. Elsewhere was somewhere Frank knew they didn't want to be.

He looked around for signs of Simeon, thinking a fearless and able member of the Black Flame was just what they required. Perhaps he was in the shadows, waiting to take down the five watchman in one, deadly move but hope was, once again, in short supply.

He heard the strike of the quarter hour. Still no sign. Simeon wasn't coming.

'We're not going anywhere with you,' said Gabby.

A ripe smile broke across the watchman's face. He took a stride towards her, lifting his hand which Gabby swatted as she tried to back away but the man at her back gripped her by the shoulder. The watchman stroked the thumb of his gloved hand across Gabby's cheek with a satisfying sneer, his bright, ice-blue eyes looking her up and down. Loitering.

'Get your filthy hands off me,' she said, stepping forward and shoving the man back.

'Oh, I know where I'd like to put my hands alright, sweetcheeks.' Growling, dirty chuckles from his four mates. 'Sadly, my orders are different, but perhaps I'll get the chance another time.'

'Mind your mouth,' said Frank, his thoughtless step forward, met with a hard shove back. The man swept the flank of his coat back and grabbed a short, heavy-looking cosh that hung from his belt, tensing his hand around it looking ready for it to see some use.

He brandished it waist-high with a look that told Frank he'd be happy to bash his brains across the Ditch, that he'd forgotten more violent confrontations than Frank would see in a lifetime.

'Perhaps I'll shove this in yours,' he spat, holding it up to within an inch of Frank's face.

Frank batted it away.

Curious eyes were now on them from all sides of the strip, drawn to the raised voices and the circle of plum-coats hemming in the three teenagers. Some had stopped, rough types dragging heavy on their pipes or the necks of their bottles, checking the game, checking the odds, hoping for something more than words to be thrown as Garrim licked its lips in anticipation.

Frank could see his clouding breath quicken, hoped the man hadn't noticed. The man's eyes swept them, then a look out into the crowds. A twitch of his long nose.

'Where's your mate?' Greeted with silence, darkening the

mood of the watchman who made a show of grinding his teeth and curling his lip at the same time before hauling up a throat-full of snot, swilling it around his mouth like a fine wine before spitting it into the gutter. 'I asked you a question.' Menace in his well-heeled voice.

More people lingered, slowing as they passed, waiting for the touch-paper to be lit. The street had trouble written right across it from gutter to gutter and these guys were the heavy ink that underlined it.

'Do we look stupid?' said Frank.

'Look and sound,' said the watchman. 'Don't worry, we'll find him.' He looked deep into the hordes, a slow sweep of the Ditch before sniffing and spitting again in defeat. 'We'll find him,' he said again. 'Meanwhile, you three are going to come with me and don't think about running. You're on my turf and I really don't want to dish out any bother.' He leaned towards Gabby and lowered his voice. 'Although, maybe I'd like to bother you. Take matters into my own hands, eh.' He straightened up. 'And no one said anything about delivering you unbruised.' He folded his hand into a fist, cracked his knuckles and flashed his teeth.

Frank's determination to front this out was beginning to crack. Not only were they in the hole of Garrim, but now they were faced with five of its meanest, and mean with the added problem of authority spelled a whole lot of trouble. Having spent a few hours in the cells in Rhaeder he doubted a similar experience in Garrim would be anything like the same.

'Who wants us?' said Gabby.

'Someone you don't want to want you,' said the watchman with a leer. 'That, you can have for free.'

'Then it would be a shame if you failed,' said Gabby. 'I hear people around this shit-hole can be unforgiving, if you give them the right opportunity.'

With the eyes of the five watchman on Gabby, Anya struck, quick and precise as the swiftest cobra, her fist finding the throat of the one who had relieved her of her dagger, sending him backwards. She reached into her boot and produced a small, brutal-looking knife – *one knife is never quite enough* – and went at him without hesitation, drawing the attention of all the plum-coats that flanked them, just enough time for Gabby and Frank turn and run. Fast.

There were no thoughts of the watchman's words, of who might have sent a party of Garrim's most violent to drag them from the Ditch, of what might happen if they got caught. Just his feral instinct to take flight.

No awareness of the colours, of the sounds, of the smells around him. Just his need to put as much distance between himself and the plum-coats as quickly as possible. There were a lot of things along the Ditch that Frank might be asked pay for, but the luxury of looking back was something he knew he couldn't afford.

He dodged through the crowds, throwing himself left and right around the swell of people, the sound of his own breaths catching awkwardly in his throat.

He lost sight of Gabby in the mix of bodies, a fatal mistake. A quick glance sideways and he missed the brace of drunks, both wielding full bottles of liquor, who stumbled out of a bar and straight into his path, propelling all three of them to the ground in a sprawling heap, Frank tumbling to an undignified stop on the hard-as-iron pavement, just missing a smoking brazier, scattering the knot of people who stood soaking in its warmth.

He was quickly on his feet, a half turn to check behind when his skull erupted in fire, dazzling lights in his eyes telling him he'd been hit hard across the head, sending him stumbling to the side and down once more.

His hand went up to deflect further blows as the tall watchman stood over him, cosh in hand, bringing it down on Frank's forearm.

A void emptied instantly on the road around him like a pebble being dropped into a pond as the crowds pushed back, anxious to be away from the fight but keen to see to whom the Ditch's latest round of violence was being dished out.

A circle of people began to form around them like the crudest of spectator sports, like fights were just another form of entertainment, one that, at least, could be enjoyed for free and without loss of dignity – as long as it was others throwing the punches.

'Get up,' said the watchman, grabbing him by the jacket. Through his blurred eyes Frank could see three other remaining plum-coats around him, two of them hauling him to his feet. Rough hands clamping his biceps. 'Leave the others,' came a growl, three words that hit Frank like he'd been coshed again as their significance quickly sunk in. They didn't want Gabby or Cas or Anya. They'd come after *him.*

A clatter from behind had the watchmen dropping Frank at their feet and frantically hammering their coats to shouts and pitched voices. Coarse, damp smoke filled the air around them and Frank felt the relief in his arms as he was let go of.

He looked behind him. They were alight, flames licking wretchedly at their backs, the brazier on its side behind them, spilt coals at their feet.

Then the harsh crash of splintering glass had the leader reeling backwards, holding his nose while the shards from the bottle that had just smashed into it crashed on the ground to his side. A crimson rush from the wounds spilled through his fingers and down his chin to cheers and howls from the crowd – a sense that some had backed the wrong horse and, just perhaps, the favourite wouldn't romp home.

Frank couldn't gather his senses. His head still pealed. A hand on his wrist pulled him away in the few seconds of distraction, enough time for him to start running again. Gabby had hold of him, the neck of a broken bottle in her hand, dragging him away, not looking back at him, just the quick, determined strides of a hunted animal.

She'd reacted quickest to the trouble, speaking the language of the Ditch with clear thinking and unfettered carnage, language that was well understood by those who sought them and those who watched on.

She let go, leading him right down the middle of the Ditch, through the crowds that he hoped would be their ally against the men he felt on their tail.

The Simbrian had always kept him running, but now he ran like his life was being dragged away from him, the deep, burning, frightened desire to keep one step ahead his only thought as he struggled to keep up with Gabby who headed aimlessly to the eastern end of the Ditch, her legs stretching, feet pounding the ground to get distance between them and the Watch.

A whistle sounded. Shrill and meaningful, a portent of more bad news, more bad luck. Four or five would be difficult enough to evade, but the whole damn Watch on their tails was the stuff of impossibilities. They'd seal off the western exit to the town, no doubt, and all that awaited anyone on the eastern boundary was Deadman's Scar and the border crossing to Kzarlac. Prisons came in a variety of shapes and sizes, but they all served the same purpose and some would have you hanging by the morning.

Garrim was too unfamiliar, a dark stranger that had hardly welcomed them and the words of the watchman stuck him like a knife – *you're on my turf.* They could run all they liked, they could hide in the doorways amongst the rabble and the filth, they could cower like beggars, they could crawl through the sewers with the vermin but they'd find them and the bruise Frank could feel grinding his forehead would be nothing compared to what lay in store for the rest of his face once they were caught.

24

Battered

There was no time for regrets or dwelling on mistakes, just for instincts.

The people began to thin as they neared the end of the drag. Quickly the street appeared bare, lacking any disguise. Short, hot breaths escaped from both of them, cold wind and the beginnings of sleet whipping their faces as Gabby turned and headed up the north-side, to a warren of foreign pavements and nameless streets, her quick strides urging Frank on.

The main roads narrowed to squalid backstreets and alleyways which funnelled out like the silken threads from the most talented spider. Spun with darkness and fear, an impossible maze in which to get jumped or, worse, caught.

Whoever had designed Garrim had been afraid of straight lines. You'd have better odds picking ten consecutive correct numbers on the luck-wheel than picking the right way, the safe way, except there was no safe way, not in Garrim, there was only the street that would do you the least harm.

The smell of coalsmoke from the braziers was quickly left behind, the reminder still on their clothes and in their hair, the air now tasting foul and corrupt, muddy slush clinging to the pavements and their boots as Gabby ploughed on with no real idea of where they were going, the scant street lighting providing just enough glow to light the way but, thankfully, not enough for their pursuers to pick them out as the shroud of Garrim's alleyways embraced them like the grim reaper comforts the newly-deceased, joining them in their flight.

They switched left and right, heading up and west in the hope the search for them would concentrate around the spot where they'd disappeared before broadening into an inevitable town-wide manhunt that would have them hung by the morning.

They headed down a narrow alley, where tired and shivering houses became a mixture of burned out hovels and abandoned, dilapidated shells, charred roof timbers poking at the vague silhouette of the looming north mountain masked in dark cloud that stared from above the rooftops in the thick soup of the night. Some houses occupied, most incapable of it.

Their frantic footsteps filled the tight spaces, echoing from the top of the high buildings that penned them in at the sides and whispered to them the warning that they should keep going and not stop to rest their heaving lungs.

Gabby pulled him into a shallow doorway, anxious glances in the direction from where they'd come even though Frank thought they'd done a good job of shaking off any chase. But he knew Garrim's surprises came in different coloured coats and were likely to show themselves when they least expected them.

They strained their ears back down the street, against the quick patter of the sleet on the roadway and on the rubble-strewn pavements. No sound of the clamour of the Ditch, no sound of the clamour of hasty boots, of hate-filled watchmen looking to bust some heads.

Frank wiped his running nose and cupped his hands to his face, blowing warm air into his palms, dabbing at the pain on his cheekbone.

He looked at Gabby, could feel the adrenaline pouring off her as her breathing calmed. He put his arms around her, an instinct he might once have thought twice about, but now wasn't the time for regrets. She moved in to him, sensing the fraying of his nerves and he knew that as long as they were in this together, they'd somehow get out of it.

'We should keep moving,' she said.

Another peer out from the doorway. Still no sounds from down the street. She took him by the hand and led him deeper into the wreckage of the neighbourhood.

No one else walked the street. Snaking rivers of smoke hurried from chimneys here and there, elusive signs of life, their reluctance to venture out welcomed as they headed further along the northern slope, through the bending alleyways that were so dipped in darkness Frank thought he might be going blind.

Quiet steps, growing in confidence, too confident as, out of a side-alley stepped a short, stocky man, blocking their path.

Even in the meagre light Frank cold make out the deep purple of his long-coat and tall hat.

Time flicked off for a moment. Frank and Gabby both turned to run but stalled just enough for the watchman to grab Gabby, yanking her backwards, bracing his forearm around her throat and dragging her two strides back, drawing a whistle from his pocket with the other.

Frank didn't think, the time had passed for doing anything as simple as that and thinking in these situations was for those who wanted their brains on the pavement.

He watched as the watchman pressed the whistle to his lips and sucked in a breath, readiness on his face, readiness to bring the whole swarm of the Watch down on their heads, readiness to see Frank get the godfather of all kickings before hauling them off to whoever had given the order to have him detained.

In the split second that it took the man in the plum coat to inhale, Frank was on him, knocking the whistle from his mouth as he sunk his forehead into the man's nose, smashing it with as much brutality as he could muster.

Blood arced out in the dark, spraying across Frank's face, the tall hat went skipping across the pathway. The man let out a loud groan like a well-rusted hinge as his knees buckled and he stumbled back.

Gabby wrestled herself free and stepped aside as Frank

launched himself, the first punch failed to land as Frank swung wildly but the second connected with the man's temple, snapping his head sideways and sending him to the cold pavement with a dull thud. Frank followed up with a towering kick to the groin, doubling the man up in the gutter but if Frank thought the watchman was going to lay down and concede an early defeat, he was badly mistaken.

Like a phoenix from a very painful set of ashes, the watchman rolled over and got to his feet, making Frank wonder if he was made of iron. The man dabbed gingerly at his nose, a poor attempt to stem the blood that flowed down his chin and onto his plum coat, now smeared and streaked in street grime.

'You broke my nose, you little bastard,' he growled, a sharp intake of breath as he touched his nose a little too hard.

His forehead was splattered with blood and shit from the street, just visible in the gloom, his thick neck and heavy shoulders just a hint of his capabilities with his fists.

Frank wasn't interested, he was disappointed that he hadn't finished the job and was now presented with the short odds that the watchman would get the better of them and they'd be in the hands of his colleagues before nine bells, odds that Frank wasn't going to take.

The man took the few short steps towards Frank, full of purpose, that purpose being to break something on Frank's face to even the score. Frank backed off, looking quickly left and right for something to use as a weapon but nothing presented itself.

A light appeared from a ground floor window before the curtain was pulled again, just another fight in the backstreets, unworthy of further attention.

The man reached inside his coat. Where Frank assumed he would pull out his cosh, a knife appeared, clenched firmly, the man's knuckles whitening. Not a small pocket knife for whittling wood or extracting a sliver of meat from between your teeth, this was the type used for hunting, for skinning and gutting rabbits. Sharp and nothing but deadly, wielded like a veteran.

'Come on then,' said the man. 'Let's see you use your fists now, boy.' Spit flew from his mouth. 'You might be wanted alive, but a few scratches here and there wouldn't go amiss, now, would they?'

He licked at the blood that still ran over his lips and lunged at Frank. Frank was on his toes, expecting it. He'd studied the way Anya practiced, how she kept her body loose and light allowing easy movement. She bent easily like rushes in the current and spun like a falling leaf on a still autumn day and he was a quick learner.

His sidestep was met by a wild arc of the blade which missed by a distance. Frank watched him stumble, he'd run the same gauntlet with Balal and this rough was a kitten compared to her.

Even so, Frank was under no illusion that members of the Watch were picked for their own assortment of abilities, ones that were used to sorting the troublemakers in Garrim, a place where lawlessness grew in the gutters and ran in thick swells off the Longshadows and it took a person with wits and menace to tread the streets with authority and without fear and the man in front of him was cast from the same intimidating mould that he'd had the unfortunate pleasure to be presented with so far.

Underestimating someone, especially in a fight, is the province of the defeated and the dead.

A battering right fist caught him full on the cheek, sending him back as the knife swept across, nicking him on the forehead. Frank felt his heel against the shallow kerb the moment before he stumbled, his head ringing from the blow, mouth dropping open. Hard stone crunched into his back and snatched his wind away. His jaw smacked against the ground setting the world spinning around him before he regained his senses.

The watchman stood over him, Frank watched him carefully adjust the knife in his hand, no hint of a smile just the look of someone who wanted to exact his own brand of retribution for his bloody nose, a debt that simply needed calling in.

There was an earthy thud and an agonising crack before the man flopped to the floor to Frank's side like a felled tree. Gabby stood in his place, a large, bloodied rock in her trembling hand. A look at each other, then at the heap of deep purple lying still in the road, face down in the filth and slush. Motionless. The alleyway hushed, broken only by the pattering of the sleet.

'Shit,' she said. 'I think I've killed him.'

25

LOST

They watched him for a few, long moments. No movement from under the pile of plum, face down in the gutter. No twitch of his legs, no groan in his throat, no attempt to get up.

Frank could see his hair, matted strands coated with filth and blood, hanging limp around his face like seaweed on a rock as the tide recedes.

Gabby still held the rock she'd plucked from the crumbled wall next to where they stood. It glistened in the night – not just from the pale sleet that whipped their faces – a simple but deadly reminder of how the Simbrian had bent and shaped them, holding them in its grasp, pushing them right to the edge, making them sink to new lows and walk the tightrope of their wits.

Frank knew the killing of a watchman would be the end of them if they were caught. No one in Garrim looked like the forgiving sort. Undoubtedly they'd just be chucked into Deadman's Scar but not before the Watch had had their fun and dispensed their own brand of retribution with objects sharp and blunt.

Gabby knelt beside the body as Frank sunk on his haunches, pressing his fingers into his head that still beat like the hammer on the blacksmith's anvil. Through his pain he could sense her hesitation before she reached forward a hand and gave the watchman a quick shove, withdrawing it as if the coat had attempted to bite her.

She reached down again, her fingers feeling for the front of the man's neck, slowly and gently, like she'd been asked to pet a rattlesnake. Then she closed her eyes and let out a long breath.

'He's still alive,' she said.

Frank wasn't sure if that was a good thing or not. Alive meant he'd wake up, probably. Alive meant difficult decisions to make. Surely the best enemy is a dead one.

Gabby let the rock roll out of her hand. Frank watched it take a few bounces to the side of the road and come to rest in the shadows, innocent and inconspicuous.

It took them a few moments to gather themselves. A few moments too long as Frank realised hanging around the backstreets when the town was searching for you wasn't a plan of any sort. That and the weather was beginning to worsen, the cold, driving sleet turning to miserable, lashing snow, relentless on Frank's face, the lifeless fingers of the cold creeping down his neck.

'We need to move him,' he said.

A long look down the alley, through the grey smudges, searching for demons before a nod from Gabby had them rolling the man over onto his back, his lifeless arms slapping the wet ground.

Frank stowed the man's knife in his belt before he grabbed him under the armpits while Gabby gathered his legs together and together they lifted.

Even with their combined strength they could barely lift him a few inches from the ground, both of them groaning through held breath as they half-dragged the dead weight across the narrow street and into one of the ruined buildings, finding a sheltered corner where they carefully laid the watchman down and stood back, watching for signs of movement. Still he didn't stir. Gabby checked again for a pulse. Still alive.

With a quick search of the battered and beaten room, Frank found a ripped and tattered length of material which looked like it had once hung at one of the now glassless windows. It shredded easily under the watchman's knife, giving enough to allow him to bind the man's hands and feet and to wind a strip around his mouth. He felt the slick of the man's blood on his fingers, silvery in the shadows, wiping the damp residue on his trousers.

Gabby hurried out and returned from the street with the man's hat clutched firmly in her hand, tossing it at his feet. Calm had returned to her face, its quiet pallor rubbing off on Frank who felt the clamp on his chest start to ease and his breathing deepen.

'I don't think anyone will find him here,' she said.

A nod from Frank. If their victim woke, they'd be long gone but still he felt the creep of discomfort in his bones, like the unconscious man still held the ace, would give them away. For a moment he wondered if leaving him alive was in their best interests, considered suggesting to Gabby that they cut his throat but easy-sounding deeds are not always easily done, and dark ones never bring any light.

'It would make us like them,' said Gabby, watching him watch the watchman, reading his mind as easily as a large-print book. Frank closed his eyes, willing the thoughts away. She was right, but he felt they were becoming more like them by the day.

Voices from down the street had them wired again. Maybe the sound of locals returning from a game of dice, maybe a group of drunks all spent out for the evening, maybe something else, something worth running from. Now wasn't the time to stay and find out.

Frank led Gabby to an opening at the rear of the building, a broken, rotting wooden frame clung desperately to the stonework where there had once been a door and they were swiftly through and out into another of Garrim's narrow and unappetising alleys, heading away. Time to put distance between them and a half-dead man.

They continued west through the endless fall of snow, away from the voices, away from the Gargoyle's Head. Quick; the occasional glance back, freezing breaths coming faster, the town gulping them down. The lightness in their footsteps began to wane as they realised they were lost to the web of streets.

Frank began to hear their faint echo become louder like someone tapping harder on a drum, realising they were becoming hemmed in on each side by heightening walls like the immovable black bulwarks of a castle, his anxiety spiking when they came to a dead end where the alley met the mountain.

Slick, moss-covered rock held its palm up to them, stopping them, demanding they turn back. Frank looked back from where they had come. Nothing but falling snow and black and the unknown. A lot to raise the senses, nothing to raise their hopes.

A look at Gabby who stared at the moving haze of night air behind them, her composure looking slightly more fragile. He could tell she didn't relish the thought of heading back, back into the arms of their silent pursuers and their sharp blades and weighty coshes.

A look around at the wall to the side, thrust up, scabbed with breaking brick, blistered with moss and lichen and scarred with black cracks.

Eight feet of rough stonework and fractured mortar. He'd climbed higher, harder looking stuff with his eyes closed, but not in the wet, not in the cold and not like his life might depend on it.

A push off with his foot had his hand gripping the top of the wall, pulling himself easily on top, taking a moment to balance himself carefully on the greasy surface which didn't want him there and would have him back on the street with a wrong move.

With care, he leaned forward, bracing his chest on the cold stone, legs straddling the wall, reaching his hand down for Gabby to take before he hauled her up, her hands rummaging for a safe hold. The alley filled with the sounds of her scrambling boots, like the scratching of rats. No one would tell the difference. No one would notice.

Gabby swung her leg up, managing to anchor her knee on the ridge, solid concentration as she centred herself. Woodsmoke from the streets below blew their way, mixing in the soup of the snow and washing through their faces, making Frank realise they were exposed and vulnerable. He lifted a leg over the ridge, pivoted round and jumped down into the neighbouring alley, realising his mistake too late.

The wall he climbed was eight feet high but, with the slope of the mountain, the lower side of the wall began six feet lower.

Unprepared, Frank felt the rise of his stomach before his legs buckled under him, his ankle rolling as he hit the pavement, pain scorching through his knees as they sent him sideways with a clatter.

He felt the hard knock of his elbow before the side of his head caught the ground, connecting in the same place the watchman had struck less than twenty minutes before. His eyes watered through the blunt thud, the smell of the gutter immediately pushed up his nostrils as he let out a yowl.

He gripped his ankle, pressing his thumbs into the flesh and bone, pointing and rotating. Painful, but thankfully nothing more.

Then the sound of Gabby coming after him. He looked up, saw how she'd lowered herself down, her hands had a fragile grip on the top of the wall as she dangled in the snow. She let go, falling the six of seven feet to the street, landing on her toes with a short exhale.

Then she was crouching down beside him. She reached her hand to his face and pushed his wet hair back across his temple, supporting his neck with the other hand as Frank opened his eyes. Only concern looked back at him through her tawny eyes. Concern and fear.

'You okay?' she said, her fingertips gliding softly over his cuts and bruises.

'Apart from nearly breaking my ankle, fine,' he said.

He pushed himself up with a long groan and turned his back to the wall leaning against it for support, finding comfort in the slick brickwork. The snow now battered the cobblestones, soaking him, soaking Gabby as she stood in front of him, the alleyway completely bereft of life, alive with the howling wind.

Frank ran his hand through his hair, so wet it was like wringing out a sponge. It had been a close call and the fact they'd managed to get themselves lost in the backwaters of Garrim did nothing to ease his tattered nerves. The whole episode had pushed him beyond his natural limits. He could see it in Gabby too.

Gabby grabbed her hair and twisted it, wringing the water out and letting the dark strands loose down her back. Water dripped in a steady stream from the end of her nose. Exhaustion gripped her face but sounds from the streets, from everywhere, from nowhere had them ready again.

26

THE PASSION

Quick glances around, not knowing if they'd drawn their pursuers closer, or if they were heading into their net, or if they'd managed to shake them before they headed away.

The oppression of the black backstreets pushed in on him. The buildings loomed like the heavy shadows of restless evil spirits, pressing inwards as they ran, the black moonless night leaving them bereft of any direction, of any good decisions as their feet hammered the cobbles.

But being in the run-down ruined area of Garrim allowed them time to breathe. There must have been a hundred broken, lonely buildings crammed in this corner of the town, left to rot like the hulking timbers of once great warships, all with their own special places to hide, small corners and recesses that only the dark could occupy. Fortune can be found in the most unlikely of places.

Frank slid to a halt to get his bearings, Gabby breathless at his shoulder. No footsteps in the dark behind them. Yet. They were stood in the doorway of a boarded-up shop, one in a line of many sad-looking frontages, its soaked, paint-peeled sign giving nothing as Frank tried the door. It was locked, but a couple of hard shoves and the old lock gave way. He willed his eyes to adjust to the darkness inside.

Gabby took a few quick steps to the side of the room where a set of freestanding shelves stood empty and started to drag them to the door with a series of grunts. Frank was instantly with her, heaving it in desperation, his breath coming in short bursts as they heaved the unit across the doorway as a makeshift barricade bringing the heavy grinding on the floor to an end. Crude, but more than sturdy enough to deter those who fancied their chances with the door and for anyone to find them here would take a break luckier than a day-long winning streak of nines and kings in the Lid.

Frank had to hope that the Watch's resources and their appetite for vengeance would only stretch so far although hope always seemed to shine brightest just before disappointment, as dusk turns to night, as life turns to death.

Silence followed, but for the muted, jagged breaths of the two teenagers who shook like new-born lambs taking their first steps.

They waited, ears alert, fine tuned to the sounds out in the street, waiting for the sound of hurried feet, silently pleading they wouldn't stop outside. Frank felt the grasping tension inside the empty shop as he and Gabby let the minutes skip by.

No one came.

Neither of them had anything to say, letting the silence eat up the space between them, knowing the fresh fall of snow would hide their tracks.

Still no one came.

Deciding it was safe, Frank lit up the Elemental ball, damping the light with a curved palm.

The shop was a lifeless empty square, the bare wooden counter and low wooden beams caked in cobwebs, the floor coated in a thick layer of dust with a door through to the rear. Even though the place looked like it had been empty for a while, the unmistakeable aroma of flour and sugar hung in the air with the cold.

Through the door the three large ovens of the bakery stood dark and idle, the dark recesses hanging open like the petrified mouths of blackened beasts. Flour sacks, scratched and soiled, empty and full lay stacked to one side with a pile of flimsy wooden packing crates.

White dust coated the brickwork, benches and washing area and the tools of the baker's trade hung from racks on the wall. It was deserted but it was dry and Frank felt the pressure in his bones loosen a little, drawing a long breath through the discomfort of his wet clothes sucking at his skin.

Gabby had started the shivers, which were only going to get worse. He grabbed a couple of crates, placing them in one of the ovens, then some more. Gabby did the same until the opening was crammed with old, splintered wood.

Frank stepped back.

'Fire,' he said, tossing the Elemental ball into the maw of the oven.

Flames erupted, dry wood cracked and blistered and joyous heat began to peel back the dismal layers of cold and misery that had begun to set firm.

Frank just stood and watched for a few moments, letting the tide of their ordeal turn and recede.

He turned. Gabby stood just a few inches from him, so close he could feel her warm breath shedding the numbness on his cheeks, her face half-lit, half-shadow, her dark features damp like the morning dew, the piercings on her face glinting in the flame, her castaway hair curled in long snaking strands around her jaw, shoulders and tumbling down her back. Drops of water melted on her cheeks.

Frank felt the sting of the cut on his forehead, the bruise that would soon sully his cheekbone. Gabby reached a tentative hand to his brow and ran her fingertips along the top of the wound, sliding her hand slowly down his face, stopping to cup the soft skin of his cheek.

Frank closed his eyes and let a long breath escape, felt her touch linger for a moment more than it should have, asking him a question he wasn't sure he was ready to answer.

He placed his hand on top of hers and pressed it gently, keeping the comfort of her skin on his, feeling the bones in her fingers, her tenderness, her warmth. She didn't pull away. He felt her other hand on the side of his neck, gliding softly to his nape. A shiver the like of which he'd not experienced before shot down his back, making him open his eyes.

She looked straight back at him, vivid and in her prime. Her chestnut eyes burned with a wildness he'd not seen, something different, something that needed no words, still asking him the question, demanding his consent.

He felt himself lean forward, the slightest of movements followed by pressure from Gabby's palm at the back of his head. He offered no resistance. He felt her face close to his, a slight movement in her lips, her warm breath a match to ignite his desire.

Their eyes locked, each knowing what the other was thinking, looking past the person and into something beyond as Frank felt his skin flare, Gabby's adolescent features emptying his resolve.

Then Gabby closed her eyes. Her lips bridged the void, soft against his, awakening something within him, her breath rapid, free of its tether. She pressed harder, both hands on the back of his head.

Frank felt his fingers in the wet locks of her wild hair, pulling her closer, his mouth hungry on hers as she responded, backing him into the wall, forcing him hard to the brickwork, pushing her body against his. Her hand went under his soaked shirt, her nails digging into his ribs, primed with desire.

Frank drew in the pain, the pleasure of it, drew in the heat of her lips, as sweet as ripe cherries, as fresh as raindrops. His hands curled along her back, tracing her shape, the line of her spine, the shallow dip in the small of her back, the exotic flare of her hips.

At her touch he felt his demons take flight. She made him feel safe, she made him feel like nothing else mattered, she made him feel alive. There was nothing else in his mind. Just her. Just them.

He gripped her tightly, drawing in her energy, her desire for him. He never wanted it to end but knew that wouldn't be long enough.

She pulled away, taking a step back, breathless, her palms pushed against his chest. There was none of the coyness that possessed Libby, nothing of the wayward nature of the girl that had betrayed him, just a certainty in her eyes, a bottomless desire and a sensual wildness that knocked the wind from him.

Her face was tight, daring him to deny her what she wanted.

Hard breaths escaped from her mouth, her chest rocked like a ship in a storm as she grabbed the front of his shirt and yanked him in once more, dragging hard and needy on his lips, pulling him down onto the pile of soft sacking, any notion of being chased and caught by the dregs of Garrim sent scattering into the night.

The snow clouds passed. The relentless sounds from the Ditch were barely audible under the crisp, starlit sky and, eventually, the abandoned shop fell silent and Garrim hushed itself.

27

THE MORNING AFTER

Frank woke. The boarded windows offered little light, just thin blades cut the flour dust through to the oven room where Frank and Gabby had slept on and under the discarded sacks, the small fire still flickered in one of the old ovens, drying their clothes which hung on a bread rack in front of the charred brick opening.

Gabby stood with her back to him, rubbing the fabric of her shirt between her thumb and fingers, checking for damp.

He watched her, the smooth feline curves of her hips, skin the colour of warm caramel, the Prismian tattoos that caressed her shoulders and spilled down her back, wondering what she was thinking.

She appeared to sense movement and gave the merest glance over her shoulder, taking her shirt and threading her arms into the sleeves before tilting her head down as she buttoned it. She said nothing.

He wondered if he'd dreamt everything from the night before, but when Gabby turned and her eyes finally met his he could still see the flaming desire, even though her face was difficult to read.

She dressed, running her fingers through her unruly hair, bending forward and ruffling it before a swing of her neck shed it from her face. He noticed the faintest of smiles tug at her mouth.

Frank propped himself up, arching his chest, pulling his shoulders back to relieve himself of any unspent tension from the previous night's chase, though most had been extinguished in the tangle of their bodies.

Gabby crouched down beside him, gently taking his chin in her hand and planting a long kiss on his lips.

'Tell me you didn't want it,' she said.

'I didn't want it,' said Frank.

'Liar.'

'Liar,' agreed Frank.

'We should get going,' said Gabby. 'Anya and Cas'll be worried sick.' She gave a cautious glance through to the front of the bakery. 'Let's go out the back. Come on, get dressed.'

She stood, taking his clothes from the rack and placing them next to him. He got up. Silence crept back, easy or awkward, he couldn't tell.

'Gabby.'

'Yes, Frank?'

He couldn't read her. She was soft and hard all in the same moment. He opened his mouth but his words deserted him. She just looked at him, waiting for him to speak.

'We okay?' he said.

He cursed himself for needing her validation, for appearing needy but she took the few steps towards him and kissed him. Then he saw the spark, the fireflies, the look that gave her feelings away and knew what they shared was real.

'More than okay.' She cupped his cheek, then wound her arm around his neck and pulled him in for a slow, satisfying kiss. She drew back. 'Never thought of myself as the sort of girl who smashes rocks over peoples' heads, though.'

'I don't think any of us set off in that direction,' said Frank. 'Trouble is, a few wrong turns and, before you know it, there you are.'

They might have been rubbish at navigating – wrong turns, wrong decisions, both they had in plenty, both would have them as Etamin's captives in Alsha Kar or heading to Balal's butchering blocks in the silent forest, but Frank wouldn't have traded any of it if it led him to a frozen, deserted bakery in the slums of Garrim, wrapped in the arms of Gabby.

'Come on,' she said. 'Let's hope the Watch will be drowsy.'

28

THE QUIET

She turned, set to head out the back before turning back to Frank.

'We should split up,' she said.

Frank knew she was right and pushed the disappointment away. After the previous night he didn't want to let her out of his sight, the same irrational thoughts that he'd felt when he started seeing Libby but, still, he realised that irrational and girls strode hand in hand ahead of him. He could fight it, but it felt like a difficult contest.

'Frank?'

'What? Yes, I think we should.'

One head was far more difficult to spot than two. Garrim might keep you anonymous, but there was no need to draw attention to yourself and he was certain word of them would have spread from the Watch who likely had a large number of businesses comfortably in their dishonest palms.

Gabby quickly and methodically started to remove the metalwork from her face, shedding her bangles before tying her hair in a loose bunch on top of her head.

Frank watched as she did it, seeing her peel away the layer that shouted anti-establishment, of the bohemian within, but left a softer, more vulnerable face in its wake, a face that had Frank wanting to draw her in and not let her go.

She wet her fingers and pushed them into the black ash of the fire, making small circles to coat her fingertips in the thin paste she'd made before smearing it on her forehead and cheeks, a little on the

z

164

end of her nose and the rest rubbed firmly around the backs of her hands and palms.

With a few short adjustments to her coat she'd transformed herself into an abandoned street urchin, a lost look of hunger and fear which didn't seem forced.

She reached out to him and brushed her fingertips over his face, sullying his skin, providing a degree of camouflage he'd need to traverse the town with any level of safety, then stood back to check her handiwork.

They headed out. Through the back and up a short set of stone steps to the street. Gabby stopped and looked around.

'Okay, be careful and take your time,' she said. 'I'll see you back at the inn.' She wound her arms around his waist and pressed her lips against his. 'There'll be more of that waiting.' Her impish smile sent a shiver up Frank's back.

'Stay safe,' he said.

She turned and wandered away, not looking back. He watched her head down to the levels, to hide in plain sight before heading up the south-side and back to the Gargoyle's Head. He just hoped the early morning would keep the knives and coshes away, felt the instinct to protect her even though he knew she didn't need it, that she'd done a much better job of protecting him over the past few years and would continue to do so.

Frank drew in a breath and looked around. Wherever their escape had taken them, they'd ended up deep in what looked like an unloved and uninhabited part of town.

Each dwelling or shop was abandoned, empty windows and doorways sadly gazing out into the rutted and damp street, choked with receding weeds, rubble and rotting timbers. Some buildings had half-collapsed with no hint of desire for repair, just withered and throttled with ivy. A committed optimist might have called the place a dive, but it scarcely deserved the name, just like the rest of the town.

Through the gaps in the buildings he could see across to the southern mountainside. It looked much the same as the north – houses bunched together, tensed against the cold, streets as dark as tar hiding unseen dangers, threats to give you the shivers. Early morning smoke lazed up from countless chimney-stacks. But he knew it meant refuge, a pinprick of safety in the sea of eyes and ears that would be searching them out.

He hoped Cas and Anya had found their way back in the dark and confusion of the previous evening, a step ahead of the Watch, and that Duckett and Cossens would keep them safe.

Gabby would be joining them soon. He let out a long breath at the thought of having to wait for long, agonising minutes before he could see her again, before he could feel the softness of her skin, taste the sweetness of her lips.

He checked himself – scuffed and torn trousers stained brown with dried blood, filth covered jacket and more bruises than a third-rate bare-knuckle fighter – the events of the previous night had left him looking more like a beggar which might play to his advantage in the early hours of Garrim's waking.

He tried to flatten his hair but without much success. Now all he needed was to guide himself back. Some tasks sound easy when you say them, either to yourself or out loud. This one did, but it was laced with holes and traps and trickiness of his own design, making him wish he'd never come. The Simbrian heir, it seemed, was making a good job of seeing to his own demise, without the help of the likes of Dagmar or Etamin.

He headed west and down, intent on skirting the levels close to where they'd entered the town. Avoiding contact with people was his plan and you always need a plan, however rubbish, and trust you can see it through – but the early hour brought the added problem he'd never thought of.

The lack of people.

The Ditch was always steaming with bodies but, as he guided himself through the deserted back streets, he could feel the touch of the inconspicuous begin to disappear and the morning begin to reveal him more obvious than a doe in the wolf's lair.

With each few steps he began to feel the creep of something at his back, like he was being watched through a window in the dark of the night by someone unseen, picking their time to grab him and squeeze his wits from him.

He stopped and looked back, immediately regretting a move that would mark him as suspicious, that would have any interested eyes or accusing finger pointing in his direction. But he couldn't help it. Had he heard something? Footsteps? Maybe. Not sure. Perhaps not.

Now the only thing he could hear was his own breath as it squeezed through his nose as the street turned itself off.

Deathly silence. The sort of silence that doesn't have you relaxing with a good book and a mug of cocoa. A thick, something's-about-to-happen sort of silence, in Garrim of all places.

He'd seen no one. Doors were shut, curtains pulled, chimneys lazed with early fires, chasing the frost from the rooftops. No one.

Again. There it was again. Something back around the corner he'd just turned. Or was Garrim playing with his imagination, not to mention his fear of being caught and battered halfway to death by the Watch.

He stilled, the heat of his anxiety no comfort against the cold of the morning. He fought the urge to walk back and look. Fought it hard but the need got the better of him and he found himself creeping back to the corner. Step by slow step. Another action that Garrim wouldn't be used to, that would have it frowning. No sounds but the crunch of his boots splitting the ice in the frozen gutters. Too quiet, like the hush of the woods before the snare yanks and the rabbit starts to scream.

He stopped at the corner, fearful of the imaginary beast that lay silently beyond, wound like a watch spring, ready to pounce on him and devour him.

A step forward had him peering round the corner, had him bracing himself and readying to run. He held his breath to the slow movements as the street corner gave way. There was nothing there but the frost-bitten street, the looming shadow of the summit far above and the familiar stink of piss.

He rubbed his face with his palm and closed his eyes, feeling foolish that he'd been beaten by the imagination of a young child, scared to sleep in the face of a towering wardrobe.

As he let out a long breath, watching it cloud in the morning chill, he was scarcely aware of the sound of movement behind him as someone stepped from the shadows and placed a rag over his face. The pungent fumes of the unfamiliar kicked at his mouth and nose to be let in. For just a few seconds he fought the hands that held it there, strong determined hands with a simple job to do, before he breathed in and yielded to the darkness.

29

THE BEDROOM

Frank's head hammered him awake. His eyes screamed at him from within their sockets for him not to lift his lids. He could barely move his neck, any attempt to twist his head to either side was met with a shot of fire through his skull. He lay with his eyes shut against the pain, warm and dry and quiet, feeling like he'd been ridden over by a company of cavalry.

The smell of the room was unusual. Sweet perfume, more sickly than honey, making something stir in his memory. Nothing good, but out of reach.

The bed was soft and warm, the sheer feel of silk on his cheek barely registering as he squeezed his eyes tighter to rid himself of the aching. Silk on his face, silk on his bare arms and chest, coating him in lavish comfort.

Silk amongst the silence.

The minutes ticked by. No sounds but his breath. Alone.

He mustered the courage to open his eyes, to fight against the stabbing that coated his head and neck and promised to stay, for now.

The room was bathed in complete darkness. Nothing moved. Frank, immobile from his thumping head, lay still, allowing his eyes to gradually adjust.

The large bedchamber became a mix of greys, the heavy drapes keeping the outside keenly shackled, not allowing Frank to absorb any colour or tell if it was night or day.

Through his daze he could make out the outline of furniture: a dressing table with elaborate bowed legs to the side of the bed, a

169

chair, a wide, full-length mirror on the wall, a cushioned seat under one of the windows. More hints at the luxurious, a faraway land compared to Garrim or the Gargoyle's Head.

He had no recollection of how he'd got there. He could barely remember what had happened the night before though the memory of the bloodied head of the watchman and the heavy rock that had beaten him senseless in Gabby's hand loomed through the haze. He stretched out his arms, reaching down to the rip at the knee of his right trouser leg, his hand stopping with a jolt.

He was handcuffed. A thin iron band circled his right wrist, from which a small but robust chain ran to the bedhead where another shackle was locked around the ornate patterned ironwork.

He tugged hard, the jangle and clank of the chain and the bedhead jarring his aching head but he knew instantly that it wouldn't do any good. Whoever had put him here hadn't intended him to be untethered the moment he woke.

He pushed himself to a seated position, a slow, difficult task. He pushed the heels of his of his hands into his temples and looked down on and across the bed, realising he was dwarfed by it. A monstrous four-poster affair that enclosed more space than his entire room back in Rhaeder. Not the blunt and cold welcome he'd expect if he'd been seized by the Watch. Quite the opposite.

There was enough length in the chain for him swing himself to the edge of the bed and sit. Still his head shook with the effort and his body demanded he lay back down and rest, chiming with pain as if he'd been beaten and kicked for an hour.

He leaned forward and pressed his thumbs into his eyes, hoping to banish or, at least, lessen the aching. The chain clinked against the mattress and pulled at his wrist as a reminder. He drew in slow, deliberate breaths, the familiar fragrance flowing through his nose, through his memory though his mind wouldn't allow him to recall where from.

In the patchwork of shadows he noticed his shirt hung over the back of the low-slung chair that sat in front of the long dressing-table under which his boots were neatly tucked, like he'd checked into a plush hotel and a valet had attended him before he'd turned in for the night.

A few items were arranged on the dresser in a neat line – a hairbrush, a hand-mirror, a round ceramic pot, other items he wasn't able to distinguish. The orderliness, the precision, gave him an uncomfortable feeling. Like the inquisitor meticulously placing his instruments of torture out in order of use before beginning his grim but satisfying interrogation of his prisoner.

The quiet lulled him and while it tried to sing him a lullaby he knew he should be wary, alert. Despite the richness of the room, the chain carried a clear message.

Frank groaned as he squeezed his eyes once more. The shadows of the night before started to leak into him. The wait for Simeon, convinced he was on to something that might lead them to Jackson, when hell had unleashed itself along the Ditch. The run into the night, the battered watchman, the fall from the wall. He and Gabby. *Gabby.*

An unfamiliar lurch in his stomach as his mind lingered, stopped there. The warmth of her lips, her passionate touch on his skin, the smell of her wet hair. Had he dreamt it? No, of that he was certain as he conjured further thoughts of them together in the abandoned bakery, wishing he was still there.

He didn't want to remember anything else, but his sore neck and battered head told him the rest of the story. He just hoped that safety had found his friends before anything happened to them but, for now, he was alone.

As wakefulness began to trickle through his veins, he knew he had to get himself free of his bonds. Waiting wasn't a plan, and you had to have a plan, however rubbish and trust you'll see it through.

Another sharp tug had the ironwork rattling, turning his head to the top of the bed to check for any weakness in the tethering or a way to slip the chain free.

Then he felt himself go cold.

He stared, checking, re-checking, certain he couldn't be right, that the image he looked upon must be built in his imagination, in a nightmare from which he was about to wake. His breath caught in his throat as it quickened. Wake up, Frank. Wake up. He backed away across the silken desert of the bed, as far as his shackles would allow as he looked again to make sure he wasn't mistaken.

He wasn't.

The iron bedhead, cast in the image of a scorpion, stood rigid before him, silent but telling him its own story. It might as well have jumped him and stung him for the effect it had.

A glance up at the painting of a woman that hung above the bed confirmed it just as the memory of the sickly aroma in the room slapped him around the face bringing with it an image of him entering the high chamber at the top of the ebony tower in Alsha Kar to be confronted with his worst nightmare. *Now* he remembered.

Etamin.

He was in Etamin's bedchamber.

30

THE VOICE

Any limited sense of composure he'd been feeling quickly dissolved. Out. He needed to be *out. Now.*

He faltered, slipping on the silk like it was covered in grease, trying not to absorb the revulsion he felt at its lush, light touch, feeling Etamin upon it, upon him.

The lure of the wraith's fingers, the exotic yet hideous feeling Frank had experienced at their previous encounters when he'd tasted the elixir of her spell, of the power she wielded, as subtle as the words of a poet, remembering how he'd been both entranced and repulsed in one slow drag of her finger down his chest.

The bile rose in his throat. Had she been there, next to him? The image wouldn't leave but the flat, unruffled sheets in the shadow on the other side of the bed reassured him though the image persisted.

But she would come. He had no idea when, but she would come and he needed to be gone before she did. The scant relief he might have felt was only that of a condemned man who knows he will not be hung at this particular sunrise.

With any calmness he could muster he looked around the room, trying to discern more amongst the shadows but his head, his fatigue and his fear kept any sensible thoughts out of reach. He'd been in more tight situations than he cared to remember, but this squeezed him from all ends.

He got to his feet, adrenaline kicking his aches aside. He took a couple of steps towards the dressing table, looking for something, anything that might be his accomplice in an escape, a weapon, anything. He could just about reach its surface as the chain of his tether tightened and called him back to the bed.

'Hello, Frank.'

The familiar rasp in the words grabbed him by the throat. The dry, coarse voice shot a burning spike of hopeless panic up his spine and had him swivelling on his feet, fighting for self-control, to not piss himself on the spot. She sat on a chair in a darkened corner on the other side of the bed, a shadow, unseen, watching him. She'd been *watching* him.

'Nice to see you again,' she said.

She stayed sitting. He couldn't quite make her out in the dark but, as she spoke, the flame around her wrist ignited and curled in a figure-of-eight like a writhing serpent, illuminating her face in a red-orange half-light, a sinister shadow over her deep eyes and the riven skin of her face. He'd forgotten how cunning her eyes were, how cold, how full of sin as if bone and blood had made her differently.

'What am I doing here?' His throat, desert-dry, barely allowed the words to pass. Etamin let out a barely audible chuckle. 'What do you want?'

No response, he could sense the rattling of her breath but she just sat there, taking him in.

Her silence sent another shiver through him, the light tapping of her long fingernails on the top of her cane beat the rhythm of terror, a slow deliberate tempo designed to feast on his fear. In just those few moments she had him begging her to break the silence, say something, *do* something. The power the ultramancer wielded wasn't just in spells and sorcery.

'You and those friends of yours were getting a little too close,' she said. 'And I can't have that. Not at this delicate point.'

She pushed herself to her feet and Frank felt himself go cold as she held her left arm out, reminiscent of the first time they'd met, when she'd launched a deep psychological assault on him as a demonstration of her ability. The flare of orange around her wrist deepened. He backed away as far as his bonds would allow, let out an audible shudder and tensed, ready for the lesson she was about to teach him but a small flame simply leapt from her wrist and set alight the candles which hung from the walls at intervals around the room.

Now he could see her.

The bent frame, the long, dark hair, peppered with grey, drawn painfully back with a look as if she'd enjoyed the experience. Her scarlet dress fell about her like the pouring of lava over a bleak hillside. Her neck bore a string of large black diamonds, gems that would normally dominate the wearer but, here, it was the other way around.

She looked at him from below her deep-set eyelids, allowing him to imagine what she had in mind, what twisted fetishes she would indulge at his expense.

He flinched as she stepped around the end of the bed towards him, brushing the flat of her hand across the sheer surface of the bedsheets. A slow, deliberate and sensual motion, a glance at the bed, then to Frank who felt the distance close like her hand around his throat. She noticed, returning his anxious look with a cobra's smile, licking her bottom lip.

Etamin stopped just a few steps in front of him, making Frank back further into the wall, folding his arms over his bare chest, the chain ringing the note of his fear and captivity.

She held her hand up, pointing her fingers at him, allowing the tip of her thumb to dance, one by one, over the tips of her fingers.

He felt her physical touch on his skin, despite the distance between them. She angled her wrist slightly, he felt her fingers running up his neck, over his cheek, back down his chest. Lower. She dropped her arm let out a low laugh, one that signalled what she had in store for him, that her warped mind was brimming with him as her plaything.

'It was lucky for you that my guards found you before that rabble did,' she said. 'I hear one of their number got quite badly beaten last night and word is it had something to do with you and your feisty female.'

His glance at the door didn't go unnoticed.

'She's not here, Frank. Nor, you'll be pleased to learn, is she in the hands of the Watch. Now, you get some rest. It was quite a potent sedative they used on you.' Her eyes roved slowly across his face and down his body. 'I have some important business to attend to this morning, but I'll be back to make sure your stay is, shall we say, memorable.'

She lingered, her hand clenched around the scorpion-topped cane, her knuckles flexing as she squeezed it before she turned, hobbled her gnarled frame to the door and was gone without a look back.

31

TRAPPED

Escape. Just the one word in his mind as the door sunk back into its frame and clunked shut.

The room hushed. He just stared in her wake, stared at nothing, at the hideous images in his head and waited until he was sure she wasn't coming back, then opened his palm, working the hair pin between his fingers.

She hadn't noticed him pick it up from the dressing table and although the padlock that held him prisoner was sturdy, it was nearly exactly the same as one Cas had shown him how to pick.

His thieving friend may be the expert, but he was also happy to show Frank a few tricks of his trade and Frank was a willing student, making sure he practised until he could silently spring the mechanism of a simple lock without too much effort.

Even so, he struggled through his trembling hands, his dexterity leaving him in the wake of Etamin's unspoken intentions, stumbling with the pliant piece of wire until, after a lot of twisting and huffing he managed to turn his lack of success around as the lock clicked and sprang open, freeing him.

He rubbed at his wrist, at the red mark that had begun to appear, thinking how safety was very much a relative concept. That being caught by Etamin's Lashken guards was a might better than falling into the hands of the Watch, although being cornered by an angry tiger rather than a pack of blood-thirsty hyenas would still have the same outcome and the certainty of what awaited him had his adrenaline climbing.

He threw his arms into his shirt and his feet into his boots, patting himself down looking for the pouch, the possessor, searching the table with quick, urgent movements. Gone.

He let out a disappointed breath before pulling the drapes back slightly. The stirring soup of black clouds still clung to the mountains across the smoking chimneystacks to the south and away to the west as the sun peered up from the horizon to the east.

Lazy orange light was just beginning to ease its long shadows across the town, barely registering on the highest rooftops as a strong wind and a brisk sky welcomed in another wretched day in Garrim.

Thank goodness.

He'd thought he might have woken in the midst of Alsha Kar, that he'd been unconscious for so long that he'd been taken across the Jixx and onward to Etamin's fortress. Even in his captivity he could feel the relief that the others were still in reach, that Gabby was out there.

He would never have thought he'd be so utterly grateful to see the cold, stinking streets even if they were tantalisingly out of reach. Yes, safety was a relative concept and the thought of being safe and well in the clutch of Garrim was, for a second at least, an amusing one.

From the window he could see he was three stories up, far below the unseen top of the northern peaks at his back that snarled at the surrounding landscape, proclaiming domination to anyone in their shadow. The view across the white rooftops, down through the cobweb of narrow streets and alleys towards the distant levels told him the house was far up on the slope. Out of the way.

He looked down to the ground, to the shadows of the street below. Cut off. Too far to jump. The downpipe out of reach, too icy, too much risk of a cracked skull but, then, risks appeared at every corner and this one might outweigh staying put.

His focus stayed for a few moments as he ground his teeth. Perhaps he could attract the attention of a passer-by, but they might alert the Watch and, anyway, the only thing likely to pass by all the way up here was a procession of rats or a stream of sewage.

He went to the door, listening through the crack, trying to hear anything that might indicate the presence of a guard, deliberating if he should open it and stuff the consequences.

His hand grabbed the doorknob, squeezing it firmly as he weighed the decision to turn it. He counted his breaths through his hesitation, then the sound of distant voices on the other side stilled him, pulling his ear to the door to listen for anything he might use as an ally, anything that could help him to calculate the risk, but luck and hope were again in short supply.

A slow turn of the wrist. A long hold of the breath as if someone might hear it through the thick wood. A decisive tug as he felt the knob halt confirmed the door was locked. He let go and retreated back into the room, sitting on the bed to draw in his wits.

A day. At least. That's how long he'd been there. He'd left Gabby in the early hours of the morning and, now, here was the sun rising once more over his captivity in Etamin's opulent quarters.

Whatever the substance he'd been forced to breathe in it was, as Etamin had confirmed, heavy handed, brutal, but extremely effective and it was still refusing to leave his body, clogging his veins and lightening his head like the back end of a heavy dreamweed session.

Frank's eyes swept the room once more, wondering if there might be another entrance, something hidden amongst the finery as sunlight began to feel its way through the windows and crawl across the ceiling.

He got to his feet, brushing off the creeping sensation the bed gave him, and started a slow walk of the room, just like Cas did every time he found himself somewhere new.

Whenever he did so, Cas was always methodical, always calm in a way Frank didn't think possible for someone who was generally scared of his own shadow and Frank found it difficult to concentrate through the thoughts of his own situation, of what Etamin would have him do for her and how long he had before she spilled her demands.

A careful pass around the room yielded nothing except the confirmation that he was a prisoner in Etamin's bedchamber although a lack of a substantial wardrobe, the limit on the riches and home comforts confirmed that whatever the house was used for, it wasn't used that much. A hideaway in the upper reaches of Garrim, much like that snake Jackson, used only in times of need, making Frank wonder what that specific need was. Why was Etamin here? Why was Jackson here?

Coincidences had the habit of not being coincidences at all, just carefully formulated plans and this bore those striking hallmarks in abundance.

Another long look out of the window, across the town. More thoughts of Gabby, swaying from her being safe with Anya and Cas to having being caught by the Watch, thoughts that dried his mouth and had him pacing. He couldn't muster a plan in his head, not one that would see him safely out onto the streets. There was nothing he could do but wait it out and hope an opportunity would present itself for him to upset the balance and beat the odds in a bid for freedom. The dice couldn't always land in favour of the house, after all.

So, defeated, he sat himself on the floor against the wall, avoiding the bed, watching the door as the sun stretched and squeezed the shadows of another terrible day.

About an hour passed. Too much time, time for Frank's mind to start looking into its corners, corners where he seldom dwelt, wishing that someone would come in and drag him away from his thoughts.

As the time dragged he even thought that Etamin's reappearance would be preferable and would at least bring whatever she wanted to a conclusion to spare him the misery of having to contemplate it. Things aren't always as bad as you think they might be, although this was probably one of those occasions where the opposite was true.

He stared at the floor between his knees, unable to bring himself to look around the room for the thousandth time, the malign feeling of captivity set his mood firmly in the basement, unable to push against the feeling that, this time, there might be no way back.

Voices had Frank looking at the door once more. Not the mutterings from a distance but the sure tones of someone immediately outside. Familiar tones, unwanted. Then the door opened and in walked the frightening figure of Dagmar Dag.

32

THE CAPTIVE

It was a familiar, yet unwanted scenario for Frank. He the one in trouble, cornered, helpless; Dagmar as poised as a tight-rope walker, untroubled and completely intimidating from the orange streak in his hair to the shiny toes of his finely-cut boots.

He eyed Frank like a seasoned boxer looks at a familiar opponent, one that he'd beaten easily on many occasions. Total confidence. No hint of sympathy. Just the desire to beat him again, knowing full well he would, that the bout would end quickly.

Frank lifted his eyes, looking at Dagmar from under his eyelids, his real father.

'Don't you dare say it's good to see me,' said Frank, edging Dagmar from his usual smart opening line.

Dagmar sniffed, looking down like a man looks at a turd in the gutter. He shook his head, whether in disbelief or disappointment, Frank couldn't tell.

'Why is it that every time you suck on life's pipe, it ends up choking you or, in this case, have you chuck your guts up?' said Dagmar, no hint of pleasure in his voice. 'Perhaps, one day, we'll meet in normal circumstances.' He cast an eye around the room, resting them briefly on the bed. 'And I guess that what takes place in this room is anything other than normal.' He looked up. 'Something that one of us will have the misfortune to experience.' An obvious glance to the discarded shackle and a raise of the eyebrows. 'I'd like to ask how in the name of Lashka you managed to end up here, but I'm not sure I'd believe any story you told me.'

'I'm looking for Jackson,' said Frank, a plucky but desperate attempt to stall, to draw out some reaction.

Dagmar gave a shallow nod, his hair glimmering in the rays from the mountain sun, no hint of surprise.

'And how's that going?'

Frank's tight look had Dagmar preparing to shovel more misery on him.

'But, now, that does make sense,' he said, a slight give-away. 'And why does the esteemed Governor interest you so much you've come all the way to this fleapit and got yourself all beaten up?'

Dagmar raised a finger, pointing across the room to the cuts and bruises on Frank's face, making Frank glance into the mirror on the opposite wall, realising he looked like complete shit.

'Let's just say I had no choice,' said Frank. 'He has something of mine and I want it back.'

Dagmar huffed a laugh.

'Well, it looks like you're all out of choices,' he said with another sweep of the room. 'And it doesn't do to be out of choices.' He folded his arms and braced his feet apart. 'No plans for escape?'

Frank felt himself grinding his teeth as Dagmar toyed with him like a cat pawing a ball of wool.

'Only if you can get me out?' said Frank. He was suddenly buoyed by the thought that if Dagmar knew he was his son, it might just present him with an exit ticket. Would Dagmar let his own flesh and blood flounder at the feet of Etamin? Maybe.

As he tossed the coin in his head he wondered why Dagmar would believe him, that it sounded like a desperate lie, one Dagmar would see right through. After all, he was all out of choices.

'That's just what I'm here to do, although not in the way you mean, I dare say,' said Dagmar. 'You see, there's been a development.'

'Development? What sort of development?'

'The sort you're not going to be particularly happy with,' said Dagmar, still statuesque. 'Which is hardly a surprise when you're stuck like a drowning man in the middle of Garrim with no one to throw you a rope.' Dagmar reached out a hand, opened the door and stood back. 'Things really aren't going your way, are they?' He rolled his head to the side. 'Shall we?'

***

The sparsely furnished room was large, larger than anyone on the street would have imagined had they been able to divert their eyes from looking in the gutter to avoid the prowling menace outside.

There were none of the fine furnishings, the sumptuous colours or heady scents of spices that filled her black tower in Alsha Kar. A scattering of simple furniture, slightly dusty from lack of use, a few plain, wooden chairs around an even plainer table, a single, high-backed chair, studded and cushioned in red velvet, bare floorboards. Functional and not the slightest bit lived in.

Flames licked at the fireplace, smoothing the edge from the morning chill that stubbornly refused to shift from the room, or any room in the town for that matter. A glass of liquor sat on a small table by the chair.

Etamin stood at one of the leaded windows, looking out. At what, Frank couldn't imagine.

He walked into the void between the fire and the table, eyes on her, conscious of Dagmar and two Lashkens at his back, his boots heavy on the wooden floor. He stopped, not really sure what to do other than wait as the door was closed behind him.

Dagmar took a step to the side, surrounding himself with as much space as the room would allow. Etamin hadn't moved, a deliberate ploy to wind up the tension and, like a single candle in a darkened room, ensure all the attention was on her.

Frank glanced at Dagmar who just looked ahead, unmoved, waiting for his leader to start directing the play. Etamin's natural show of authority began to work its way onto his skin. He wanted to speak, to break the silence, but knew that would break the rules of her game and might have consequences best avoided.

'I believe you have something that I want.' Gone was the grating in her throat, her voice was smooth and like her shadow – dark and cold, the sound providing some relief against the chafing

184

silence. She turned towards him and took a couple of steps towards the high-backed chair, her black eyes danced over him, opening slightly wider. Frank felt himself flush. 'Oh, not that. Something else. Something...of interest.'

She sat with a surprisingly elegant movement, both hands resting on the scorpion at the top of her walking cane. She looked nothing but business-like and serious, her face focused and unemotional.

'I'm not sure I have,' he said.

She took him in for a few seconds, as if giving him a chance to re-think, but Frank couldn't fathom what it was she was getting at. A slight shrug of his shoulders had her unsmiling face turning even more solemn.

Etamin nodded at the guards, one of whom opened the door and vanished down the landing, the sound of his boots receding as the room hushed once more.

'What's this about?' said Frank.

No answer. Etamin looked into the fire and waited.

A minute or two passed, though it seemed to stretch much further until the sound of approaching boots from outside had Frank looking at the door, hoping the current mystery of why he'd been summoned would quickly be solved.

The guard entered, ushering in two more, each gripping a third man under the armpits. The familiar figure gazed dispassionately at Frank whose face dropped as he looked into the battered face of Simeon, stripped to the waist, hands tied to the front.

Simeon shrugged the heavy hands off, flaying his elbows as best he could, his two sentries not backing an inch. He looked at Frank and gave him the slightest of winks through the eye that wasn't closed, bloody and bruised. He shifted on his feet, eyes sizing up the room, the occupants, the escape routes. Frank knew there were none.

A slow turn of the head to Dagmar followed by a nod of acknowledgment, like he'd just turned up late for a meeting of the golden intake. To Frank's surprise, Dagmar dipped his head in return.

Simeon flexed his shoulders, his wrists working his bonds, the sinewy muscles that contoured his torso flexing and folding.

'You know Simeon Peth, Frank?' Frank didn't answer. 'Very adept at shielding from mind-reading, even under the most invasive of methods. Exactly what I would expect from a Black Flame but, fortunately, I managed to extricate something.' The muscles on Simeon's torso tightened slightly. 'You see, every man is a vault of secrets and vaults take many forms. Some take the brute's way to crack it open, but I prefer a gentler approach – the right pressure applied at the right moment – in the right place. It's a delicate thing.' Simeon tensed, his face blank. He stared at Frank who noticed a very slight shake of the head. She turned to Simeon, stepping around him in slow, intimidating strides. 'Perhaps you threw it to me to try to save your skin, hm?' No response. 'No matter.' She turned to Frank. 'I managed to see it, just, but there it was, there *you* were.' She waited, tapping her black fingernails on the ivory scorpion, the silence tugged hard on Frank. 'The key, Frank. You know, the key of darkness.' She raised her eyebrows, an understated display of triumph. Frank tried not to look at Simeon but was unable to resist the impulse to swallow, drawing out Etamin's serpent's grin. 'I know you have it, and it's probably in this clever little pouch of yours.'

She dipped her hand into her pocket and produced a small leather pouch, pulled tight at the top. The possessor.

An image of Gabby giving him the key for him to put in glanced across his mind. Now his eyes fixed on it, instantly giving him away.

'So perhaps you'd be so kind and get it out for me.' Words that showed she held all the good cards.

She weighed it in her hand as if it were filled with gold and she was assessing its worth, but no amount of gold would see good the price of what was inside. An object beyond value.

'No,' he said, finding calm in his voice in the face of his nightmare. 'It's not in there,' he lied.

Etamin smiled, he knew she'd expected him to refuse. Her scheming mind would have all the plays set out in front of her like a chess champion. He waited for her to make her next move, to play her next ace.

She walked in awkward steps over to him. Frank felt his breath shorten as she reached out and gently took his right hand. He watched the red flame skirting her wrist and waited for whatever she was about to throw at him. He could take it. No, he wasn't sure he could but he was never going to give up the key without a fight.

She rubbed her thumb over the back of his hand in slow, seductive circles.

'I wonder if I could get it if I cut off one of your hands and used it to retrieve whatever you've put in there.' A delicious look spread across her face, pressing hard on Frank's determination to keep calm. She increased the pressure before stopping and pressing hard into his skin with the tip of her nail. Her eyes drilled into his as he felt the burn as she pressed harder. 'What? Do you think I wouldn't?' He couldn't work out whether to nod or shake his head but knew she would do anything to get what she wanted. She let him soak up her words. 'But perhaps I can offer you a better incentive.'

She took a step back and tapped her cane on the floor twice. A wave of crimson light spread across the floor in a wide circle, throwing up a cloud of dust.

Immediately, a huge scorpion, the same as those Frank had encountered during his nightmare time in her palace, appeared.

The rush of its claws on the floor sent ice through Frank's veins. It approached, the size of a large dog, and stood at Etamin's side, tail held high and still, completely under its master's control. Frank glanced at Simeon, who looked down at the hideous, oversized beast with astonishing calm.

'Now, Frank,' said Etamin. 'I need you to listen carefully because I don't like to repeat myself.' Frank's eyes flicked from her to the scorpion and back. He tried to control his breathing, tried to concentrate on her words but could feel the tremors in his body and the clouding in his head. 'My request is simple. I give you the possessor, you give me the key. Do I make myself clear?'

He glanced at the scorpion again. It hadn't been summoned for decoration. He hesitated, then opened his mouth but no words came out. Etamin just waited, impassive in the face of Frank's paralysing indecision.

'Perhaps I should make myself a little clearer.'

She tapped her cane on the ground once and uttered a command with a look at Simeon. The scorpion pushed itself up, took the few steps towards Simeon and raised its tail high in the air, the point of its sting angled directly at his chest. It stilled, awaiting the next, deadly command.

Simeon looked the beast up and down in one passive move of his head, still but still unafraid. He looked at Etamin with unbelievable contempt, a thin smile on his bloodied lips, one that told her she could threaten him all she liked, but he would never be beaten.

'Now, Frank. The key, please.'

She handed the possessor to him, one word away from commanding her beast to skewer his uncle if he didn't comply. He felt the tick tick ticking of the clock counting down in his head.

Hand Etamin the key to the Simbrian or watch Simeon die. That was the silent choice she offered. The life of one man against the lives of many and the tyranny that would be unleashed on the world as she neared her goal of possessing the Simbrian.

He looked at Simeon, the man he'd been led to believe had betrayed his family, who had taken the responsibility on his angular shoulders because of the love he had for one woman. A lifetime of solitude and exclusion for a love that hadn't been returned, but still burned bright within him. A man who'd been protecting the world, who'd run the gauntlet of Balal in the silent forest, who'd saved his life and the life of his friends without hesitation. He'd risked much and asked nothing in return. Perhaps the best of men.

Frank felt a long breath leave him under Etamin's demanding stare and reached into the pouch.

'No, Frank,' said Simeon with unerring calm. 'I'm not worth it.'

The guards' fingers pressed tighter into his arms even though he just stood with passive calm. The scorpion flexed its body. Simeon stared it down.

But Frank barely heard him as he pulled out the short iron rod, an arrow etched into one end, and held it in the flat of his palm. The object they'd nearly been killed for in their escape from Irundi. That had been so out of Etamin's reach until they'd brought it out of the silent forest. The key she needed to ignite the Simbrian, once it was complete and Frank had brought it gift-wrapped straight to her door. What a fool. What a complete idiot.

He stared at it as Etamin held out her hand with a silent order. He looked at Simeon, guilt and sorrow on his face as he handed it over. Some fight.

'Good boy, Frank,' she said, pocketing the key, her face lit with power, tight and triumphant.

She tapped her cane on the ground. '*Hrak,*' she said, her voice full of menace and gravel. The word flew as true as a freshly fletched arrow right at Simeon. The scorpion reared on its hind quarters, steadied itself and thrust its sting straight through Simeon's heart.

33

Unexpected

Air exited Simeon's lungs in a long, quiet whisper. His eyes clouded, closed and he slumped forward, propped up by the guards who let his limp, lifeless body fall to the floor.

Frank watched through his horror as a thick crimson pool spread from under his uncle and across the floor, blackening the floorboards. He felt his eyes mist, tears forming and falling at the man who had saved him and his friends, whom he had misjudged but had never taken the opportunity to express his gratitude. Now he would never have the chance and he felt a small piece of himself break.

Now his body started to tremble. Now his insides burned, turning his fierce unforgiving eyes to Etamin who just studied him with interest as if she'd just finished the day's mundane chores and was looking for some thanks.

'Now, now, Frank. Don't go all sentimental on me. We're all put here to rot away and be forgotten, eventually. Some sooner than others.'

No look at Simeon, as if he was already forgotten, a spent object thrown in the rubbish, discarded. She returned Frank's stare with a level of challenge he'd yet to see.

'You monster,' he said. She simply laughed as if he'd paid her a compliment. He lowered his voice. 'You coward.'

The words were slow and pointed. He knew the slight would cut her, on the surface at least. He wasn't wrong. Some words were not designed for the powerful.

She thrust her hand out towards him, flooring him instantly, slamming the air from his lungs. A cord of red flame entangled him, like scorching spider's silk, the heat from his bonds sinking into his flesh as he writhed in a helpless heap at her feet.

A burning scream echoed from his throat as the fire cut through him, choking him. Then it was gone, leaving his body seared and shaking.

Etamin stood looking down on him, then turned away and walked across the room. Frank wrapped his arms around himself, the remnants of scorching alive on his skin, watching her gnarled ankles receding to the door as he fought to find his breath through the spasms that wouldn't let him go, gulping in and spitting out at the same time.

'You have much to learn, Frank,' she said as Simeon's body was dragged out.

He thought she would leave, let him fester in his own mess but she turned and walked back.

'Get him up,' she ordered in calm, confident tones to the Lashkens that stood at the door, behind Dagmar who remained impassive.

Heavy, highly polished boots approached in his blurred eyes before he was hauled to his feet by rough, unconcerned hands, a hissing suck of a breath through his teeth as the guards clamped him under the biceps.

Frank felt his legs begin to dissolve beneath him and he wasn't sure how he managed to keep himself upright, but a few deep breaths and his head began to clear.

The Lashkens resumed their positions at the door, three of them, composed, expressionless. Frank looked down where Simeon's body had been, at the dark stain, the last remnants of his life. The scorpion had disappeared but the fear in the room remained. Dagmar hauled in a breath and flexed his shoulders, unscathed by the whole, unpleasant episode.

Etamin stood in front of the fire which spat and cracked as if in protest at what it had witnessed as those in the room clung to her next words. She took in a breath, composing herself before she looked at Frank again in her unpredictable fashion, making him wonder if she was going to bed him or kill him. At this point, the latter held more appeal.

'I thought I would show you how we deal with traitors here in Kzarlac,' she said, a barely covered barb in her voice promised the spilling of more blood. 'Those that come to Alsha Kar and stand before me with the sole purpose of destabilising what I and my ancestors have assembled over centuries.'

Her hawk-like stare rocked him slightly. Was she referring to her brutal dispatch of Simeon? Or was it something else?

Something inside him crept to the surface, a gradual understanding of what her blunt tone meant, that she'd had enough of him and his interference in the Simbrian. She must have reached the end of her tether with him long ago and now he'd snapped it altogether with a resounding flourish.

And now she had the key from him.

As far as she was concerned she'd finished with him, not understanding the blood that ran through him, blood she would be spilling to teach a lesson to anyone else foolish enough to go up against her.

His throat closed, each dry swallow closing it further like a rabbit struggling in the hunter's snare. He saw her eyes upon him, bereft of the salacious intent she'd left him with in her bedroom, replaced by the soulless look of revenge.

'There's no room for sentimentality here, Frank,' she said. 'When someone has come to the end of their usefulness I have no alternative but to act.' She screwed up her nose, her words reminded him of how Dagmar had described Sapphire Hark in the aftermath of the raid on her house, and he knew they meant. 'I get so disappointed, but not surprised. Nothing surprises the Dahke dynasty. From the day Kester cleaved Rossia in two, it has been the destiny of Lashka and her line to restore what was rightfully ours. Joleyon was never fit to rule. Weak, and people need strength.'

'People don't need a tyrant,' said Frank, trying to quell the shakes in his body. Trying to delay what he knew was coming. She ignored him, pouring herself a glass of liquor and sucking in a mouthful.

'My priority and that of my predecessors has been focused on one thing – the creation of the Simbrian and those that stand in my way deserve to reap my very own brand of displeasure.' *Shit.* 'It's important that anyone who thinks they can stop me possessing the power that the descendants of Lashka deserve understand the consequences, however regretful. The Simbrian is mine by right.'

She was matter-of-fact, solidly certain of her ground, her purpose, her unfailing destiny. *Everyone thinks they are on the side of the right.*

She stepped away and Frank saw the glance at the guards standing behind Dagmar. The slightest nod of the head. All three of them stepped forward. Frank said goodbye to any last lingering thought of freedom, knowing that the glimpse of Garrim from Etamin's bedchamber had been his last and he was about to be hauled away to live out his life incarcerated in her ebony tower, to serve Etamin in unspeakable depravity or, more likely, to have his neck stretched by the hangman's noose.

He felt himself take a step back, eyes pinned to the guards as they moved.

But they stopped short of Frank, clamping their hands around Dagmar's arms and binding him in shackles before he could react, relieving him of the weapon that hung at his side. Frank watched through disbelieving eyes as Dagmar began to struggle until one of the guards drew his sword and pointed it directly at his chest, the tip an inch away from slicing him open and spilling his guts on the floor. He stilled, face tight, looking down the blade.

A slow raise of Dagmar's eyes asked Etamin the question.

'Dagmar,' she said. 'How disappointing.' A slight shake of her head. A faint tut under her breath. 'You bring shame to your bloodline in seeking to cross me, your rightful sovereign.' Dagmar attempted a hefty tug against his captors but they held him still. 'Not going to deny it?' Dagmar's eyes darkened. If looks could kill. 'Not that denying it would do you any good.' She took a step towards him, though Frank noticed how she didn't get too close. 'You think you can possess the Simbrian, that you are more worthy than I?' Dagmar stared her down, resolute. 'You may be sharp enough to slice the wings off a dragonfly, but when will you learn that underestimating people is your soft underbelly, hm? And to underestimate me, well, I must say I never had you as such a fool.'

'I serve only you,' he said, voice low. 'For the glory of Kzarlac.'

His voice didn't waiver, but Frank detected a note of untruth. He was sure Etamin felt it too and she'd already made up her mind in the face of his short and terribly unconvincing rallying cry.

'So you will have your reward,' said Etamin with a smile written with sarcasm.

She jerked her head towards the door and the Lashkens escorted Dagmar from the room.

'You can't do this to me,' said Dagmar over his shoulder. Etamin watched as the door shut, not a hint of regret crossed her face.

'Yes I can,' she said under her satisfied breath.

The room went strangely quiet. After everything that had happened in the fifteen or so minutes Frank had been in there, it felt like even the walls and furniture were ready for a break.

Still Etamin watched the door.

'Why did you do that?' said Frank. 'Dagmar's single-handedly served the Simbrian to you on a plate.'

She turned, making her way to the high-backed chair.

'Don't be a fool. Dagmar serves himself, as do I, and if you think he was tracking down the guardians for my benefit then you're an even bigger fool than I thought.'

Frank hesitated. Of course he could see the lies in Dagmar whenever he talked about the Simbrian, the confident look of someone making all the right moves to win the contest, the undignified air of conceit and composure that he wore like his favourite pair of boots,

194

that left Frank under no illusion that he would try and claim it for himself whatever words spilled from his mouth.

'What will you do with him?'

She stopped, surveying him, barely any movement in her eyes.

'And why the sudden interest?' Etamin narrowed her eyes, trying to pinpoint the weakness in Frank's words. 'I would have expected you to thank me for doing you a favour.' Frank offered no answer and refused to let Etamin draw one out. 'It doesn't matter if you're a beggar or a prince. Traitors all smell the same and you know their fate, Frank.'

Perhaps she was right, perhaps the world would be a better place with Dagmar's head on a spike but Frank had already felt the stir of something unfamiliar, something unexpected. Dagmar wasn't just Etamin's latest obstacle, her next kill, the last in a long line of those she looked to control.

Dagmar was his father.

Etamin sat.

'My journey is nearly complete,' she said. 'I have the key, the heir and now all I need is to add the seventh part of the Simbrian to the others and I can ascend my rightful place. If only Lashka could be here to see how mighty I have made her dynasty.'

It was as if she were addressing herself, or no one in particular, like Frank was temporarily forgotten and she was giving words to her thoughts and there was much about her words that Frank could have feared but one in particular had his breath still.

'Wait,' said Frank. 'The heir?'

Did she know? Frank's skin flared before Etamin clarified.

'Of course. My true daughter, Valaine De Villiers.' *Thank the stars.* 'Unfortunate, but necessary and nothing can stand in the way of my destiny.' Etamin drew in another mouthful of liquor. 'She is here and will make her final journey back to Alsha Kar with me, once the seventh part is secure. Such is the bravery of the Dahke dynasty and her sacrifice will be of the worthiest kind.'

As far as Frank was concerned, sacrifices were always

significantly overrated and generally considered worthy by the people who didn't have to make them. It was considerably easier to be poetic about it if someone else had their head in the noose.

Frank's loathing of Valaine De Villiers ran close on the heels of Dagmar. As part of Emerald's gang she'd done nothing other than easily earn his disrespect in the couple of years he'd known her. Rude, obnoxious, spiteful were just some of her more appealing qualities and, if Emerald wasn't such a bully he was sure she'd run her own pack of wolves to make people's lives at Excelsus and in Kzarlac a misery.

Undoubtedly she'd want to set fire to the world and watch it burn and Frank struggled to think of any redeeming characteristics and had long since wished her dropped from a high cliff.

But death? A death he would, at least in part, be responsible for.

He was the Simbrian heir, yet Etamin had mistakenly identified De Villiers in his place and whatever his feelings towards the young misery-maker from Emerald's little clique, the obvious dilemma had taken seed and started to grow in his mind.

Her sacrifice wouldn't be noble or worthy or any of the hollow words that spilled from Etamin's mouth. It would be useless, unnecessary and a complete waste of time.

34

THE THREAT

In the wake of Dagmar's arrest, Etamin had disappeared, leaving Frank to be led back to her bedchamber by two Lashken guards, wordless and worried, the sure click of the lock sealing him in once again where only one fate and many dark thoughts awaited him.

Simeon's final look promised to stay with Frank forever. Steel in his grey eyes, like smoke behind glass, refusing to be cowed, brave to the very end, an end that had been entirely Frank's fault, something else that would stay with him.

There was no denying that, had they not been in Garrim, had he not spotted Frank in the Ditch being thrown out of the Lid, had he not decided to track them to Duckett's, he'd be alive. Fatal decisions had followed quickly on the heels of more fatal decisions and, when it came to it, Simeon had rolled the wrong dice, the same dice that Frank and the others had been rolling, except they'd escaped a fatal spiking by a huge arachnid, leaving Frank with his conscience irreparably skewered instead.

Frank was in no doubt that Simeon had meant to protect him to the end. Maybe he thought his sacrifice would in some way spare Frank, give him a reprieve, but he was mistaken and he'd given Etamin a glimpse of the key of darkness. A rare error from the methodical and meticulous Black Flame that had left Etamin more powerful than even she might have imagined when he awoke to find her drooling over him.

He'd never forgive himself.

He paced the room in a hopeless ritual, rubbing his biceps,

gripping his hair as he relived the moments in Etamin's presence.

There was something about Dagmar he didn't get. He was as cunning and disciplined as Simeon, more so and wouldn't have been so stupid not to understand the risks of a double-cross in the face of Etamin.

His reputation strode confidently before him in brash, unapologetic strides. Ruthless and unwavering in his desire to find the Simbrian guardians, to rid them of their curse with the sole intention to make it his own.

Etamin had probably seen right through him from the start, even if he had left no scent. But something still puzzled him – why had he let Sapphire Hark go?

Her story hadn't made sense when she'd told him, nor did it make any sense now. Everyone knew he'd slain Montrose Menetti and had obtained the other parts of the Simbrian from the grasping, greedy Eli Chetto, by the misplaced love of his aunt Rachel and, by reasons yet to show themselves, his mum.

There was something out of place, something he'd missed in the passing of time, since the very first step on the ladder that led him here, but in the silken bedchamber his mind couldn't close upon it and answers were as rare as a warm welcome in Garrim.

He went to the door and pulled on it. Definitely locked. He hammered it with the flat of his palm which echoed away as the door opened and he faced one of the guards, face of solid hostility, eyes daring Frank to make another sound. Frank resisted the strong urge to take a step back.

'Can you take me to see Dagmar?' he said, straight and confident, the tone of someone who has nothing to lose.

'I don't think so,' said the guard, bracing his hands either side of the door frame, looking like he would push it through. Frank gave him a nod.

'Etamin said you should see to any requests I had. I guess you'll be the one answering to her when I let her know you haven't been helpful.'

The guard huffed.

'You think she meant every stupid request? Like taking you to see Dagmar?' He nodded his head to the bedroom. 'Be a good kid and get back there. And stop your noise.'

He reached for the door handle.

'You haven't complied with any of my other requests,' said Frank.

The guard gave him an odd look.

'You haven't made any.'

'Do you think that's what I'm going to tell Etamin?' Frank let the pause hang, letting the guard colour in the picture. 'I'm the one she wants in her bedchamber, and I'm sure she won't want to incur any distractions.' The guard's face stilled. 'She'd get very angry.' A short pause. 'With you. I'll make sure of it.'

A final look into the guard's eyes, watching as uncertainty took hold. Frank took a step back into the room, laying the gauntlet squarely across the threshold.

With his hand still on the door handle, the guard looked behind him at a second sentry, who gave a shrug, then back to Frank, looking like he was considering his options, eyes searching Frank's face for the bluff.

'What do you want to speak to Dagmar for?'

Frank tilted his head to one side and widened his eyes – *as if that's any of your business* – the guard sucked on his teeth.

'Ten minutes,' he said.

'Fine.'

35

THE PRISONER

The guards led him down three flights of stairs to the ground floor.

They entered a long corridor where he was marched right to the opposite end, stopping a dozen paces from the top of a final flight of stairs that looked like they descended to a level below the house.

Another guard stood waiting, having raised himself to his feet on seeing their approach, a look of relief on his face that it was just them and not a different sort of bother.

'Wait here,' said one of Frank's guards, fixing his eyes on Frank before heading down the passageway.

A hushed conversation followed, the guard looking back to Frank then to the jailer who kept shaking his head, jabbing the air with his finger and whispered words. More looks back to Frank between animated sentences. The guard stilled, pointing a finger to the jailer's chest, followed by a nod, then turned and beckoned Frank down as the jailer reached to the collection of keys, set on a ring attached to his belt.

'Ten minutes,' said the guard.

The jailer, looking less than composed, jerked his head at Frank and led him down the stairs to a solid door. He picked a key without even examining the bunch, looking as if he could select the correct one even if he were blind. He slotted it into the lock and turned it. A weary clank sounded, mournful in the tight space as the jailer pushed the door open, the stench of rotting straw and human waste hitting Frank squarely in the nose.

'Ten minutes,' said the jailer.

If he'd expected Dagmar to be mired in pity and self-reflection, he was mistaken.

Propped up on a long stone plinth that acted as a bed in the small cellar, one wrist shackled by a long chain that was attached to the wall, his arms folded across his chest, Dagmar hardly seemed to notice as the door opened, although Frank sensed his eyes on him instantly, undiminished by the misery of his situation.

Then Dagmar gave a slight lift of his head, his piercing stare nearly picking Frank up and dumping him against the wall. Not even the raise of an eyebrow.

The squalid room was dimly lit by a small, barred window set high in the wall, letting in a fraction of the early winter. He could smell the moisture on the grim, irregular stone walls, the space hewn from the rock under the house and into the side of the mountain. Stone that gave no warmth or optimism, that dragged out the misery for anyone unfortunate enough to find themselves locked in here, but Dagmar didn't seem to mind.

Frank looked across at him, the man who had caused so much misery across foreign lands, with no regard for the suffering of others was now supping on his own medicine.

In other circumstances Frank might have decided that destiny had carved out this final path for Dagmar, had rubbed its chin at him, sitting as judge and jury and given him no reprieve. They were the dice that someone like Dagmar rolled each day. But, as the jailer closed the door behind him, Frank felt himself begin to wrestle with the sight of him chained. He deserved it, certainly he did, but it felt awkward seeing a sharpened hunter caged and tethered.

'Did you have something to say, or are you just going to stand there?' The semi-dark devoured Dagmar's words. He could feel Dagmar's sharp eyes, slitting him open, revealing his guts. Frank searched himself for a response. He'd asked to be brought here, to ask about Sapphire Hark's re-reading of his character, but he could feel his courage ebb in the face of his real father. 'I'm not sure who should be more worried, me, here, awaiting certain death or you, set for something of an interesting experience at the hands of Etamin.' He inspected his fingernails. 'I know which I'd prefer.'

Frank broke his stare, looking around the cell with feigned indifference.

'I guess what goes around comes around.'

Dagmar huffed a laugh under his breath, sending a small cloud of mist out into the void.

'A well-worn cliché, Frank, but there was nothing to go around in the first place,' he said. 'That's what no one understands.'

Dagmar had a point, Frank didn't understand.

'No escape plans?'

'Worried about me?'

A probing grin. Frank shrugged. A thin smile awakened Dagmar's face, not an ounce of concern infected him, not on the outside, at least.

'Looks like you're all out of choices,' said Frank. 'And it doesn't do to be out of choices.'

'Very good,' said Dagmar as he swallowed his own words. 'But what makes you say that?'

'Perhaps it's the chains, or the thick stone walls, or the guards,' said Frank. 'What do you think?'

Dagmar didn't shift, he just continued to pin Frank to the door with his stare.

'Remember, Frank. If they try to drown you, you grow gills and fins.' He looked both certain and uninterested, and decidedly unflustered. 'If you catch my drift.'

Frank felt himself completely drop Dagmar's drift as his brows dipped at his casual words, as if being chained and locked up was a familiar occurrence.

'I know you're descended from Lashka, Etamin won't harm you.'

Dagmar shook his head.

'Do you really think so? We're all the unfortunate descendent of some old queen or other, Frank. Don't think that buys you any level of credit with Etamin Dahke. Valaine De Villiers, her own daughter, will certainly be agreeing with me very soon.' Dagmar hadn't moved since Frank had entered the room, the shadows across his face making a deeper demon of him. 'And I don't think becoming Etamin's plaything will cut you an inch of slack.' He paused. 'You and I are in similar boats,' he said. 'And I've got a bit of a sinking feeling? You?'

Frank gave a shrug.

'My Dad'll come for me.'

It was a lame response, one Frank had used in the face of Dagmar before, thinking it might have some salvaging quality, but he'd even given up believing it himself. Even in the semi-dark Frank saw the roll of Dagmar's eyes.

'Spare me that old chestnut. Surely you haven't asked to come here to lecture me on Lawrence Penny's character, or lack of it. You still choose to believe in your father, but you should reconsider giving loyalty to someone who can't give you honesty back.'

The words dug deep and Frank didn't move.

'So, let me tell you again,' said Dagmar. 'Your father's a coward and has absolutely no interest in anything. Not even you.'

'Why don't you like him?'

Dagmar just lay there, unmoved and Frank began to rip at himself for allowing Dagmar to lead him down a side-street, away from the reason he'd come but Dagmar was the master of control and Frank, for his part, felt himself eager to comply.

'Spargo told me you and my Dad were best friends.' Still no response but for a shallow snort. 'What happened?'

Dagmar drew in a long breath, perhaps sensing Frank would continue shaking the Lawrence Penny stick in his face until he grabbed it and tore it into pieces.

'Faithless is he that says farewell when the road darkens,' said Dagmar, as much to himself as to Frank. He let the words settle. 'Did you ever wonder about those of us in the golden intake and our paths to the Simbrian? The four of us – Simeon set out to gather information – to become a scholar of the Simbrian, if you like. His way of protecting it – and he kept Irundi close.' Dagmar sniffed. 'We never really got on. Spargo decided to protect it from Byeland's side of the border by ascending the ranks and keeping close to Jackson; me from this side. Then there's good old multi-talented Lawrence. We get taught about the one most powerful, fascinating object in the entire history of our nations, one that's known to be true but has survived in murky waters for centuries, hidden from view and, despite being a guardian, what does Lawrence do about it?' Frank found himself unable to move. He knew the answer. 'That's right – absolutely nothing. The supreme student, scholar and swordsman who breezed his way through Excelsus with an enquiring mind and an intellect as sharp as a freshly whetted blade sits on his pathetic, disconnected backside and does absolutely nothing except milk a few cows.' Once again, Dagmar drew the air long behind his comment. 'And none of us have been able to figure that one out.'

Frank paused his thoughts. Dagmar was trying to get into his head, like he always did, dropping subtle hints and innuendos, wielding the stick of doubt and pointing it straight at Frank.

He knew his dad was up to his neck in the Simbrian, that much was obvious in what Dagmar had just said but that he'd decided to turn his back on the whole thing and concentrate on bringing Frank up on the farm wasn't something to mutter behind his back about.

He'd explained that to Frank a number of times since he found out he went to Excelsus. So why would Dagmar think he should be doing something else?

'Maybe he lost interest when you got his part of the Simbrian. Maybe being released was a relief. I hear being a guardian comes at a price.'

'Not for someone like Lawrence, and I never asked Rachel to get it.'

'I know, but she got it from him anyway, just for you. She told me she loved you.'

'Yes, but I never led her on. I just wasn't interested in her.'

A thought ran through Frank, no, not her – *perhaps you loved someone else?*

'But she gave you what you wanted, no wonder my Dad didn't want anything to do with the Simbrian after that.'

Dagmar shifted slightly.

'You think so?' Dagmar let his comment hang, purposely, expertly making Frank itch for him to deliver the punch line he knew was in the back of his throat. 'But I was quite happy for him to keep it. In fact I offered it back to him, but he refused.'

Dagmar tapped a finger on his knee, allowing his words to sink in, though they hit Frank like a newly fletched arrow.

'You did *what*?' said Frank.

No response, just a penetrating, searching stare into Frank's mind, a steady, well-executed game of chess. Check-mate.

'You see me as a villain, Frank, yet you make that judgement based on the tales of others and choose to look no further.'

His words had all the essence of a bluff, yet there was no reason for him to lie, not now he stared death in the face. Everyone saw him as a villain. Everyone. Yet there was something in his tone, the level of his voice that pushed the questions back down Frank's throat and he couldn't think of one to puke back up.

'A lot of interesting chat, Frank,' said Dagmar, still with studied calm. 'Although I sense it's getting us nowhere. What's done is done and my attention should really be on my immediate future, or lack of it and I don't have many minutes to waste. So, why did you ask to come and see me, if not to see me in chains?'

Dagmar's words brought Frank back level, had him looking at the reason he'd been brought to the cellar, feeling he'd been side-swiped into a river of irrelevance and was being swept along with the current.

'I saw Sapphire Hark in the town.'

A raise of the eyebrow. 'An unusual choice but, then, perhaps a wise one.'

'You let her go?'

'What else did you expect me to do?' Frank's silence gave him the answer. Dagmar's eyes, unyielding, searched Frank's face with simple understanding. 'You take me for a butcher.' A statement, not a question.

'Everyone takes you as a butcher.'

Dagmar let out a self-absorbed laugh.

'And you found Wordsworth Hums,' said Frank. Dagmar nodded, his brow creasing in curiosity. 'You said so to Etamin when I was in Kzarlac.'

'Then why are you asking me? You're not using your ten minutes particularly wisely, Frank.'

'Did you kill him, too?' Again Dagmar gave a slight, casual shake of the head, like a dog owner who's just seen their pet take a shit in the corner of the room. 'I don't understand, you've been killing people to collect and assemble the Simbrian. And Etamin's right, you want it for yourself but she saw through your plan.'

'And that's why protecting the world isn't a game for children. You'll end up losing because you have no idea of the rules and don't know what you're dealing with. Do you really think I'm in this so I can dominate the world? If I were you I'd be asking me different things, like *why* I let the Hark girl go, or why your great father didn't want his part of the Simbrian back, or why, now that I have six parts, Etamin has decided to come to Garrim.'

The words were past Frank and gone before he could digest them. He couldn't believe Dagmar was painting his own portrait in colours quite opposite to those everyone knew suited him best. If it was anyone but Dagmar sitting in chains in front of him he'd think it was just a typical ploy to gain sympathy before he met his inevitable end. But this was Dagmar, with no reason to tell Frank anything but, then, a dead man's words can never be properly disputed.

'She knows, doesn't she?' said Frank.

He felt the words turn breathy on his tongue, hoping he'd throw them back with denial but knowing he would confirm what he thought. Etamin knew the identity of the seventh guardian. That's why she didn't need Dagmar anymore. Dagmar sniffed.

'That's more like it.' Dagmar gave an exaggerated smile. 'Yes, Frank. Etamin knows and the world has just become a more dangerous place.'

'Who?' Too much eagerness in his voice. 'Who am I looking for?'

This time Dagmar raised an interested eyebrow.

'Says the boy currently imprisoned by the world's most deranged person, about to become her whore.'

'Oh come on, Dagmar. Now is not the time for games.'

Dagmar swung his legs off the bed, the sudden, liquid movement catching Frank, making him rock on his heels as he flinched. A captive ring filled the room as the slack chain fell against the wall, then tightened as Dagmar placed his feet on the floor, bracing his elbows on his knees, leaning forward. He cracked a smile.

'Games? I think the games are all but over. There are very few moves to check-mate, now.' He was still difficult to read but Frank detected a note of defeat in him, a faraway sound that didn't fit with the focused and determined bastard he'd come to know. 'I've known for a while,' said Dagmar. 'I just couldn't find them. They'd disappeared, just like Hums, but Garrim has since offered up its shiniest piece of shit.'

'Then why did you tell her?'

'Tell her? Have you not heard anything I've said? Here I am, waiting for the axe to fall and you insist on racing ten streets ahead and get run down by a passing wagon before you stop and think. Telling Etamin is the very last thing I would have done. Handing over that information would be gifting the keys to the world to a lunatic, and I had no intention of unstoppering a bottle of certain death.'

'Then who...?' Frank felt his voice trail off as his mind thumbed through what he knew, what he didn't quite know. Pieces of the puzzle fell around him, taking shape until he could see it in his mind. 'Jackson.'

'Clever boy, Frank,' said Dagmar with a thick slice of cynicism. 'You must have wondered why the likes of Alfred Jackson hauled his way to the arsehole that is Garrim for his holidays. When you think of it, it's a puzzle that solves itself, really.'

'Jackson's a guardian?'

Dagmar let out a chuckle.

'No, Frank. He's merely the go-between. The broker of absolute power and the future of all you and I hold dear, just to keep his place at the highest seat, to strike a deal. People like him are simply interested in just two things – getting into power and staying there. He's been protecting the final guardian and he's held the trump card for many years, knowing my quest would force him to play it at some point and my guess is that with you and your friends taking your seats at the table, he knew that time would come soon. I take it he's not been thanking you for your recent interference.' The slightest of nods from Frank who felt himself drowning in the river of disbelief that swirled around him. 'Only now, when his own authority is under threat, when he knows I hold six of the guardian's powers, has he chosen to play his ace and climb between the silken sheets of Etamin's bed – metaphorically speaking, of course. The reality, I'm afraid, remains with you.'

'If not him, then who? Who is the seventh guardian?'

'Too late, Frank. Knowing who it is won't stop this. Of course, keeping the key out of her possession might have been a good idea, but your carelessness is yet another hand on the lever of the trapdoor.'

'Please. Please tell me.'

Dagmar remained expressionless, chewing on the inside of his lip, allowing valuable seconds of Frank's ten minutes to slip away, his hand firmly in the game as if he was at Sapphire Hark's table in the Lid.

'I've known ever since I was a student at Excelsus,' he said, then hung the comment out for Frank to contemplate.

Someone at Excelsus, that made sense. Still Dagmar didn't

move. Frank wracked his brains for anything he might have missed but knew he could stew on it for weeks and still be no closer. 'They were there, I had them in my sights, ready to approach them at the right time...and then they were gone.'

'Who?'

No response.

'Like I said, it doesn't matter. It's too late. Etamin will have all seven pieces, she has Valaine De Villiers, the Simbrian heir, and now she has the key.' Dagmar clasped his hands together. 'I'm sorry about Simeon. Clever man, loyal. I thought he'd kept Irundi and the key buried but it seems like you and your band of fools brought it out and now she has it. Not your best moment and now you're destined to remain her captive until she tires of your youth and dispenses with you in her normal way.'

'Why don't you just...'

The cellar door opened, Frank turned his head.

'Time's up,' said the guard, jerking his head at Frank. Frank looked at him, then back to Dagmar as dozens of questions flooded into his mind, questions to which only Dagmar knew the answers, ones he'd not been clever or prepared enough to ask and, as soon as he'd left the cell, knew the chance would vanish.

Dagmar, just lifted his legs back on the bed and threaded his fingers together over his raised knees, closing his eyes.

'Wait,' he said. 'Just a few more minutes.'

'I said time's up,' repeated the jailer through his teeth. Frank turned his back to him, facing Dagmar.

'I don't get it,' he said.

'You heard the man,' said Dagmar. 'Time's up.'

Frank felt a firm grip on his arm but shrugged the jailer off, turning back to Dagmar.

'Gills and fins,' he said as the jailer grabbed him a second time and hauled him out and away from any answers.

36

The Wrong Heir

The guards led him away, up the cellar stairs and into the light of the open hallway. He paused, glancing back, head jumbled with Dagmar's words, the riddles, wishing he'd asked for more time.

Absolutely, he had him as a butcher. He'd been intent on ending Gabby's life in pursuit of Zanmir's eye which was the only evidence he needed, a vivid reminder of Dagmar's capabilities in the face of his reshaping of his own image which could only be a ruse, one that should be forgotten and not pick at him.

More than that, the threat that they'd been trying, badly, to avoid now loomed ever nearer. Etamin had the final guardian within reach. He couldn't quite remember Hums's words when he'd narrowed his enormous white eyebrows and told them they had to keep the world safe, but he could imagine the ancient caretaker shaking his riven head with a disappointed sigh in the knowledge that Frank had let Etamin take the key from him, the key that would fire the Simbrian and imbue her with power never previously encountered.

He and all the other guardians would have him as weak, that protecting peace and averting tyranny ranked well above the love and friendship of individuals. Each of them, and their ancestors, generations past had undoubtedly faced the same unenviable and impossible dilemma and had always chosen the same path.

The key was gone, getting it back was like throwing a rope around the sun, finding Jackson or the elusive seventh guardian equally so.

Not for the first time, Frank could feel the peace and security that Byeland had enjoyed since the days of Kester sailing towards the horizon, barely visible to the naked eye as it headed out of sight.

The guards guided him up one flight to the bottom of the second staircase, one step behind, blocking any route down and out, not that Frank had the appetite. Engaging his flight reflex seemed impossible while his mind was brimming.

He couldn't shake the brief encounter with Dagmar – lies or truth – or the moment Etamin had murdered Simeon. The image kept replaying in his mind, each time willing the ending could be different. An earthy mix of grief, fear and anger twisted itself around him, standing in the way of any other thoughts or plans he might otherwise have had.

He'd never seen himself as vengeful. He'd been brought up to be forgiving and always thought grudges were a waste of breath, for those who raged against the world and everything in it but, monster or coward, he knew he wouldn't rest until he'd paid her back.

Movement at the top of the stairs distracted him and had him looking up. He felt himself draw in a breath and hold it as he stared at the odious figure of Valaine de Villiers heading down.

She stopped, gripping the bannister like she wanted to strangle it and snap its neck and stared back, sporting her customary scowl, looking like she wanted to rip the world into little pieces, a look she immediately fastened on Frank with the usual heavy dose of suspicion and loathing.

'As if my day couldn't get any worse,' said Frank with an undiluted lick of animosity.

'What the fuck are you doing here?' she spat.

He could ask her the same question, but Frank already knew.

'Pleased to see me, as always,' said Frank, mirroring her dark look. 'Aren't you meant to be at Excelsus?'

'And? Aren't you?'

Her narrow eyes, the deep ruts in her forehead, the bitter edge of her words, the look of entitlement. All the hallmarks of Etamin, all owned keenly by De Villiers.

'No, I left,' said Frank.

'Huh, why don't you tell me something that might surprise me? Always had you labelled as a drop-out. I see that wimp of a friend of yours isn't there, neither are those two stupid fruit-loops you hang around with.'

Frank pushed against his instinct to grab her by the throat. Maybe he could save Etamin the trouble. He'd forgotten just how naturally jarring she was, how she had no words of praise, just a vocabulary full of grievance and mock superiority. 'How come you've decided to join Kzarlac? Hate being a loser?'

She stood a couple of stairs up, looking down at him as if that were the way things should be, her familiar expression of contempt spread across her face showing she relished her feeling of superiority, making Frank want to slap it off immediately. He wasn't going to tell her he was there against his will.

'Etamin sent for me,' she said with a sneer of self-importance, a backward tilt of the head.

'I know,' said Frank. 'She got me here, too.'

'You should know I'm related to her.'

'I know that, too.'

De Villiers descended a stair, coming as close to Frank as she dared, staying a safe distance, typical of her and the rest of Emerald's gang, only brave in the company of others.

'So you'd better mind your manners or I'll just have to ask her to let me use you for target practice.'

Frank took a breath; whatever he thought of her, however much he wanted to grab her by the hair and smash her face into the wall, he could never bring himself to be complicit in her murder, though he fought the feeling, imagining the final look on her face as Etamin shrugged her shoulders and had her skewered by one of her giant scorpions as had been Simeon's fate before realising she'd got it all wrong.

He held his hands out, palms facing De Villiers.

'You need to leave. Right now,' he said, immediately questioning his judgement.

A dark cloud instantly spread over De Villiers's face.

'What? Where do you get off telling me what to do?'

Frank looked behind her, then back down past the guard to the room where Etamin had murdered Simeon, straining to detect any sounds, anyone approaching.

He knew as soon as Etamin and Jackson had completed their immoral and sordid dealings, cementing their place in whatever vision of the future they had concocted, she would head to Alsha Kar, complete the Simbrian and dispatch De Villiers as quickly as the poacher breaks the rabbit's neck.

'I mean it, you need to get yourself as far away from here as you can. *Right now.*'

Whether it was the heat in Frank's voice or the tight look on his face, De Villiers seemed to trip over herself. It was apparent that, in a skip of her dark heart, something had registered and Frank saw her face drop.

She looked around, then behind her, as if expecting an imaginary arm around her throat or the hiss of an arrow before it pierced her neck.

'Now you're beginning to make me nervous, Penny.' Her thin layer of bravado cracked a little. She waited, a second drew itself out between them.

'She's going to kill you.'

The words were out before he had a chance to check what he was saying, but De Villiers needed to hear them, to understand that she hadn't been politely invited back here for a family reunion, that she was to be the unwilling lamb on Etamin's sacrificial altar.

Silence enveloped De Villiers as she drew in the sincerity on Frank's face. Her usual façade, like a band of angry crows, fell away.

'She wouldn't.' Her voice lacked any measure conviction as she struggled to keep the veneer intact. Frank's silence gave her the answer. Her dark features paled and Frank could tell that she knew her family connection could never act as a safety valve against the rampant ambition of the Dahke dynasty. Dagmar had already suffered that fate. 'Why?'

Frank hesitated. He genuinely felt nothing but hate for De Villiers, it would be the easiest thing for him to simply walk away and leave her to whatever end Etamin had planned – her brave and worthy sacrifice – but as her sharp eyes searched his he knew he couldn't do it, knew he had to do the right thing, save her from the fangs of the viper.

De Villiers's eyes watered slightly, still they asked Frank the question.

'Because she thinks you're someone you're not.'

'Someone I'm not. How can I be someone I'm not?'

Frank hesitated. To tell or not to tell. To save her or cast her to the wolves. How much to give away.

'She thinks you're something called the Simbrian heir.' A puzzled look washed over her face, as if Frank's words had been spoken in a foreign language. 'Look, it'll take me too long to explain it to you.'

De Villiers narrowed her eyes, screwing up her nose.

'Do you think I'm thick or something?'

A typical lash-back with the sensitivity of a brick. Frank held back what he really thought, he couldn't tell if what he'd just said had sunk in or if she was winding herself up for a fist-fight as she pushed her bitten nails into her palms. The switch from abject concern to characteristic aggression was seamless.

She took a step forward. For a moment he thought she would just push him down the stairs but Frank held his ground, feeling the heat of her circling hostility. She stopped, the tell-tale paralysis of fear anchored her to the spot, daring her to run.

'Did you get what I just said?'

He could taste his own frustration but any words on his or her lips were suddenly extinguished by a voice from behind him:

'And what did you just say?'

214

37

THE RIGHT HEIR

Etamin's voice, low and throaty, pierced the tension from the bottom of the staircase, all attention now plainly focused on her and her badly-timed and unwanted appearance.

She approached them slowly, the confident look of an apex predator filling her dark features, the stark twist of orange-red on her wrist. Her walking stick tapped expectantly on each of the wooden treads as she ascended. Slow and deliberate.

Frank glanced down at her then back up at the still-riled De Villiers, willing her to be complicit, to keep the silence and the secret he'd betrayed, knowing she suddenly had a winning hand to play.

But the second he looked at her he knew he'd chosen the wrong playing partner, one who would cheat and scheme to win the game and needed no excuse to willingly throw him to the dogs. Killer dogs.

'Penny says I'm not the Simbrian heir,' she said, a slight, forced smile as she dodged her own death. Like the executioner had just lifted the noose over her head and planted it firmly around Frank's neck.

Etamin didn't break her hobbling stride, nor change her expression. Her breathing rattled as she absorbed De Villiers's tiny but invaluable nugget of information, a short sentence made of gold.

Frank's mind immediately raced ahead, frantically trying to figure out how this was going to go as he felt the shadows of the corner he was being pushed into start to close in.

De Villiers appeared emboldened by Etamin's appearance, the smallest pack of ravenous beasts waiting for their moment to pounce.

'Is that so?' said Etamin, her voice laced with interest. She stopped next to Frank, her eyes wandering over him, keeping him alert, tense. He ran the scenario, knowing what her next question would be before she had time to ask. 'Then who is?'

Her voice was nothing but demanding, as hard as stone and twice as heavy. Her nightmare eyes stilled and ground into his, a look that demanded his compliance.

A glance to the swirl of flame. His silence didn't appear to shake her but, then, knowing she could wait until she got what she wanted, by whatever means she considered appropriate, was sufficient to relax the hungriest predator. Knowledge to dry Frank's throat.

'What's the Simbrian heir?' said De Villiers, chewing at a finger, her brow knitting.

'Quiet,' snapped Etamin.

De Villiers recoiled as if she'd been slapped, hunched her shoulders, looking like she wanted to smash a fist into anything within range. Etamin growled under her breath as she eyed Frank with the quiet intent of an executioner anxious to get on with the business of death. Frank urged himself to keep quiet.

'Penny's not going to —'

'*I said quiet.*'

Etamin remained focused on Frank. Her eyes gleamed in anticipation as she looked him up and down. She touched the top of her cane to Frank's chest, watching the carved scorpion effigy move slowly back and forth with his breathing.

'I seldom repeat myself, Frank. So please be a good boy.'

Frank bit down, clamping his teeth together. He watched the red flame twist along its slow, sinister path around her wrist ready to turn him to cinders where he stood. Etamin sniffed.

'Perhaps it's that Prismian girl,' she said. De Villiers laughed under her breath but Etamin's face remained dark and poised, studying Frank for a sign of weakness, of betrayal – something she wasn't going to get. A thin smile cracked across her withered face. 'It was easy enough to get you here, Frank. There'll be little difficulty bringing her.' She looked at the guard standing two steps down, his attention immediate. 'Gabriella Asaro,' she said. Frank flinched as her voice whetted itself into a sharp edge. 'She's here in Garrim. Have her found and brought here.' The guard nodded and turned to leave but Etamin raised a finger to stop him before looking back to Frank. Her face darkened a shade, unlit by the thin smile that tugged the corners of her lips as she began to press carefully and skilfully on Frank's pressure points. 'As a little welcome gift, I'll make sure to throw a party for her with the roughest of my soldiers the minute she arrives. What shall we say? A dozen? Unfortunately, they lack the usual physical comforts men need, as well as any semblance of gentleness but, believe me Frank, they *love* a party, especially involving young flesh and they'll have no trouble keeping her occupied for many, many hours. I doubt she'll be able to walk by the time they've exhausted their lust. I'll see to it, personally. Maybe you and I can watch.'

Frank boiled at the thinly veiled amusement on her tongue. He didn't try to hide it. He wanted to dare her, but knew Etamin was ten steps ahead of him and that she'd roast her own mother to have the Simbrian. She signalled to the guard with a jerk of her head and he turned with a cursory nod.

'Wait,' said Frank, springing the simple trap.

The guard paused. Etamin widened her eyes, knowing she'd pushed the one button she needed to. He held her gaze, resisting the futile urge to slap the triumph off it and grab her by the throat, knowing she was genuine, that using his friends as a weapon against him would empty his reserves. He'd shown it with Simeon, shown how he put the people he cared for before all else, regardless of the consequences. She saw it as the perfect weakness, one to be exploited, one to throttle him with and she'd win every time, just like his gran had warned.

Still she waited, unmoved by the anger in his eyes, anger to pin her to the wall and rip her throat out. A long breath left him as he felt himself fill with resignation.

'I'm the one you're looking for.'

38

THOUGHTS

There'd been no decision to make.

He'd revealed himself as the Simbrian heir in half a heartbeat to save Gabby with zero hesitation while, at the same time, sealing the fate of the world and he knew he'd do it a hundred, a thousand times over if he needed to.

But once was enough and he knew he'd never see her again. That was the worst of it. He could face his own miserable slaughter, or so he thought, could face down Etamin in the seconds before she sent him to his grave, but knowing he'd looked into Gabby's warm eyes for the last time, that he'd never breathe in her scent again or hear her voice hung a weight on his heart.

He closed his eyes and pictured her as she walked confidently away from him the previous morning, turned the corner and was gone. Gone forever. No more laughs, no more warm embraces, no more teenage dreams. The world couldn't be a bleaker place.

Etamin, on the brink of landing the seventh guardian, now had the key and the heir in her possession. The set was hers, nearly. She wouldn't let go – not him, not the quest she'd set herself, not the lust for power. Talons so sharp he could feel the vicious points burning into his skin. Centuries of Kzarlac searching, of focus and effort were bound to this single moment and she'd been wordless as Frank had been led away under the relieved eyes of De Villiers who had pleasure rolling off her in smug waves.

Back in the prison of her bedchamber, Frank sat on the edge of the bed, filled with resignation and defeat.

He braced his elbows on his knees and dug his fingertips into his scalp, feeling tired beyond description, resisting the temptation to lay down, knowing the luxurious feel of the silken bedclothes would pull him in close and draw the sleep from his weary body and he'd wake to the whim of the monster that would now use him as her toy before slashing his throat. Depraved didn't seem like an adequate description.

Now it was simply a matter of waiting. There was no plan, no trying to bust himself out. There was now a guard in the room with him, at least one more outside and a leg-busting drop out of the window if he dared.

He felt completely coated in a sticky layer of misery and hopelessness as he tried to grasp on to the possibility that she wouldn't destroy him once she had the seventh guardian. Maybe he could get through to her? Certainly he appeared to hold an unfathomable allure and, however unpalatable, he started to wonder if he could use it to his advantage, turn the fight in his favour. Devour or be devoured.

He'd noticed Etamin's eyes go cold as he told her, as if she'd been expecting it but, even through her evil stare, didn't want to believe it.

He even thought he detected a hint of sorrow on her sour face, a barely detectable drop of the mouth and eyes but, as much as he thought about using her apparent liking for him to his advantage, she had been specific about where her priorities lay and in her overall scheme knew he featured some way down the list. She would have killed her own daughter just to open the gates to absolute power, killing him would require less from her.

But he had time. When Esryn had explained about the power of the Simbrian heir passing to whoever kills them, she was clear that could only happen once the Simbrian was complete and fired.

Exactly how time much depended on how keen Jackson was to complete a deal that would see him stand alongside Etamin as the Simbrian play entered its final act.

The irony of resting your life on a weasel like Jackson had Frank shaking his head, but he could see the sands starting to run quicker than they ever had before. Knowing he had an undefined amount of time to play with had zero sobering effect, especially now he was her captive once again and, although Etamin had left him unshackled this time, he knew that was because escape was impossible.

The guard sat watching his every movement, no weapons drawn, but primed. Frank threw him the occasional look back, each one a reminder of his captivity, of the ticking clock.

He fought the running of his thoughts – of Gabby, of Etamin, of death and tried to find something he might use to eke out more hours or turn the onrushing and overwhelming tide.

He mentally retraced his steps in the useless pursuit of trying to think how the confrontation with De Villiers and Etamin might have gone differently, how he might have steered it along another path had he had time to think. But it was all a waste of time, a waste of the limited time and energy he had left.

His brief encounter with the incarcerated Dagmar, the man he'd most feared since all of this had begun, seemed long ago and wholly blurred.

How their fortunes had suddenly smashed into each other.

Now they were both shackled to the mast of a sinking ship, watching the waters rise slowly around their feet, outcome assured.

Frank studied the palms of his hands in a futile stab at summoning some inspiration from his conversation with Dagmar. He'd looked his real father in the eye and had, just briefly, felt something, felt his emotions shift ever so slightly.

Even now he could feel the unsettling hands of pity on his. Pity for the man who oozed power like others breathed in the air, reduced to a convict, a condemned man and Frank wasn't sure whether to feel revulsion or disappointment in himself for letting Dagmar get under his skin, even in his final hours.

He hadn't intended to feel sorry for Dagmar, not in the slightest. Frank only had to conjure images of Gabby fleeing Kzarlac's pillaging of her homeland, or the butchering of Montrose Menetti, or poisoning Gabby when they'd been locked up in Alsha Kar, but he'd left Sapphire Hark alive and helped her escape. Why? It made no sense.

He wished it had been a simple case of reaffirming his opinion, that Dagmar was a circling, heartless beast with nothing but an appetite for glory and suffering but something unseen stood before him, telling him to think, to consider what he'd witnessed in Etamin's room and down in the cellar and, as he focused and unfocused on his hands, the conversation began to pick at him.

You have me as a butcher?

Then something he'd nearly missed – *I protect the Simbrian from this side.*

Protect? No way. Says the man who has made it his life's work to assemble the power to crush cities. Who would do that unless they wanted it for themselves? And why even utter the words?

The road was littered with numerous signs as well as many more corpses and a more obvious attempt at a bluff he'd never seen. The only thing Dagmar was capable of protecting was himself, yet it nagged him that Dagmar had chosen the moment when he was most vulnerable to tell him something so different, so unexpected, something that he had no need to fabricate in the face of his own execution, as if he needed to reveal something to Frank in the moments before the final axe was swung.

He thought about what Dagmar said about his dad, what Simeon had said about him – talented, enquiring supreme student, scholar; a coward. The doubts, the unanswered questions that had them scratching their chins, but neither of them had lived alongside Lawrence Penny like Frank had, had seen him dedicate himself to bringing Frank up, keeping him safe and working hard on the farm in blissful detachment from his Simbrian past like he never knew the thing existed.

A life of loyalty to the Simbrian wasn't for everyone and, perhaps, forgetting about the whole thing was for the best, so why did those who knew him best see things from a different end of the spyglass? Not that Frank thought he was ever going to get the chance to ask him, but the questions wouldn't go away – *ever the mystery, Lawrence.*

And Dagmar had willingly been handed him something he wasn't expecting, though he should have guessed.

Jackson. The self-serving head of Byeland Council.

Frank had harboured a creeping suspicion for a while and his disappearance with their book had confirmed he was up to his neck in the shit the Simbrian spewed, for sure. But Dagmar's revelation that he was harbouring the seventh guardian with the sole intention of elevating himself even further had hit him hard – and Dagmar knew who it was and Frank cursed himself for not finding out. Now he'd never know, not that knowing would steer his ship in a different direction.

They'd failed. *He'd* failed. Hums had been wrong to entrust the secret of the Simbrian and the safety of the seven guardians to their incapable, fumbling hands. They'd dropped every catch thrown at them and no one wins a game if you can't get the basics right.

It was over. Etamin would fulfil her self-appointed destiny, Jackson would join her and the world as they knew it would be bent and twisted into a different shape. Perhaps it was a blessing that he wouldn't be alive to see it all burn.

A muffled noise from beyond the door dragged his thoughts back and had him looking up. Immediately the guard was on his feet, a question on his face, but he didn't draw his blade. Frank got to his feet, drawing the guard's attention.

'You stay put,' he said, a moment of distraction as the door to the bedchamber opened, distraction so the guard was unable to react, or cry for help as a small dagger found his throat, sending him stumbling against the wall.

His hands went to the hilt, pulling at the leather-bound handle with the instinct for survival, a sucking sound filling the room as he pulled it free, releasing it from the severed artery in his neck.

It would be the last thing he did. All Frank could see was dark and crimson and death. Arcing, flowing, bubbling from the deep wound as the blood left the guard's body like the flow of water from a drainpipe in a storm, leaving him slumped on the ground, silent. Dead.

Frank's skin rippled in the moment of confused violence but he felt the tension instantly melt away at the sight of the slight figure of Anya standing in the doorway, blades drawn and bloody.

'Frank,' she said, relief but no smile on her face. 'Not expecting me?'

39

THE ESCAPE

She hauled the body of the second guard into the bedroom. A deep wound in his chest, inflicted with frightening precision, spilled the last of his blood, leaving a black smear on the floor as she dumped him next to his colleague. She retrieved both her knives – one blade is never quite enough.

Frank barely had time to process what had just happened, such was the speed and efficiency with which Anya went about her task.

'How did you know where I was?'

She looked up, a focus in her eyes yet brushed with emptiness, her breath steady yet caught on the edge of the danger that stalked the rooms of the house.

'This is Etamin's house,' she said. 'A girl who came and told us you might be in trouble, that you'd been brought here.' A glance to the door. 'Come on, let's go.'

'Girl? What girl?'

'Not now, Frank,' she snapped. 'We need to go, quick.'

She turned, eager to be away while Frank found himself rooted, looking at the doorway.

'Where are Gabby and Cas?'

'Come *on.*'

She turned and stepped back into the corridor. This time Frank was on her heels.

She moved like a gazelle on the wind, swift and sure, hugging the shadows, as quiet as the ghost she was becoming. In Esryn's mould. Movements that confirmed time wasn't their companion.

Frank kept as close to her back as her could, stepping where she stepped, weaving where she wove, as if the route away from his nightmare were inked on her skin.

They moved from doorway to doorway along the long landing before Anya stopped at the bottom of a flight of stairs. Voices up above, from the next level.

'Shit,' she said, fingers raking her hair. A look back, past Frank, re-calculating her next move. 'They go up to the attic. I got in through the roof.' A scratch of her chin and flash of her teeth revealed she hadn't bargained on an interruption. 'They'll see the rope.' Said to herself.

Then she was past him, back the way they'd come. If there was urgency before, it stepped up a notch.

Down one flight of stairs. Not once did Anya look back to check if Frank was keeping pace. She could sense him on her tail, he was sure of that, summoning an awareness Frank couldn't comprehend as they traversed the landing to a second staircase.

The whole interior was far bigger than any house Frank had seen in the town from the outside. Every building he'd seen in the whole miserable time they'd been here was small and tawdry and stinking yet here they were, firmly in the backstreets of Garrim, as if this was four or five houses knocked through to make a large, single dwelling. As much of a palace as you could get in this mountain town.

Anya paused, adjusting the knife in her hand before setting off down the stairs to the lower level, street level where Frank had been led following his request to see Dagmar.

She peeled left at the bottom, at the end of a long hallway that ran parallel to the side of the mountain. Then she stilled. An outstretched palm had Frank doing the same as he caught sight of two hefty Lashkens further down, their attention buried in conversation with someone at the front door. No look towards the teenagers.

'I thought she'd be gone by now,' said Anya, to herself, before snapping her head round.

Then he heard it.

Voices. Voices at the top of the house, coming down behind them, towards them. Excited and irritated, a sign that Anya's entry had been exposed, that whoever was in the attic was now heading to raise concerns that someone had entered the house through the roof, just a matter of time before Etamin had someone check on Frank. Just a matter of time until someone found two butchered guards. Just a matter of time until they were caught.

They pushed back a couple of steps up the stairway, out of sight of the Lashkens but towards the approaching sounds from further up. The guards along the hallway would be in earshot of the commotion in no time and there was nothing like curiosity to cure the boredom of guard duty.

He could see Anya calculating, calmly laying out their options in her mind but Frank could see that they were stuck, out of choices and it does you no good to be out of choices.

A look up, a look along. They lay trapped between. Anya looked across the corridor. Five paces down a door on the other side stood slightly ajar. Five long, heart-rending paces. It was easily in reach, a second or two away but bound by the risk of being seen by the guards. A risk to weigh, one with the finest of margins.

He heard Anya draw in a breath as if she were about to dive into deep water then she was across the hallway and through the door, silent, steady, unseen.

Frank knew he had to follow but his mind fought against him, lacking Anya's poise and cool head, certain he'd give them away, his mind laying out the alternatives if he stayed put. Twist of stick? Either way the house was bound to win.

A look down the passageway. The guards, all but standing statues, still in conversation, paid him no attention as he took a breath and headed to the door.

He was through and closing it behind him before he could blink, ear immediately at the crack between the door and frame.

He waited. Waited for something evil to follow them in, for someone beat the shit out of them and drag them to the cellar to be imprisoned with Dagmar.

Footsteps outside came and went. Frank kept his breathing tight until he was certain no one was going to enter, then stepped away and turned to the room. Not safe, not yet.

The small room was dark and smelled of dust and neglect. Frank knew it backed onto the mountainside, not the safety of the street, not the promise of a window through which they might make their escape although it was lit in meagre tones by a thin strand of light which lanced through a small pane of glass in a door at the rear at which Anya already stood, looking out.

A small desk, on which sat a pile of books, a few sheets of writing papers and a discarded pair of glasses occupied the middle of the room. Bare walls with little else, unloved and unkempt.

Anya turned and took a pace back to the desk, bracing her palms on the top.

'Come on,' she said, an instruction to Frank to help her move it to the door.

Frank nodded and, together, they lifted the desk, placing it as a flimsy barricade against someone coming in. Probably the worst barrier Frank had ever seen, one that a Lashken with half the usual muscle would knock out in a stroke of his forearm.

'How did you find me?' he said as Anya gave the desk a shove to make sure it was as tight to the door as possible, sending the pile of books to her feet in the process. Unnecessary sounds to lure a search-party.

'Like I said, a girl, at the Lid. Young, white hair, hungry-looking. Gabby went down there —'

'Gabby, she's okay?'

'Yes, Frank, Gabby's fine, except for pulling her hair out wondering where you are, she's not slept or stopped prowling the streets looking for any sign of you. She went to the Lid thinking you might have gone back to see Sapphire Hark, it was an obvious place to look.' Anya looked at the door, eyes focused. 'She wasn't there but the girl heard her asking and managed to stop Gabby as she was leaving. She told us where to find you.'

Frank felt the pin-pricks on his skin. Gabby hadn't given up on him. He knew she wouldn't, that every filth-covered rock in Garrim would be turned in her desire to bring him back to her. She knew he was in trouble and he knew she wouldn't rest until she knew he was safe. He knew that, because that's exactly what he would have done for her.

'Etamin's here,' he said, feeling the hot spike of anxiety that had always accompanied the mention of her name.

Anya nodded, no sign of fear as her attention was taken by something on the floor, at her feet.

She bent down, a slight pause, a knitting of the eyebrows before she picked something up and stood, holding it out for Frank to see.

A book. Purple cover. *Their* book.

Their frayed and battered book.

In the stack on the desk, it had been ordinary and unassuming. Easily missed.

Frank nodded and immediately felt a wave of anger crash over him. Jackson had been here. In fact, he was probably still here, in the house, a guest at the top table. His anger tugged hard on its leash, had him reliving his conversation with Dagmar, how the old man was selling out his country and his people with his knowledge of the identity of the final guardian and using it to strike a deal with the most odious and barbaric of partners. Unforgiveable.

Frank looked at the pair of spectacles, slamming his fist down and breaking them with a heavy thump, too late to realise his stupidity. A look at the door, then to Anya whose eyes were silently berating him.

'Let's get out of here,' he said, heading across the room to the back entrance.

He glanced back. Anya was giving the single desk drawer a quick search before she moved quickly to join him. Frank pushed on the door handle. There was no lock and the door eased itself open with a groan like it had a hangover, revealing an open space, the outside world, but as they stepped through the door, any spark of relief was quickly extinguished.

40

The Courtyard

The tiny yard, cloaked in deep shadow, hewn into and surrounded by the unforgiving rock of the Longshadows, offered no hiding place. A cold, bleak square no more than five paces across. The ultimate dead-end, the perfect snare.

Frank stepped across and ran his hand over the sheer, glass-like rock surface, planted vertically, deeply, disappearing skywards into the dark clouds that veiled the peaks. He felt the cold trying to anchor his palm, withdrawing it quickly.

The flagstones on the floor sweated ice crystals, smooth and glistening, tidy, providing nothing of use with which to try and wedge the door shut. There was only one way in and one way out.

They were cornered, minutes away from discovery. The house was being searched and staring blankly at the door wasn't going to do them an ounce of favours.

This time, though, Etamin would have him in chains along with Dagmar and he couldn't begin to imagine the severity of the punishment she would inflict on Anya.

Two guards lay dead in the house. She would demand recompense and it would be served with uncompromising brutality. She knew Frank's weakness and she'd be sure to exploit it, making him watch as she broke Anya's body before slitting her throat. She might even ask him to do it to save others he loved in the twisted game she insisted on playing.

He looked at Anya, she was composed, thinking, planning, doing what he should be doing despite his absolute certainty that the clock was ticking down on their capture.

He started to pace, checking the rock-face for the unusual, the way Cas would scout a room, for anything that would help them and delay the inevitable.

Nothing. Just the dead-end that spelled violence and death in large letters.

He cupped his hands together and blew the salve of warm air into his palms as Anya suddenly held her hand up, cutting the sounds of his feet on the stones as he stilled.

'What's that?' she said, her senses heightened, eyes weaving one way then the other. She didn't look at him, just descended further into concentration. Frank held his breath. 'That noise?'

Her eyes darted to the flagstones. Frank watched as she stepped back, then to the side, focused, trying to locate the source of whatever had caught her attention. Then she was down on her knees, dagger drawn, the material of her trousers darkening where it rubbed against the wet ground. She adjusted her grip on her blade, holding its tip down, then dug the point into the loose earth surrounding one of the stones before drawing it hard along the edge, excavating a narrow, shallow trench between the two flags.

Frank was instantly down at her side, his fingers picking at decades of dirt and decay. Then he heard it too. Above the wild scraping of steel on stone, he heard it. The rush and echo of running water.

Anya didn't rest, digging frantically until the whole edge of the flag was exposed, stopping for a fraction of a second to wedge the point of her knife under the stone, prising it underneath, trying to lift it.

Frank wedged his fingertips into the gap, barely wide enough for him to get any purchase on the edge, the cold and wet pushing him off with a snarl.

The scraping from the point of Anya's dagger intensified, dragging out the remaining debris, all other sound stripped from the enclosed space except for the heavy breaths of the two teenagers which punctured the air like a frightened animal, growing wilder, agitated, good reason to be frightened, keeping their eyes off the door.

Tick, tick, tick.

The feverish digging around the flagstone stopped as they both grasped the exposed edge and heaved against the weight. The stone stretched Frank's bones in its attempts to keep itself flat to the ground but he wouldn't let it win.

They wrestled it until they managed to lift it above the lip of the adjacent stone. Quickly, Anya shoved the length of her dagger underneath to stop it dropping back as Frank strained to hold it, fighting the numbness in his fingers, the burn in his wrists and forearms.

Inch by inch the flagstone fought, holding its ground, slowly giving up its struggle until they finally had it vertical, flipping it onto its back like a beaten turtle, the loud slap of stone dumping both teenagers onto their behinds.

Anya was on her feet, rubbing her grazed fingertips in the palms of her hands. Both of them stood by the space vacated by the flagstone and looked at the rusting frame of an iron grate underneath.

Frank knelt, praying that the grate wasn't bolted down. Through the crude fretwork he could just make out the flow of water. Water to freeze the sun. He stuck his fingers through the metal, feeling the cold bite from the years of penetrating ice and snow woven through its fabric.

A sharp yank and the grate lifted, flooding him with relief as he pulled it up and dropped it onto the upturned stone with a hefty clank, followed by a loud crash from behind the door, the sound of someone weighty shoving the laughable makeshift barrier off its wooden legs.

Frank stared down into the circular hole, the hollow thrum and splash of running water filling his ears and the courtyard around him. A ladder, rusted to ruin and looking as brittle as an eggshell ran from the rim into darkness while the purifying scent of ice-water and tang of damp minerals sprang from below.

'Storm drain,' said Anya, looking into the hole like it was the jaws of a ferocious beast.

She looked at Frank, both barely able to hide their shivers, both counting down as the sound of the door opening filled the cold air and a uniformed Lashken guard appeared, a look of cool disbelief on her face.

Neither of them looked up, Frank just gave a single nod before Anya grabbed him and jumped.

41

THE STORM DRAIN

There was the briefest moment when the world switched off. Just silence and darkness before they were pitched into the searing cold of the ice-water that flowed recklessly from the mountains and shook its fist at the town from beneath its filthy streets.

Nothing could have prepared Frank. Standing in the courtyard had been cold, Garrim was constantly cold, but the meltwater breathed a completely new meaning into the word. It grabbed him and drew all feeling from his body, right down to the marrow in his bones the instant he hit, submerged for a second that lasted much longer, ripping the warm air from his lungs.

Frank gasped. Deep gulps of burning water flooded into his throat and down into his lungs. He surfaced, still clutching Anya who coughed like she was trying to shed her guts or in the death throes of the plague, the noise echoing through the passage hewn from the rock under Garrim, drowning out the sharp voices from the courtyard as they left it behind in the swell of water. No sounds of anyone else joining them, but he didn't have time to admire their luck, the drain might have been their accomplice, but it was no sanctuary.

The current wasn't a torrent, but still fast enough to carry them swiftly along the subterranean passage, bound in a seam of dark rock, smoothed by decades of the cold flow which bore them, running straight as an arrow and sweeping them forward just as fast.

Frank could barely steady himself, now ahead of Anya, losing his grip on her in the run of the drain as she still coughed and floundered in the churning chill. He looked through the blur of water as it tossed him round three hundred and sixty degrees, picking out the unmistakeable silhouette of a ladder approaching quickly. The bent and mangled strands of broken metal dangled in the distance, brushed by the flow of the water and bathed in a cream-coloured shaft of light from the grate that opened to the street above.

He'd have one chance.

He was on it in a matter of seconds, much quicker than he had anticipated, too quick.

He thought he'd misjudged it as the side of his head clattered into the side-strut of the ladder, snapping his neck back before he raised his arm, grabbing the bottom rung, barely feeling the rough, rusted iron as his deadened fingers wrapped around it, ignoring the constant pinpricks of icy water that peppered his face.

Flakes of forgotten metal fell onto his cheeks and into his gaping mouth as he fought to hold on. The ladder groaned under his weight as he managed to wrestle himself up to the next rung, his arm burning with the effort, mouth spitting rust.

Anya bashed against his legs, bringing her to a stuttering halt, latching onto his ankle, sending up a scything arc of water to the roof of the tunnel. Frank felt himself slip against her weight and the drag of her body in the water. He reached down with his free hand and Anya, through the freezing, unrelenting spray that rode over her body, grabbed his wrist, sending a potent and painful jerk through Frank's shoulder.

The menacing water frothed and spat, trying to take them both down, as if it sensed the building cramp in Frank's legs, his arms, his desperate fingers as he clung on, silently begging Anya to adjust herself and find the bottom rung, any rung, as safety called them from above.

Frank looked up through the metal grate that led to the street, feeling the sinews in his neck stretch. It was so close, yet it might as well have been a mile.

Anya let out a stifled scream and her hand slipped down his wrist, the cold and wet loosening her grip. The rush of the water pulled at her, grasping at her ankles. She turned her head, staring down at the freezing water as it gushed past. Deep churning eddies, growling and sizzling, spun unbridled beneath them and tempted them on into the black.

They both knew what lay beyond. Somewhere. The point where the drain exited the mountains into the jaw-dropping depths of the gorge. Distance unknown, outcome certain.

She looked back up, the calm wintry sunlight lit her terrified face. Small, jewel-like droplets sparkled on her skin as she tried frantically to haul herself to the safety of the bottom rung.

The rage of the water twisted Anya's kicking legs one way then the other, testing Frank's grip, beginning to kill it. He couldn't feel the tips of his fingers but Anya had managed to steady herself and swung her free arm up, latching on to the tattered iron cylinder at the bottom of the ladder, forcing her fingers tight around it and heaving herself from the icy waterway which refused to give her up, just as Frank's grip failed him.

He saw the flex of Anya's bicep under the soaking material of her shirt just as the crack of brittle metal echoed through the smooth rock as the rung snapped from the vertical side rail of the ladder, dropping her down, her hand slipping, slivers and scales of dry rust falling into her eyes and mouth.

Frank went to grab her by the collar. Too late. She let go. Frank watched as Anya, the unassuming girl, the master of combat, the girl who'd been with him from the start, was dragged down and under, resurfacing once before she disappeared from view, swept away to her death.

42

THE DROP

The groan of twisted iron filled the void as the entire ladder threatened to prise itself from its fixings. Frank looked up to the safety of the street, then back down the drain. How much longer before it emptied into the Jixx from the indescribable height of Deadman's Scar?

It wasn't a choice.

A split-second later he was back in the freezing water, after her, churning it with great strokes of his arms in an attempt to pick up speed, to try and reach Anya before the water took her over the edge and smashed her young body on the rocks at the bottom of the chasm.

He had to try. She'd come for him, he'd do the same for her. He'd not be able to look himself in the mirror otherwise and the value of his friendship with Anya – with Cas and Gabby – was worth all the coin on the Ditch, all the power the Simbrian contained, worth his own life.

The tunnel took a sharp turn to the left. The flow of the water smashed him into the unyielding rock wall, slicing at his back, spinning him sideways in the dark and submerging him momentarily. He spluttered out a mouthful of icy water, pain shoving itself into the roots of his teeth as he looked down the run of the drain.

Then he saw her, clinging with utter desperation to the final ladder.

Beyond, the water rushed toward a large, distant opening with the promise of the winter sun. Their last glimpse of daylight, the first glimpse of death.

Anya had both arms entwined through the bottom few rungs, the white clouds of her breath coming in short bursts. The tell-tale signs that she was all but spent but refused to yield to the watery onslaught and the cold.

Frank suddenly sensed a shift under him, an increase in the rate of his descent through the channel, the gradient of the tunnel and the speed of the water changing in the flex of his frozen fingers, drawing him quicker to the ladder, quicker to the deadly exit.

Now it was his turn to panic. His momentum was too much, too fast, the passage too wide. He spread his arms and legs, a frantic attempt to slow himself as he approached.

Then he was on it, grasping at the air, pushing like a salmon, his fingers craving the safety of the ladder as he barrelled into the tired metal frame. He managed to get both hands on the second rung but the momentum of the water carried his body under the ladder, bending his tired arms against his elbows, his grip deserting him in a second, sweeping him under the ladder, under Anya. She tried to adjust herself, clawing the water, trying to get hold of any part of him before he was lost to the current.

As she reached, grabbing the shoulder of Frank's jacket, she lost her grip and fell, letting out a high wail that followed them both as the water devoured them once more and rushed them on to the end of the drain.

Frank's fumbling hands grabbed her by the waist as they were dragged, feet first towards the approaching daylight.

He could sense a subtle change in the sounds around the mouth of the tunnel as the water tumbled out into the gorge. He could sense the clean air, but struggled to breathe it in, the last breath he would ever take as the thrashing water hauled them to the lip of the outlet.

Frank clung to Anya. He screamed as the air sucked the water out of the rock, over the edge and down. Down and down.

Then they followed.

43

NOTHING LEFT

The sound changed in an instant. The relentless pounding and throbbing of the rushing water in the confines of the storm drain disappeared as it frothed like a good head on a pint of ale before plummeting away beneath Frank's dangling feet.

Everything about his frantic passage under the town meant he should be following it down as part of the deadly cascade, but he found himself hanging in mid-air. Not falling. Not tumbling into the ferocious jaws of the gorge that would see him bitten in two with a snarling clench of its teeth.

He looked up to see Anya, arms at full stretch against his weight, dagger up to its hilt in a large, rotting piece of timber that had wedged itself at an angle to the side of the opening, the wide aperture in the rock that disappeared back into darkness, the gawping mouth of the foulest monster that spewed ice-water and misery over them and into the abyss.

She'd seen it. He hadn't. She'd had the grace to trust her instincts and lance the wood just at the vital moment and, now, both her hands clung to the hilt of her blade, to their lifeline. Below his swaying feet he could see nothing but a cauldron of crushing death as the cascade disappeared into mist and rock.

The situation offered no words, just another countdown against her wiry strength while his numb fingers clenched themselves tight to the belt of her soaked trousers.

A desperate look to either side. An inspection ladder hung to the right against the slick, sheer cliff, mercilessly out of reach. Rigid, emotionless. He looked up at Anya, through the pouring water that slammed against his face he could see the rigid contours of the muscles up the entire length of her arms, arms that couldn't bear the weight of two people for long.

He didn't have time to think. He looked at the ladder again. He was naïve to think he could get to it, but it was their only route out alive.

He reached up, stretching his arm and fingers as far as he possibly could, the shift in his weight making Anya yelp in terror, the mind-bending drop rubbing its hands in anticipation.

In one movement he pushed the toe of his boot into the rock-face under the opening and half swung, half launched himself up, feeling his guts drop through his feet as he plucked the air and slammed his hand into the length of timber into which Anya had plunged her blade, folding his blue fingers onto it, forcing them to find any sort of grip that it would allow, the surface of the wood soft enough to butter the tips of his fingers and send him down if he made a fraction of a wrong move.

His fingernails offered only the most tenuous of grips, but he wasn't there the hang about. A quick shift to the right managed to buy him another yard, close enough to attempt a swing to the ladder.

One swing. One swing would do it. If only he could trust his freezing hands. All of a sudden it looked too far and in his moment's hesitation he was brought back by Anya's pallid shriek.

'I can't...' she cried. 'I can't hold on.'

He stared into the frightened face, saw the desperation looking back at him. Freezing, uncompromising water washed over the patchwork of blues and purples that were her hands, looking like they belonged to a beaten corpse, the water pummelling her face and shoulders.

Frank didn't wait. He leaped without thought, propelled himself across, his hands grabbing a rung. The ladder was solid and held his weight with ease but with the blood having left his fingers long ago, he couldn't be sure of his grip. Even so, without hesitation, he dropped his legs, hanging them loose and swung them back to Anya.

'Grab my legs,' he shouted, his voice barely audible over the relentless pounding and outpouring from the drain. She looked across. The gap between her hand and his right ankle was mere inches yet it must have looked like an impossible distance.

She'd need to let go of her dagger, the hilt of which she was completely bonded to, her hands locked onto it as she held on to life. Just the effort and the trust she'd need to put in herself to do what he needed her to do was enough to drain the most resolute person, someone with all their wits intact and pumped with unebbed strength while she looked completely spent, like she had nothing left to give.

The fear of a condemned woman approaching the scaffold had spread across her eyes, the deer waiting for the jaws of the wolf to lock around its neck. Final moments.

'I can't,' she hollered.

'Yes you can.' He shifted his position on the ladder, moving another dangerous inch to her. 'Look at me, Anya.' Her eyes, drained of the fight, met his. 'Yes you can. I'm not leaving here without you.'

'Frank, I can't.' He saw the slip of her hand, loosening, her cold, lifeless fingers gradually failing, sliding serenely from the dagger. 'I'm sorry.' One hand slipped away. She looked down, closed her eyes, accepting her fate as she prepared for the broad shoulders of death to bear her weight. 'I'm sorry.'

Then she fell.

44

From Death

Frank swung from the lower rung. In the split-second that Anya's hand abandoned the hilt of her dagger, he anchored his feet under her arms, crossing his heels behind her back, latching on to her like a newborn.

She let out a shriek as she grabbed him and clamped her arms to his calves, grabbing him behind the knees with nothing but blind instinct and hot, relentless terror as her companion. Shrieks followed by sobs, the hopeless sobs of someone on the edge of losing, convinced nothing can save them, disbelieving in miracles or mercy.

He felt the full pull of her weight, fought the burning muscles in his upper arms, the pull at his shoulders for as long as his momentum took him back, swaying like a frail sapling in a storm.

Anya hung from his legs, still hundreds of feet above the beckoning fingers of death. As they dangled above the yawning maw of Deadman's Scar, Frank was still certain that she'd drop, that all of her energy had been dragged from her and spat out by the melt-water and that she'd take him with her, but his last-gasp action appeared to pump new energy into her.

She pulled herself up, hollering, screaming with the effort as death pulled against her, gripping the soft flesh just underneath his ribcage, hauling herself further as Frank ground his teeth against the burning pain.

She forced herself up, her other hand clamping onto his shoulder before she found the security of the ladder, dragging her soaked, spent body over Frank, her knee connecting resolutely with his cheekbone.

A look up. The ladder disappeared at the top of the cliff, thirty feet or more above him. Thirty short feet; no distance, a laughable distance, a distance only a fool would scale, knowing a slip would end in a broken body being swept away by the Jixx. But they were both beyond that, now.

Then she was heading up. He watched her for a moment before following on Anya's sure and deliberate heels, rung after rung, water dripping steadily onto him from Anya's drenched clothes until they reached the top and collapsed, face down on the rocky surface of the cliff-top, guts heaving, nerves shattered, bodies broken. Wordless. Safe.

It took a few torrid, timeless minutes for the world to rest easily, for them to be sure they'd awoken from the nightmare before they pushed themselves to their knees, heavy breaths in the way of speech.

Anya grabbed him. She buckled her arms tightly around his neck, the weight of her arms on his shoulders, her forehead pressed against his, water running in a stream off the ends of their noses, eyes tight shut to try to banish the memories. He could feel the shivers running through her as she fought to level her breathing, could feel it in him, too.

Then they both burst into tears. Slow, heavy sobs prevented any words even though none were needed, none could begin to paint the picture of their escape from Etamin's house, minutes of their lives that he knew would never leave them, minutes that would forever be a stain on his memories that no amount of scrubbing would diminish.

They'd survived when they shouldn't have. Death had rushed at them from all angles and they'd dodged it. Just. A cat with barely one life left. But they'd survived.

Anya unwound herself and they both sat, knees high, heads bowed down between, hands clasping the back of their heads, drained beyond description, dragging themselves slowly back. Anya patted her hip, a movement to reassure herself. Their book, sodden and dishevelled, was miraculously still intact in her belt, pages crimped, purple leather cover mottled like the skin of a drowned corpse.

They'd got it back, they'd done what they'd entered Garrim to do, but Frank felt no sense of achievement or elation. The price had already gone beyond the means of the richest man in Byeland and would keep increasing all the time they were hemmed in by the mountain town, especially now Etamin sought him for a different purpose.

He raised his head and looked out across the gorge. The mouth of the storm drain exited at near right-angles to the main cliff face, shielding them from both the town and the alert eyes of the Kzarlac border post across the deep divide. Some fortune amongst their misfortune.

They sat on a small, flat and narrow plateau of rock away to the north east of the town, a dozen rough stone steps led up from the flat and on to the lanes of the eastern fringes, down to the bridge across the Jixx to the border.

They could stay there for the rest of the day and no one would know they were there. Only the wind found them as it whistled in from the east, had their teeth shaking and their soaking, chafing clothes clinging to their exhausted bodies.

Frank felt his muscles begin to quiver. Short spasms that he couldn't see coming, that twitched and twisted him as a reminder of their ordeal. Short spasms that would become continuous, uncontrollable shakes in no time. He knew it would be short minutes before the cold took hold, buried itself beneath his skin and he'd begin to lose control unless they got moving and found somewhere to thaw themselves, to dry themselves.

Safe they might be, but Garrim was intent on rubbing itself into their skin and settle in their lungs without hesitation.

The thought of Etamin's guards tracking them overground to the edge of the abyss set in his mind. It was unlikely they knew exactly where the storm drain exited but it wouldn't take them long to find out and, given what he'd revealed to Etamin, she would undoubtedly send a large arrest squad to see if the two of them had somehow made it out or, more likely, watch as they were catapulted to their deaths.

Waiting there was the strategy of fools.

He pushed himself to his feet, his clothes sagging heavy with the claws of meltwater that sunk back into his skin.

A quick look across the stone steps and down to the town. No sign of Lashkens or the Watch. Not yet.

'We need to go,' he said.

Anya just nodded and got to her feet, her skin like paraffin and her lips turning the colour of a fresh bruise. She looked in dire need of warmth, her face wan and wretched, half the girl who'd entered Etamin's bedchamber less than an hour before. The look of a candle flame that had nearly burnt out.

Frank, too, was completely penetrated by sour and painful cold. So cold he thought he would never be warm again. His fingers felt numb and weak, his nose endlessly running, the air cut his throat and nipped at his lungs and the wind blew cold through his clothes, sticking them to his flesh. He struggled to think straight. Cold and delirium were cosy bedfellows.

As if their teeth hadn't been kicked enough, snow started to drift down around them, swirling in the empty air beyond the cliff-edge, turning the brown and black rocks into grey ghosts. His only thought was to get back to the Gargoyle's Head as quickly as their circumstances allowed. Easy when he said it in his head but words and deeds can have different outcomes, even at the best of times.

He took Anya by the elbow and heaved her towards the stone steps. She sagged but then he saw her eyes sharpen, some light among the freezing fog as she shook him off.

'I'll be okay,' she said. Her voice shook unconvincingly. 'We need to get moving.'

245

45

THE COLD

If anyone had told Frank that, at some point in his life, he would sell his soul for the warmth of a fire, he would have laughed himself hoarse, but extreme situations bring with them the most humble and basic of cravings and he knew, at this point, he would trade anything he was asked without thought or hesitation just to rid himself of the cold.

Each step along the back alleys and pathways of the north-side came complete with the torture of the bitter wind and stinging snow as it snapped and tore at their soaking clothes, sticking them to their limbs like freezing, hungry leeches.

His shirt hugged tight against his skin and his trousers sagged at the waist with weight of water. Worst of all was the sucking of his sodden socks in his boots that slowed him down and numbed his toes.

He'd never been so cold. He'd never been so wet. It was in his bones, in his blood. It coated his skin and stung his eyes. It rolled down his neck and caught in his throat. It spoke to him and told him it would never leave and delighted in the great spasms it inflicted on his flinching muscles.

It would have been easier to tolerate had he been wearing nothing at all and all the time he fretted that he and Anya, conspicuous in their wretched condition, would be noticed. There were many sights in Garrim that were as unusual as they were commonplace but he couldn't say that two drenched and shivering teenagers would have been one of them.

The shakes were small, at first. Small, but he could feel them like the first burst of tiny bubbles as the pot starts to boil and knew they wouldn't stop, that they would only get worse. He could see it spreading over Anya as they edged across the levels towards the southern side and up through the mazey back-alleys towards the back entrance of the Gargoyle's Head which never seemed to get any closer.

The streets were deserted enough, the wind appeared to keep everyone from the eastern edge and, as they gradually climbed the southern slope, he had no idea if they'd been spotted, if the Watch had seen where they went but he was too desperate to care. He just needed to get to safety and safety didn't sit whistling on Garrim's street corners, nor did it show itself from the greys and blacks of the shadows. It had to be found.

Gradually, as swiftly as they could, they found themselves at the eastern entrance to the narrow road along which the Gargoyle's Head sat.

The back entrance to Duckett's kitchen was locked, bolted. Natural precautions, seriously taken.

Frank could have wept at its sight, a beacon of hope among all the shit, and hope had been in short supply since they arrived in the town.

He should have been careful, but his common sense had left him at the exit to the storm drain as he hammered hard on the thick wood, so hard he felt the pain from his fist through the numbness of his entire body. He didn't care if anyone along the street heard, he was beyond that and his tolerance for being out in the cold had long since left him.

Cas's face appeared at the window, then he was frantically clawing at the door's shackles, opening it and ushering them in.

They entered into the kitchen in silence, Cas's mouth unable to bring forth any words, concern immediately lighting his face.

For a moment he looked unable to think what to do first before he grabbed two stools and placed them in front of the fire, guiding them over before running for help and blankets while Frank and

Anya slowly prised their sodden, frozen clothes from their spent bodies, unable to stop their hands from shaking, their fumbling fingers not quite up to the job.

Though the fire blazed, the heat just seemed to bounce off him. Frank could barely feel it, so chilled as he was, but he knew it was there, prayed that it would start to kick life back into him and bring feeling to his toes and fingers that felt ready to drop to the kitchen floor.

Their dreadful ordeal was behind them, being in the dry comfort of the inn had been a distant dream since he awoke in Etamin's bed that morning, since he'd watch her butcher Simeon and put chains on Dagmar.

He felt the heat of his tears, the squeeze of his eyelids as he tried to keep them tethered. Yes, it was all behind them and, yet, there was more out of sight down the trail in front, ready to greet the Simbrian heir as he stuttered in his attempts to evade those that sought him.

Right now, though, it was difficult to think past the next minute, past the cold that seemed determined to stay firmly put, past the sensations of the swirls and eddies in his legs.

He and Anya sat, half-naked, staring into the snaking orange of the flames, icy water pooling on the floor around them, their bodies not allowing them to thaw. He turned to her.

'You okay?' Two short words that spoke a hundred.

She didn't look at him, just continued looking at the fire, fighting the shakes that were determined not to leave, contemplating two more deaths at the end of her blades that would leave their shadow, just as Simeon had said.

'Yeah,' she said, without conviction.

Pale faces and bluing lips still trembled as Cas returned, Duckett in his shadow, wrapping the two teenagers in dry, warm blankets, peeling them away from the outside which now seemed very far away, a different world. Few words but much concern to drag their freezing bodies back and stop the shakes from setting in.

The warming process was slow. Hot soup, whiskey, fire and more whiskey gradually bringing Frank and Anya back to life. Frank just sat there as Cas and Duckett fussed around him, paralysed and numbed to the core but he had never felt so grateful and was certain he would never feel so again if he lived to be a hundred.

'Take your time,' said Duckett, his words full of gentle concern. 'People here die from the cold if they're not careful.'

Frank gave him a grateful nod, thinking how the cold was well down the list of things that were likely to kill him here in Garrim. A thought to sober the staunchest drunkard and as Frank pulled his blanket tighter around his shattered limbs he knew this was no longer just about him.

They'd always looked out for each other, the four of them but, now Etamin knew he was the one to hand her the power she hungered for, the sole possessor of the ability to fire the Simbrian, he knew the rules of the game had shifted irrevocably.

She wouldn't just come after him. Now everyone who he'd ever known was a target in her brutal game and he knew she'd win at the first attempt, just as she had done with Simeon and the threat to Gabby. Gabby?

'Where's Gabby,' he said with an irrational sense that, because she wasn't in the room, she had been taken by the Watch or was running from a Lashken patrol. A baseless panic had him alert and eager like a rabbit anxious at the stilling of the breeze.

'Out looking for you,' said Cas. 'She was pacing like she had shards of glass on the soles of her feet. I said she should wait, that Anya would get you back, but she wouldn't listen, surprisingly. Went out again about an hour ago.'

As he spoke the door from the bar opened and Gabby walked in, wrapped up against the cold, her face dropping once she saw Frank sitting at the fireside. The sight of her lit a spark and untethered the butterflies in his stomach. For a moment he couldn't feel the cold and her appearance had tears rolling down his cheeks once more.

She didn't wait. Her coat and scarf fell in a heap on the floor as she shook them off and rushed to Frank, throwing her arms around him, drawing him in tight and burying her face into the blanket at his neck. He rocked on his stool, steadying himself against the passion, against the heaving sobs she swallowed like she hadn't eaten for a week. For a minute, Frank thought she was never going to let go, not that he would have minded.

She unwound herself and looked at him, tears spilling down the fawn skin of her cold cheeks. The pain and relief in her eyes were clear. Utter relief. He'd come back, part of her had clearly thought he wouldn't, all unspoken. The candle of hope had burned right down, but she made sure she kept the flame flickering for as long as she could, damned if she'd let it die out.

She leaned forward, pressing her lips hard to his, drawing him in, letting go only when she knew he understood. Then a smile, the fireflies.

'Nice to see you too,' he said, low and even as Gabby turned to Anya and threw her arms around her, pulling her in, wordless in her relief, her gratitude.

Frank noticed Gabby close her eyes tight and tighten her arms, imbuing Anya with warmth and love, with the thanks for a debt that could never be repaid before she loosened herself and kissed her on the cheek.

Anya's eyes met hers and something unspoken passed between them. A slight exchange of nods, a slight watering of the eyes. Frank knew Gabby would have wanted to be the one to venture to Etamin's house, that she would have insisted on being the one to prise him from the warped mind of the Kzarlac monster, but Anya had talked her out of it, presented herself as Frank's best chance for escape, the shadow that would slip in and away with less emotion, less chance of an error for which there was no margin.

Anya had been right, just. Only just.

Frank felt the comfort of the relief in the room, here with his closest friends, together, alive. They'd not hesitated to come for him, to risk their lives for him, a bond that would last a lifetime, one of which he'd never felt deserving, but he'd done the same, in the rush and twist of the storm drain, he'd abandoned his own safety to go after Anya despite the risk that they'd both be shattered at the bottom of Deadman's Scar. And he'd do it again, do it for any one of them, every time, without hesitation.

'What the hell happened?' said Gabby in a near-whisper, kneeling on the floor next to Frank, her hand on his knee.

Duckett stood back, his hard eyes diverting for a moment to the back entrance as Frank began to tell them about his few waking hours as a captive, Anya joining in when he tried his best to describe their escape and their nightmare in the drain, words faltering on his lips.

Recreating the details inside Etamin's house, though fresh in his mind, brought images Frank would have rather kept securely locked away. Images he knew he'd have to lock in a box, the lid to which he hadn't a hope of keeping shut. The bedroom, Dagmar, De Villiers. Simeon.

Simeon.

Frank found himself stumbling over his words as he relived the dying light in his uncle's eyes. He saw the mix of tears and cold steel in Anya's eyes as he described the savagery dealt on him by those who sought power. Not just Kzarlac. Not just Etamin. But Jackson. He was equally guilty and he could tell by the way her fists balled in her blankets and the steady stream of silent tears that ran down her pinking cheeks that Anya's desire for revenge would have her gut them all.

'I'd lay odds Simeon was compromised,' said Duckett. 'How many times have I warned you to be careful with your words?' Many. Too many. *Even the beer glasses have ears*, that's what Duckett would say to them. 'You can be as careful as you like, but there'll be spies everywhere. There's no shortage of villains happy to have a few crowns pressed to their palms for information. He was just unlucky.' Matter-of-fact from the ex-military man. He looked at the back door for the umpteenth time before walking over to it. 'Let's hope he hasn't attracted the wrong attention to my door.'

He checked it, an uncharacteristic look of uncertainty on his face, his steady hand pushing at the handle twice and rattling it in its frame to be sure it was secure even though he must have known trouble was more likely to just walk in through the front door and buy itself a whiskey.

46

THE SWITCH

It hadn't even the slightest scent of mission accomplished even if the book, the object that lay in the centre of their Simbrian journey, now resided safely in their hands, although safety, as he'd discovered the hard way, is a relative thing.

No relief, no feeling of the job having been done. Frank may have begun to feel warm and dry but, inside, he was hollowed out and cold and to add to everything he was now a marked man with a price on his head the size of which would give the jitters to any one of the gambling houses on the Ditch.

But having retrieved the book, they had no reason to stay.

It seemed easy when he said it, thought it – leave, go home. But things are usually harder in the doing.

The Watch would be in someone's pocket, probably Jackson's, but Duckett had tried to reassure them that there would be plenty of places they would go looking before they landed on his doorstep. Encouraging words that gave them no encouragement.

As the early winter light began again to fade and the inn became busier, Duckett left the four of them alone, all hung out in front of the fire, allowing Frank to spill the details about his weird conversation with Dagmar – how he knew about the seventh guardian and his assertion about protecting the Simbrian. Even as he recounted, he found himself wondering if he had been spun a tale, unconvinced. Dagmar was difficult to read, didn't show the usual signs and tells of dishonesty. He was far too adept in the pale arts for Frank to be sure if he was telling the truth in the face of his looming death.

'If he's protecting it, he's doing a pretty rubbish job of it,' said

Cas. 'Protecting doesn't mean going around killing guardians.'

'But he let Sapphire Hark go,' said Frank.

'Yes, but he killed Menetti and Ludlow Hums,' said Cas. He let out a confused breath. 'So it doesn't all quite add up.'

Anya coughed, a barking, throaty cough that ripped at the room. She pulled her blankets tighter.

'More whiskey?' said Gabby. A nod from Anya, dry swallows as Gabby poured her a glass. 'I think you should go to bed. And you, Frank.'

Frank didn't feel he could get to his feet, let alone climb a full flight of stairs even though the thought of lying in the comfort of his bed began to cushion his thoughts but he knew he had to, but not before he'd given them the bad news, another detail he'd left until Duckett was elsewhere.

'There's something I need to tell you,' he said, stirring images of Etamin. His eyes swept the three faces, anticipation written there. 'Something bad.'

'Bad,' said Cas. 'Like what you've already told us *isn't* bad. How can there be anything worse?'

Frank drew in a breath, not sure how this was going to go down, not after their near-death experience in the silent forest, an episode from which they were still healing, one that had cost them enough and undoing the good they'd done was yet another of Frank's mistakes.

'Etamin has the key.' He looked away, then felt himself wince. A glance back, the others looking at each other but offering no words. 'I had to, she was going to kill Simeon if I didn't so I handed it over...'

He couldn't finish, they knew the rest.

Anya stifled more coughing, her fist over her mouth.

'It doesn't matter,' said Gabby.

'Doesn't matter?' said Frank. 'Of course it matters. I've let us all down. Again.'

'No you haven't,' said Gabby.

'Yes I — '

'No, Frank,' said Cas. 'You haven't.'

Frank's quickly rehearsed apology stalled on his tongue, not quite understanding their understanding. He might be battered but he knew he didn't deserve their sympathy. He looked at Anya, who sat staring into the fire; surely she was imagining her hands around his neck or thinking she should have just left him to the whims of Kzarlac's finest, but she looked like she couldn't care less.

'What do you mean?' he said.

Cas took a step and crouched down beside him, a comforting arm around his shoulders. Cas looked up at Gabby, who gave him a slight nod.

'Look, mate, what you gave Etamin wasn't what you think it was.'

Frank was sure he couldn't have looked more puzzled.

'It was the key,' said Frank. 'I put it in the possessor before we left. Gabby gave it to me and I —'

'It was a fake,' said Gabby.

A what now? Frank felt his lips move but no words passed them. He looked at Cas, then to Gabby.

'The key I gave you. It was a fake,' said Gabby. 'You can thank Cas.'

Frank's eyes quizzed Cas, demanding he conjure some sense into the room.

'I thought it would be safer not to take the key with us,' said Cas. 'Just in case.'

'Turned out to be a good idea,' said Gabby, a glance to Cas. 'Perhaps you should become a seer?'

Cas smiled, no movement from Anya, just occasional sniffs.

'Sorry,' said Cas. 'I discussed it with Gabby and Anya and we agreed it was for the best.'

'No good having the heir and the key all in the same place,' said Gabby. Wise. 'So I got Blackburn to knock us up another.'

'Then where's the real key?' said Frank.

'Safe,' said Gabby.

By the way she said it, Frank could sense that was all he was going to get, that she had closed the cover and held it to tight her chest. A move to protect him.

Frank drew in a breath and nodded. Cas had done it for him, they'd all done it for him, he just wished they'd told him. He knew it wouldn't have saved Simeon, that Etamin would have slaughtered him anyway just to teach Frank a lesson, a lesson of which he would be the subject now he'd reprieved De Villiers.

'By the way,' he said. 'About the heir thing.'

47

LUCKY STARS

As things turned out, Duckett needn't have worried about them trying to leave immediately.

The night heralded the shivers and ended with the onset of cold sweats. The following morning Frank's throat felt like he'd been feasting on broken glass and his limbs felt like they'd been staked to the ground and hit with a hammer, keeping him from peeling himself from his bedsheets.

After the terrors of the previous day, the long frozen dunking in the chill of the storm drain, perhaps it was inevitable. A mark to let them know they hadn't escaped unscathed, that their liberty had a price but descending into the misery of a cold and fever was just loose change compared to the alternative he'd faced.

Still, his head drummed and just the thought of getting any part of himself out of bed drained any remaining energy from his bones.

Anya, too, had succumbed and lay curled in the warmth of her blankets, unmoving.

If the Watch or Etamin arrived now he'd probably agree to go with them as long as he could sleep his illness off in the soft and quiet of a comfortable bed, even one with silk sheets.

Duckett had told them to stay put and, as if in collaboration, the town was warning them to do the same until they had a sure way of getting through those that sought them, knowing there would be eyes everywhere.

Not only the Watch, a member of whom they'd half killed, but Etamin's Lashken guards, two of which Anya had dispatched – a pitiless, relentless cocktail of thugs and killers hungry for revenge with a passion for punishment, the thought of which made Frank's small room above Duckett's bar seem even smaller, with a large, bright target painted on his door.

He quickly reached the bottom of the curve, the heavy and penetrating aches in his limbs starting to feel less tender as the days passed and the level of phlegm in his throat receding to an irritating and persistent trickle. Gabby and Cas did their best at playing nursemaid, supplying hot drinks laced mildly with honey or generously with whiskey and keeping out of the way as much as necessary to stay any spread of fever while all Frank could do through his sniffing and raw coughing was look out of the small window at the bright, early-winter sky that had settled over the mountains but failed to bring much in the way of cheer to the four of them, locked inside the inn, awaiting recovery.

But he soon began to feel his old self stepping into his tired and restless body which, in turn, led to fresh thoughts of what Garrim had served up for them and the scant likelihood of getting through the western pass untroubled.

They would soon outstay their welcome and, as each day passed there was always the looming certainty of a knock at the door, of another Manville Symes poking his filthy nose around, a kind of sixth sense that had Frank wired, primed to run despite the viral aches that played heavy tunes on his bones.

On the positive side, if that's what you could call it, he couldn't believe Etamin or Jackson would think he and Anya were alive, knowing they'd pitted their luck against the shuddering ice-water under the town, knowing where the storm drain led. If they'd gone over the edge, no one would find their bodies for days, weeks. Perhaps that might give them the window of opportunity they needed once they were all fit enough to make a run for it, to keep surviving. Being dead had its advantages.

But Etamin wasn't easily fooled and the vile ultramancer was the refuge of abilities of which he had only scratched the surface.

They had survived the storm drain, but he feared she had the cunning and acumen to make her suspect any reports of his death might well be premature.

***

His scars were healing on the outside, bruises fading, cuts vanishing – but not all wounds are visible. It had been four days since he and Anya had arrived back from the north-side. Four days since the freezing waters had tried hard, but failed to carry them to their deaths. Four days that had Frank sleeping fitfully, waking to the sound of echoing water, or Anya's screams or Simeon's face as the life disappeared from his eyes.

He relived all of it a hundred times, deep wounds that showed no signs of growing scabs, promising to rob him of the rest he needed to make a decent fist of getting out of Garrim. He knew fighting it was pointless and he had to hope they would fade in time but hope had disappeared into the distance, had run ahead of him with little chance of catching it up.

Where the enclosed space of his room up in the Gargoyle's Head might have had him pacing, he found unusual comfort in it, as soothing as the honey that Gabby periodically brought to him. And, as the threat of contagion receded, she stayed with him, easing him back to normality.

Sometimes she'd sit on his bed and simply let the silence bind them, sometimes she'd just stay for a minute or two, tending the fire or fussing around his windows or bedclothes, but she always checked he was healing and he knew, when she disappeared from his room, that she and Cas were doing the same for Anya.

The weather amongst the Longshadows had calmed. For now. Bright azure skies that wouldn't have looked out of place above a silken sandy beach on a summer day breathed some normality into the shortening days and brought nights filled with wondrous starlight.

He knew the time was approaching when they'd make the collective decision to leave. It wouldn't be hard, all of them had choked on a gut-full of Garrim and slamming the door in its face would be nothing but a pleasure. Just another day or two, then the running would start.

***

He watched Gabby as she stood at the window, using her hand gripped in her sleeve to wipe away the cold moisture that had become a permanent fixture on the small panes of glass.

She looked out and up, bunching her shoulders.

'The stars are bright tonight,' she said before pulling the curtains shut and clambering onto the bed next to him, shifting herself up to the pillow and settling in the crook of his arm, lacing her slender fingers through his. He sensed her quiet, slightly detached, something on her mind.

'You okay?' he said.

She shrugged, curling her knees up, pressing her shins against him. She didn't offer a response, instead he could feel her building up to something. So he waited.

'I remember the clear nights,' she said, like she was referring to a ghost that haunted her from time to time. 'The clear nights when we were drifting across the sea, after we escaped.' She paused. 'Funny, such beauty in the middle of the nightmare.' She stilled for a moment. Frank tightened his grip around her shoulder and went to draw her in but she pushed herself up, tucking her legs underneath her, her eyes on the curtains as if something sinister lurked outside, waiting to shatter the glass.

'A starry night always brings the memories back. Sometimes, on clear nights, I can feel the swell of the water at my feet even though I'm nowhere near the sea.'

Frank struggled to find any meaningful words. She looked at him, her eyes filled will sadness and distant fear.

'During the nights, while we drifted, my Mum used to say that there was a star that shone for everyone. For me, for Elly. We just had to keep looking until we found it and it would keep us safe.' Her eyes watered and she looked away. 'It was her way of keeping the terrors from our young minds, distracting us, playing games. So we would spend the night looking for one to call our own but I could never choose. So many. Always too many and there was always something wrong with the ones I picked out. Too bright, too dim, too close to another.' A rueful smile. 'Then, one night, the night before we were rescued, there was this terrifying storm and someone fell from the boat and we lost him.' She paused and Frank could almost feel her trying to tiptoe through her thoughts. 'I didn't think I could ever be so frightened but when the clouds cleared and the stars shone again I picked one out straight away and spent the rest of the night wishing it to deliver me safe and sound somehow. I don't think I closed my eyes once. I watched it until dawn, making sure it didn't disappear, that it was keeping watch over me. Then a boat spotted us and we were picked up.' She looked at him through the tops of her eyes. 'It's still up there and I still believe its watching over me, keeping me safe.' A glance to the window. 'Sometimes I can't bear to look, just in case it's gone. Silly, really.'

Frank knew that some of the simplest stories were the most difficult to tell, kept locked in a box for no one to hear, or just a select few. Brave deeds aren't just the domain of the battlefield.

'I think it's a beautiful thought,' said Frank. 'I keep forgetting you've been through so much and still you've never stood back from what we're doing.'

Gabby played with her knuckles and shrugged.

'Perhaps it's in my blood, now. Like I've been marked. I didn't know why I was spared and others died, but I suppose it was so I could do this. And I'd have never met you.'

The words filled him up.

'If you believe in fate and that sort of stuff,' he said.

'Do you?'

'I'm not sure. If I did, I'd have to say it's got a pretty rubbish sense of humour, the way it's played my hand.' He looked back towards the curtained window. 'I doubt if there's a star that shines for me or, if there was, it burned out years ago.'

She smiled sweetly.

'Then you can share mine.'

Her eyes sparkled brighter than anything in the sky outside, their beauty offloading some of the weight and, for a minute, the world seemed a better place.

Whatever star was shining over them in the aftermath of his ordeal at the hands of Etamin and the whole gutter-swilling stay in Garrim, it would have used a lifetime of luck already and, as Frank lay next to her, he knew a hundred more couldn't lift the death sentence that was part of his existence and had been since the day he'd been born.

He knew it, she knew it, they all knew it but in Gabby's telling of her story, he didn't want to bring it up, didn't want to think about the difficult, unknown road ahead. All he wanted was to be with her.

The following morning ushered in more bright sun that poked at the curtains, sending a long sliver of light across the bedroom ceiling. The weather had obviously had enough of pissing all over Garrim, for now at least, and decided to smile for a while, doubtlessly brewing more of the hard stuff for the coming days, confirming to Frank that they needed to be away before they found themselves trapped by a dump of snow that might block the western pass.

He braved getting out from under the covers and away from the warmth of Gabby's body to pull the curtains slightly open, brightening the greys in the room, not staying out of the bed for longer than the freezing morning needed.

As he pulled the covers back over him he felt Gabby's arm across his chest, pulling him over pressing her lips to his. She propped herself up on her elbow, her wayward hair tumbling in dark ringlets over her face which he brushed aside.

'Sleep well?' she said with a slow, fond drop of her eyelids.

He nodded. He hadn't. Etamin had followed him through the night, chasing him through his breathless dreams, red flame tethering him, death not far behind. He pushed the thoughts back, hoping Gabby wouldn't notice the disquiet on his face when a gentle knock at the door had both him wired and looking up.

A spike of irrational dread was followed by relief as the door opened slightly and Anya's face appeared. She pushed it open, Cas's scrawny frame at her shoulder following her in.

It was the first time Frank had seen her since they'd returned, soaked and frozen, to the Gargoyle's Head.

'Sorry to intrude,' she said. She looked at Frank. 'You look much better.' A smile, slightly forced.

'So do you,' he said. She didn't, she looked like a wax figure. A pale imitation of the girl who'd been his saviour, who had come for him with teeth bared and steel flashing but had barely made it out the other end.

Frank and Gabby propped themselves up as Anya took a short stride to the side of the bed, their book gripped firmly in her left hand.

There was something in Anya's manner that drew him. Not the slow, pasty movements of someone raised from the dead as she sat on the bed, not that. She was normally relaxed and languid when it was just the four of them, not taking too much too seriously but he could see the tension on her brow and it was clear in her voice as she said:

'I think you should take a look at this.'

48

THE BOOK

Certain words demanded your attention and she immediately had theirs. The stiffness in her voice, the serious tone she took as she sat herself next to Gabby were rare things on Anya. Cas dropped himself at the foot of the bed, propping himself up on an outstretched arm.

Anya tossed the book on the bed, its leather-bound cover frayed and slightly tattered at the edges, war wounds from its travel alongside them, but the pages were undeniably unscathed despite being carried submerged in the frozen waters under the town.

Frank had forgotten about it, like pretending it didn't exist would allow him to think of fonder things, not that that was going particularly well.

It should be falling apart, the paper soiled and crumpled, the strange writing smudged and faded but, even now, it looked unharmed by anything the Simbrian journey had thrown its way.

Frank and Gabby looked at the book, then back to Anya, asking her the question. Anya dipped her hand into her breast pocket and pulled something out.

Even among the assorted greys of the shadows in Frank's bedroom there was the immediate flash of aquamarine as the scant light from the gap in the curtains found the smooth body of the familiar stone that Anya held up between the thumb and forefinger of her right hand.

Zanmir's eye.

The fabled gemstone that they'd prised from the gutless hands of Manville Symes, that Dagmar had been prepared to kill Gabby for and that Jackson had pocketed once they'd returned to Byeland with the black stag. Frank had forgotten about it, but he could feel his interest shaking down any remaining malaise in his bones.

'It was in the desk in Etamin's house,' said Anya. 'I thought I'd rehome it again, seeing as Jackson appears to have kept it for himself.'

A nod of appreciation from Cas. Anya drew in a lengthy sniff and barked a dry cough into her fist.

'But that's not it,' she continued. 'I was thinking why Jackson would have it. Why he would bring something so rare and valuable to meet with Etamin. You remember the conversation at your gran's cottage when she said it might help read and understand the Simbrian.' Nods from the others, Frank's mind conjuring images of the last black stag and Jackson's untimely visit after they'd returned from Kzarlac. 'And that Hoffs created it with the sole purpose of allowing Zanmir to read and decipher coded messages.' Frank felt his face crease into squint, not sure of the path down which Anya was leading them. 'Well, it got me thinking. I remember Jackson saying it could be used for enchanted texts.' She looked at Gabby. 'Your mum told us the strange marks and blots in our book were definitely an enchanted text, even though its translation was beyond her.' She paused, looking at the gemstone that sat in the palm of her hand. She looked up. 'So I thought I'd have a look at the book through this.'

She turned the gem back and forth as the room held its breath. Frank just stared at Anya as what she was saying began to filter through. The smug, scheming Jackson had tossed them a different gem, one contained in his words, one that they'd not caught at the time. How they hadn't made the connection at the time immediately annoyed him, his disappointment in himself making him focus more blame on the Byeland chief.

'I think Jackson may have done the same,' said Anya. Her voice beginning to split as she gulped down dryness to avoid coughing.

Frank sat up further and let the blanket fall away, heedless of any chill in the room. He picked the book up from the bed as if it would fall apart in his hands, a delicate pressed flower that would disintegrate if he were to drop it.

With care, he opened it to the first page, to the image of two crossed arrows underneath a star, the symbol of Hums and his dynasty, then on until he reached the pages of purple and black blots and marks that littered the end of the book, pages that were bound up in, and protected by, an unholy curse.

He stopped at the first of such pages, pressing his thumb up the centre to keep it open while he looked at Anya once more.

She held her hand out to Frank who took the gleaming gem in his hand, letting it rest in his palm and weighing it carefully. Beyond riches. Beyond understanding. Did Zanmir's eye hold the key? Anya's unspoken words told him it did. Gabby dipped her head, a sign for him to get on with it.

'Go ahead,' said Anya.

Frank got up and stood at the window, pushing the curtain fully across, adjusting his position so the light was behind him, holding his hand up until the early winter sun latched on to the solid gem, cutting its way through swiftly and surely.

A vivid ray of turquoise light filtered through and dazzled the dusty wooden floor.

He lifted the book so the beam of light struck the open page, bright light danced in blue sparkles, offering up the book's secrets and inviting him on.

Frank moved the stone in front of his eye, careful not to subdue the sunlight, until he was looking directly through the middle of the gem, just as Zanmir would have done during her daring and dangerous forays into Kzarlac.

He remembered Jackson's telling of the story and felt like he was stepping back, feeling the spirit of the courageous spy at his shoulder.

Through the stone the light bent and twisted in a spiritual path, a vortex illuminating the paper, drawing Frank into a different world beyond. He knew both the stone and the book were imbued with enchantments, were mystical beyond his understanding but nothing could have prepared him for what he saw.

49

REVEALED

The moment he'd seen movement on the page, Frank felt like he was entering a different plane of existence, that or the delirium of his illness still stalked him. The signs of the otherworldly beckoned him in with a spectral flick of its head.

The odd flecks and pen strokes that had forever been beyond their understanding picked themselves up and assembled themselves on the page.

It wasn't possible, yet they began to tell Frank their story, gathering themselves into a small, transparent sphere that lifted itself from the page and rotated slowly before his eyes.

It was the thing of dreamweed. He was tripping, hallucinating, surely.

He'd stretched his thumb to where the orb hovered and tried to touch it, only to see the tip pass through the spectre of an image that the eye had pulled from the surface of the page. A glance to Anya.

'You see it too,' she said.

A statement, not a question from the girl who had performed the same ritual, her face loose and wondrous, a sign that she, too, had grasped at the air in an attempt to touch the sphere that had appeared out of the depths of the page.

'Turn the page,' she said.

Frank adjusted his grip on the eye, feeling a tentative sensation in his fingertips, Anya's words setting him on edge as she simply nodded for him to have a second look through the gemstone.

Once again, Frank positioned the stone in the daylight and peered through. Once again, the lines on the page bonded, mutating into the orb. Anya flicked her head to the side, a silent request that Frank turn the page.

Frank obliged, an unexpected flurry of nerves gripping his stomach as he watched the orb lift itself away from the book and travel slowly from its previous page and settle on the new one, rotating, waiting.

The lines and blotches on the new page began to churn, caught in their own current of sorcery, spinning like a child's top until they fused to form a long shaft which angled itself out of the paper, making Frank jerk his shoulders back to avoid it.

The book was only slightly bigger than Frank's palm, but the shaft appeared far longer and Frank resisted the urge to reach down and grasp it, knowing whatever had been conjured from the pages was an illusion, not meant for idle or uninterested eyes, aimed only at those who had ridden the journey, who bore the scars of the Simbrian quest and had survived to tell the tale. The Simbrian had served up many strange things, but this had to be the most bizarre by far.

Then both images moved, the orb circled before settling itself on top of the shaft. The image stilled, waiting once more, a silent whisper for Frank to continue, urging him to turn the page.

He flicked at the edge of the paper and as the page settled, the combined three-dimensional picture lifted itself off the book and came to rest on the new page with an easy flow.

Frank waited, his eyes flicking from the image that held itself with authority in mid-air through the lens of Zanmir's eye, to the page.

This time the flecks and blots twisted themselves into what appeared to be a small piece of cloth which floated to the top of the page, its surface rippling as if it were caught in a constant breeze, then out and over the top of the orb, wrapping itself tightly around it, covering it completely.

Frank could feel himself shaking his head, could feel the others' eyes on him.

Words; that was what he and the others had expected from the enchanted text. Words that took the challenge of the Simbrian at least a pace forward, words that gave the answers to the questions they'd not been near solving, but the vivid images that passed before his eyes had him reaching into himself, stretching his fingers to find some sense in the bizarre picture show that played out through the centre of Zanmir's fabled jewel.

The spectacle, wrapped in wonder, continued as, with a slow hand, he slid the next page across. Once more the image followed, a slow glide to its next position where a small, pointed object, like a large needle, gathered from the bruise of ink stains on the paper. It lifted itself above the covered orb, then, unhurried, pushed itself through the top, sinking down and through, securing the small sphere to the shaft.

The image hovered, awaiting Frank's attention, patiently asking him to turn the next page so it could tell him more of its story, its riddle. He could sense the questions on the lips of the others, their desire to quench their thirst for the knowledge he was unwrapping, but Anya stilled them with a slight raise of the hand until Frank had finished what she'd asked of him.

He lifted the page, the unusual assembly followed silently and obediently and all the time Frank asked it for a response, asked himself to try and decipher what he was being shown. He could feel the movement in his lips but was sure he'd stopped breathing.

The next page showed a flat disc being threaded onto the bottom end of the shaft, travelling all the way up, stopping just below the orb, followed by a second, similar object that also threaded itself on and stopped an inch or two below the first before the final image revealed an oval-shaped object which circled the shaft in a slow, deliberate motion, finally coming to sit between the two discs in a snug fit.

The image lingered before the oval opened to a tar-black aperture, drawing Frank's eye, grabbing him and holding him still.

For a second he thought he heard screaming, deep pitiless

screaming. The unholy sounds of the damned and deranged filling his head, spilling from the page. For a second he thought it was going to consume him, draw him into its world and bind him to the pages of the book. A shudder ran up his spine, nothing to do with the cold. He'd imagined it, surely. It was only a picture. Yes, he was sure he'd imagined it.

He looked up at the others, mouth open wide, the book and its unfathomable contents robbing him of speech.

It took a long few minutes for both Gabby and Cas to conduct the same ritual with Frank and Anya watching in silence as they delved into the warped and absurd world created by his mother. A world none of them were conditioned for, that meant nothing to them, despite their long Simbrian journey.

Finding guardians was one thing, being party to the wild enigma that was Rebecca Forbes catapulted them to a different level of understanding, a place where they had previously been uncomfortable visitors but were now expected to inhabit, to decipher and Frank knew the book, thus far so shrouded in enchantment, was revealing a new pathway for them to take.

'This is impossible,' said Gabby. 'No one, no one normal that is, could even begin to do this.' She turned to Frank. 'I remember the script in the book was beyond even my Mum's knowledge, but this. Who enchants a book and has it run us a picture show? And why?'

Frank nodded. The book had played its masquerade, hiding its true self like the dapper rogue who silently steps among the gambling tables in Garrim, relieving people of their coin and wallets while standing beside them like an innocent. It had done its job well.

'I've no idea what is this telling us?' he said.

Anya looked up from the book.

'They're instructions,' she said.

50

IMPOSSIBLE

Instructions? Instructions for what?

Frank could tell they all thought it, that none of them were even beginning to put the pieces of this one together.

The odd pictures in the book might once have set the touch-paper of Frank's curiosity alight, might have had the natural interest of youth heading to find out more, to work out the riddle. But not now. It had all the promises of another quest and he couldn't face another, not when Etamin was about to gather in the seventh and final guardian and start her own journey to find him or anyone associated with him and end them all.

He didn't possess the energy, his brain was still fogged from illness and wouldn't allow him to think beyond the rest he still needed, let alone search for a meaning to what they'd all just witnessed. There was no need for a wave of disappointment to wash over the room, but there it was, sapping them of any remaining interest, not that there was much to go around.

He looked from Gabby to the floor, eyes unfocused in a sorry attempt to drum up an element of fascination from his battered and fatigued body, but whichever way he turned he ended up down a dead-end, keeping him silent.

'I'm going back to bed,' he said, dumping himself down and pulling the blanket up, hoping they'd take it as their cue to leave him to his gloom, until Cas spoke.

'You know,' said Cas. 'I can only think of one sphere we've come across in the whole of this mess.'

So could Frank. The only orb remotely associated with the

entire Simbrian adventure was that which sat confined in the possessor on the small table in his room and, despite his reluctance, Cas's observation stirred his interest, albeit with a very small spoon.

'What about it?' said Gabby.

'The first picture in the book,' said Cas. 'The orb.' Gabby nodded. 'There's only one orb we've ever run into during the whole of our Simbrian saga.'

Frank sat forward and checked himself, pressing his fingertips into his scalp, digging deep into his memories to confirm there'd been nothing similar, something he might have missed or overlooked before. There wasn't. Cas had already sifted through the dirt and debris and managed to pull out a needle.

'The Elemental ball,' said Gabby.

'I was given the Elemental ball by Wordsworth Hums,' said Frank.

He drew back the blanket and stood up next to the small table where his stuff lay. He fumbled in the possessor, drawing out the small sphere that had been part of their lives since that fateful day under Excelsus academy, in Hums's hideaway, when Frank had been handed it with instructions to keep the Simbrian safe. The ball that clasped the elements, that held them, waiting to be unleashed, that only responded to him. Why?

He inspected it, turning it around in his fingers before laying it in the flat of his palm where it made its mesmerising transformation from a dull brown ball to a vivid and colourful living object, full of mystery, full of trickery. A conspirator, awaiting Frank's spoken command.

'Hums gives me the ball. The ball appears out of the enchanted scribblings in our book. The book that was put together by my Mum, her pathway to the guardians. But to what else?'

They all looked from the sphere to the book as if either of them might cough up some answers.

'But he didn't give you a rod or a stick of any sort, though,' said Cas.

Frank pursed his lips and shook his head. Cas was right, perhaps there was no connection, perhaps it was just the nearest straw at which he was able to grasp. Still he considered the ball, floating an inch off his open hand as the picture in the book had mimicked.

'No, but Felix Menetti did,' said Gabby, bringing Frank to his senses.

'What?' he said.

'Felix Menetti let you keep his dad's staff, the one he made into a makeshift oar when we came back from Unwanted Island, the one with the strange markings carved into it.' She looked at Cas. 'Coincidence?'

Cas shrugged.

'Two gifts from the first two guardians that exactly match the first two pictures. What odds would we get down at the Lid?' He looked at Frank. 'Have you still got it?'

A nod. He still had it.

'It's under my bed at Polly's,' he said.

Frank felt himself nodding, more to himself than the others, drawing up as much recollection as he could about his encounters with the remaining guardians – Edwina Chetto, Sapphire Hark, his dad, his mum.

'She gave me her handkerchief,' he said, not quite believing the words as they passed his lips. He looked at the faces of the others, one by one, noting the furrow appear on Gabby's brow. 'Edwina Chetto, when I was consoling her in her room. She gave me her handkerchief to wipe her tears. I kept it. It's in my bedside table.' The change in their mood was unmistakeable. Frank didn't need to draw on his senses to detect it as it thickened around them, a friendly beast that walked amongst them, that prowled in between them and cut the sound from them. Frank could tell they were on the edge of something important, the slow creep towards the verge of the book's secret, its purpose.

Whatever journey it had taken them on, it had guided them to this point, stood them shoulder to shoulder, side by side on the edge of something dark, staring into a pit of discovery, inviting them to jump.

Frank couldn't shake Edwina Chetto from his head, of him taking the handkerchief and putting it into his pocket as her breath jerked with her sad, pitiful sobs, trying to understand the significance of the simple action that connected him to her and to the book. No one offered an explanation until Anya spoke, pouring a bucketful of oil onto the already raging fire of his curiosity:

'The skewer,' she said. 'The thing Sapphire Hark used to lock herself in and open the door to the hidden room in her house. Remember?'

Frank locked his eyes on to hers, moving another piece of the puzzle into place.

'She gave it to me,' he said, not quite believing himself. 'And she was caught before I could give it back.' He looked at Gabby. 'I still have that, too.'

The piece of cloth in their moving images, the small pointed object that speared the ball, securing it to the shaft. Four items, four gifts from four of the guardians, four exact matches for four images in the puzzle the book had laid bare.

'What's it all about?' said Gabby, her voice hushed as if she spoke any louder she might awaken something she'd regret. 'How can the four guardians give you four random objects that then appear in our book? Not just appear, but combine to form some weird object. How is that even possible?'

It wasn't possible. Frank knew that and he could see it in the expressions of the others. His mother had put the book together as she was creating the first form of the Simbrian that she then destroyed, along with herself, over fifteen years ago.

There was no conceivable way she could have known that it would fall into Frank's hands, hands that would touch items from each of the guardians she had so secretly disguised in its first seven pages. It wasn't possible, not by anyone's hand and yet here they all were, bringing the whole story to life in the absence of any credible alternative.

One coincidence may have been okay, but four? And it wasn't just four, not as Frank's head took the next few strides amongst the puzzle's untwisting vines. There were three more guardians.

'My Dad hasn't given me anything,' he said, but as he said it he immediately realised that wasn't true.

He lifted his hand, stopping as he reached chest height, not wanting to bring it any further. A memory filled his head, a long forgotten image of him as a seven year old boy, sitting under the oak at the top of the wildflower meadow on the farm with his dad, both looking out over the shallow valley. Lawrence Penny had lifted the locket over his head and placed it tenderly and carefully around Frank's neck. *'It's time you had this,'* he'd said, his voice as gentle as the lambs in the field across the stream.

It was the only object that his dad had ever given him that had belonged to him and there it was, hanging against Frank's beating heart, a passenger throughout their journey and a talisman that had steered Frank through the most delicate and most deadly of situations. Now he felt the weight of its guilt, its collusion.

Frank threaded his fingers around the silver chain and lifted the small oval pendant so it rested in his palm, the delicate fretwork warm against his skin. The oval object that appeared as the final illustration in their book. It was hard to comprehend. Five images, five guardians, five objects.

He looked up.

'I don't get it,' he said.

No one offered anything. Not a surprise, they didn't get it either.

'But that leaves your mum?' said Cas.

Frank could detect the unsaid meaning in his words and it was plain on his face – she'd been dead for all but a year of Frank's life. She'd taken a fragment of the Simbrian from Moonhunter's mother to spare her teenage lover from the cheerless burden it heralded and used it to set herself on a path for something he was yet to fully understand.

Yet Cas was right. She was the sixth guardian.

She'd borne the mantle and willingly headed into the dark maw of Kzarlac to give it up to Dagmar.

She'd sacrificed herself and left him nothing, nothing but a soulless hollow deep inside him that could never be filled, a painful slice from the thinnest blade that refused to heal no matter how he tried to bind the wound, she'd robbed him of the love to which all children were entitled and still he didn't know why.

He felt the tears, felt the emotion run hot over his skin until a soothing hand on his arm began to staunch the flow of his mixed feelings.

'It's okay, Frank,' said Gabby.

'Don't worry,' said Anya. 'We have each other and, somehow, we'll all make sense of this together.'

But Frank barely heard them. His mind replayed the pictures in the book, the two missing pieces of whatever strange thing it was showing them – two flat discs.

He placed the Elemental ball carefully back on the table and looked down, realisation rising from his toes.

His hand hovered over one of the Dahke passes that lay to the side of the possessor, thinking back to his gran's cottage, shaking it from the small wooden box that contained his mum's love letters from his dad.

He could feel the reluctance in his hand, had to dare himself to pick it up and admit to himself that it fit the puzzle.

'She left it for you,' said Gabby.

Frank looked at her.

'But I found it by complete accident,' he said.

'Frank, none of this is an accident,' she said.

'Six coincidences,' said Cas. 'That's some accumulator.'

Six completely random objects, given over by six specific people, all of which had shown themselves in the small, unassuming book that Frank's mother had meticulously put together. Completely impossible, implausible yet, there it was.

That left the second flat disc. The final part of the bizarre animation.

Frank dropped the Dahke pass in his hand, letting it clatter on the small table before reaching down and picking up the other, the one he'd been handed by Dagmar during their ill-fated ordeal in Alsha Kar.

He held it in the flat of his hand, thinking, digging deeper and deeper into the confusion in his mind. It would make sense except it didn't, it didn't fit. He knew through his unfinished conversation that Dagmar had never been a guardian and although he was up to his neck in the whole saga, Frank knew that wasn't it.

'Dagmar's not the final guardian,' he said. 'He told me he knows who it is. It's not him.'

'But he gave you the Dahke pass,' said Cas.

'I know,' said Frank, fingering the black disc. 'But this is in the book.' He looked up. 'I don't understand.'

'Frank,' said Cas. 'This is the Simbrian. When have we ever understood?'

Frank had never known how clever or ingenious his mother had been, but the book, the small unassuming object that they'd come to Garrim to retrieve had them scratching their heads for the rest of the day until they thought it best to put it down and forget about it, no further down the pitch-black road than when they started and now it felt like someone had turned the lights down further.

If only he'd inherited some of her gifts. Perhaps he had; could use them to help but had no idea of how to ignite them, like staring at a locked door having no clue where the key might be. He could tug on it all he liked, try to kick it in or batter it off its hinges but access to the world his mother had inhabited undoubtedly required more finesse.

He'd thought Moonhunter's notion of something lying dormant inside him, waiting to be roused from its slumber, was fanciful, that she'd just said it in the heat of their conversation although perhaps that's what the head of Excelsus could detect.

Excelsus never makes mistakes, that had always been drummed in to them during their short tenure at the academy, that there was always a reason why someone got an invitation. He'd never had any talent, not in the way Gabby, Cas and Anya had, but now the faint notion that the whole Simbrian quest had called to him from within Moonhunter's carefully penned letter had him reconsidering.

And so another day passed within the limits of the Gargoyle's Head with thoughts of heading home scattered amongst the lack of ideas about the book and the message it was trying to wipe off on them.

The dark drew in early now, a match for Frank's mood as he finally felt himself rid of the fever and aches that had sucked his body dry of energy and left his brain mired in a cosy blanket of fog but he still needed an early night in the hope that a new morning would pump fresh ideas into him.

That, and it was time to leave to search for the secrets that lay in his bedroom back at Polly's.

Gabby came and sat beside him on the bed, a rush of anticipation, the crackle of desire as she slid up to him, placed her hand on his cheek and turned his face to hers. He drank in the softness of her eyes, the colour of freshly ground coffee, and the contours of her perfect lips as she drew him towards her and pressed them to his. Her mouth opened slightly and he felt the warmth of her tongue on his, the light pressure of her hand on the back of his head pulling him deeper before releasing him.

'Stay with me,' he said.

'What makes you think I was going anywhere,' she said, turning to the candle, extinguishing the flame with a short, hard breath.

The morning was gearing itself up for another fight, threatening to spill great chunks of snow from the fresh batch of dark clouds that had brewed once more over the fissure in the Longshadows.

Frank had woken in darkness an hour ago, content to just lay and watch Gabby as she slept, tracing the outline of her jaw with his eyes, the stretch in her neck and slender collar bones, wondering if sleep still held him in a sweet dream as he watched the gentle rise and fall of her chest, the delicate flicker of her eyelids.

The untethered coils of her dark hair had fallen over the soft skin of her cheeks and he resisted the urge to brush them away. The grey shadows in the room, lit only by the dying embers in the small hearth, stirred the thick silence, bringing Frank a moment of calm in the middle of the Simbrian storm. Gabby brought him calm. She always had.

He lay there recalling the many times he'd nearly lost her, both to the twists of their bad decisions and by his own petulant behaviour, but here she was, unwavering in her loyalty to him and their friends, ceaseless in her compassion.

He knew that under her harsh exterior and formidable attitude lay something else, the frightened girl who had fled from Prismia at the age of seven. She kept her hidden, mostly; refused to let it define her and he loved her for that. Not just for that, for everything she stood for.

He pushed himself up, careful not to wake Gabby, and brought his knees to his chest, allowing his eyes to adjust to the creep of the dawn.

He looked out of the window through the half-pulled curtains, wondering if they'd be shackled to the town by another unrelenting tumble of snow, that they might have to put off any plans for an escape back to Rhaeder. Not that they had a plan, and you always need a plan, however rubbish, and trust you can see it through.

Bad weather meant the transport wouldn't make it to the outskirts of Garrim. It would be forced to stop at one of the villages in the foothills further down and any travellers would be left with the decision to make the rest of the journey on foot or turn back.

The idea of having his feet frozen and relapsing back into the pitiful aches and coughs of the last few days made him pull the blanket up and draw his shoulders together but they needed to get out, get back home so they could recover the remaining items in Frank's attic bedroom and try to start piecing together what the book had shown them. It was definitely time to move on.

He couldn't shake the book's images, couldn't think what his mum had meant, what she was trying to tell them. The early hours were never a great time to be thinking, not for teenage brains but he knew looking for the final guardian was like like trying to push the snow back up into the sky. Pointless. Etamin had them.

Still the book's collection of objects picked at him and wouldn't leave him alone as if it still had a final card to play.

His weary eyes travelled to the small table where his stuff lay dumped in a pile, ready to be packed and taken back to Rhaeder.

The Elemental ball, the possessor, the Dahke passes sat together. Two black discs, each edged with gold, one of which he understood, one of which made no sense, just a solid reminder of the connection between his mum and Dagmar, of the blood that flowed through him, blood that would be spilled and savoured unless he could get out of Garrim.

Dagmar was bound to the Simbrian, more than they ever were, it ran in his veins, controlled his waking hours. The image of him pressing the pass into Frank's palm persisted in Frank's mind. But he wasn't a guardian, so what was he missing?

Gabby stirred, turning herself onto her side with the sort of murmur it's only possible to make in your sleep. He looked at her, silhouetted against the bed, wondering what she was dreaming.

He ran his fingers along her exposed shoulder with a gentleness he'd forgotten he possessed. For a moment he thought of their future, of a life with her. But, then, it doesn't do you any good to dream of the things you know you can't have, not when you're a hunted man and he was sure Gabby didn't bargain for a life on the run.

He closed his eyes, allowing himself to give in to the fatigue that wouldn't leave. He'd make the most of their time, for however long it lasted, at least he owed that to himself.

He lay back on the bed, turned and curled himself into Gabby and fell back to sleep.

51

THE POSSIBILITY

He had no idea of the time when he woke. Through the open curtains the charcoal sky told him nothing. Frost gripped the inside of the windows, announcing another cold-as-stone day in Garrim. There was nothing to get out of bed for and even if there had been, weariness kept him firmly anchored to the sheets.

Gabby still slept beside him, no reason to be awake, less hours spent doing nothing. He wished he'd not woken and even though he willed his body back to sleep, the more he tried, the more awake he became.

He knew another dreary day meant waiting; waiting for Duckett to give them as much assurance as was possible that they'd be safe if they left, waiting for a knock at the door from the Watch, the odds of which were shortening by the day while no one down the Ditch would be betting on their successful escape.

The wind rattled the glass in the window frame, stirring Gabby. Frank disentangled himself from the blankets and went to the window, peering down onto the empty street below at the mix of browns and blacks and greys, at the wet and even wetter, at the hostile eyes of the town. Just another shit day in Garrim.

He glanced in the mirror. He looked like utter crap. Just a few days in the town had the dark circles advancing under his eyes with little sign of stopping, let alone retreating and his battered face was barely mending. No wonder Lily, the working girl at the Lid, had seemed twice her years.

A look down at the two Dahke passes, the deep mystery that had him wanting to shake some sense in it. Maybe he'd missed something in Dagmar's words but it was too late, he couldn't remember and Dagmar might have already breathed his last.

He picked up the possessor, an absent-minded action, thoughts of Simeon as he'd handed the key over to Etamin, lust and thunder in her murderous eyes, a sure reflection of what was to become of the world unless he could keep her from his door.

He went to lay it down again when another object, sitting innocently on the table, something that had been hidden under the pouch, caught his attention and he heard a faint click of something falling into place.

He nearly dismissed it, nearly covered it up again and answered the call of his bed until he felt himself clawing at his memories, images of where he'd come by it. He looked down on it, considering, wondering.

The one-crown gambling chip, given to him by Narvi with the naked warning that he'd rip Frank's throat out if he ever laid eyes on him again, daring him to re-enter the Lid.

A flat disc.

He looked from the chip to the Dahke pass with the scorpion emblem cast onto it. They were more or less the same shape and size.

The threads of a connection began to twist into a single, unlikely strand. That he hadn't really found the objects pictured in the book. Had they, in some way, found him?

They had all been randomly obtained, each a result of chance, a spin of the luck-wheel. All unplanned meetings with people he'd never met. All complete coincidence. But coincidence is just an explanation offered by fools and liars and he'd given up on believing in them months ago.

He picked the playing chip up, holding it between his thumb and forefinger, rolling it slowly.

'Something interesting?'

Gabby's words brought him to his senses. Frank turned, watching her uncoil herself from the sheets, yawning like a cat and blinking the sleep from her eyes. She pulled the blankets back over her against the morning chill and closed her eyes.

Frank closed his hand around the chip and got back into bed, immediately feeling her warmth as she wrapped her arm over his chest and kissed him on the cheek. He felt himself calm, the tension in his bones that simply fell away at Gabby's presence.

She glanced down at his hand through her tired eyes and yawned.

'You got me a present.'

Frank pushed her hair from her face.

'Yeah, I just popped down to the gift shop and got you the best thing they had. Hope you like it.'

Frank opened his hand and passed her the playing chip which Gabby took from him. He felt the warmth of her hand as it lingered deliberately on his. She looked at it, her heavy lids struggling.

'Lucky me,' she said with a playful note. 'Just what I wanted. How did you know?'

Her teasing drew a smile from him.

'I hear a girl can never have enough of them,' he said.

Gabby rolled onto her back and held the chip up. 'Narvi got you worked up again?'

'No,' said Frank, looking down at his hands. 'I just thought… it's something that it can't be.' She turned it over in her hand. A slight shrug. 'The book,' he said. Gabby appeared to shake off her drowsiness. 'I was wrong. It's not the Dahke pass.'

'You think this is the missing picture?' said Gabby. 'Not Dagmar?'

'I don't know what to think,' said Frank. 'But it's too random, surely. I only met him by complete accident.'

'They're all random, Frank,' said Gabby, putting her arm back round him and closing her eyes. 'All of them.'

And the coincidences weren't just wearing thin, there was a dirty great hole right through the middle of them which left him staring Narvi right in the face.

'Yes, but we sought out the others – Hums, Menetti. We sought them. We never sought Narvi. He doesn't fit the pattern.'

'If you think about it, we never really sought any of them, except Sapphire, maybe. And when was there ever any pattern?' She opened her hand and the chip fell on the bed and rolled to the floor with a clink. 'But you think he's the final guardian?'

Frank didn't respond. Is that what he thought?

He started mulling over the absurd notion that they were all part of an elaborate play, where all the players knew their roles except them, that the script was already written but they didn't even know the next line.

But something snagged in his mind. Wordsworth Hums, content in his underground hideaway, Felix Menetti, pacing on his lonely island, Edwina Chetto, confined in a drug-induced torpor in her bedroom and Sapphire Hark, barricaded in isolation in the middle of Alsha Kar. All out of sight. All hidden.

It's easy to hide yourself in Garrim. You're damn right it is.

'Perhaps we should risk certain death and pay him a visit,' said Gabby.

52

THE RETURN

They hadn't come to Garrim to hunt guardians but, then, most of the time the best stories don't end up how you think they will.

The early morning could just as easily have been midnight, such was the mood of Garrim – cold and testy, a day fashioned from ill-temper and the brittle existence in the palm of the mountains.

Dark snow clouds snarled at the town which looked back and dared them to throw anything they had at the ground. A cold, wet sleet covered everything in icy moisture and the whole town wore its familiar frozen look.

Anya led them away from the inn and through the unwelcoming narrow streets, down the south-summit towards the Ditch. Their boots crunched and slurped at the half-frozen filth, their breath smoked and their noses ran. Frank's ears tingled, beginning the process of numbing. After days of recovery in the warmth of the Gargoyle's Head, it was an unpleasant reminder of his escape from the backstreet house and of how quickly his fortunes could change.

Perhaps venturing back out, where the eyes of the town would be glaring at them, was the province of fools. It certainly seemed like one of the most stupid things they could be doing and Duckett had growled when they refused his counsel to stay put. Wise words, badly ignored.

Surely they would have been better running in the other direction, back to Rhaeder and its calm normality, but they had no choice, no good ones, anyway, not if they were to quench themselves of the question Frank had posed.

Despite the best attempts of the weather to keep Garrim's

residents bound to their homes once again, the streets were busy. Drunks finding their way home after an all-nighter, others up at dawn to catch an early scam. Garrim never slept.

Wariness walked alongside them, its eyes alert as theirs, primed for trouble, for a repeat abduction but this time they'd be prepared if Etamin came calling.

Frank gripped the Elemental ball inside his pocket, his mind half lost in its puzzle as he dug his fingernails into its pliant surface. The moving images from the book replayed before his eyes, the connections, the whole construction involving the gifts he'd been handed by the guardians, something totally beyond his grasp.

But he was close; *they* were close and he wondered if Narvi would provide a further important piece of the puzzle or, as Dagmar had warned, they were too late and Jackson had finally laid his cards on the table.

They were a line of hunched shoulders in the face of the bitterness. The warmth of the pub quickly left them, seeking a different host, leaving them to the chill of the streets as they approached the Ditch, the now familiar tones of bawdy music and the sea of bodies loitering all along the pathway, cheap whiskey in the air, fending off the bite of the cold although Frank doubted it would deter anything in a plum-coloured long-coat.

They split, with a rendezvous inside the Lid.

Cas moved in the shadows, the consummate thief, blending seamlessly with the dregs. Anya swept along the street on the heels of the locals, trailing one, then another, close to their coat-tails while Gabby idled by a brazier, taking in the lay of the strip, watchful for the sharp eyes of spies and informants before moving innocuously to the next.

Frank turned his collar up and took a mock swig from the beer bottle he'd grabbed from Duckett's empties and strode comfortably along the path, stopping occasionally at a doorway, feigning interest for just long enough to not arouse any attention, politely dodging the vulgar advances of the barely-dressed.

This morning the Ditch was kind. Frank arrived at the tasteless entrance to the Lid without the slightest hint of bother, his eyes immediately falling on the young girl doing her shift touting in the freezing doorway, a different girl to the one he'd encountered on his first visit, relieving him of an opportunity to show his gratitude for telling Gabby where he'd been taken. A risk much higher than the few words she'd uttered.

The girl was occupied with one of the fattest men Frank had ever seen. His ample belly spilled over his trouser-top like a batch of proving dough in a container too small. His face, all ruddy cheeks, thin veins and hefty jowls was pushed into the girl's and, even at a distance, Frank caught the waft of the stale liquor about him.

The girl looked ready to cry, or puke, or both but a job is a job and he knew the eyes of the house would be on her, expecting her to draw in the punters or offer them something else, even at this hour and regardless of who was asking.

He looked through the door. Cas, Gabby and Anya were already inside, sitting at different tables but close enough to each other.

Frank swept his eyes across the inside of the Lid, taking in the punters. The air punctuated with the occasional yelping at a win but, predictably, the rot of losses and the sunken shoulders of those debating whether to play another hand was the order of the morning.

Then he saw her moving through the misery. Slow, clipped strides, black dress swaying with each step, the ample Mrs Burns approached the table where Cas rode the luck-wheel. Cas had clocked her the minute she'd started her rounds, her checks on the dealers and players and as she walked past his chair Cas raised his hand and stopped her, then looked up and spoke to her, slow and sure, delivering his message as well as the folded piece of paper they'd arranged in advance.

Gabby and Anya looked on.

The floor manager hesitated, looking first at Cas, then at one of her heavies and, for a moment, Frank thought their plan had collapsed at the first turn until she opened the note, revealing the

Dahke pass, before he watched her read the single word Frank had written on the paper – *Simbrian.*

Her eyebrows dropped and she said something to Cas, no hint of understanding on her face. They exchanged a few words before she straightened, gave Cas a look and headed towards the staircase and up to the small office where Frank had been threatened with a gut-spilling on his first encounter. Frank's cue to enter.

Gabby and Anya rose as he walked to Cas's table. They all hoped they'd baited the trap just enough to lure the largest rat.

Through all the morning trade, through all the people that came and went, Frank was sure he'd not be recognised. It was a week since he came face to face with the man who he'd have as their missing guardian. Dozens of the lonely and inept and displaced had stumbled through the doors and lost their dignity in the interim, and Frank didn't bother a look to any of the watchful eyes as he headed across the floor, confident of his anonymity.

But it seemed those that kept order at the tables had a trained eye for those not welcome in the Lid and he felt movement at his back as soon as he met the others.

The first heavy made a grab for him but he ducked and pulled back, batting his significant forearm away, allowing Anya to step forward. A smile cracked across the doorman's face, one that spoke his pleasure in tackling a young waif-like girl as he gave a slight shake of his head.

His smile remained intact just long enough for Anya to rid him of it with a right cross so powerful even Frank thought he saw stars. The heavy sunk to the floor, the punters around him stepping back to avoid his hefty frame as he fell, startled eyes on him as his bulk rattled the floor and didn't get back up.

Tension and violence were part of the Ditch's landscape but, among the disciplined tables of Narvi's gambling den, it appeared to spark a round of concern as, in the throw of a right hook, the cards stopped being dealt, the dice stopped rolling and the small metal ball on the luck-wheel came to a stuttering halt, anxious eyes in their direction from all around, the sudden silence telling Frank things were going wrong already.

A crack of the knuckles from a second thug had Frank looking up.

'We're not looking for trouble,' he said but one look at the face told him they'd clearly already found it although a quick glance at Anya made him pause. A downwards look to his partner, spark-out on the casino floor, then back to Frank, before the bark of a familiar voice had his head turning.

'Back to your business.' Mrs Burns stood at the top of the stairs, her gaze sweeping the room, aimed at dealers and clients alike. 'There's nothing to see, here.' The whole room hesitated. 'Go on.'

She trotted down the stairs and over towards them. Those at the tables shrouded themselves in low murmurs before turning their attention back to losing all their money, the queasy sound of gambling quickly filling the void left by the brief punch-up at the hands of the teenagers.

A fight in a gambling den. Nothing out of the ordinary along the Ditch.

Mrs Burns came to an abrupt halt a pace from Frank. She looked at the burly doorman, the one still standing.

'Back to your post, Jarred. And make sure no one speaks to the Watch.'

A nod from the gorilla before he turned and walked away. Mrs Burns sniffed and looked at Frank.

'I thought Mr Narvi made it clear to you the consequences of returning to his club.'

She clasped her hands to the front, looking set to throttle him.

'I'm rubbish at consequences,' said Frank. 'Really.'

She looked at the man stirring on the ground, her lips a severe thin line.

'I'd appreciate it if you took your fights elsewhere,' she said.

'Oh, that wasn't me,' said Frank with a nod of his head towards Anya.

'Do that again and I'll have you all skinned.' She looked Anya up and down before doing the same to Cas and Gabby. 'I take it you're all together.' A collective nod. 'Then if you'd like to follow me.'

53

Unaware

A vivid sense of déjà-vu filled Frank as he followed the short strides of Mrs Burns across the gaming floor and up the bent wooden staircase, though this time he had the comfort of the others behind him.

No one paid them the slightest bit of attention as they headed up, too intent on the next win to have any interest in four youngsters who, outwardly, were about to be lectured by the reclusive owner who would probably have them all thumped and thrashed and spat on before chucking them out.

A heavy took up position at the bottom of the stairs doing a bad job of trying to keep his eyes off of Anya as they headed to the top, to the closed door behind which they hoped lay some answers.

Mrs Burns cleared her throat with a guttural rasp in keeping with her personality. She knocked and went in without a look back, holding the door ajar as a sign that they should enter, that their presence had been requested.

The sight was a familiar one to Frank. The small office that hemmed Narvi in, anchoring him to his receipts and ledgers, kept him counting his takings, witness to his burgeoning fortune.

He watched as the others swept the room, absorbing the books crammed shoulder to shoulder at their owner's back and sides.

Narvi sat facing them, lips pursed, immaculate in his irritation at having been disturbed although there was something different about him in the way he fingered his glass while deliberately ignoring the Dahke pass and note that Cas had handed Burns, both of which occupied his desk. He flexed his shoulders and let the silence in.

'I thought I made myself clear?' said Narvi, swilling the contents of his glass around before taking a sip of the amber liquid, his eyes sharp over its rim, aimed directly at Frank. 'You know one word from me to the Watch and you'll all be wishing your mothers had never given birth to you.' The light skimmed off his slick, greying hair, the tone of amusement in his voice wasn't reflected in his face. Narvi looked at his floor manager. 'Thank you, Mrs Burns, that will be all,' he said through a forced smile, though not as forced as the one she gave him back, one that barely hid her annoyance, obviously hoping she would get to stay and witness whatever was about to unfold rather than being dealt with and dismissed like a schoolchild who'd run a simple errand.

She swallowed and gave a curt nod.

'I'll call if I need anything,' said Narvi, perhaps as a way of softening the blow.

Another nod, then she left, closing the door carefully behind her.

Frank knew Narvi was right, that he could just summon the Watch and make them disappear, but the fact he hadn't gave Frank some kind of reassurance, or perhaps Narvi, bored counting his coins, fancied playing a game to liven up his dreary day.

Narvi studied the door, letting the silence set hard, a look of stone on his face. The room bent with tension. Frank was gripped by an unshakeable feeling that something nasty was about to happen even though Narvi showed no sign of moving, he just sat and eyed them all. He set his fingertips on his glass, turning it left and right. Frank glanced at Anya and noticed Cas take a slight step back.

Narvi turned to Anya, drawing in the long breath of a tired man.

'Don't ever try to mix it up in any of my businesses again, understand?' Anya didn't move. 'You might be good one-on-one but I've learned a significant number of ways to turn even the best fighters inside out when they're least expecting it.' He didn't look for a response, but turned his eyes to Cas.

'You have some influential friends in Kzarlac.' Narvi fingered the Dahke pass that lay on his desktop. A slow, deliberate motion a match for his self-assured tone, the tone of a conductor about to orchestrate the whole symphony.

The note lay to the side, as if he was working up to the main attraction.

'No,' said Cas.

Narvi turned the corners of his mouth down.

'So you found this in the gutter?'

'No,' repeated Cas.

Narvi shifted forward in his seat. He picked up the disc and tapped it hard a couple of times on his desk, the way a squirrel checks the quality of its next meal.

Frank could already see the direction of the conversation's travel, heading towards them, carefully steered by Narvi who looked set to relieve them of as much information as possible.

'I think we all know that you don't come across a Dahke pass unless you've had the pleasure of holding hands with either Etamin Dahke or Dagmar Dag.'

He set the disc spinning, drawing the focus of those in the room. They watched, listening to the rumble on the desktop as it slowed and clattered to a halt.

'So, which was it, hm?'

The challenge in his voice was clear, as was his continued probing for details, details he would turn on them in a twitch of his finely waxed moustache.

Now Frank felt the hesitation in the room. They'd entered the lion's den with a plan, a confrontation in mind and with a deft swerve and a few well-delivered words Narvi had them sweating over how to play their hand. Stick or twist? Either way might end in bother, but Frank was spared the decision.

'Dagmar,' said Gabby, sending a quiver through Frank. She'd said it from nowhere, like she'd broken an unspoken promise between them but Frank knew she would have played the odds in her mind before speaking, that she wouldn't place their entire quest at risk without understanding how revealing their hand might, at last, bring down the house. 'He and Etamin are looking for you.'

'For me?' A raise of the eyebrows.

'Of course,' she said. 'We know what you are.'

Narvi looked down into his glass, a slow blink in contemplation, considering the bluff. He drew the silence out once more with slow, solid breaths. Frank watched him, mapping the path ahead, a path that needed careful navigation. A wrong step and Narvi would have them face down in the shit. Narvi knew it, but did nothing.

'And what am I?'

Words delivered coolly and confidently. He lifted his glass to his mouth, another unhurried, deliberate move, though he stopped as Gabby nodded to the note on his desk.

'The Simbrian, we — '

'Ah, yes. I was wondering what that meant,' He placed his glass back down, picked up the note and held it at arm's length. 'The...' He paused. 'The...Sim-bri-an,' he said slowly and carefully, drawing the word out like he was explaining it to a foreigner. He looked to Gabby over the piece of paper. 'What's that then?' No answer. He put the note back down. 'I must say it sounds very mysterious and there's nothing more I like than a bit of mystery to sharpen my day.'

Frank stalled. A glance to the others.

'Well?' said Narvi. 'Are you going to tell me?'

He leaned back, folding his long arms across his chest and waited.

Frank was blindsided by the den owner's words. They'd rolled the dice and thought they'd win whatever way they landed but now, in the face of Narvi and the way he spilled authority, he could feel creeping cold of doubt, that they'd got it wrong.

And now Narvi was fishing for information and information had its very own market, especially in Garrim, especially where the Simbrian was concerned.

Narvi raised a hand to his chin and rubbed at it.

'Perhaps I should just get the Watch down here,' he said, a look of imminent conquest in his smile, one that told them he had them just where he wanted them, cradled seamlessly between them telling him about the Simbrian and handing them over to the band of thugs that kept order on the streets. A well-played hand.

Narvi got to his feet, taking a few languid strides to the door. He opened it. Mrs Burns stood outside, suddenly bolt upright, feigning innocence, a look of mock surprise on her face.

'Mrs Burns, I have an errand for you to run.'

A last look at the four teenagers corralled in his office before he fed them to the dogs.

54

IDENTIFIED

Mrs Burns stepped into the room, a willing messenger for her boss's words, words that would have them in the hands of the Watch within the next few minutes. All she would have to do is flag one of their number down in the street but a voice beat Narvi's to it.

'I recognise you.' Everyone turned to Anya. She looked at Burns with curiosity, with narrow eyes. 'I thought I did, downstairs.' Frank clocked the sideways look from Burns to Narvi. Anya took a step forward, raising a pointed finger, wielding it as if it were one of her knives. 'You were who I saw talking outside the house.' A look to Frank. 'It's her, I'd bet my blades on it.'

Narvi remained calm and poised but, if he was unmoved, by the same measure Burns suddenly looked uncertain, her naturally possessed look of someone in charge shifted before she regained her composure. But they'd all noticed.

'I think you must be mistaken,' said Burns.

Anya gave a slight shake of her head, examining Burns who picked at her fingers but just managed to hold on to her practiced look of office as Anya looked set to wrestle her to the ground and extract the truth in her own way, despite Narvi's earlier promise of Garrim-style reprisals.

'Mrs Burns thinks you must be mistaken,' said Narvi, slick and assured.

Frank looked at Anya, waiting for a response, but it was Gabby who spoke.

'How did Lily know where you were being held?' she said. Frank could see her mind still turning, as if she was unwrapping a parcel only to find more paper underneath. She looked at Burns. 'How? How does one of your good-time girls know that?'

Burns opened her mouth but tripped fabulously over her words. Narvi's still features, his calculating and unruffled features, remained expressionless.

'Held?' said Narvi, interest in his raised eyebrows.

Frank clenched his teeth.

'Spot of bother with the locals?' said Narvi with a smile. 'Well, well, the mystery deepens.' He drew another mouthful. 'Perhaps we should get Lily up here and ask her,' he said. 'Mrs Burns?'

'She's not working until tonight.'

'Shame,' said Narvi. 'I'm sure she'd put us all straight. You know how some of the girls like talk, I'm sure she and a bunch of others know about the goings-on in the Dahke house. Either that or a punter making small talk on the way to getting his paid-for pleasures out of her.' He picked his glass up. 'Maybe you could drop in later, or tomorrow and we'll see what she says.' *And you'll make sure she has her story very straight*. Narvi took a mouthful of liquor, a savouring breath as the swallow warmed the back of his throat. 'So, unless you're going to enlighten me on what this Simbrian thing is all about, I suggest this meeting is over.' A challenging raise of the chin.

No one spoke, like Narvi had produced an enormous pin and stuck it right into their fully inflated balloon.

Frank felt twisted, chewed up and spat out, even though Narvi hadn't so much as raised a finger or his voice to them.

What had started as a plausible explanation for the picture in their book, what had seemed like the sole candidate with the label of seventh guardian sewn into the inside of their collar now had him staring at Narvi's desk, not knowing which way was up, such was the way Narvi had of tipping his words left and right so you never knew which were straight.

'Who said anything about Etamin's house?' said Cas.

The timid tone from Cas might well have gone unnoticed in

different circumstances, but Narvi's face froze, just for a second, then a twitch of the nose, a twitch of the mouth. Frank looked at Cas, a slight nod from the thief, confirmation of the tell on Narvi's face, the tell of a liar. Narvi chewed the inside of his mouth.

'No one said anything about Etamin's house,' said Cas. 'So how do you know that's what we meant?'

Now Narvi looked like he wanted to inflict some damage, tripped up by his own words that had him sprawling face first in the filth of his own lies.

'A lucky guess,' said Narvi. *Liar.*

'Luck?' said Frank. 'I think we both know that luck doesn't exist within the four walls of the Lid. Just speak to any of your regulars. And you don't seem like a man who plays at your own tables.'

He thought he saw a muscle tighten in Narvi's jaw. Time to grab the tail of the fish before it jumps off the boat and away. Some moments need to be seized. Sometimes you have to nod to the dealer for another card.

'I know you're in Jackson's pocket,' he said.

'You have no idea what you're talking about,' said Narvi, the bland, cover-all response when someone knows exactly what's being talked about.

'No?' Frank grabbed hold of the moment of indecision like he was spearing a fish, and he meant to eat today. 'Dagmar told me about Jackson, how he's been keeping the last guardian to himself, and Dagmar doesn't seem like the sort of person to get things wrong.'

Still Narvi projected a smooth and unruffled front. Goodness, he'd make a great poker player if only he didn't run the tables, but Frank could see the baize on the table beginning to thin.

'I said, you've no idea —'

Frank grabbed his locket and stepped forward, opening it and holding the picture out for Narvi to see. 'This is what I'm talking about,' he said, voice battering the books around the office, the lid off his temper at the side-stepping and word-twisting of the well-presented den owner.

Even the smallest of things can illicit the greatest surprises and Frank knew the power of what was confined in the casing that hung from his neck. He'd used the tactic to corner Moonhunter as she dodged and weaved around his questions and accusations and he hoped Narvi wouldn't be immune to the same. He wasn't wrong.

Immediately Narvi paled, froze.

The smug veneer peeled a fraction. He gradually raised his eyes to Frank, studied him for a few seconds, then dipped them again to the portrait of Frank's mum.

'What in Kester's name...'

His voice knotted, his eyes glazed, his face froze. Frank had flicked a switch, just like he knew he would, one that Narvi had thought out of reach.

'*She* found you,' said Frank. 'Didn't she?' No response. '*Didn't she?*'

His raised voice brought Narvi back. He paused, then slowly, very slowly, offered a nod. He opened his mouth but only a dry, indistinct sound came out. He looked at Gabby.

'What kind of sorcery is this?' he hissed, placing a steadying hand on his desk.

He made a grab for the locket but Frank was alive to it and took a step back.

'Hands off.'

Narvi looked like he'd seen a ghost, one that had haunted him, unseen, for years but only now had shown itself and bared its fangs. The haggard look of the gambler whose luck had just run dry.

He turned to Burns.

'Thank you, Mrs Burns. That will be all.'

'But —'

'I said that will be all,' his tone daring a refusal.

Burns gave a nod of the head, a tight look at the four teenagers before leaving the room.

'She knew who all the guardians were,' said Gabby. 'She visited them all.'

'So we know she must have visited you,' said Anya.

Narvi still looked like he'd been hit with a rock. Dazed at the sight of Rebecca Forbes's image as if she were still fresh in his memory, still flesh and blood, standing before him.

He reached for his glass and drained it, immediately filling it from the bottle on the desk and draining it again, letting out a gasp as a drop dribbled down his chin.

'Tell us again that we don't know what we're talking about and I'll get Anya to show you her knives,' said Frank.

Narvi didn't seem the sort who would flinch at idle threats, confirmed by the chuckle he let out, a chuckle that turned to a laugh, a mocking, superior laugh that had Frank boiling inside.

Schemer. That's what Frank saw as he stared at the superior face looking back at him. Narvi was just another conspirator in the whole Simbrian construct, just another conniving weasel among a whole sorry bunch of weasels who wanted something for themselves in return for selling out just about everyone else.

He felt himself grinding his teeth and his mood dip in the midst of the office. Narvi appeared to notice.

'Your mother?' said Narvi, his head tilting to the locket. A nod from Frank followed by a raise of the eyebrows from Narvi. 'Who'd have thought it? Please don't think you understand my motivation, Frank.'

Frank swallowed his urge to tell him exactly what he thought. Again Narvi appeared to read him, the wily old den owner with years of experience at studying people, Perhaps a one-sided contest. 'You'd have me as a greedy bastard?'

Gabby huffed loudly.

'Owning a gambling house might be a contributing factor,' she said.

Narvi let out another laugh and aimed a look in her direction.

'Very good,' he said. 'But this has nothing to do with money.'

Nothing to do with money? He had to be kidding them. Sitting there at his ledgers, counting his takings as much as he counted the fools at his tables, he'd have them all as mugs if he wanted them to believe that.

Everything about Narvi smacked of the finer things – the cut of his clothes, the weight of his crystal, the quality of his liquor, his books, the elegance of his manner – and those things weren't bought with the mountain air, they were bought on the misery of those that came through his gilded front door and as far as Frank could see, he couldn't get enough of it.

'Then what is it to do with?' said Frank.

Narvi paused, chewing at his mouth, the hesitant look of someone who has something to say but then knows they couldn't unsay it.

'You're the last one,' said Gabby. 'The seventh.'

Narvi gave a shallow nod and sat.

'I know,' he said.

'We've been through so much,' said Anya.

Narvi looked at the sullen faces of the four teenagers standing in his room, in the dark heart of the gambling den, in the middle of the town that would hang them as much as put its arm around them.

Something akin to sympathy crossed his face, something which told Frank he might have an ounce of understanding about the punishment they had taken to get this far, the cost and that someone, for once, might take pity on them although pity in Garrim would be a lonely place, a place where not many would dwell.

Narvi closed his eyes, his face suddenly looking tired, long lines showing his years. Frank could tell he was standing right on the edge, knowing he should jump but needing that last piece of assurance that he'd not crush himself at the bottom, that there would be a soft landing.

'We've *all* been through so much,' he said. Another refill, another drink. He leaned back in his chair. 'Years in Garrim doesn't do for one's health.'

He looked up, eyes resting on each of their faces for a few seconds, a pause as the silence ate the room. He expelled a decisive breath, the sort of breath that signals that the flood waters are about to breach the riverbanks.

'I was told to wait,' he said, inviting the question.

'Wait? Wait for what,' said Cas.

Narvi leaned forward, braced his elbows on the desk and arched his fingers to his mouth, considering his next words.

'It doesn't matter,' he said. 'I was told to wait, that this day would come and I was to surrender my part of the Simbrian.'

'You've surrendered it?' said Frank.

A slow nod from Narvi as he scanned the confused faces opposite. 'Jackson now has it.'

'Jackson?' said Gabby. 'Are you —'

'Mad?' said Narvi. 'No.' A pause. 'It would take a lifetime for you to understand. Although, you...' He studied Cas. 'You'd know. You can tell if someone is lying?' A nod. 'Garrim teaches you that some people just lie for a living, so much so they'd swear up is down and down is up. But you can always tell, if you know what to look for.' He paused, eyes still on Cas. 'So it should be of no surprise that, conversely, there are those who you know are telling the truth. *Know*. And a small number within whom the truth sits so comfortably that you believe what they're saying without any doubts, *any*, however fanciful that truth may seem.' A flick of the head to Frank's chest. 'That was her. That was...Rebecca Forbes.'

Something passed across Narvi's face as he said her name, like the two words were spoken from deep down and had trouble surfacing, spoken from a place he'd kept shut tight for years, away from the prying and the curious, where only his distant memories stirred at the soft breath of something not forgotten. Of something lost.

'You were in love with her,' said Gabby. Not a question.

The look on Narvi's face spoke of the story he didn't want told. No denial.

'There are many things in life that will catch your eye,' he said. 'She was certainly one of those. But very few things will ever capture your heart.' He looked at the object that hung around Frank's neck. 'Life is unsure. Love is not.'

No more words, like he'd closed the book.

An uncomfortable quiet hugged them all. A low-life businessman in the shit-stick of Garrim was the last person they expected to confess enduring love for Frank's mother – another person – but there it was, as loud as a screaming child and just as painful on the ears. Not quite what they were expecting, as if anything predictable had ever been handed to them since they'd first encountered Hums.

Frank looked at Gabby. Something akin to understanding passed between them, but Narvi's words still left him with an itchiness that any amount of scratching wouldn't rid him of. Whatever he thought he was meant to say, it was clear that another apparently sensible person had joined the lengthening line of those who fell for the charms of his mother, a long line whose thirst for the sorcerous beauty had been left unsated, knowing the well had run dry and would never be replenished.

'It was her. She told you to wait?' said Anya, breaking the deadlock.

Narvi nodded, regaining his senses.

'That's right.'

'And she told you to relinquish your fragment of the Simbrian?'

Another nod.

'It's difficult to describe her, explain her. I had to believe she was telling me something that transcended truth.'

In all honesty, Narvi looked like he'd been turned inside out by Rebecca Forbes, a slavering puppy eager to please its master, made to beg and whine or jump through fire.

'I never had the pleasure,' said Frank.

'Then you must believe me when I tell you she knew exactly what she was doing.'

'You want us to believe you?' said Frank. 'We're running from most of the stink that Garrim has to offer, as well as Etamin, while you're sitting in your counting house about to flush the world down the toilet, so you'll excuse us if we appear a little bit sceptical.'

'I should have known you'd be sharper than a freshly whetted blade.' He chewed the inside of his cheek as he contemplated his next words. 'Knowing who your father is.'

The last thing Frank would have expected from the mouth of the club-owning thug and the words slapped him hard around the face.

'I don't understand,' he said, trying to search his mind for how a down-town Garrim gangster would have the faintest idea who his father was, who *he* was.

Smug satisfaction spread over Narvi's face, the same look he must have witnessed a thousand times at his tables as the ball on the luck-wheel stopped on the right number or as the player slowly places a pair of aces on the table. A winning hand.

'How do you know Frank's dad?' said Cas.

'The same way I knew *your* dad.' Another coal on the fire. 'And your brother.' Narvi turned to Anya. 'And I remember your sister and brother.' A look at Gabby. 'Though I'm ashamed to say I never had the opportunity to preside over anyone from Prismia.'

Narvi let the words hang, like he'd thrown them all the pieces of the puzzle and now wanted them to fit them together.

'You're Hector Baggus,' said Gabby.

A perfunctory nod.

'Clever girl,' said Baggus.

55

THE SIMBRIAN SCHOLAR

Hector Baggus, the former principal of Excelsus, replaced by Aurora Moonhunter, then vanished nearly five years ago. No one had seen or heard of him since, no one knew where he was, what he was or even, it seemed, who he was. No one except Alfred Jackson, and the head of Byeland had come to pluck his golden goose.

Frank had never seen a picture or portrait of him and it wouldn't have been a surprise if that was by design, a carefully crafted exit from the limelight of Excelsus to the guaranteed anonymity of the Ditch, perfectly executed.

It's easy to hide yourself in Garrim. You're damn right it is.

'What are you doing here?' said Gabby.

'Waiting,' said Baggus. 'Like I said.'

'Couldn't you wait somewhere more...more...'

'Agreeable?'

'That would be one word.'

'No one knew me here, and I keep myself to myself. I have my books, and my memories and, of course, a living to make.'

'And no one recognises you?'

'You grow your hair, grow a moustache, grow a reputation for being a nasty little hermit bastard. Easier than you think. I would ask how you found me, but I'm not sure I'm altogether that interested.'

'I'm not sure you'd believe us if we told you,' said Anya. 'Although Frank's mum kind of led us to you, as she did the others.'

A sorrowful look of longing brushed over Baggus's face at her mention. Frank gave an uncomfortable shift. Baggus regarded them for a minute.

'Excelsus never makes mistakes,' he said, a faint smile plucking his lips. 'You said I was the last. You know who the other six are?'

Frank looked at the others, seeking approval or otherwise. Gabby nodded.

'Yes,' she said. 'We found the others.'

Baggus raised an admiring eyebrow.

'And may I ask who they are?'

Gabby reeled off the names – Wordsworth Hums, Montrose Menetti, Edwina Chetto, Sapphire Hark, Lawrence Penny, Rebecca Forbes. Frank watched Baggus's face carefully, checking his reaction to the prestigious club of which he was a member, noting the increasingly curious look in his eyes as the list fell from Gabby's lips.

'An interesting collection of names,' he said. Baggus rubbed at this fingers. 'Perhaps I could have guessed at someone like Wordsworth, but the others? I can't imagine the Carey girl having the strength to do what was necessary. Clever, but timid as two mice.'

'Carey girl?'

'Edwina Carey. That was her before she married that detestable Eli Chetto.' Baggus huffed, though Frank could see him sifting the individuals, the names on the register. 'Sapphire Hark? Is she related to Piotr Hark?' For a moment, Frank fought the urge to tell him that she was dealing cards just a few dozen yards away, down the stairs, but just nodded back. 'You know they were all in Rhaeder at the same time. *We* were all in Rhaeder at the same time,' he said, a note of puzzlement in his voice. 'Hums, obviously, Menetti taught under me for a year, at the same time that Edwina and Lawrence were there and Piotr Hark had a silversmith's in the town.' He looked at Frank. 'Of course, your mother was there.'

It was the perfect hand, one with the longest odds, all the players in the Simbrian game sitting at the table at the same time. High rollers indeed, and those with much to lose looked like they might have been participants in a game, one of which they were totally unaware, one for which Frank's mum dealt the cards and made the rules.

'Rebecca was always around. She'd just walk around the academy as if she owned the place. Brazen as anything. Even when I asked her to refrain she just completely ignored me. She, on the other hand, wasn't so easy to ignore. I remember she lived down by the lake with her mother, fearsome woman. She still with us?'

A nod from Frank, the comfort of the cottage looming in his mind, warm and safe. Far away. A place that had given life to whatever implausible scheme filled Rebecca's mind and left her obsessed with the Simbrian, an obsession that would see the end of her. She'd planned it, of that he had no doubt, the reason for which was still tiresomely, inconveniently elsewhere.

But Baggus's observation that all the guardians had been in one place made him wonder if, among whatever abilities lurked within the enigma of Rebecca Forbes, his mother possessed the ability to sniff them all out, or was it just luck knocking? He couldn't believe it was; he'd seen enough to know that luck always seemed to be against the man or woman who depends on it and his mum didn't sound like the sort who needed it.

'So why did she tell you to wait and hand over your segment?' said Anya.

'You don't know why?'

'Surely it would make more sense to tell you to hide yourself, protect yourself? To stop Dagmar getting to you?'

'Dagmar?'

'You know Dagmar's been wreaking havoc all over to recreate the Simbrian,' said Gabby. 'So why just give up your piece?'

'Dagmar? No, that's not right.' Baggus spoke with the assured authority of the schoolmaster he once was. 'The golden intake were all clear on their desire to protect the secret. They swore on it, for as much as that means.'

'It doesn't mean much,' said Gabby. 'He's been murdering Prismians and probably his own people to get it.'

'No,' said Baggus. Nothing else. Straightforward and to the point. *Do you have me for a murderer?* Frank felt himself swallow.

Something in Baggus's manner had his mind taking a step back.

'You must be joking,' said Cas.

'My boy, the Simbrian and the fate of the world has not the room for jokes.'

'What makes you so sure,' said Frank.

'Because Dagmar is the one person who can make sure the world is kept safe.'

There were, perhaps, many words that might have surprised Frank, even at this stage of their quest, but none were more likely to strike him speechless than those Baggus had just spoken, that simply rolled off his tongue and across the room. The continued unbundling of Dagmar's murderous character had Frank silent, wondering whether the box did not contain what was written on the lid.

Dagmar was the one person the world should fear, the one person to run the leather off your boots, the one person to elicit the sort of nightmares that had plagued Frank since he'd first set eyes on him. Keeping the world safe was for people other than the notorious, dark-haired villain from Kzarlac who had built his reputation on foundations of blood and death.

'I can see you have your doubts,' said Baggus. An observation, mildly put. 'But you'll concede I know Dagmar better than most, having taught him and been party to his thoughts and tendencies across those formative years. He made sure the Simbrian was always part of the golden intake conversation. I consider myself somewhat of an authority on the subject and I suspect not many people know more about the legend than me. I couldn't shake him off the subject. A right ferret with the scent of rabbits in the air.'

'So what did you do?' said Frank.

'We shared as much information about it as possible, from the events leading up to its creation, its splitting, the road since. Just about everything. From Kester's relationship with that demon, Everbleed, to the desire of the Dahke dynasty to one day possess it. The only thing I kept from them was that I was a bit more involved in the legend than they'd believe. It seems that your father was also keeping his lantern hooded, assuming the guardianship had been passed to him by then.'

'Hang on,' said Gabby. 'Everbleed, a demon?'

'Of course. I understand your empathy with all things Prismian, Gabby, but Everbleed...' Baggus gave a grave shake of his head. 'Has there ever been such a cunning and ruthless seer and sorcerer? You might think Lashka, and her descendants through the Dahkes, are murderous and brutal beyond the limits of most men, cutting the throats that stand in their way but Everbleed made the most single-minded person seem like a confused and rambling idiot. She stood for one thing – the dominance of Prismia. The Prismian prophetess, sick to her gums with the grandstanding of Rossia and looking to slay the beast in the most inventive of ways. I know a good number of her prophecies by heart.' A glance to his impressive array of books. 'She talks of light and dark, but her and her bloodline have strayed well beyond the blackest shadows – bunch of thieves and poisoners, madmen and bandits. Garrim rolled up and presented as flesh. If I were her descendent, I'd watch myself closely.'

Her blood, bad blood, *Frank's* blood.

'So the Simbrian was her way of elevating Prismia?'

'I don't know, but I wouldn't be surprised if there was something like that behind it. The Simbrian was her idea, originally. A few sweet whispers in Kester's ear and he bought it, for the right reasons but, if she had further plans, they were thwarted. She never knew who all the guardians were, despite what some think, although in some of her scribblings she gives the impression that she knew how to control the Simbrian, such is the foolishness of those blessed with foresight.' A disappointed shake of the head. 'No one can control it. Even if you wanted to you'd have to bring it back to life and so Dagmar, Simeon and Spyro all agreed that the Simbrian should never see the light of day. It was only Lawrence that seemed completely indifferent about the whole thing, like he couldn't care less.'

'Then why has Dagmar got it nearly fully assembled in an impenetrable tower in the middle of Alsha Kar?' said Frank, knowing

Dagmar wouldn't see it in its full glory. 'Face it Hector, he's fooled you. You and all of those around him.'

'No.' Baggus's granite face was unmoved. Not even the slightest shake of the head. 'I know Dagmar. He's far too bright a man to take such a risk. He, more than anyone, is aware of the unimaginable power of the Simbrian. No one has ever possessed it in its pure form.'

'My mother did. How?'

'Yes, but only to destroy it. Everbleed foretold it. How? I can only guess. Each fragment of the Simbrian has a core, surrounded by an essence that keeps it contained. Some of the core's power permeates the essence. If she somehow managed to split each guardian's part, siphon some of it off, if you understand me, that would do it. In that way an incarnation of sorts, the first incarnation, could probably be assembled. Certainly it wouldn't have been beyond her ability.'

'So it must be possible to make a second?'

'Of course, maybe even a third, but no one can be sure precisely what would be unleashed on the world should it come into being once more. I can't even start to imagine. Death, destruction, control. A parasite. The darkest, foulest and most manipulative creation that would see mankind swept from the face of the earth with a flick of its wrist. I have no idea what Kester was thinking about, but Everbleed undoubtedly got into his head and convinced him it would be a good idea to have it created on the absurd basis that it would keep the peace between Byeland and Kzarlac.'

'But it's worked. The two nations have been at peace ever since.'

'My guess is that that would have happened anyway. No one wants conflict, not really. Too messy, too expensive, too risky. No, everything I've read points to Everbleed wanting to stoke the boiler. Bad blood, that was Everbleed, the creator of all things malevolent only this time she took the whole thing too far. Anything like the Simbrian is far too unstable, too unpredictable and only the Simbrian heir can put an end to it. For good.'

'We thought the Simbrian heir was the one who could control it?' said Gabby.

A three-way glance to Frank that didn't go unnoticed by Baggus.

'Control it? Have you been listening to anything I've just said? You can control a dog, you can control a horse but you can't control the darkest forces forged by powers from a different age, power beyond your imagination. Control is the last thing the Simbrian is capable of, the last thing it wants. Everbleed's prophecy tells you all you need to know.'

'A child from the dark and the light,' said Gabby.

'Will choose between a better future and eternal night,' said Baggus with a shallow nod.

'I don't understand.'

'That's because this is far beyond the comprehension of young minds.'

'Surely eternal night refers to handing the power to someone like Etamin Dahke.'

Baggus gave a shake of the head. 'Choosing between a better future and eternal night has nothing to do with whose side you're on. This has nothing to do with choosing between Byeland and Kzarlac, Joleyon and Lashka, Jackson and Dahke. Nothing. Whoever has it will forever be its captive, in its keep, under *its* command. Can you imagine being ordered to set fire to the world in your every waking moment, to be able to think of nothing but destruction, of darkness... of death? Can you?'

Blank faces gave him the answer.

'Then what's your point?' said Gabby.

Baggus's face was as dark as the words he'd just uttered.

'If the Simbrian is created, the world will forever be in eternal night. *That,* is my point.'

'Then how can there be a better future? Everbleed said there would be a choice. That doesn't sound like a choice to me.'

'As the prophesy says, the Simbrian heir will choose. A better future is the final destruction of the almighty power. Final. To rid the world of a truly malevolent force that should never have been created in the first place.' He looked right into Frank's mind. 'The

Simbrian heir, whoever they are, must destroy the very thing they are the heir of…along with themselves. There is no other way. That is the choice, even if, as you say, it isn't a choice at all.'

Frank felt the slap of the words, thought he heard Gabby stifle a gasp as his mind began to cloud. The quiet thrummed in his ears. He knew what they were all thinking; he was thinking it too. He caught their looks, each unable to quite meet his. Baggus fixed his eyes on Frank, a passive look of realisation on his skin.

'Like I said, Frank. Excelsus never makes mistakes.'

56

ABSOLATUM

It's one thing having the wind knocked out of your sails, but something else completely when the sails are ripped from the mast and shredded into small pieces before your eyes.

Destroy the Simbrian, along with yourself – not words Frank ever expected to hear as he turned sixteen, not words he might have guessed would be part of his young existence, but there they were, knocking him sideways and he had no idea how he managed to keep himself upright.

The way his luck had turned, he felt he shouldn't be surprised, but the cat had been stripped of its ninth life. He'd laughed to himself about the number of people looking to end his life but he hadn't thought about adding himself to the list.

He wasn't sure he could do it even if he got the opportunity. The Simbrian resided high up in a warded tower in Etamin's citadel. Unreachable.

'How would you go about it?' said Gabby.

Frank could sense the shift in her voice, a string that had been tightened a couple of notches. She hadn't wanted Frank to be the one to ask but had already run ahead of him, not wishing to delay the formation of a plan, their next steps, steps that might keep them alive although Baggus's words had just opened up a trapdoor.

'Destroying the Simbrian?' said Baggus.

Gabby nodded. Baggus rubbed his eyes with the thumb and forefinger of his right hand, looking like the conversation was beginning to take a chunk of him with it.

'There is a single word, a power word that bends the Simbrian's will, that will make it wither and die, destroy it once and for all.' Their faces asked him the obvious question but Baggus shook his head. 'I'm afraid that's the one piece of information that's eluded me.' He turned to Frank. 'I don't know, but she did.' A dip of his head to Frank's chest. 'She must have known it to have ended the first incarnation. The final destruction would require the same thing, the same sacrifice. If the Simbrian is to be created again, as Everbleed has foretold, then it is the duty of the heir to see to it that it never sees the light of day. As a guardian, I knew this day would come, maybe not in my lifetime, but at some point. That's why it's important for me to hand over my part.'

'Important?' said Gabby.

'Of course.'

'Why do you think that would be anything like a good idea?'

'Don't you see? It must be done. Only with the construction complete can the beast be slain.'

A simple shrug at his statement of the obvious and there was no arguing with his logic, however dangerous.

But Frank had felt the tug of something in his head. A gentle voice at his ear whispering in the stillness. A word that he'd heard but not quite grasped in Edwina Chetto's bedroom, at Sapphire Hark's table. But he had heard it clearly as a peeling bell more recently, when Aurora Moonhunter had placed her hand on his chest in her office and grasped onto something that dwelt within him, something of his mother, her lover. The word, so often just out of reach but now laid out in large lettering before him.

'Absolatum,' he said to himself. Louder than he'd imagined, but quietly so not to expose the world to danger.

He could see himself staring back at himself. Could see his mother at his shoulder whispering it over and over lest he were to forget it. Reminding him. Nothing else allowed itself to enter his mind. Just the word. The word he knew would end all of this. The power word, as Baggus called it. As simple and coy as it was frightening and he dare not breathe it again for all the sands of time ran around it, waiting for it to be wielded and smite the greatest power ever to have been conjured by those foolish enough to think they might one day make it succumb.

It never would, everyone and everything would yield to it first. That's why it had to be destroyed, destroyed using a solitary word, four syllables, and only he could use it, could drive a stake through its beating heart and condemn it to the darkness where it belonged.

Together with himself.

Death now looked at him from both sides – from Etamin, from himself – closing in, giving him the most laughable of choices.

He saw Gabby's face drop, saw her placing the final part of the Simbrian puzzle into place. The part that confirmed his death, that they would be ripped from each other before they'd had a chance to start.

'What did you just say,' she said, but she knew, even though he'd not told any of them about that particular part of his meeting with Moonhunter. He could see it in the lines around her face. They thought he'd been shielded up to now, shielded by their knowledge and their wits and their luck. That he was from the dark and the light didn't mean he had to destroy anything, that, maybe, he might use the power held by the Simbrian to create a better world, for prosperity and harmony.

But that wasn't what the Simbrian wanted. In their audience with Hector Baggus, ex-head of Excelsus academy and, as it had turned out, guru and keeper of all knowledge of the Simbrian, Frank's future had been sliced off at the knees. Whatever life he thought he was going to lead after all of this had finished, he could forget it, screw it up and throw it in the nearest dustbin. It wasn't going to happen and any happiness he and Gabby thought they were going to share could take the next transport out of Garrim.

He looked at Gabby.

'Nothing,' he said. 'It doesn't matter.'

57

RESCUE

Baggus wasn't the happy ending they might have expected. That he wasn't still in possession of his part of the Simbrian was, at best, chilling, more chilling than the bitter wind that blew down the Ditch and had people pulling their collars up and heading for shelter.

He knew a lot, more than any individual they'd encountered so far but it was clear there were forces at work that even he didn't completely understand even if he was doing his bit to ease them along.

Whatever they had expected to achieve in his upstairs office inside the Lid, hidden away from his past, had disappeared down the drain with all the other shit and sticking their hands in the filth wasn't going to do any good.

It was too late. Jackson was now in control, with the imminent and inevitable closing of the loop of power by handing the final part of the Simbrian to Etamin, leaving Frank as the last part of the puzzle. The whetstone on the blade of power, the blade that would let his own blood as Etamin wielded it at his throat to claim her place as sovereign over any land she cared to crush.

Baggus had put his faith in words uttered to him fifteen or more years ago by Frank's mother. Not something you'd bet your house or your last silver crown on, something he would be wiser to than just about anyone else and Frank hoped he was right, that, in the final analysis, he'd played a winning hand, for all their sakes.

***

Back in his room, Frank flicked through the book, studying

each of the symbols as he turned the first few pages – the rose above two crossed arrows, the star cradled in the stag's antlers – all of them from Hums to Baggus, wondering what they'd all been told by his mother. Had they, too, been told to wait and hand over their piece of the Simbrian like Baggus? Perhaps, or maybe they didn't believe in Rebecca Penny's words though her charisma shone around the guardians like the midday sun.

He closed the cover and, with it, thoughts of understanding what it was telling them. Anyway, concentrating on anything other than the number of ways he was going to die was proving difficult in the wake of their conversation with the ex-head of Excelsus.

In the space of a few minutes he'd confirmed just about everything Frank had hoped he wouldn't, including the pedestal upon which Dagmar had belatedly placed himself. But it had been years since he taught Dagmar, years in which it was possible that even the brightest of minds had been grabbed and moulded to the greed of Kzarlac, yet Baggus was immoveable on Dagmar's motivation, giving weight to Dagmar's own words, adding a pinch of confusion to stir slowly into the mix.

But to shake Baggus's exposure of how the Simbrian story should play out was the thing Frank would never be able to do.

Absolatum. One word. Absolatum.

It had always been there, stalking him, like everything else, just biding its time, waiting for its own moment in the light, handing Frank and his friends its personal invitation to place its own unique piece into the puzzle.

And this was the final piece.

The final piece.

The destruction word. The power word, designed to kill, to destroy the Simbrian, to rid the world of the monster that stalked it. But not just the Simbrian. It would take the Simbrian heir with it. The word held Frank's destiny in its fist, goading him to action, daring him to finish what he, Gabby, Cas and Anya had started. The word that was only visible to him, the one person who could use it, the word that signed his own death warrant.

If he refused the challenge, if that was what you called your own death, there was only one other pathway. He'd be on the run forever and the hunt would never stop.

Etamin knew. Etamin who was in league with Jackson, a combination who could muster entire countries against him. Where could he go? He had no contacts or allies in Nahor, Aradusa or beyond and he couldn't ask the others to go with him, although he suspected they would, without hesitation.

Then their families would be in danger, as would Polly, Norris, Maddy, even Phoebe; Phoebe whose father had been butchered before his eyes. How many would they kill before he was shamed into giving himself up?

There would be nowhere to hide.

What would they do when they found him? He wouldn't let anyone control him. There was never any way he'd do the bidding of those who only sought power for the wrong reasons, those who had no idea from what unfathomable planes of power the Simbrian might conjure its force and if they couldn't get him to do it, then he was certain his young life would end so that someone else could take his place, Everbleed's prophesy fulfilled.

With the book back in their hands and their meeting with Baggus having borne the sourest fruit, they were done with Garrim.

In fact, they'd been done with it days ago but Duckett had cautioned them against leaving until he could be sure there was no danger, opening the door for boredom to enter and kick them all in the shins and they'd all had a bellyful.

Restlessness had been their companion in the wake of their visit to the Lid, but the western approach was the only one way out of the town and they knew they needed to make their getaway by themselves and not look to the local smugglers for help. The stink of Manville Symes still hung around them as a warning but Duckett and Cossens had told them there was no other way out.

As the worsening winter approached, the transport to Rhaeder only ran one day every week but, according to Cossens, it was as reliable as the word of a drunk. Its appearance was dependant on good weather and the town's eyes were bound to be on it, waiting for the emergence of the four teenagers, such was the reach of Jackson and the influence of Etamin.

They could wait it out if they wanted. Jackson would have to return to Rhaeder at some point soon and the Watch, rid of their paymaster, would doubtless tire and turn their attention to other, more lucrative matters.

But waiting was Etamin's game. She'd waited a long time to get this far, for Dagmar to bring her to the edge before she'd brought him down. She'd wait some more, that's what predators are conditioned to do if they are to stay at the top of the food chain and, where Frank was concerned, she was very, very hungry.

Frank knew he was being particularly quiet. He knew the others could tell. All of them tried, at various times, to draw him into a conversation about what to do, to create a plan. You always need a plan, however rubbish, but Frank's plans just involved his own death – at his own hands or those Etamin would have around his throat, either way the outcome was just the same.

'We'll find a way through,' said Gabby.

She meant it, even though she knew it wasn't possible. Her feisty determination remained intact, he could see her thumbing through whatever options she felt existed, planning. But Frank was beyond that. Only thoughts of the Simbrian's last moments clouded his mind. Either way the noose was already feeling tight round his neck, waiting to be hunted down by Etamin's forces, a hunt that would continue until she'd won, or he'd somehow manage to end this whole, sorry mission with a single word.

He'd have to head to Alsha Kar, find a way into the citadel, do the impossible to get into the room that housed the dais within which the Simbrian resided, fire it with the key and then destroy it before anyone noticed him. Completely impossible. Completely insane.

Kill it. Kill himself so the world could breathe easily. And all the time Etamin would be waiting. Of that he had no doubt. He'd observed plenty of spiders, motionless at the edge of their web just waiting, a natural instinct, knowing that it was simply a matter of time until a fly found its unsuspecting way into the deadly silken threads and met its end. And so it was with Etamin, with no prizes for guessing who the fly was.

At least the Gargoyle's Head monotony had one benefit. It gave Frank more time with Gabby. Waking up with her each chilled morning pushed the misery of the town back down its throat. Each hour spent entwined with her was bittersweet. His hunger for her doused with the stifling realisation of what approached. It might be months or years but, if you look for the downside, you'll always find it and Frank could only think of the future in terms of days.

They all sat in Frank's room doing not very much, which was all they had left to do as, outside, the dull, unvaried chug of snow from the sky wrote the story of their confinement. Conversation had run dry and none of them felt very much like breaking ranks to try and lift the mood.

A knock at the door didn't shake them, they were used to either Duckett or Cossens checking on them throughout the day, although they were doing it less and less, giving Frank the feeling of being a forgotten man in a forgotten town but he knew they were the thoughts of fools and forgotten was the one thing he would never be.

No one looked up as the door opened. It could well have been the whole company of the Watch standing there but the four of them were beyond caring.

'Don't bother getting up.'

Frank's head jerked up at the sound of the familiar voice. Spyro Spargo, dressed in a battered old overcoat, unshaven and looking like he'd fit right in down on the Ditch, stood in the doorway, leaning casually against the doorframe, arms folded, his boyish face beaming as if he'd just turned up late for a party.

They were on their feet, a sudden upward shift in the mood of the room at the thought of the rescue party having arrived.

'Spyro.' Frank could taste the relief on his voice. 'What are you doing here?'

A nonchalant shrug.

'Looking for four missing teenagers. What are you doing here?'

'It's a long story,' said Gabby. 'How did you know where to find us?'

'Knox,' said Spargo. 'I checked with him and he put me onto this place after I'd checked in with Frank's grandmother. She told me you were headed here.' Frank nodded, recalling how Knox had set them up with his old friend Duckett on their first visit. 'Unfortunately for the Alphaen, despite our customary attention to being brilliant, we've never been welcome in Garrim, so I thought I'd come on my own. Oh, and bring in the cavalry.' Spargo unfolded his arms and stepped into the room as the tall figure of Lawrence Penny appeared in the shadows behind him.

58

THE AWKWARD REUNION

Frank felt the instant drying of his mouth, the rise of something like anger in his throat as his dad ducked under the frame of the door. As warm emotions hit him from one side the sense of being caught off-guard had him biting down on his teeth. He sensed the looks from the others and the slight squeeze of Gabby's fingers on his arm.

'Dad.'

He could have been angry, might have wielded the silent treatment like a surly adolescent but, in that moment, after weeks fighting the chill of Garrim and all it had thrown at them, after having a death sentence declared on him that he was never likely to shrug off, Frank thought he had never felt so grateful to see his dad and, despite all that had passed since he last saw him, Frank got up and gave him a hug. Lawrence hugged him back. Just like old times at the farm, except it wasn't.

'Spyro said you might be in a spot of trouble.'

Frank and his dad exchanged looks. Frank had nearly forgotten the kind eyes and powerful build of the quiet, unassuming farmer.

'No, we're fine,' said Frank, confidence waning over his few words.

Spargo let out a laugh. 'If your definition of fine is being holed up in a tavern in the backstreets of Garrim because the Watch or worse are looking for you,' he said through his pristine teeth. 'Then I'd say you're doing a pretty decent job. If you want us to leave?'

'Only if you take us with you,' said Cas.

'Okay then boys and girls,' said Spargo, sweeping his eyes and charm across the room. 'If you want to get your things.'

'We're leaving now?' said Anya.

'Right now,' said Lawrence. 'Unless you'd rather stay.'

No, they'd not stay a minute longer and once they'd shut the door on Garrim, they'd make sure it stayed locked and the key disposed of.

Lawrence and Spargo gave the four teenagers time to pack their things, not that it took long, just a few belongings stuffed into a bag although they would all have gladly not bothered if it helped them to navigate a safe route through the western pass.

They headed down the stairs and into the back room where Duckett and Cossens both waited, ready with their farewells and probably hoping they'd never see Frank and the others again for all the potential bother they might have brought to the doorstep of the inn.

'Seems like there's no one looking out for you,' said Cossens with a glance to Lawrence and Spargo.

'We spent some time checking the western exit,' said Spargo. 'Nothing but your usual bunch of bandits and criminals, a couple I recognised, but no Watch or worse.'

Frank felt the churn of his stomach calm a fraction.

'But we can't take chances,' said Lawrence. 'I think it's best if you don't all go off together.'

'I think you're right,' said Duckett. 'No point drawing attention when you don't need to.'

'Thanks for taking care of them,' said Lawrence, his voice genuine and warm.

Duckett nodded an acknowledgement.

'No place for youngsters, Garrim,' he said. A look to Frank. 'So it's nice to see you, nice to see you leave.'

He gave his departing guests a warm smile.

Frank knew the words didn't exist that would convey their thanks to him. For the risks he'd taken in harbouring them and the safety he'd willingly provided. Duckett knew it too. Sometimes much can be said by saying nothing.

Lawrence put his gloves on, stretching his fingers right down to the ends.

'Frank, I'll take you out first, then I'll come back for the others. Spyro will wait until we're sure there's no issues.'

'And if there is.'

'Then I'll have to whip their sorry arses all the way to the Jixx, Frank,' said Spargo.

Lawrence pulled his coat on and went to the door, a hand on Frank's shoulder.

'Wait,' he said. 'Gabby's coming with us.'

'Frank, we can't risk the sharp eyes and slack jaws on the street. It'll only take one person to see you and before you know it you'll be in the hands of the Watch.'

'Then I'll stay,' said Frank. 'Take Anya first, she deserves it.'

Lawrence exhaled through his nose, a vexed breath. He looked at Gabby with a jerk of the head.

'Okay. Come on,' he said. 'Some choices are set up to regret. Let's hope this isn't one of them.' He nodded at Spargo, the sort of nod you give someone with unspoken wishes of luck. If their Garrim adventure was anything to go by, they'd need it but, in Frank's short experience, luck always seemed to be against the man who depends on it.

'Ready?' said Lawrence to nods. A look at Frank. Another brisk nod. 'Then let's be quick about it.'

59

PUZZLED

It was the first time they'd set foot outside the inn since their encounter with Baggus and Frank felt the reluctance in his boots, as if criminals and murderers were waiting at the door for him, hugging the shadows, blades ready for a throat.

Gabby grabbed him firmly by the wrist and followed Lawrence along the narrow backstreet and down the slope. There was no hesitancy, no fear in the man who had passed through Excelsus as a first-class swordsman and student of all things out of the ordinary, slipping back in time, into a role very different to anything Frank had seen of him as he grew up, radiating reassurance.

The rush of the southern storm drain sang a sweet melody as they crossed over a grate in the pavement, inviting Frank back. He felt the rise of bile in his guts, the clinging hands of fear as he relived his ordeal. It wouldn't have him again, not the bone-chilling water, not the biting cold, not the brute of a town.

Across the filthy streets to the western fringes, eyes alert, keen over their collars. Just yawning locals, scratching dogs and the stench of dishonesty and exploitation.

No one gave them a second look as they reached the bottom of the slope and headed through the suburbs, past the tight knots of slums, past the unfortunate residents that were past caring, past the foul-smelling slaughterhouse hidden on the outskirts, where offal was being sluiced into the drains and out towards the Jixx, the stink the only thing bothering around the residential parts.

No Watch, no Lashkens, no trouble.

Within fifteen minutes of brisk walking they were at the stables to the rear of the Troll's Cudgel.

Frank stopped and looked back at the town. It looked down on him, ready to puke its worst in their direction, but nothing moved, nothing came.

It had been so easy. Too easy.

There were two horses already saddled, reins wrapped around a rail, prepared for a quick getaway.

'Can you ride,' said Lawrence to Gabby.

She nodded.

'A bit.' No confidence in her voice which matched the wary look she gave the mounts.

'You can ride with me,' said Frank.

A nod and a smile from Gabby.

'I'm going back for the others,' said Lawrence.

'Do you want us to wait here for them?' said Frank.

Lawrence placed a reassuring hand on Frank's shoulder, his quiet eyes a balm to the knot of nerves in Frank's stomach.

'No, you need to head west, back to Rhaeder, I'll make sure Cas and Anya follow.' He looked at Frank. 'You remembered the book?' A nod. 'Okay, I'll see you at Polly's. Wait for me there.'

With that he turned and headed back through the filthy suburbs, towards the southern slopes, leaving Frank and Gabby alone.

They'd not be back, not for all the gold in Byeland. The town that ran to its own rules wouldn't miss them, but had taken more out of them than they would have imagined and as they thought of heading west through the mountain gorge he knew there would be no looking back, no smiling at the waning landscape and no hope that their memories of the Ditch would fade.

Frank placed his foot in the stirrup and swung himself up with a grace that surprised his bent and aching body. He held out his hand, which Gabby took before he pulled her up behind him. She leaned into him, pressing herself to his back and wrapping her arms around his waist.

'This is cosy,' she said.

'I could get used to it,' said Frank.

He pulled on the reins and gripped the horse with his legs, giving it its cue to move out, away, for good.

They moved fast, the mountains penning them in from both sides, but they were leaving, each step down the western valley, between the receding peaks, was a step towards something brighter, something more hopeful. And it was just the two of them, what might have been a carefree moment to savour for two teenagers in the early throes of romance, except death was at their backs and that didn't make for a pretty story.

Gabby gripped him tighter, pushed in closer, her lips at his ear.

'You told your dad about the book?' she said.

Frank stalled, drawing the horse to a stop. A pause for reflection.

'No,' he said. 'I never did.'

'But he just asked if you had it.'

He stalled a bit more.

'I never told him.'

60

The Objects

They spent the night hunkered down in a woodland, stars through the tree canopy, one watching over them, one that looked down upon their escape from Garrim and ushered them west with a slow sweep of its protective hand.

Freedom tasted good. Freedom they'd not enjoyed since they'd left Rhaeder on the transport weeks ago. But it was a freedom that wasn't written into his destiny, thrown to him so he should savour every fresh drop of it. A freedom Frank knew they ought not to get used to.

Leaving Garrim shed a hundredweight of all things bad and desperate from Frank's shoulders, yet there was something that left pin-pricks on his skin.

The sight of his dad, too brief for him to have absorbed what it meant to him. Years of love and care, guiding and protection, memories tainted by feelings at odds with the man who had brought him up as his own, despite knowing the woman he loved had born Dagmar's child.

Perhaps it took courage beyond Frank's understanding to do something like that, to agree to raise a child that wasn't yours because the person you adored asked you to and you asked nothing back of them.

Perhaps it was as simple as that and nothing else mattered, perhaps if he'd known from a young age it wouldn't have mattered. He'd thought about it in the quiet of the night when he was with Gabby knowing, without doubt, without hesitation, that he would do the same for her.

They woke early, just at the breaking dawn. No signs of Cas or Anya. Not yet.

He was sure they'd have got away, judging by how easy it had been for them and that they were in the finest of hands but he knew his restlessness would stay close by until they were reunited, confirmed by the continual glances back along the road.

They were on their way as the sun broke on the horizon, the mountains at their back, the long shadows of their ordeal receding fast, a near seamless move from his brief experience as a caged bird, hidden among the shadows and tension of the upstairs rooms at the Gargoyle's Head to the open landscape of Byeland. The fading greens in the onset of winter, a different breed of winter than that which had whispered its promises to Garrim.

By the time they reached the outskirts of Rhaeder, the sun was being claimed by the late afternoon. The comparison with Garrim was stark. Like comparing a meadow full of wildflowers with a pile of shit. The smells were so much better – expensive tobacco, no urine, no cheap perfume or garbage rot. Even the tang of coalsmoke seemed fainter and less likely to clog your throat. Clean streets, smiling faces, faces that didn't want to see you battered, robbed and left in the gutter. A world apart.

Despite the subtle warmth and the familiarity of the streets, there was no comfort, not even in the sea breeze on his face. He knew Etamin would find out he was there and come for him but he had the small luxury of knowing he had a head start, time to make a plan to delay the executioner's axe.

Polly didn't ask too many questions. She never did and Frank was grateful for her restraint as he and Gabby came through the door.

There were many things she or Norris could have thrown at them, but the fact she kept the conversation on warming them up, cleaning them up and feeding them up was a minor mercy and they were soon out of her way and in the small attic room as the early winter light dwindled.

They wouldn't stay long, only until Cas, Anya, Spargo and his dad had returned safely from Garrim. To stay longer would just be inviting something more bothersome through the door.

He knew he'd need to distance himself from those who had cared for him since he arrived at Excelsus. He needed to stop Etamin getting to anyone who had brushed his life, who might be used as the worm on the hook. All the Quigley's, Blackburn, Moonhunter, even some of his Excelsus classmates like Meredith, the Maddison twins, Eric and Jamie. They all stood as symbols of his existence, to be gutted one by one for no good reason other than they had known him. Not a cause to die for.

But there was one thing that couldn't wait as they closed the door to his attic room above the teashop, alert to the sound of anyone approaching up the stairs.

Gabby sat on the bed. Frank knelt in front of her, placing a comforting hand on her knee as he reached under the bed, reaching for the long wooden shaft that he'd brought back from Unwanted Island nearly a year ago and where it had lain untouched since, an insignificant length of timber that would have been destined for the fire – until now.

As he grasped it a cold spasm seized his arm, a burning chill ran up to his neck, scattering into his chest, making him wince. Gabby put her hand on his shoulder.

'You okay?'

Frank gave as convincing a nod as he could, but knew there was something different, something unusual about its touch. Like it was alive, like it was waiting, waiting for something that the centuries had kept from it, which only the passing of time had brought. That the heir of its power was about to feed it.

Frank held it in his hand, running his fingers over the grooves that had been carved into its surface by skilled hands from long ago. Gabby brought him back.

'Frank,' she said. 'The Elemental ball.'

With a nod, Frank retrieved the ball from his pocket with his free hand. Immediately he felt the sphere pulling against him, pulling itself toward the pole. Frank felt its power, had to fight to stop it wrestling itself from his grip, battling an invisible but toxic, binding force.

As slowly as he could, and with little finesse, he brought the two objects together, exactly as the book had shown them. The ball adhered itself to the end of the shaft, bonded in brotherhood, welcomed in from the dark. Immovable. Frank tugged slightly on the Elemental ball; it didn't budge, wouldn't budge and he could feel its energy, its gentle pulse through the length of wood.

He looked at Gabby.

'The cloth and the skewer. They're in the drawer, there.' A nod of his head had her opening the drawer to his bedside table. She pushed her hand in, moving it left and right before she removed both objects.

'I'm not sure what's going on,' he said, but he could detect the lie in his voice, the undercurrent of the tone that told Gabby he knew exactly what this was, that they all knew what this was from the moment they'd played to its tune through the magical prism of Zanmir's eye, yet not one of them had dared say it.

Frank held out his hand to Gabby who lay the small, square handkerchief in the flat of Frank's palm. The material pulsed, as though it had been caught by a gust, signalling to Frank to join it to its new sisters.

Frank curled his fingers, folding the material slightly so it rested in the crook of his palm before turning it over and placing it on the top of the ball. The material instantly flared, red flame burst through the gaps between Frank's fingers as the cloth wrapped itself around the sphere, twisting like a vine around a dying oak. Frank drew his hand back but the flames ceased as quickly as they'd appeared, like a trick from an adept magician except this was beyond illusion, beyond magic.

Gabby passed Frank the thin metal skewer, Sapphire Hark's

special possession; the thing that kept her safe from discovery now glowed cobalt in Frank's hand, offering him an invitation. Frank thought of the picture in the book, how the straight length of steel pushed itself through the top of the Elemental ball, securing it to the wooden staff. He hesitated, wondering if there was any way not to complete the ritual, how not to take it to an end where none of them could be sure what was going to happen but something had infused the air in the room, making demands which he was unable to refuse.

'You know what this is,' said Gabby, her voice rigid, tense.

'I can *feel* what it is,' said Frank, tightening his grip on the construct in his hand, offering up the skewer.

It wanted him, wanted to possess him. He could feel the power probing his fingertips, tapping at the windows looking for a way in, the spread of darkness, like a spill of water finding the cracks in the dry earth.

He could feel a change in the weight of the locket, felt it straining to be free, the chain at the back of his neck beginning to bite.

In his pocket he felt movement, the movement of something trapped, working its way out of their bonds, pushing to be let out.

'I'm not sure I can do this,' he said. His glance up at Gabby had her reflecting the creep of terror he was beginning to experience.

He'd been focused until now, unwavering. They all had. They'd pursued the guardians, tracked down Zanmir's eye, the key of darkness and now he knew they'd been doing all of that without an eye on the endgame, of what this was all coming to and without a plan of what they would do when they arrived at their destination, a destination at which they were about to disembark. Right now.

'Then we should stop,' said Gabby. An instruction rather than an option. 'Look, we know how this all fits together, right? So we don't have to do this.'

Frank nodded, forcing back the desire to continue, a desire he knew, for certain, wasn't of his making. He fought it, fought for control, for dominance until whatever had him caught up in the battle hissed and stamped its feet, receding a petulant step – this time.

'But it's not a question of doing it,' said Frank. 'It's about why, or what we're doing. This can't be the Simbrian. It *can't* be. Etamin has it in her fortress, probably complete by now. She has all the original parts from each of the guardians, we know that, we know what Dagmar was doing. I've seen it. Felt it. That's how it works. What we have is...something else.'

Whichever way he cut it, it made no sense. Everything they'd discovered about the Simbrian from the very start of their quest pointed in Dagmar's direction. Each guardian, Irundi, Jackson – they all knew what was at stake and what they needed to protect or seek.

Not once during the last few years was there anything that mentioned a random collection of objects, disconnected, ordinary, objects that his mother had so carefully arranged in their enchanted book. She'd shrouded it so thickly that no one could decipher her text, no one except them.

She was cunning beyond measure, had planned everything thus far with an ingenuity beyond the cleverest scholar, with a precision beyond the brightest engineer, always with a specific purpose, that was something of which he was completely certain. Nothing of the trail she had left was random or a matter of chance. It was seamless, slick and deliberate.

They were missing something, something fundamental, something important, something that would finally put the riddle of the Simbrian to rest but what they had was unquestionably real and all the time the thought tumbled around and around in his head, something Baggus had mentioned – is this a third incarnation?

The assembled pieces broke apart in Frank's hands, like he was breaking bread, as if each part could sense they no longer needed to be bound to each other and as they dropped to the ground he could have sworn he detected the faint mutterings of the sinister, obscene ancient curses with the promise it would be back.

The bits lay on the floor at their feet, motionless yet primed with a life force Frank couldn't comprehend. He could feel the spasms in his biceps, through his chest, the sweat patching under his arms and trickling down his back.

Whatever he'd just roused, he knew he'd barely nicked the surface, knew he hadn't had a sight of the raw mass of heaving energy that thumped and pounded to be released. He hadn't even put all the parts together and it had set itself to take him apart and reassemble him in any way it saw fit, like he was just clay in the hands of a frenzied but talented sculptor.

'I wish I knew what was going on,' he said, looking at Gabby. 'This....' He swept his hand over the collection of objects. 'This scares me.'

They'd been through much – Etamin, Dagmar, Balal, Irundi, all of which would test the most valiant and fearless of men – there was much Frank could have been afraid of throughout their quest but nothing that had gone before scared him this much.

Whatever he had before him was a nightmare made real, the sort of prowling evil that answers to nothing and no one, that's best kept buried lest it tense and pounce and rip out your throat. The problem was that he could hear the faint knocking of destiny at his door and keeping it shut was getting more and more difficult.

'We should get all of this away from here,' said Gabby. 'Maybe find somewhere...' She paused.

'What?' said Frank.

'I was going to say somewhere more secure, but I'm not sure where that would be.'

She was right. Safe wasn't something the Simbrian understood. Untethered, the world would suffer and only one end was befitting for such a monster.

'I don't know what to do,' said Frank.

He looked at Gabby, could tell she had no answers.

He couldn't pull it all together in his mind. Either that, or he didn't want to. Both he and Gabby knew where the signposts were pointing. He had his destiny now, his direction and a path that led away from her. It sat unspoken between them, a block of lead weighing him down.

He never wanted to let Gabby go, but knew he'd have to. The Simbrian heir was his burden to carry. No one else deserved to be dragged down through the earth with its weight and as he looked at her he felt the dark door open inside him and through it fell all the things he wanted to remember about her.

'We'll find a way through, Frank.'

She meant it. It was hopeless, but she still meant it. He nodded as convincingly as he could. He felt a little lost, like a child in a crowded market, strangers everywhere. But he had her and she was stronger than he would ever be, would guide him through this.

'I can't put you in danger.' His voice cracked slightly, giving her a glimpse into the pain he felt inside.

'I'd be disappointed if you didn't.' Her eyes flashed. He knew she'd go to the extremes of time for him, would fight to keep him safe.

'You're the only one I ever want to disappoint,' he said.

She was the one he wanted to hold, to make laugh, to bare his scars to, to watch the sunrise with, the starlight, to share his secrets but something inside him kept telling him, reminding him he never would.

'It's late,' said Gabby. 'Why don't we meet back here tomorrow? The others should be here by then. We can make a plan.' And you always need a plan, however rubbish, and trust you can see it through.

She made to push herself up, but Frank made a soft grab for her hand.

'Stay,' he said, urged.

He thought she might resist, that she might have had enough for one day, goodness knows most people would have had enough for a lifetime, but her eyes told Frank the opposite. She understood him, that he couldn't make sense of this all by himself.

He needed her now and always would. It had started with the storm of the Simbrian and it had never ended or let up. She'd blown into his life on the wind and rain and their quest had had him off balance ever since but she provided a gentle hand on the tiller and now he needed her more than ever.

She got to her feet and pulled the curtains, thrusting them into shadow. She turned to him, something reckless in her face. She moved quickly and cat-like to him, pushing him back on the bed, straddling him and pressing her lips hard to his.

'Let's worry about it in the morning.'

61

THE INTRUDER

Frank rolled out of bed, careful not to wake the slumbering girl laid out beside him, and pulled on a pair of trousers. Thirst clawed at his throat. Rain softly patted at the window.

He glanced at the floor, at his bag, where he'd placed six of the gifts the night before, ready to take them as far away from Polly's as he could. The wooden shaft sat propped against the wall by the door.

Gabby stirred. He took a minute to watch her, to imprint her on his mind. He knew he could stand and watch her until the house crumbled around him and never tire of the bold contours of her face, the smooth curves of her hips as she moved slightly under the covers.

With a careful pull, he closed the bedroom door behind him and descended the two flights of stairs to find Polly, Norris and Maddy by the back door, putting on their coats.

'Hello darlin',' said Polly. 'Didn't want to disturb you.' Frank glanced at Maddy who immediately turned pink, avoiding his eyes. 'You take your time, we're off out for the morning. We'll see you later.'

'Have a nice time,' said Frank, reaching into the cupboard and taking down two glasses. Polly looked at him, then at his hands and back to him with raised eyebrows before heading off.

He followed them through to the shop and watched as they left through the shop entrance, slight relief that he wouldn't have any award questions once Gabby emerged from his room, excitement that he now had time to pass with just him and her until Cas and Anya arrived, images he let linger as he set the two glasses down on the counter and grabbed a jug of cold juice from the shelf, slowly filling the glasses before heading back to the small hallway and the bottom of the staircase.

Frank started up the first flight, eager to be back next to Gabby, to feel the security of her warm body next to his when something made him stop. He turned and looked back down the stairs. A prickling sensation pulled at the nape of his neck, drawing him back down to the front door, rarely used by the family who preferred the ease of the shop entrance.

He placed the glasses on the bottom step then stared at the door, the seconds stretching out, his hand reaching for the handle. He paused, then pulled on it.

Open.

A slow dip of the head to the floor.

A wet boot-print.

He backed away a step, his eyes pinned to the large, dark prints on the carpet, following them to the foot of the stairs then...up. Up the first flight.

He retraced his steps back to the first floor landing. Slowly, slower than was good for him, hand pushing absently on the wall, his anticipation getting the better of him. Perhaps Norris had popped out that way for something and forgotten to close it, but he'd been pulling his boots on in the kitchen five minutes ago.

He fought his senses for another explanation as he reached the first floor, tracing the line of prints as they headed along the landing to the second flight. The flight that led to the second floor, to his room.

Gabby.

Frank abandoned all good sense and ran. Along the landing and up the stairs, taking them two at a time, hot breaths exiting his lungs as he stopped at his bedroom door.

Open.

Frank stood in the doorway. Dagmar stood pressed back against the window, Gabby held tight in front of him, his forearm anchored around her neck, a finger held to his lips, undiminished by his time in captivity at the hands of his paymaster. Both of Gabby's hands gripped Dagmar's arm, trying to wrestle herself away but strength was his master and he didn't budge.

'Shut the door,' he said. For Gabby's sake, Frank didn't hesitate.

Then, to Frank's surprise, Dagmar let her go. Gabby stepped away and was standing next to Frank in an instant. Dagmar propped himself against the window sill, rainwater still dripping from his coat and hair, relaxation written across his face, despite a deep cut to his lip and painful-looking lacerations across his neck.

He pulled at his gloves, making a nonchalant gesture of taking them off and placing them on the sill beside him. He crossed his ankles, a short wince as Frank noticed the tear in his trouser leg. Dagmar cleared his throat and folded his powerful arms across his chest, raising his eyes to them, eyes where the devil danced.

'What do you want?' said Frank.

'How do you know this isn't just a social visit?'

'Don't —'

'Play games? And why would I come all the way here to do that?'

'I'll call the authorities.'

'That would be a shame,' said Dagmar, a complete lack of concern in his words. 'Then you wouldn't get to hear what I have to say.'

The room paused, Frank latching on to the crumb that Dagmar had just thrown, the master tactician. Dagmar pursed his lips.

'I thought I ought to at least thank you for the help, Frank.' He glanced at Gabby who looked on, unsurprised.

Frank had filled her in on everything that had happened at Etamin's house in Garrim, explaining he'd dropped the lock-picks on the bed in the cellar, shielded from the guard, giving Dagmar the edge of an escape. Not that he thought he needed it. 'I must say I was slightly surprised, and I'm never surprised.'

Frank knew Dagmar's game, a game he needed to play. Back

in the cellar he'd fed him the barest of details he knew would pick at Frank from the moment he'd uttered them and he knew Frank would be unable to resist the opportunity to try and understand, that he'd wrestle with the questions Dagmar posed. Questions to which only Dagmar undoubtedly had the answers, and only if he was free.

Dagmar noticed the look on Frank's face.

'Something on your mind?'

He knew, knew he had Frank on the hook.

'You said you protected the Simbrian from the Kzarlac side,' said Frank. Dagmar just waited, not even offering a nod, not the slightest reveal, holding everything just beyond Frank's grasp. 'But you've been assembling the parts of the Simbrian, surely you don't deny that.'

'Of course I don't,' said Dagmar, like he'd just been asked the stupidest question. 'I showed you after all.'

'You can't be doing that unless you want to use it for your own ends,' said Gabby, thunder brewing on her face. 'If you were protecting the Simbrian, you wouldn't track down the guardians. You'd leave them be.'

Dagmar's face gave nothing away.

'You mean that's what *you'd* do.' He stretched his wounded leg, gritting his teeth with the challenge. 'Doing what everyone expects can lead you to the outcome everyone expects and I've always prided myself in doing things differently. After all, what's the point otherwise?'

More teasing words.

'You're a liar,' said Gabby.

'Are you sure?'

Frank felt Gabby shift, a note of hesitancy rang out in the doorway.

'Of course, rumour and lies have fed my reputation, which seems to have been to my advantage,' said Dagmar. 'The greatest camouflage.'

'Then what have you been doing?' said Frank.

Dagmar's hand went to his beard. His dark eyes drank down the two teenagers.

'I knew that the Simbrian would be rebuilt, we all did, as Everbleed's incessant rambling confirmed. Believe me, Frank, no one wants that. Well, nearly no one. I'm sure Hector Baggus would have told you that it's a pathway that should never be trodden, but people like Etamin Dahke think they have the shoes for the job and would have themselves believe they could master something so chaotic and powerful.' A disappointed shake of the head. 'Why is the world so full of fools?'

Frank felt himself falter on Dagmar's words, solidly spoken. He looked at Gabby who wore the face of the unconvinced.

'So what are you doing if you're not seeking the Simbrian to conquer the world?' she said, throwing down the challenge.

'Well, since you're so interested, I've been trying to execute my well-thought-through, though highly dangerous plan which, to my regret, appears to have backfired right as I dip for the finish line.' He stroked his beard, taking in Frank and Gabby as their silence asked him to go on. Dagmar paused, water falling in steady drops from his hair. 'You see, the problem with having the guardians scattered all over the place is that someone, some-when, would eventually discover who they are and hunt them all like new-born fawns.'

'They've kept themselves hidden for centuries,' said Gabby. 'Who's to say they couldn't keep hiding?'

'Because things change.' His eyes rested on Frank. 'With each generation the guardians get more careless, as if they don't take their duty seriously and with carelessness comes danger. Do you deny that your mother found them all?' A slight raise of the eyebrows that Frank tried to ignore.

'That's different,' said Frank.

'In what way?'

Frank struggled for a response. He didn't know. He had no idea why his mother would embark on a fool's pathway to find them all. In all of this, he'd yet to understand what drove her to her death at the end of Simbrian road and he wasn't about to concede a point to Dagmar.

'She evidently did it, as have I,' said Dagmar. 'And so have you. It would be a matter of time before people with more sinister motives would do the same.' Gabby huffed, she had Dagmar pinned all over with sinister motives, as did Frank. 'It might be in a hundred years, it might be next week, but it would happen, eventually. I knew that from my years at Excelsus and knew I needed to act, one day.'

If Dagmar could see the scepticism in Frank and Gabby, he didn't show it.

'So, what was your plan?' said Frank

'Simply, collecting all the parts and keeping them completely hidden so that no one would ever find them. All under the ruse of the glory of Kzarlac. Only Etamin and I knew where they were and I planned to kill Etamin once I had them all. Then the world would be safe, the guardians would be released from their burden and, after I'd gone, no one would ever be able to find their legacy buried high up in a warded tower and the legend of the Simbrian would once again become just that. Simple, and I love a bit of simplicity.'

'How very noble,' said Gabby to a shrug from Dagmar. 'Painting yourself as the unsung hero.'

'I was never very good at painting,' said Dagmar with a smile.

But Frank felt himself hesitate, trying to find a crack in the plausibility of Dagmar's words. In a few sentences Dagmar had thrown a blanket over what he thought and to sort the truth from the lies in the face of the man with the orange streak in his hair was the thing of impossibilities.

'Except you didn't fool her,' said Frank.

Dagmar shook his head.

'A knife edge. I just needed Baggus to agree to give it up, but I couldn't find him and Jackson had him in his pocket. That self-serving bastard knew how far I'd got and rather than siding with me, opted for the heady aroma of supremacy and the blinkered trappings of power. A rather stupid coin toss, wouldn't you say? Now he and

Etamin have all seven and will have us begging for mercy or digging our own graves. Neither of which appeal to me. I'm not very good at begging. Or digging.'

'Then it was a stupid idea to start looking for the guardians,' said Gabby, still looking for the weak point on which she could hang Dagmar's words. 'Maybe you shouldn't have started for all the trouble it's led to.'

Dagmar turned his mouth down and shrugged.

'The road was always going to be dangerous,' he said. 'And I concede that you may be right. Even I thought it a foolish idea at the start and would put it back in its box, only to open the lid again. I'd mull over the consequences over the years and never quite got to the starting line.' He paused, checking himself, his next words. 'But every bonfire needs a match and it was someone else that eventually convinced me I should do it.' His eyes latched on to Frank who knew exactly what the next words would be before Dagmar uttered them. 'Your mother.'

62

THE REWRITING

He knew the words would find their target, would have Frank thumbing through his already brimming mind for an appropriate response, but silence was all he offered.

'Why?' said Gabby.

'Why what?'

'Why did she bring a piece of the Simbrian all the way to your doorstep, then contrive to create it and kill herself? It makes no sense.'

'As you say, it makes no sense.'

'Then why?'

'I wish I knew.'

Where Dagmar had always displayed the self-possessed look of someone at ease with whatever he faced, Frank detected the subtle change in him, the look of someone who can't find their door-key and doesn't know where to start looking for it. Something lost.

'She convinces me to locate the guardians, then does it herself anyway, like some sort of twisted game with no rules or boundaries but, then, that was Rebecca.' His eyes lost their focus. 'Rebecca,' he said under his breath. He looked down, clasping his hands together, his mood changing with the beat of his heart. A moment passed. Frank glanced at Gabby before Dagmar looked up again. 'Ever seen a shooting star?' Frank nodded. Plenty. 'It dazzles you, you follow it. A thing of unparalleled beauty. You watch it, can't take your eyes off it. The most wondrous and fascinating thing you ever had the pleasure to have witnessed.' He paused. 'But as you follow it, it turns black, disappears into bottomless night. All you see is darkness but still you look, sure it will return, just for you, just for your eyes and all the time you wonder how something so breath-taking could turn into something you can't even see.' He gazed through Frank. 'Even now you wish you could bring it back, knowing you had it for just a second and that it lit up your life for a moment. But then you realise it's turned dark forever.' His eyes focused on Frank. 'That,' he said. 'Was your mother.'

Then Frank saw it in Dagmar's face. The same look Moonhunter had failed to keep tethered, the same look they'd drawn from Baggus.

'You loved her?'

'Some people aren't capable of feeling loved.' Not the answer to his question, but Frank saw the faraway look that briefly hung in Dagmar's eyes and he knew. The words Dagmar had said to him back in Etamin's citadel: *I know from bitter experience exactly what it's like to have lost the one thing you desire more than anything else*. Frank had thought he was referring to the first build of the Simbrian, that he burned at the loss of the power that had been within his reach, but that wasn't it. It was something else, someone else.

'She'd always taunt me that she would do something – change the future, change history, would have those that hold power running in different directions. She kept on, provoking me to do the same, like rebuilding or destroying the world was some sort of game, just a contest to simply be won or lost, one she could walk away from with no conscience about the outcome.'

Dagmar's face, animated until now, darkened.

'Then she did the impossible.' He didn't have to spell the words. 'I was there, the day she created it, the day she destroyed it. It was as if she created it from nothing, as if she'd just wished the thing appear. Such dark talent, drawn up from the earth, through the blood that ran so vividly through her veins. She wanted me to know she had it, to set me a challenge that she knew I wouldn't win.'

'Which was?'

'To stop her. To stop her fulfilling the first part of Everbleed's prophesy. If I could prevent her from destroying it, it would mean the second part wouldn't follow, not for now at least.'

'But she still killed herself.'

'If you mean she won the game, then yes. I failed and, as you well know, just the thought of failure sticks in my throat but I never expected to beat her. Not her.'

It was unlike Dagmar to speak in the reflective tones of defeat. It was like he turned up for a fight, expecting to be knocked out by the first punch but Frank could sense Dagmar felt he'd met his match.

'Not much of a prize, though,' said Dagmar. 'Your own death but, looking back, I shouldn't have been surprised by anything she did. Though, strangely, she left me a picture, a clue to one of the guardians, a picture of two crossed arrows underneath a rose.' The symbol for Wordsworth Hums, the first page in their purple book.

'Like she was sending me a message, a final jibe, telling me to find them, to do what she wanted. I kept it for a while, then, one day, when Etamin rose to power, I accepted the challenge she'd left me, like she still taunted me from the grave, but I only did so to rid the world of the Simbrian, forever. So I went looking for the others under the guise of doing it for the supremacy of Kzarlac, if ever that was a cause to brag to your grandmother about.'

'And you found them,' said Frank.

A nod.

'It's interesting, isn't it, that when you start searching for something so special, all of a sudden that which you desire happens to find its way into your hands. Perhaps I should have wished for something more exotic.' A smile at his own attempt at humour. 'Rachel Penny gave me Lawrence's, your mother gave me hers and I came by Edwina Chetto's via that poor excuse of a husband of hers. Then you led me to Sapphire Hark. Menetti volunteered his —'

'You killed Menetti,' said Gabby. Not a question. Dagmar shook his head and huffed a laugh.

'I never killed him.'

'What?' said Gabby. 'Everyone knows you killed him once you'd stolen his part of the Simbrian.' *You have me as a butcher?*

348

'Rumour and lies,' said Dagmar. 'He handed me his fragment of the Simbrian, then took his own life.'

There are some words you never expect to hear, not strung together in a sentence, one that makes no sense, yet there they were, put on a plate for Frank and Gabby to pick at. The truth? Who knew?

'Handed it to you?' said Gabby. 'Why would he do that?'

'Why indeed,' said Dagmar. 'He didn't say, but I got the feeling he'd been waiting for me to come and get it. He appeared unusually pleased to be getting rid of it, as if the final act of his life was a meaningful one. Perhaps the strain of being a guardian does that to you.'

'But you invaded Prismia.' Now Gabby's temper flared, hatred in her eyes colder than the rooftops in Garrim. 'You slaughtered my people.'

Frank could feel the emotion boiling inside her, that she would take her chances in a fist fight right there. Dagmar shook his head, his constant rebuttal of anything they threw at him trying to push Frank off balance.

'I'm sorry Gabby,' said Dagmar. 'But I had nothing to do with any of that. It was all part of Etamin's empire building. In fact, I tried to stop her.'

In the face of Dagmar's denial, whatever insults and threats Gabby had poised died in her throat, a tiger in mid-leap.

'I couldn't have her killing Menetti before I found him,' said Dagmar. 'I'm sorry about Prismia. It was all so unnecessary, like most things touched by her evil hand.'

The edge of compassion on Dagmar's words was undeniable, the sympathy in his eyes tangible. Gabby took it in, a glance at Frank who was equally astonished.

'But didn't you kill Ludlow Hums?' said Frank, feeling the certainty move and start to crumble under his feet. Dagmar's face tightened.

'Have you listened to anything I said?' A sharp edge to his voice, a raise of the volume. 'You could have saved me a lot of bother had you just told me where he was, instead I had to convince that stuff-ball Herbert Lanks to get a message to him which was like extracting all of my own teeth, followed by my eyeballs.'

'So where are they?'

'Ah. The Hums brothers are living out the rest of their lives in a beach house down near Copperhead Sands. Like Miss Hark, they were both happy to dissolve into anonymity, although I am a little surprised at her choice. Garrim, I'd rather shit in my own mouth.'

Frank wanted to disbelieve every word that came out of Dagmar's mouth, that he stood there spewing lies to save his skin but he was his usual sure, measured self and his skin needed no saving. He owed them nothing, had no reason even to be there, let alone tell them anything and nothing about him indicated he was speaking anything but the truth.

'That doesn't explain why you're here,' said Frank. 'Nor does it explain why my Mother did what she did.'

'No, I guess it doesn't.' Dagmar's eyes fixed on the door. He bent his leg, pulling on his facial muscles before standing and brushing himself down. 'You know, fleeing across Byeland with the spectre of death on your shoulders is thirsty work but, then, you'd know that. A drink would be good.'

63

THE INTERRUPTION

Down in the kitchen, Frank pulled open the door of Norris's well-stocked drinks cabinet, propping the staff up against it, his bag at his heels. He'd picked both up as he'd left the room, leading Dagmar down the two narrow flights of stairs, Gabby at the rear, holding the book.

Dagmar limped slightly, but if he was in pain he didn't show it. From the severity of his injuries, Frank could tell he'd fought hard to prise himself away from the murderous grasp of Etamin, an episode that had left him battered and bloodied but one that hadn't stopped him making the journey to Rhaeder, nor would it stop him making whatever onward journey he had planned – a similar one to Frank, no doubt, away from death.

Dagmar slumped into a chair, flexing his foot as Frank placed a bottle of whiskey on the table in front of him. He and Gabby remained standing, still a natural precaution despite Dagmar's condition and revelations.

'Don't worry about a glass,' he said, pulling the bottle towards him. He pulled out the stopper and took a long draw. 'Ah, that will do nicely.' He raised the bottle like a waning drunkard. 'Join me?'

Frank gave a slight shake of the head.

'I think I need to keep a clear head,' he said.

'Well, as long as it remains on your shoulders,' Dagmar gave a shallow smile. 'The landscape has certainly changed since we first encountered each other behind the walls of Excelsus, don't you think?'

Maybe the best of understatements.

'Where will you go?' said Frank. 'Not Kzarlac?'

'No, although I don't think Etamin will bother with me, now. The only way I'd be welcomed back to Kzarlac would be with a noose around my neck.'

'What about those loyal to you?'

'Ah, loyalty. Perhaps the most overrated of qualities. Loyalty belongs either to the highest bidder or to those armed to the teeth and I think Etamin has cornered the market in both and, when you think about it, most find it better to side with the winners. Even the most loyal of dogs can change their masters, with the right encouragement.' He took a shallow swig, sucking in a long breath. 'So, Frank, before I head away and out of your life for good or meet my inevitable end, I thought it would be the right thing to do for you to understand a thing or two about your father.'

'And you're all about doing the right thing, aren't you?' said Gabby.

A wry smile.

'My Dad?' said Frank. 'But you haven't seen him in years.'

'Maybe that's the point.' Dagmar turned the bottle in his hand, inspecting the label, inspecting the glow of the liquor inside. 'Whiskey ages well, gets smoother with the passing of the years, tastes so good that you'd be forgiven for thinking it always tasted that way. But what you have now isn't what you started out with.' He looked up. 'In fact, the flavour was once bitter and difficult to stomach.'

'You've always called him coward.'

'That's right.'

'Why?'

'Because we all knew – me, him, Simeon, Spyro – that the Simbrian should never see the light of day, that's why I was happy for him to keep and protect his part. It was just us, just the four of us that could make the difference if we all stood together. *All* of us. I thought we were all alike.'

Dagmar's words slowly brought the dawn to Frank. There was

352

so much at stake, so few to wear the mantle, yet Lawrence Penny had waved his farmer's hand in Dagmar's face and told him he wasn't interested in protecting the world from the horrors the Simbrian would wield if Everbleed's words ever came to pass.

'But he stepped away and the question I've been mulling over for as long as I can remember is why?'

The same question Simeon and Baggus had thrown his way.

'Why does he have to be part of it? Any of it?'

Dagmar pursed his lips, considering the question, considering the answer.

'We don't always choose our responsibilities, Frank.' He looked from Frank to Gabby. 'If the past couple of years have taught you anything, they will have taught you that. So you'll forgive me for thinking your father should have shouldered his share. I know he's told you that he lost interest, but I don't see how that can be.' He let the comment hang, opening the door and inviting Frank through. 'You see, when someone so intelligent, so talented, so vain is surrounded by something like the Simbrian, not only that, but also happens to be a guardian, it's not possible to be agnostic about it. You're either in, or you're out.'

'So he was out.'

'You'd think so, but there's a problem with that.' Frank waited. 'Why, then, would he pursue Rebecca? The Simbrian obsessive, hm? The only other person I've known to be in so deep is the person who now wants me half-way up the blade of a longsword. You want nothing to do with the Simbrian, then you want nothing to do with Rebecca and Lawrence wanted *everything* to do with her. Every. Little. Thing.'

'He loved her,' said Gabby. 'Surely it's as simple as that.'

Dagmar shook his head.

'Simple things can cover all manner of complexities. There was something more to it,' he said. 'She didn't feel the same way. She'd come to me when she was supposed to be seeing him, full of cunning and desire, then she'd leave my bed and go back and, all the time,

Lawrence stayed interested and, unusually for him, forgiving.'

    'Perhaps I'm the forgiving sort.'

    The voice from behind Frank cut the room.

    Lawrence Penny stood in the doorway through to the teashop.

64

THE CONFRONTATION

His short, greying hair glistened with moisture, drops of water fell slowly from his chin. The nasty bruise that stained his cheek and the bloodied collar under a thin, painful-looking cut gave voice to his unspoken story of his exit from Garrim.

All eyes landed on him. Lawrence looked at Frank.

'You made it back,' said Lawrence, his face showing the kind of fatherly concern Frank had grown up with. 'No problems?'

Frank shook his head.

'Where are Cas and Anya?'

'Spyro's with them. We had a spot of bother getting away. Don't worry, they'll be here soon, we just have to wait a while.'

He'd already swept the room with his eyes, as if he was checking the odds ahead of a fight, his gaze coming to rest on Dagmar.

The man may once have been his closest friend, but there was no sign of that in the look that passed between them, in fact, sworn enemies would have looked at each other with greater cheer. However many years that had ground by since they last set eyes on each other, the passing of time and all of its crimes hadn't healed any rifts.

He took two paces into the room, closing the space between him and Dagmar, shedding his coat and draping it over a chair. He ran his palm swiftly back and forth across his head, spraying droplets of water like a dog shaking its coat after a dip in the river.

Frank felt the grip of Gabby's hand around his bicep as well as the acute rise in tension in the room.

'Well, well,' said Dagmar. Measured words, a touch playful,

fixing on Frank's dad, watching him like a fox watches a hare, waiting for it to bolt. 'My old, old pal, Lawrence Penny. It must be, what, twenty years?' Lawrence pulled at the fingers of his gloves. Crisp, urgent movements. 'Some might call it a pleasant surprise, but I'll just call it a surprise. Not going to say hello?'

'Dagmar,' said Lawrence with a curt dip of the chin. 'Looks like you cut yourself shaving. No wonder you grew a beard. Can't say it suits you.'

Dagmar nodded to Lawrence's face. 'That looks painful. Someone shove a cactus in your face or did you find a bit of rough down on the Ditch? You always struck me as the sort.'

Dagmar was unable to resist a broad smile at his own words. Lawrence's nose twitched, unimpressed.

'If only your boots were as smart as your mouth.'

Dagmar stretched his good leg out and looked at his foot, pivoting his heel left and right.

'Vurrian leather, these,' said Dagmar, leaning forward and wiping at a patch of invisible dust down the length of his boot. 'Hand-made. A thing of quality – honest to a fault and have never let me down.' He looked up and fixed his stare on Lawrence, letting it settle. 'Some things let in the wet far more easily, don't you think.'

Lawrence huffed. He stepped to the table, pulling out the chair at the opposite end from Dagmar and dumping himself onto it before grabbing the bottle of whiskey. The room silenced as he dragged a mouthful from the neck, letting out a satisfied gasp as he swallowed, wiping his knuckles across his mouth.

Frank stood back, fascinated by the trade of insults cutting through the air before him, a look at Gabby who raised her eyebrows at him.

'What's this about,' said Frank.

Both men just looked at each other, each waiting for the other to break or offer an explanation.

'Don't believe anything this liar tells you,' said Lawrence, eyes fixed across the room. 'He'd do just about anything to see my name in the gutter. Isn't that right?' Stillness from Dagmar. 'You see, he's still sore. I think he has a nasty cut that won't heal properly, that chafes and gnaws, that has irritated him since back then and he still blames me.' A shake of the head from Lawrence. 'Like you say, Dagmar, over twenty years and I can still smell it festering.'

Dagmar's surface cheeriness faded a touch, he gritted as if the dentist had unwittingly brushed an exposed nerve.

'More like a boil that needs lancing,' said Dagmar through his teeth. 'If only I had my sword and the use of all my limbs, I'd happily put an end to you, you scheming son of a bitch but, quite frankly, I'm not sure I could be bothered. We could always fight with pitchforks, if you'd prefer.'

'I don't think you'd want to fight me, Dagmar,' said Lawrence. 'You know it wouldn't end well.'

Frank felt himself tense. He couldn't remember all the tight situations he'd been squeezed into since his Simbrian quest had begun, but this was beginning to feel like the most uncomfortable.

The bag of items sat behind his heels. He was conscious of it whispering in his ear, pleading with him to be away, like a haul in a robbery where he was still in the victim's house.

He pushed the voices away and flicked a finger at the book in Gabby's hand, drawing Lawrence's attention.

He eyed the purple leather binding as Gabby turned it over in her hands, her eyes questioned Lawrence.

'How do you know about that?' said Frank with a dip of his head to the book.

'What do you mean?' said Lawrence.

'I've never told you about it, yet you knew I had it. How?'

Frank saw the hesitation in his dad. Briefer than a blink, but he noticed. Lawrence's eyebrows dipped.

'You told me when I was at the festival.' *Liar*. 'Or when you came home last. You showed it to me.' *Liar – liar, liar, liar.*

Lawrence shrugged, certain in his words, not thrown or wavering in his conviction that Frank was mistaken. But Frank had learned the lessons of the Simbrian – sometimes complex, sometimes obvious, sometimes harsh – lessons learned the hard way. He'd learned from early on not to let others try and bury the foundations of truth. Those on the Simbrian trail might want to throw him off the scent but he knew to trust himself.

'No I didn't.'

Silence.

'Seems like he didn't, Lawrence,' said Dagmar with a lick of mischief. Lawrence wasn't put off.

'I'm sure you did.'

'Frank seems to think you might be hiding something,' said Dagmar, leaning back in his chair and lacing his fingers behind his head. 'And, knowing you, I'd have to say he has a case.' He turned to Frank. 'You see. Like I was saying, your great father is quite the expert when it comes to concealment.'

'Why don't you tell that to someone who gives a shit,' said Lawrence. 'Same old Dagmar. Always overthinking, always coming to the wrong conclusions and look where it's got you.'

Dagmar wasn't put off.

'Perhaps Frank might wonder if there is anything else you might not be telling him, telling any of us, hm?'

'Always the clever mouth, Dagmar.'

'Of course, but don't forget my clever mind. Remember that? The one that could never understand your relationship with the Simbrian – a guardian, Rebecca's favourite – and you gave them both up, willingly, and have shirked your responsibilities ever since. Now, that's something to consider.'

'What of it?'

'Well, I have my theories.'

'You always liked to theorise, didn't you. What would the world be like if this and that happened, blah, blah, blah. Drove us all bloody mad. You just need to accept that the Simbrian was never something I was interested in.' He levelled a piercing look at Dagmar, one Frank had never seen in all his time growing up, one that would have seen most men shrink in their boots, but not Dagmar who looked in good shape for a war of words.

'Yet here you are, riding in to take your seat when the performance is almost over,' said Dagmar, the question posed.

'What's that supposed to mean?'

'I don't think I'd need to be the sharpest pin in the cushion to think there's more to this than a desire to save your son.' He turned to Frank. 'You're good at puzzles, Frank. Why don't you try and solve the riddle that is your father.'

'Like you should question me over my motivations. You'd sell your own mother if it meant you could have a taste of the Simbrian, so don't act like I'm the one lacking honesty here, Dagmar.'

'Oh, come on Lawrence, your honesty wouldn't cover the head of a goose. There's something going on that I don't quite get but, as you know, I'll get there eventually.' Dagmar leaned forward, bracing his elbows on the table. 'Eventually.'

Frank looked on, the sharp sparring beginning to lay in his stomach like a heavy meal.

Lawrence leaned in, mirroring Dagmar, pinning him with his stare.

'You were just jealous of me, Dagmar. I had the talent, the accolades, the looks. *I* was a guardian – not you. All through Excelsus I could taste the green on you, and, as if you could've predicted, it was me that got the girl in the end. Not you. How's that festering wound of yours, hm?'

Frank saw the wince on Dagmar's face. Maybe it was the pain in his leg or, more likely, a fresh wound, one not inflicted by sharp steel.

'Testy, that nerve. Admit it, Dagmar, jealousy drove you to want to burn the world, to smash your fist on Prismia and recreate the Simbrian, all because she wanted me instead of you. A high price for everyone to pay.'

Dagmar shook his head as Lawrence's words had Frank shaking his. In a few well-delivered sentences, he'd cast a shadow over everything Dagmar had told them up in Frank's room.

'Don't flatter yourself, Lawrence,' said Dagmar. 'No one ever got Rebecca, not physically and certainly not whatever resided in that mind of hers. It was always she who got them. I stepped aside as soon as I knew what she was.'

'Like anyone would believe that?' said Lawrence, looking like he held a library of knowledge on Dagmar and had only just flicked to the first page. 'Not still hurting? Not still feeling that razor-sharp edge of rejection? The one that drove you to kill and torture your way through life as Etamin's ferocious little pet.'

Dagmar threw his fist down on the table, driving the sound through the room, nearly sending the bottle to the floor.

'Don't you dare call me that.' Words delivered slowly, deliberately, murderously. 'You have no idea what I had to endure at the hands of that woman.'

Lawrence chuckled. Point scored.

'I think you had more luck with Etamin than you did with Rebecca,' he said, not bothering to hide his amusement, turning the blade he'd just wedged under Dagmar's skin.

'And look where it got you with Rebecca,' said Dagmar. 'She destroyed herself, she paid the price for her meddling and her vanity and whatever was in that scheming mind of hers. Perhaps she killed herself rather than spend another minute with you?'

'Nice try, Dagmar,' said Lawrence. 'A poor effort, but a nice try. Her mind was pure, clean brilliance, deeper and shrewder than all of ours put together. She was something to behold.'

'She was that, alright. She was as obsessed with the Simbrian as you are indifferent and that's what I don't get. I know opposites are meant to attract but that's ridiculous. So, Lawrence, what is it you're hiding? I'm sure your son would like to know. After all, he and his friends have risked much in their quest to keep the world safe, as have I, while you've been sitting on your fat, apathetic arse doing nothing. Until now.'

Lawrence leaned back, flexing his broad shoulders.

'Well, Dagmar,' he said. 'Since you're so interested, there is something you don't know.' Lawrence turned his head to Frank. 'Isn't that so, Frank?'

There were, perhaps, many things Frank knew that Dagmar didn't and much of it wouldn't trouble the man with the orange streak but, from the look on his dad's face Frank instantly knew there was only one secret about to come out of his mouth.

'No,' he said, catching the plea in his voice.

But the corners of Lawrence's mouth twitched upwards as he turned back to Dagmar.

'He's not my son at all. He's yours.'

65

THE BETRAYAL

Whatever interesting or incisive words Dagmar had prepared simply dissolved on his tongue. The man who was never dumbfounded was completely dumbfounded. Such was the edge on Lawrence's words that Dagmar appeared sliced open as he swallowed them whole.

He just stared at Lawrence, stared past him. He looked at Frank, urging him to contradict but Frank just looked back. Any words Dagmar had clung to the inside of his throat, withered and died.

Lawrence simply leaned forward, took another swig from the bottle and sat back again, looking like he'd just wished Dagmar a happy birthday.

'How dare you do that,' said Frank. He could feel the emotion bubbling to the surface. 'It's not your secret to tell.'

Lawrence looked at Frank, no regrets on his face.

'Yes it is, Frank. Mine and your mother's.'

Dagmar looked from Frank to Lawrence, questions in his eyes but not one he could raise through his mouth.

'Are you taking the absolute piss?' he said.

Lawrence just threw him a triumphant smile. Dagmar got to his feet, any pain in his limbs quickly forgotten.

'Is this true?' A look right through Frank. A reluctant nod. 'And you've known this for a while?' Another nod.

'Any theories you'd like to propose?' Lawrence's voice was full of relish for the upper hand he'd just dealt himself. Four aces, gloating like the worst of winners.

Dagmar looked like his house had been blown away in a storm

and he was left holding a single brick. No hope of filling in the many blanks left by Lawrence Penny's reveal.

'To create the perfect bloodline,' said Frank, filling them in.

Dagmar opened his eyes wide to Frank, like a dog that's just been offered a treat.

'You're descended from Joleyon and Lashka,' said Gabby. 'She from Everbleed. It was your blood she needed.' A nod toward Lawrence. 'Not his.'

Fury erupted in Dagmar's eyes as he turned them to Lawrence. 'She did this on purpose?' he said.

'Come on. Dagmar, everything Rebecca did was for a purpose,' said Lawrence. 'If you mean she used you, then yes. But, then, as you said, she was always pretty good at that.'

Frank could see Dagmar quickly fitting the pieces together, the sharp mind of someone used to getting to the answer ahead of others. His eyes swept the others in the room, landing on Frank.

'Then you're the heir?'

Frank nodded. Dagmar nodded back.

'Then Etamin will kill De Villiers and nothing will happen.'

'No,' said Frank.

'No what?'

'She won't kill De Villiers.'

'Of course she will. She thinks De Villiers is the heir.'

Silence from Frank, the sort of silence that both poses and answers a question.

'You mean she knows? How?'

'I told her.'

As he said it, Frank realised how foolish he must have sounded, a child in an adult's world.

'You told her? Have you lost all grasp on your senses?' said Dagmar. 'What in Lashka's name did you think you were doing?'

Frank couldn't offer anything. Trying to save De Villiers seemed like the right thing to do at the time and he had no regrets. Regret had fast become a pointless emotion, not for those who'd learned life's lessons the hard way, and he was brimming with those.

'Then she'll come after you,' said Dagmar.

A statement of the obvious, maybe, something that needed to be aired, definitely. Frank had barely thought of anything else since the moment he'd revealed himself to Etamin, but he still had a card to play.

'There's a good chance she thinks I'm dead,' he said, although he could feel himself mentally crossing his fingers as he said it. 'And she won't know I'm here.' Of that he was confident. 'So I'm a step ahead, at least.'

All he needed was to ask them for their help. Two of the greatest minds, the greatest swordsmen Excelsus had ever produced. Maybe, together they could outrun the galloping death that would try and run him down.

He looked at Dagmar who looked like he was still processing, then to his dad who sat in reflective silence, tapping his fingers on the table.

The sound of hurried feet outside and the clatter of the door opening had Frank backing off. Neither Lawrence nor Dagmar moved, aside from a slight shift of the head, as they watched Cas enter the room, followed closely by Anya.

Cas bent, hands on his knees, heaving in chunks of air like he was drowning. Anya looked calm and poised, but Frank noticed the bruising on her left cheek, the cuts across her brow and the way her left arm drooped unnaturally by her side, like the branch of a tree sheared off in a storm.

It looked like there'd been some fight, one which hadn't quite gone their way. Both looked wired, primed to danger as if their appearance wasn't something to be pleased with, the sort of looks that are the forerunner to bad news and unwanted bother.

Gabby was at Anya's side in an instant, wordless in her relief. She opened her arms and went to embrace Anya, but Anya winced and stepped away.

'You made it,' said Frank.

'Just,' said Cas.

But Frank could see something in their eyes, eyes that looked across to the table, at the men sitting there, as if another step into the room would be like approaching a hungry wolf and running would be a much better option. He noticed Cas's eyes come to rest on Dagmar, noticed them widen at the beast who'd preyed on them for years. He opened his mouth slightly as Anya spoke.

'He was going to have us turned over to the Watch, to stop us leaving Garrim,' she said.

She offered no expression, her face looked buried in the detail of whatever had happened after Frank and Gabby had left the previous day.

Frank looked at the two men sitting opposite one another, turning his head to Dagmar, disbelief on his tongue as he wondered how he could have been taken in by his lies. How, in the few minutes they'd spent listening to him in his bedroom, he'd begun to believe his rewriting of the Simbrian story. He'd been duped, violated and he felt the rise of anger in his throat. Dagmar looked nothing but relaxed.

'You were going to do *what?*' said Frank.

But Dagmar just raised an eyebrow and looked at Anya, an invitation of sorts.

'Not him,' said Anya. '*Him.*'

Some things you are prepared for, and accusing Dagmar of something that fit right in with the man they'd come to know and loathe was one of them, he wore the coat so well, but as Anya raised her good arm and pointed directly at Lawrence, Frank didn't quite know what to think.

'He beat Spyro up, knocked ten bells out of him until he was unconscious, then he was going to turn us in.'

Lawrence didn't move, he just languished in his chair, fingers tapping on the bottle of whisky, calm and self-possessed in the face of Anya's words that bounced off him like the rain on a Garrim rooftop.

'But Anya had a go,' said Cas. 'We got away, but I can't believe we made it.'

Frank looked from his friends to his dad. The bruise on his cheek, the cut on his neck. He thought back to their exit from Garrim, how easy it had been. No one waiting to skin them. No Watch. No Lashkens. And only two horses prepared.

Dagmar looked at Lawrence, started a run of shallow nods as if the dawn had just broken over an unanswered question.

'Funny when things don't go quite your way, eh, Lawrence,' said Dagmar. 'I know the feeling. You could say we were kindred spirits but that would be like me admitting to crawling in the gutter or being a lying bastard.' Lawrence remained passive, unreadable, fingers drumming quietly.

'You always did that,' said Dagmar. 'That finger tapping, keeping quiet when you knew what was going on while the rest of us were playing catch-up.' A look at Lawrence as if he could see the mist clearing. He turned to Frank. 'You said a moment ago that you were one step ahead of Etamin, but I'd lay odds that Lawrence is two steps ahead of you.' A pause, both men locked eyes, both giving the other a knowing smile. 'I think you'll find she knows exactly where to find you and she'll be here very soon, won't she, Lawrence?'

66

GOODBYES

No denial. Lawrence looked at Dagmar, a look of congratulation at having solved a conundrum too difficult for the brightest of minds.

To Frank's disbelief, something resembling a smirk revealed itself on his dad's face.

'Well, Dagmar, you always did want to be top of the class,' said Lawrence, leaning back and stretching his legs. 'Perhaps you'll get on the Wall of Exemplars after all.'

Frank had been nothing but cold in Garrim, but the bitter wind across the Jixx and the meltwater from the Longshadows were nothing in comparison to the ice that shot down his body. His dad, the one person he should be able trust, whose loyalty shouldn't be in question had handed Etamin the knife with which she would cut his throat and the total lack of anything resembling remorse had tears welling in his eyes.

'Why?'

The word caught in his throat. A look of nonchalance that would have put a cat to shame appeared on Lawrence's face.

'Destiny is a cruel master, Frank,' he said with a sniff. 'And who am I, or you, to stand in its way.'

'You want it for yourself,' said Frank.

'For myself? No,' said Lawrence.

'Then —'

'You have little time,' said Dagmar, cutting Frank off.

Each person in the room turned sharp, calculating their next move and Frank only had one thing in mind. The running would have to start sooner than he'd hoped. Lawrence's adept eyes appeared to read him.

'You can't stop this, Frank,' he said.

Frank could see his dad's limbs tense, anticipating, ready. Frank grabbed the bag, grabbed the staff and went for the door.

Lawrence was on his feet with striking speed, moving to block his route out through the shop but Dagmar sprang, two steps ahead, as if he'd been waiting, calculating how this was going to play, coiled like a sleeping viper but alert to the scent of trouble.

He caught Lawrence with his shoulder, sending him spinning into the large dresser against the wall, sending a cascade of crockery splintering to the ground, tripping Frank in the process.

'Run,' he shouted before landing a solid punch across Lawrence's temple.

Out through the door, through the blur of red and white chequered tablecloths, pushing tables and chairs to the ground behind him, makeshift obstacles to the danger at his back.

Then he was out on the street, Gabby at his back, Cas and Anya further back, the thuds of falling fists left behind in Polly's backroom.

Having some time to think would have been handy. Having a plan of any sort would have been handier still but both had made themselves absent. Haste had perpetually run into bad decisions but Frank knew he needed to put as much distance between himself and nearly everyone else. That's all he could think of, no plan, and it's best to have a plan, however rubbish, but not at this moment. Just survival would do for now.

Out of Murgatroid Square, feet falling quickly on the pavement as he headed into the town centre through the persistent drizzle. No looking back. No time for that, no time for bad ideas, not that he had any good ones.

A hand on his elbow stopped him as he entered the town square. Gabby pulled him to a halt, Cas and Anya joining them.

Gabby swallowed a breath, a glance over her shoulder. No one coming. Yet. Nothing at his back, nothing except the grasping hand of destiny, the one thing he knew he couldn't shake off, the one thing he should be afraid of.

Anya drew in a sharp breath through her nose, her eyes alert, dodging around and through the buildings as the muscles on her neck stiffened.

'She's close,' she said, her seer's senses on fire. No guesses as to who she meant. 'And she'll have half an army with her.'

Frank wiped the moisture from his brow and looked at Gabby, his eyes bereft of any worthy clue of what he should do next. The sea hemmed them in from the west. Etamin and Jackson could be anywhere.

'We need to get to Blackburn's,' said Gabby.

Frank shook his head, glances around the square, eyes on each of the roads that led to and away from the wide, open space in the centre of Rhaeder, a space that now seemed surprisingly small.

'No, we can't involve him,' he said.

He started across the square, not really knowing where he was headed. Away, just away. She was coming, coming for him.

'But I already have,' said Gabby in his wake.

Frank stopped and turned. Gabby hadn't moved.

'Already have what?'

'Involved him.'

She raked her fingers through her hair, shedding it from her face. Even now she looked unfazed, like she was there to guide him right through this and bring him safely out the other side.

'How?'

'He has the key.'

'What?'

'The key. I left the original with him. He doesn't know what it is, but I thought it would be easily hidden there.'

It was a decent idea. Anyone venturing into the inventors workshop – not that any did – were generally faced with a whole host of half-baked, half-assembled but usually unfinished contraptions.

Pieces thrown together at the whim of the eccentric who presided over them, fashioning and shaping wood, heating and bending metal, blending and mixing many concoctions in the hope of giving birth to something new and useful.

'Can't we just leave it there?' he said.

There were so many off-cuts and odd bits of many types of material that finding the anonymous, rectangular key would be beyond just about everyone.

But that was the problem. Just about everyone, but not everyone and Gabby had grasped the outcome.

Etamin would stop at nothing. She already wanted him as the heir, was about to hunt him down in his own backyard and he couldn't imagine her reaction once she found out that the key she'd taken from Frank was a dud.

Gabby had been right to hide it, had prevented the dog from biting this time, but she'd overlooked the danger she'd put Blackburn in. Now she realised and her expression spoke the words – once the hunting had begun it wouldn't stop, not until Etamin had it and Blackburn would pay the price.

'I guess not, then,' said Frank.

Another round of anxious looks at the four corners of the square, at the pavements and buildings slick with the wet. Which way would she come?

'You get to Blackburn's,' said Cas. 'I'll wait here. If Etamin or her men come, I'll come and find you, or throw them off the scent. It'll give you time to get as far away as you can.'

Frank was caught off-guard. He knew his best friend so well, knew that each time the Simbrian bit them he had to find a different strength to push through, to cover his fear and stop himself running. Each episode took a little more out of him and, rather than become more fearless in the face of all the danger, he had to mine even deeper to keep himself going.

'No,' said Frank. 'We're in this together.'

'Except we're not,' said Cas. 'It's you she's after. Look, Frank, you're the best friend I ever had, so let me give you this, yeah?' A tear formed in the corner of Cas's eye as he looked at Frank, urging him to flee yet not wanting to see him go, knowing it might be the last look they'd get of each other. A final moment of the most worthy of friendships.

Frank took the few steps over to him, wrapping his arms around him and drawing Cas into a tight hug, the sort of embrace reserved only for when words are too hard, where only those involved know its true meaning, where letting go is the hardest of undertakings and, as Frank pressed his hands into Cas's back and kissed him on the temple, he felt another piece of him break and fall into the abyss.

'Love you,' whispered Cas.

They held each other, not long enough, until Cas stepped back, appearing to sense the passing of valuable moments that might keep Frank from death. Moments he was prepared to give up in the name of the closest of friendships.

Love has many forms and Frank felt the moment begin to overwhelm him as he looked at Cas, the depth of the pain in his eyes, the tears that ran unfettered down his sallow cheeks, the leash he kept on the sobs raging to be let out. No more funny comments, no more teenage moments, no more words.

This was goodbye.

'Now get going,' said Cas with a flick of his chin towards Iron Lane.

Frank looked at Gabby. She had no words. It had been the four of them. They shared a bond like no others, like no others ever would but it was over, at least for now, until Frank could find a way out, something he wasn't sure existed.

'I'll stay with Cas,' said Anya. 'Better the two of us to keep a look-out.'

She studied Frank as he hesitated.

'I can't,' said Frank. 'You saved my life.'

'And you saved mine,' said Anya. Nothing else, nothing but the certainty that she'd do it again.

Her look was straight and level, a sign for him and Gabby to run, to leave their two friends to face and divert an enemy against overwhelming odds. An impossible challenge but one they'd take on without question. Undoubtedly the best of friends.

Gabby stepped forward. Quick hugs for Cas and Anya.

'See you later, dummy,' she said.

'You bet,' said Cas.

'None of us are going anywhere,' said Anya with a faint smile. 'You go, we'll take it from here.'

67

THE SIMBRIAN

Frank and Gabby headed to Iron Lane, through the sea of morning shoppers and up to the plaza, towards Blackburn's. No looks back, not to see if Cas or Anya were still there, not to see who had emerged as the victor in the fight between Dagmar and his dad, not to see if Etamin was sweeping through the eastern fringes of the town.

There was no time to look at the shop fronts, the high-class tailors, jewellers, art galleries and the rest. None of it mattered any more. They didn't deal in life and death, and death was the greatest leveller, it didn't matter who cut the cloth for your suit or set the diamonds in your necklace, you'd lay in a coffin just as easily and rot as well as everybody else.

They quickly arrived at Blackburn's run-down shop, the fading and rotting façade shrugging its shoulders at them.

A sign hung against the inside of the grime-covered glass. Out. Blackburn was out.

Frank pushed the door. It opened and he and Gabby stepped inside, commencing an immediate search, hoping to quickly find the key of darkness and be on their way, to put more distance between them and the hand of death.

But, where Frank had thought it would be difficult for anyone to find it in the chaos of Blackburn's workshop, he hadn't considered that that also applied to him. Shelves, cupboards, workbenches – all familiar, all set out or filled to the brim in Blackburn's unique and chaotic way, hiding everything in plain sight.

The whole inside was strewn with bottles and jars, boxes and parcels, off-cuts of wood and strips of metal, all with their own unique place, all appearing to have been thrown or placed at Blackburn's whim.

Now Frank cursed the inventor. Speed is what he needed, not a shop full of shit and rubbish so thick he hadn't the first notion where to begin. And even though Gabby had started to brave the task, futility was all he could see as she cleared, clattered and picked through the ocean of randomness.

The noose was tightening. Whatever motive his dad had in alerting Byeland's greatest enemy and inviting her across the threshold, he knew she wouldn't be far behind. She'd be swift, cutting through the country before there was time for anyone to react. Not that they would. Jackson was with her, allowing her to access the corners of his domain with a sweep of his deceitful hand – a task far simpler than having the whole of Blackburn's imagination to contend with.

But, in the clenching of his fist, he felt it, heard it. A bell in his head, clearer than he might have imagined. Had he imagined it at all? It knew he was there, that he'd come for it.

It called to him from the cluttered row of shelves right at the back of the workshop, just by the small forge that Blackburn slaved over in the pursuit of discovery.

'It's over there,' he said, his words immediately stopping Gabby from her search, heading after him to the rear of the workshop.

He found it instantly, its mutterings and curses giving its location away, its snarling demand to be taken and bonded with the other parts, a brotherhood of carnage and bloodshed waiting for Frank to bring them together.

For a moment, Frank felt like throwing it into the hot coals of the forge just to see what would happen but something in him knew it would have no effect, that the object was forged by different forces, not known to this life and neither fire nor ice would prise its power from it.

'We should go,' said Gabby, still calm, still there for him.

A look at the door, at the waning minutes.

Frank felt himself being pressed tight into a corner, the pressure building, searching for an outlet, a reprieve.

He took a few strides to Blackburn's long workbench in the middle of the workshop and stopped, his mind blank yet clear.

'Frank?'

Frank dropped his shoulder, letting his bag slip to the floor. He placed the staff on the bench and crouched, retrieving the pieces from his bag before laying them out on Blackburn's large workbench, along with the key.

'Frank, what are you doing?'

Gabby didn't try to hide the hint of alarm in her voice. He looked at her.

'Time to see what I can do with this,' he said.

'Do you think that's a good idea?' said Gabby.

'I'm all out of ideas. You?'

She paused, then shook her head.

'I guess I am too.'

Perhaps Baggus was wrong, What if the heir could control it? And then there was the other thing, the one that he tried to push away, that if he needed to destroy it, it had to be complete.

Time wasn't their ally and quickly he started to fit it together, just as he had done in his bedroom though, this time, he didn't stop with the skewer.

He held the Dahke pass to the end of the shaft, a small hole appearing in the centre, allowing him to thread it on. The playing chip followed in the same fashion.

Throughout, he could feel it taunting him, words beyond his understanding, but taunts without doubt. Vile, abusive words that urged him on before he took the locket from his neck, shedding the chain, holding it to the gap between the two discs.

The force with which the locket pulled at his hand was astounding, unstoppable. It had one purpose – to be bound to the others to complete the construct, complete the journey, complete the nightmare.

As Frank pushed it in between, it adhered itself fast to the shaft, quelling the voices that filled Frank's mind with a deep, satisfied breath.

The room calmed, as if a crying child had fallen asleep, ready to wake at the slightest sound.

He looked at Gabby, looked at the key and looked at the fully built object in his hand.

The Simbrian.

No doubts, no questions, just certainty. What he had was real, he could tell by the way his blood bent towards it. Even in its slumber he could feel himself struggling for control, against something unhinged and blessed with a might unknown to the ages.

The serpent might be asleep, but it was dreaming of death and terror and the spilling of blood. If it awoke, it would take everything to darkness, of that Frank was certain and, as he looked from the staff to the key, he knew he was but a step away from shaking it awake.

He and Gabby were stuck in silence, neither quite believing. The end of their long and careless quest, well, not quite the end, but all they'd been through had led them here, witness to something so benign-looking, so ordinary and unremarkable yet knowing it contained mystery and power of an inconceivable magnitude and, for a moment, Frank felt humbled by its presence.

He grabbed the key and placed it in the possessor before he looked at Gabby.

'Let's go,' he said just as the door flew open, a broad, dark figure appearing in the doorway, blocking their only way out.

68

LASHKENS

Frank froze. He sensed Gabby still, too, but he breathed easier as he realised who had entered the shop.

Dagmar heaved in great gulps of air from what must have been a lung-busting run from the teashop, through the square and up Iron Lane. No sign of the wounded leg though he bared his teeth as he leaned against the frame of the door.

His face bore the marks of recent close combat although Dagmar looked like that was already in the past, that he was focused on what to do next, until his eyes came to rest on the construct in Frank's hands.

His face stalled, his eyes lifting to Frank's. Whatever words he had stayed in his throat, however foolish he thought Frank, he decided not to say it. He just looked back to the street.

'They're here,' he said, calm, possessed, matter-of-fact.

'Who?' said Frank, like he couldn't have guessed.

'Lashkens. All over town.'

Dagmar wiped his mouth on his knuckles and ran his fingers through the orange streak in his hair, made slick from the light rain, eyes returning to Frank's hands.

He didn't need to say they were looking for him and, if they were here, she was here. Here to end him.

Dagmar had been right, his dad knew, had tried to keep him tethered to Polly's. Now he knew it was to await her arrival, to be turned over to her like a wanted criminal. His own father, sending him to his fate as if he'd carefully planned it from his fields back in Smithwood – planned it since Frank was born, a thought to shake him down to his boots.

'We need to go,' said Gabby.

There she was, cool-headed and thinking ahead, doing all the things that Frank should be doing but he hadn't the wits to find the door, let alone straighten his mind and come out the other end with a plan.

A nod from Dagmar who stepped out into the plaza without a look back, knowing the only sensible option for them was to follow.

'My Dad?' said Frank.

'Farming's slowed him down,' said Dagmar. 'Lucky for me. He'll be out of action for a bit.'

As they ventured back into the open, the distant sounds of shouts drew near, commotion fuelled by panic heading their way like an vast wave careering towards the beach on which they were all stranded.

Lashkens swarmed in left and right, scattering locals who yelped and shouted in a mix of terror and alarm.

The first one stopped in front of Dagmar, to be met with his crushing fist. The guard went down, Dagmar grabbed his sword and looked in each direction, brandishing the weapon against the oncoming tide of soldiers.

All routes from the plaza were quickly stoppered with the tough and mean from Kzarlac, their orders clear.

Only one way remained open and Frank had no hesitation in legging it across the slick marble that hugged the ground towards the academy, Gabby and Dagmar alongside him.

Dagmar ushered them across the bridge, a sprint through the yawning shadow of the huge stone vulture, over the river that cut the academy off from the rest of the town, running for their lives, heaving in the ragged breaths of the hunted.

Frank fumbled in his pocket, the thought of destroying the bridge before any of Kzarlac's soldiers crossed behind them, just a throw of the Elemental ball and the whole, ancient crossing would disappear into the rolling current, taking the enormous statue with it and buy them immeasurable, valuable time.

It was only then that he remembered. No longer a bewitched ally, one that had helped in the tightest of situations, but part of the Simbrian, part of the construct he held in his hand. Without it, the bridge would remain intact, the soldiers would soon flood the square and swarm across, cornering them.

He had no idea if the Simbrian would help. He'd have to fire it with the key. Only then would he know what it was capable of, but to unleash the unholiest of monsters with a frivolous flick of his hand was a fool's plan, one that might see the town and the people he loved reduced to cinders. Perhaps it had come to that, after all, he had nothing to lose and you should always beware the man who has nothing to lose.

Dagmar didn't head into the building itself, perhaps to avoid the potential of being trapped inside. Instead he headed left, in front of the academy and over towards the cliffs and the waterfall, allowing them to skirt around the back, out into the woodland where they'd have a far better chance of evading capture under the cover of the trees.

They turned to head along the side wall only to be faced with a dozen Lashkens, all of whom drew their weapons the instant they saw Dagmar who looked set to fight them all with his bare and bloodied hands if it bought Frank and Gabby some more time.

More Lashkens were now crossing the bridge, sealing off their route back, corralling them like errant sheep who had escaped the butcher's knife but had only delayed the inevitable outcome.

Dagmar looked towards the woodland, then to the river. Lashkens everywhere. Nowhere to run.

'I'm sorry, Frank,' he said, still looking out at the overwhelming force stood against them as though a way out would present itself. He held up the blade in his hand and inspected it. 'Not sure this sword is quite up to the job.' A smile cracked on his face. 'Might have been a bit of fun to be had, don't you think?'

But Frank barely heard him in the face of the enemy who had

them surrounded, pushing him, Gabby and Dagmar slowly to the cliff edge, to the waterfall, to the final corner where his life would end.

69

CORNERED

It was over.

Whatever this had been, whatever he thought it was, whatever it might be, it was over.

He was cornered, the running had stopped before it had even a chance to begin. The waterfall spat and frothed at his back, the cliff-top beckoned him closer, his only escape route.

His world was now but a few dozen square yards of ground between him and the damp stone walls of Excelsus academy. The last place his feet would feel the comfort of the earth. The final scents and sounds and colours. He half expected the huge stone vulture to turn its head, waiting for the opportunity to pick over his corpse.

Gabby held onto him, her eyes wide, panicked as they closed in. Dagmar stood to the side, still calculating the odds.

A look across the river, the wide marble plaza. Cas was held by the huge Lashken while three more surrounded Anya, all with ferocious blades drawn, each glinting in the wet and set to gut her at a wrong move.

Lashkens everywhere, let loose in Rhaeder by Jackson with permission to end him. Two dozen of them stood between him and the bridge, spread out to the academy walls, cutting off any last route out. A powerful band of Etamin's thugs, ripe for the fight, keen to smash some heads, but Frank saw the unease on their faces, how they regarded him and the object he held with almost god-like deference, with the fear that it wouldn't go their way.

Two teenage kids, some fight? One sided. But he could tell by the distance they kept that they knew this was nothing ordinary, perhaps they'd all heard the stories of the slaughter of Dagmar's men in the foothills of the Longshadows years ago as they faced down a striking young woman who, like him, had to be stopped at all costs. Men like them, turned to ash.

A legend born in their lifetime. They might tell the stories and sing the songs, but no one looked keen to be part of it.

Then he saw her. Crossing the bridge, her crooked frame uncomfortable astride the blackest of horses. He watched her all the way as she came to a halt just behind the line of guards facing Frank off in front of the cliff edge.

She dismounted. Slow and assured, like this was only going to go one way, her way, the hush of the orchestra before the conductor taps his baton.

The Lashkens parted, allowing her through. The short strides, the clip of the cane, the sound made by approaching death.

Etamin stepped through the ranks of armed men, each not looking the slightest bit reassured by her appearance as if the biggest bully was likely to bring the fiercest bother.

Dagmar squared his shoulders and sheathed his sword in his belt but Etamin took her time, stopping ten paces from them. Dagmar's look sliced right through her throat, unwilling to waste his words on her, knowing he'd be the first to die.

'I'd like to say you're changing sides like the wind, Dagmar,' she chuckled. 'But we all know you've been on your own side from the start and all traitors of Lashka will reap their full reward.'

She thrust out her arms, fingertips pointed directly at Dagmar. No hesitation, no time for him to respond or plead, not that Dagmar was the pleading sort.

Red flame shot in hot, raging torrents from her hands and slammed mercilessly into his chest, lifting him off his feet and thrusting him twenty feet backwards before he could blink. Another stab of her arms had Dagmar writhing in agony where he'd fallen, the venom in her eyes speaking a dozen languages of vengeance in her determination to end him.

His cloak erupted in a plume of smoke and flame, Gabby shrieked as Dagmar burned.

With a rush of blood, Frank stepped to the very edge of the cliff and held his arm out over the drop to the ocean.

'Stop.'

He felt the painful rasp in his throat, the force in his voice that emptied his lungs in one short powerful breath. The jet of flame ceased, her look would have killed him on the spot, of that he had no doubt, but she'd forced him to play the only card he had.

He looked across to Dagmar's prone shape, a bundle of black rags smoking in the cold and wet of the early winter morning. Etamin's ferocious assault had all but set him on fire but faint movement from under the charred cloak told Frank he'd survived.

'Don't think I won't,' he said.

A venomous smile tugged at her mouth. She licked her bottom lip, eyes on the construct in Frank's quivering hand.

'So you do have it,' she said. 'And there was me finding it hard to believe that your father was telling the truth. Allowing me to end his own son, now that's something to be admired and rewarded and so it will be once my destiny is complete. As you can see, I have two of your friends in my hands. Unfortunate for them, but one man's misfortune always brings a benefit to another.'

She held his gaze but couldn't prevent her eyes from coming to rest on the object in his hands. The Simbrian, her destiny, the only thing she wanted to take away intact and now just a few yards of grass and Frank stood in her way.

'Now, Frank. I need you to hand it over, then we can discuss how you can extricate yourself from this very difficult position you find yourself in.'

Extricate. Is that what she'd really said? Whatever words Etamin might use to draw him in, however she wanted to describe it he knew there was only one way this was going to go.

She wanted the Simbrian. He had it in his hand. He had the key. He was the heir. Very few pieces of the puzzle to put together now. In fact, there seemed but one to manoeuvre into place.

How she must have thought all her dreams had come true in this very moment. Kill his friends, kill him, become the new heir and control the power. Power that would bend the world to her will. He could sense her desire, breathing in the mesmerising elixir of the Simbrian like a junkie craving their next fix.

He looked out to the cresting waves, then down the sheer face of the cliffs as it dragged the water over to its fate, then back across the river to the town, its bright but narrow lanes and to the academy, the bright blue-grey stone and the green lawns that surrounded it.

Lashkens everywhere. Enemies everywhere. Defeat and death everywhere.

'There is no way out, Frank.' The crowing cockerel in Etamin's voice was sharp and triumphant. Frank turned to Gabby, her determined look shovelled coals on his fire, telling him she wasn't going to go down without a fight, but this wasn't her fight, he wouldn't let it.

'You need to go,' he said, the edge of pleading in his voice. 'Please, Gabby, I can't let you stay. You have your life to live.'

But Gabby didn't move, her look, her slight shake of her head told him everything – *not without you.*

'You can't let her have it,' she whispered.

She held his chin delicately in her soft hands and turned his face to hers. Her beauty swept him up, took him away from all his troubles and in that moment he knew everything would be alright just as long as he had her by his side.

He locked his eyes on to hers. Nothing else mattered. Power, fortune, influence. None of it mattered as long as he had her.

Tears sprang in her eyes, lighting them up in her sadness. They ran untethered down the satin skin of her cheeks. He wanted her to be the last thing he saw, like this, looking at her in a way he'd never looked at anyone, her frightened but brave face. He'd seen it a hundred times before, but this time it was reserved just for them, for him.

'You have to destroy it.' A determined squeeze of his arm. 'You have to destroy it *right now*.'

She didn't need to say anything else. There was nothing left to say. He knew the word, what he had to do. What it meant.

Death. Death for him, death for Gabby.

Death wasn't for people like him, like them.

Etamin dealt in death like the Ditch dealt in misery, dispensed her unique brand of tyranny without a blink of her evil eyes, but that wasn't his world, nor was it the world he wished to inhabit.

He knew those he loved would forgive him. He looked out at Cas and Anya, at the friends who'd travelled the road from the start, who would have swapped with him without hesitation if they could, if destiny had guided them a different way but the dark clouds of fate hung squarely above his head.

He could just read their faces, faces that urged him to finish what they'd all started, to save their world in the only way possible despite knowing it would end them too. They knew destroying the Simbrian in front of Etamin wouldn't be without its consequences, that she would rain retribution and her own brand of hell on anything within reach. The screaming, raging tyrant would set the world on fire and those closest to him would be the first to pay the price. She'd butcher Cas and Anya before they'd have a chance to run, of that he was certain and he knew they'd expect it. Still they willed him to carry through.

Gabby placed her hand on his chest, an attempt to quell his burning nerves and he felt a run of calm in his veins. They pulled each other in one last time. She gripped her arms behind his back and turned her head into his chest. He pressed his face gently into her hair, drawing in her sweet sweet scent for the very last time. Then he let go.

He gave her the slightest of nods, leaning in to kiss her one last time as he tasted the warm salt of his own tears. Gabby nodded back, her silent declaration that she was with him, that she would die with him rather than let him be hauled into the abyss alone. Her eyes shone through her tears, through her attempts to keep her breathing steady as she fought against the constricting hand of fear. They had started this together, they would end it the same way.

Frank reached to his belt, loosening the drawstring of the possessor, reaching in and pulling out the key. The construct in his other hand answered, a slight tremor, an invitation as Frank flipped the locket open, revealing the aperture, black as midnight, a cold, bottomless pit of misery and untamed power heaving and wrenching at its tether. It would not be denied, it would be set free.

Suffering souls from a hundred generations howled, drawing his life in. A hot wind from nowhere whipped the cold air, lashing Frank's face, the messenger of what was to come.

He swore it spoke to him, urged him in many tongues to insert the length of iron, to possess it, to let it possess him. For eternity.

Frank froze, his hesitancy carved from knowing there would be no way back, that he was tightening his own noose. He had no notion of time. He might have been waiting a second, or an hour, he couldn't tell. He looked up at Etamin, a coiled viper in the open waiting patiently for her prey to appear. Then a gentle hand on his.

'Do it, Frank.' Gabby's fingers gripped him tighter. 'Do it now.'

He looked at her. One last time. Just once more. Once more his eyes lingered over her. But he knew, knew the book was written, the game was ended, the song was sung and he would never sing another. He was out of choices and it doesn't do to be out of choices.

'I love you, Gabby.' Emotion and fear. A final crack in his voice.

'I love you too,' she said, her hand on his, the one that held the key, light pressure helping him on.

The moment everything had been building to was on his shoulders, just a small movement away from the unknown. Terrifying. Frightening. A dreadful sense of falling, out of control, of being buried or burned alive, of trying to take your last breath but failing and letting death consume you.

Frank fought for calm, found it as he looked into Gabby's still and resolute eyes.

Then he pushed the key in.

70

THE END

Instantly the earth shifted, the world bent skywards as the Simbrian spat into life, lit up, swallowing the air around them.

Fierce light, the colour of a thousand stars yet darker than a starless night sky and flame whiter than the hottest iron on the blacksmith's anvil encased the whole object, twisting around the shaft, the voices of a million tortured dead leaped into the air, blocking out any other sound.

The ground shook. Everywhere, those around fought to steady themselves, fighting to keep their balance as a pulse of death and terror shot out from Frank's hand, rolling across the plaza, sending up dust and debris.

He fought to control it, thought his whole body would fall to pieces with the tornado of unbridled energy that wielded itself around him, that moved to assemble itself and control him as quickly as it could.

He could feel it growing, grabbing, eager to be out and away, a beast without rival incapable of feeling with no gratitude for being let loose, just death and destruction on its mind.

He was immediately exhausted by the chaotic, undiluted power as wave upon wave of deep, hollow throbs pulsed through him. Sweat tumbled from his face, his teeth rattled in his skull, his entire body felt knocked in on itself, turned upside down. He could feel it grasping at his bones, his soul. Impossible strength tumbled out, the wellspring of a thousand years unstopped, shattering.

Then everything went quiet. An aura of blue mist swirled around him like the delicate lace on a bridal veil. He could feel its touch, its amused taunts of the boy who stood like a frightened child, waiting for it to crush him. Still the Simbrian whispered to Frank, words from the edge, beyond his understanding, pushing him, asking him, demanding him. He fought it, fought the creeping presence that tried to bind him, tried to hold him prisoner. It would. He couldn't stop it. It was no contest.

He didn't want to control it, had never wanted to, or knew what it would even take to steady the fear and fight it, but it wanted to control him, its subordinate, its servant. The malevolent spirit, imprisoned for a thousand years, had awoken and now had idle hands.

He looked round. Etamin stared straight back at him. Dark eyes. Dark, evil eyes that gladly welcomed an old friend through the door. A triumphant look on her face as she raised both arms, the red flame binding her wrist burned with a venom he'd never seen before. Venom to kill, to kill him. To release him from his brief bonds of the custodian of the Simbrian so she could take the mantle from him and wear it to possess and cower the world. He felt Gabby's hand grip his arm. Etamin opened her mouth, throwing an arm back behind her head but before she could utter the words to send Frank to his grave, Frank raised the Simbrian with both hands.

'*ABSOLATUM,*' he cried, Gabby's final scream in his ears, before slamming the tip of the shaft down into the ground with the last ounce of energy within him.

A blinding blue light flashed skyward, pulsing out, ripping through the academy and across the town, a bone-shattering explosion ripped the guts out of the earth and the sky then...

Nothing.

71

DREAMS

Is this what death feels like? Is this where all souls pass through when it's time?

There was nothing. Just brilliant blue light, nothing else as if he was suspended in a cobalt sea without feeling the lap of the waves or in a cloudless sky without hearing the refreshing sigh of the wind.

He couldn't feel anything, not even his own body, as if he'd been turned to vapour but he was there, he could see his hands, his legs.

He could hear faint cries and the distant smell of the tart acrid scent of cinders, yet nothing was burning.

He felt wrapped up by the blue; warm, yet there was no fire, no sun. Just calm.

So he stood still, alone, wondering if he was meant to do anything, to take his first step in whatever afterlife he'd been propelled into, wondering what the rules were, if anyone was going to show him the way.

He drew in a long breath then lifted his hands to his eyes, inspecting the lengths of his fingers, looking for any signs, any differences but there were none. His heart still beat in his chest, his breath still felt warm on his palms, his feet still had the ground beneath them.

He looked around himself as the blue began to shift like the waves on the sand, began to break apart. Small cracks began to splinter the nothingness, then peel itself down, shedding like a snake sheds its skin.

The blue light faded as the burning smell rose quickly, making him place the back of his hand to his nose and mouth. He could feel himself, feel the warm skin of his cheek. Not the cold flesh of the dead but the heat of his blood.

Was this really death?

The mist began to clear, slowly, a thick fog that refused to be banished but thinned so he could see a yard or two in front of his face. It faded, gradually, but it was then he saw it. Blurred through the smoke, through his squinting eyes but gradually the shape of a person began to form as the fog around him pulled itself reluctantly away.

She stood before him. Tall, elegant, poised. Beautiful. Her long blonde hair cascaded wildly down her back and around her shoulders, her alabaster skin perfect, her vivid blue eyes hypnotic. Then she smiled, a warm familiar smile that stilled his breath and prickled his skin.

Not once did she look away, her eyes swallowed him up. She was totally consumed by him. He was totally consumed by her.

Disbelief ran hot in his blood as he felt his defences wither at the realisation. A white-hot spike of raw emotion shot through him and he felt himself begin to crumble into tiny pieces.

'Mum?'

72

REBECCA

Her smile broadened. An acknowledgement, an affirmation. She took two barefoot steps towards him, liquid movements like nothing he'd seen before, as if the world were smoke and she was merely passing through it. Her pristine turquoise gown, with just a fascinating hint of transparency, shifted with the passing breeze, her long golden hair tumbling down her back save for a few strands that wound artfully around her breast and face, like she had been preparing herself for this moment.

She lifted her arms, holding them loosely outstretched, inviting him forward. He didn't resist, couldn't resist. He ran. Only a few paces but he ran, grabbing hold of her in case she disappeared.

She wound her arms around him and eased him to her chest. He felt the comfort of her embrace, her fingertips as they slid silently through his hair, the completeness of her warmth running through him. The matchless touch of a mother. Sunshine to his rain. Salve to his agitation. Calm to his trembling body.

He breathed her in. Deep, soothing breaths. Bathing in the sweet scent of honeysuckle that surrounded her, that emptied from her pores, summoning the tears from the deep wellspring of longing and loss that he'd felt his entire life.

He clung, harder, not hard enough, digging his fingers into the soft material of her robe, feeling it bunch in his hands, listening to the quiet beating of her heart, making sure she was real. He wouldn't let go. Wouldn't let her go. Ever.

She held him close, letting the full palette of his emotions pour from him. He felt her soft lips gently kiss his hair, easing him, allowing him to be the young boy, the motherless infant who never knew her who, somehow, had brought her from the bright embers of the Simbrian.

'My beautiful boy.' Her voice, whispered into his hair like an angel in his dreams. He'd never heard it before, only imagined and it dripped on him like warm syrup. 'My beautiful, beautiful boy,' she repeated. He thought the shiver that shot through him would never end, that the tears would never stop. He knew moments came and went, but some stayed with you forever. Moments like this.

She held his head gently between her hands and turned his face to hers, stroking a thumb across his cheek to sweep a falling tear away. As he drank her sweet sweet smile, he shed all of his troubles. She was with him. Safe. He was whole, complete, instead of being half of something.

'Am I...'

'Dead? No.'

'But you...you died.'

'No, Frank. I never died. I was always here, just on the other side, just watching. And waiting. But always here.' Her mellow tones made him feel far away, like she was there but not. But she was real and he was afraid to let go in case he lost her again.

The charring mist continued its sluggish retreat. He looked to where Etamin had stood. Nothing but black, choking ash. No flesh or bone. No life, just the evil remnants of the person who would have slain him without blinking.

On the edge of the clear air Frank's eye was drawn by a figure laying prone a dozen yards away, face down in the earth, long dark ringlets dismantled by the destruction of the Simbrian. Frank ran to her, knelt by her, not knowing where to put his hands in case he damaged her.

'Don't worry, Frank. She'll be okay.' Frank hadn't needed to tell her it was Gabby. 'The blast will have protected all those you care for. All of them. It knows, such is the nature of the power you unleashed.'

He hadn't noticed that she'd walked to him until she was offering her hand. Frank rose, sucking in the acrid smoke, feeling the tart taste of cinders on his tongue and the roof of his mouth.

He looked up and around, at the devastation. The utter devastation. Destruction of the Simbrian had fashioned the same on the town and the haze of dust thrown up by the final act hung heavy.

Buildings clung to life, to their crumbing walls and shapeless roofs. The streets now a maze of fractured masonry like a war had been waged and no one had emerged victorious.

The whole west wing of Excelsus was in ruins, thumped to the ground and churned to rubble by the blast. The great glass dome, built at the time of Kester, was gone. Only a bare, broken framework with jags of broken glass hung precariously over the library, set to drop at the next meagre gust of wind.

The great stone vulture, emblem and talisman of the academy, stood headless, its once mighty wings shorn pitilessly from its body, leaving ugly grey stumps with no sign of the once magnificent sight that graced the bridge at the entrance. Its head lay shattered in the middle of the marble plaza which was covered in a thin film of pale powder, like the face of an elegant woman.

The shops across the plaza were all blown in, including Blackburn's ramshackle workshop.

Slowly, gradually, faces started to appear. Cautious and timid like mice who sensed the presence of a cat, as if they feared a second explosion might rip them to bits. Quick glances across the rubble-strewn roads had them hugging doorways and street corners, knowing they'd be safer running but, at the same time, not wishing to miss the drama that was unfolding itself on their doorstep.

'I always knew you'd be brave enough to see it through.' His mother's voice wound itself around him once more.

'Then have I destroyed the Simbrian, for good?'

Rebecca smiled, but offered no response as their attention was drawn to someone rising to their feet, unsteady at first, then the slow, deliberate motion of someone checking each limb to see if they were still working, movement for signs of damage, hair coated in ash but the orange streak still visible.

Dagmar stood with his back to them, his blackened cloak emitting slow, lazy streams of smoke. He shook the senses back into his head, black dust falling around him then, as if he sensed their eyes on his back, he turned. Silence, but for the whistle of the breeze. Stillness, but for the steady movement of Dagmar's head as he looked Rebecca up and down. His heavy breaths bringing on deep raking coughs until he spat whatever he'd drawn up to the ground at his feet.

She gazed straight at him, a slow sly smile on her mouth that didn't quite reach her eyes but conveyed a message across the void, one that Frank didn't understand.

Dagmar straightened, with difficulty, like he'd been punched several times in the ribs. He wiped the back of a blackened hand across his face and drew his fingers down his beard.

Frank didn't believe in ghosts, but Dagmar looked like a complete convert, the way he looked at Rebecca, unable to look away, rooted like a mature oak but bearing the unmistakeable hallmarks of someone wanting to run very quickly in the opposite direction and never look back.

'No.' He looked at Frank, a slow shake of the head. 'No. No. *No*. What have you done?' he said through his teeth. Back to Rebecca. 'This...this can't be. *You*...can't be. I saw you destroy yourself on the foothills of the Longshadows.'

'And you took me for a foolish young girl, Dagmar.' She remained still, calm, in control, a slight breeze picking at the ends of her hair. 'But here I am, not so foolish, to deliver what I promised.'

'No. You killed yourself. I saw it. No one could have possibly survived. Not you. I can't...I don't...surely...'

He looked at Frank again as a daze of realisation spread over his face. Frank could tell something had suddenly dawned on him as his jaw slackened and something resembling horror filled his eyes.

Dagmar wasn't scared of anything as far as Frank could tell.

He'd been unfazed about double-crossing Etamin but here, in the ruined outskirts of Rhaeder, there was something different about him as he faced his mother. His slight, unassuming and waif-like mother who looked like she could calm storm-wracked waters with her look alone.

'What have you done?' he said again. Doubt coursed through Frank. There was something going on that he didn't understand and he could sense the confusion on Dagmar's breath.

'You knew, Dagmar, don't deny it,' said Rebecca. A neutral look. 'We even talked about it. About how we might have done this together, remember?'

'No,' said Dagmar. 'No, I don't believe you.'

'I know you don't, but Lawrence did.'

'Lawrence? What's he got to do...'

Dagmar's voice didn't just trail off, it slipped and fell over the cliff-edge.

'I couldn't have done it without him and it might have been you, had you believed me. Just think, you wouldn't have missed bringing up your own son. Instead, Lawrence promised to keep him safe until the time arrived. Love can always be relied on to make decisions for you.' She gave a wayward smile. Dagmar looked like he'd been punched, very hard. 'I said you hadn't seen the last of me, remember? Just before you tried to stop me destroying the first Simbrian. Still you didn't believe me and yet, here I am.' She was the epitome of serene, self-possessed.

'How?'

Rebecca took a step towards him, her hand still on Frank, a movement that had Dagmar reaching for his sword. His hand tensed on the hilt. Rebecca looked at the weapon and clicked her tongue. A shake of her head. Frank looked at Dagmar who retreated with the care of a cornered animal. A second step back, a third, eyes never leaving Rebecca.

'I visited them all, Dagmar. Splitting each part was child's play.' She was calm, nothing but self-assured. Nothing smug or gloating about her. 'I transferred part of the power back to the guardians themselves, not that they would ever have known. Of course, I took a little for myself so I could create the first Simbrian.'

'No.' The slightest shake of the head from Dagmar, frozen by Rebecca's words. 'Who does that?' he whispered.

'Then I made certain it would pass to Frank through an object, any object, that they passed to him.' She stared right into Dagmar. 'But not only that.' He stared right back as she paused, drawing the silence out, a flicker of something to come. 'I took something else. The core.' Her smile, so enchanting, invoked nothing but heightened dread in Dagmar's face. 'I kept that bit for myself. Why no one thought of splitting the power I'll never know but, then, Everbleed's blood can give you such a different perspective on things.' *Bad blood.* 'The bit I left, the bit for you to take, to carry back to your secret den in Alsha Kar is...nothing.' A shrug. 'Impotent. An illusion. I'm afraid you've been running around making your own little collection, like I knew you would. I even started it for you. And why? To keep the Simbrian safe? Out of my hands?' Dagmar's silence and gritted teeth gave her the answer. 'A valiant attempt to thwart me, but no match. It was never a match.'

'Who does that?' whispered Dagmar once more, bitterness sharp in his eyes. He drew his sword.

'Don't,' she said, iron and stone suddenly in her voice. Harsh promises frozen in her words. 'You know I'll tear you into pieces.' He hesitated, then something in his eyes that Frank had never seen. Fear. Dagmar looked shot down with fear. Unnatural, unholy fear like he was looking upon the beast of his most intimate nightmares. Still his grip tightened. 'Don't,' she said again. 'You know I will. Underestimating people is your weakness, Dagmar.'

She splayed her arms, inviting him to deny it, letting him know that he'd committed the one mistake that would have stopped any of this happening. He'd underestimated *her* and the world had shifted as a result.

'You expect me to believe you?' said Dagmar.

Rebecca shrugged.

'No,' she said. 'But that doesn't matter. All that matters is what happens next.'

'But the Simbrian *has* been destroyed,' uttered Frank through the stand-off. Rebecca looked at him. Soft, kind eyes. A disarming smile. A mother's smile. She cupped his cheek and looked him directly in the eye.

Then he saw it.

As plain as the sun that tried its best to cleave the sky.

The simmering of something tainted. A silent rage, tugging restlessly at its leash, barely contained, emboldened by the flickering of a red flame. Wildfire in her eyes. *Wildfire.*

'No,' said Dagmar. His body slackened like the condemned man being lead to the gallows accepting his fate, knowing there would be no reprieve.

'No, Frank.' A contaminated edge to her voice. 'The Simbrian lives.' She turned back to Dagmar, who backed further away, uncertainty firmly etched on his face, the look of someone who knows they need to run but can't take their eyes off the rush of death heading towards them. 'For all the wrongs that have been done to me, I *will* inflict my revenge.'

The fire in her eyes ignited. Frank felt his breath fail him as his mother, so long the one missing part of his life, pulled him close, her light touch on the side of his head, her sweet smell still fragrant in his nose, her love for him a pure, binding force.

Then he felt it. Felt it though her fingers, her slender arms, the slight bow of her hips.

He felt the heat, felt the rise of the red flame, the burn of rage, of sin, of revenge.

She lit up. Pure brilliance shone through and out of her. A dazzling, unedited power of something beyond the boundaries of Frank's imagination. Some things are not meant to be understood but he could feel it leaking out of her, a wrath to send the skies tumbling in on themselves. A fierce, sharpened wrath.

Only then did he understand.

He hadn't destroyed the Simbrian.

In that moment he knew what he'd done, what his mother had set in motion with her astonishing power, her unrivalled ability, all of her plans. Everything she'd gone through, everything he'd gone through, was always meant to lead up to this moment. This specific moment.

Her tracing of the seven guardians, her flight to and from Irundi, her building and destruction of the first Simbrian, the book, conceiving and bearing a child with Dagmar's bloodline, a bloodline that, mixed with hers, had created the heir. All of it just so that she could guide him to its second incarnation.

She'd planned it all, right down to the last, intricate detail and had his dad raise him like a suckling pig, ready for the slaughter.

Now he knew what his role in this was all about.

He'd summoned her.

And only the heir could do it. Only *he* could do it.

However she'd bent the destiny of the ages, however her unimaginable abilities had managed to reshape the fortunes of the world, he'd summoned her, summoned the power within her, the sheer power that she'd kept closed off from the world until, as she'd so meticulously prepared and planned, he'd hauled her back from a different time to live again.

He was but a small, battered and weary cog, along with the seven guardians, his dad, his friends, Dagmar, Etamin. That's all they were, and he knew why. Knew what she'd done.

The Simbrian was, as Baggus had described it, a living, breathing thing. A restless and unrepentant animal that wanted nothing but to bring the world to its knees.

He stared at her, his mother, the lost part of his soul, feeling the love and comfort he craved, wondering if it would start to slip from his grasp, to disappear from view. So he held her tightly, his emotions tangled.

The burning, unquenchable love he felt for the woman who

bore him ached inside. The sudden fear of someone he didn't know, someone who bore love and hatred, dark and light, a mind full of talent yet stoppered with a rage he hadn't barely the wisdom to understand.

She was magnificent. Utterly beautiful. Utterly terrifying.

She let him go, taking a step back and held out her hands, burning with the intensity of a hundred suns as her voice echoed violently across the ruin of the town, across Byeland to the Longshadows and beyond into Kzarlac for the world to hear. She spoke with the clarity and certainty he'd knew he'd never hear again:

'*I* am the Simbrian.' Her look of triumph was stuff of nightmares. 'There will be no forgiveness and, for the world, there will be no happy endings.'

Milton Keynes UK
Ingram Content Group UK Ltd.
UKHW021822010124
435297UK00017B/1142